THE S_. APPRENTICE

BG KNIGHT

Copyright © 2023 BG Knight

All rights reserved. No part of this publication may be reproduced, stored in a retrieval system, or transmitted in any form or by any means, electronic, mechanical, photocopying, recording, or otherwise, without the prior permission of the copyright owner.

This is a work of fiction. Names, characters, businesses, places, events, locales and incidents are either the product of the author's imagination or used in a fictitious manner. Any resemblance to actual persons, living or dead, or actual events is purely coincidental.

If you have enjoyed this book, then BG Knight would be grateful if you would leave a review on Amazon.

"Smoking Revolver" by Sam Kahn © 2023

PART ONE

Sri Lanka

Late Autumn 2000

Chapter 1

The narrow path sloped downwards, its surface bisected by roots that grew rough nodules and loops that hid beneath the leaf litter as if intentionally to trip the unwary. The trunks of the numerous trees that flank the path were straight, their bark smooth, thrusting out wide buttresses at ground level to provide stability for the enormous canopy that over-shadowed the solitary figure that passed beneath. His bare feet trod soundlessly over the ground; the thin colourful sarong tied at his waist flapped in the light morning breeze. The sun had yet to rise but a familiarity with the route guided the slight figure flawlessly down the hill.

Gradually the trail widened and pushed the thick vegetation back into the forest. The distant roar of the river rose to meet him with every step. Before he saw it, he knew that the monsoon rain of the previous night had filled the channels between the rocks with surging torrents of water. The levels would be too high and too perilous to allow him to take his regular morning swim.

A small grove of geranium bushes offered from bowed branches dark, ripe berries that he collected, putting them into a soft forage bag that hung from his shoulder. They joined the various other blooms, shoots, fruits and roots that had been picked earlier in his trek down to the river.

The ground opened out and any vegetation was sparse, with detritus from last night's flood lying caught in the surface roots and low-lying branches of the trees. Where the young man stood surveying the fast-flowing water had been submerged a few hours ago and the earth around him showed the evidence of the abrasive nature of the incursion.

This morning the river was angry, torrents of swirling water streaming over flat slabs of grey rock as the sky began to lighten in anticipation of the appearance of the new day's sun. The young native inhaled the humid air, the damp smell of the forest floor infused with a fine mist from the earthy water. He raised his arms and stretched; his feet planted slightly apart. Not so much a solar salute, but an acknowledgement that nature was all powerful and he was fortunate to be able to witness its bounty. The pulsating roar filled his ears as the speeding river bubbled and boiled down small falls and consumed boulders that tried to stand in its path. Future surges would undoubtedly shift these huge lumps of rock further downstream, but for the moment they were lodged and confounded the passage of the water that spun and leapt around them.

Circling the bushes that still clung to the riverbank, he climbed to the top of an outcrop of rock that rose above and overlooked the heart of the rapids. The raised peaks of some of the underlying slabs of rock were still exposed. He scrambled down the slippery incline to the edge of the water and hopped from exposed rock to exposed rock until he alighted onto a long finger of stone that ran parallel to the flow of water. It sheltered the bank from the main force of the river, although narrow channels continued to find a way between some of the slabs. The eddies of gritty water had worn the rocks to a smoothness that made progress across their surface treacherous. In the face of these monolithic stepping-stones, where millions of years ago there had been deposits of softer rock, deep round hollows in the shape of narrow commas had been created, the tail pointing downstream. Grit and shale were held in suspension in the water filled pools, grinding and scouring the rims to a polished finish.

At the bottom of each one was a deposit of lees that has been washed down from upstream as the river carved its course through the land. The man knew the location of each hole, but when the water was this high and this fast, most were inaccessible. However, some sat higher than others.

He placed his long-handled axe by the side of one such pool and bent down to scoop a handful of the shale from the murky depths of the hole. Holding the material in his cupped hands, he turned to wash the contents in one of the more gently flowing channels. The water ran through his fingers and the smaller, lighter stones were washed away.

When he was satisfied that enough had been removed, he emptied onto the rock surface what was left in the palm of his hand and studied the grit carefully. He prodded and sifted through the little grains with his forefinger until he saw a glint of light blue. Not large, but smooth and unmistakeably a shard of sapphire.

This morning was not intended as a serious expedition. As with most other mornings, he dug in the rock pools out of habit rather than any wilful or financial intent. He enjoyed the experience and every time the little gems appeared it gave him a buzz of excitement.

Carefully he picked through the slivers of sapphire, until he detected a couple of more sizeable pieces that might have a little more intrinsic value. In the bottom of his forage bag, he kept a small chamois leather pouch, sealed at the top with a leather draw string. He eased the top open and into it he placed these stones. He selected only the best of the remaining shards, even though he knew that they would be ground down and used for industrial purposes.

There was one more pool that he realised would still be accessible. He replaced the pouch in his bag before setting off again across the slippery surface of the rocks. The depth of the turbulent water across the smooth surface increased as he proceeded, splashing his calves and tugging at his feet as it hurried past him. He could see the hole but to get to it he had to jump across a channel of boiling water that, if he lost his footing, would beat him senseless before sweeping him downstream.

He had been across this gap many times when the water was calmer and he hesitated slightly, wondering if, on this occasion, it was a wise move. The hole was full of water that ebbed and flowed over the edges as the river swept past, the contents twisting around the smooth rim of rock that encompassed it.

After a brief pause, he took a deep breath and launched himself across the divide. He dropped to his haunches as he landed to steady his balance before rising and cautiously moving on through the thin veneer of slimy water that skimmed across the surface of the slippery rock. This pool was deeper than the others, the water within it clouded by the mud and silt that has been ripped from the land upstream. Once again, he lowered himself onto his knees by the side of the hole. The entrance was smaller than most and he could only use one hand to explore the interior.

He stretched his arm down. Unable to feel the solid bottom, he slid his fingers deep into the shale that had been deposited. The grit was coarser to the touch and hence the weight of each handful far greater. He shaped his hand like a shovel to extricate it from the hole and then with his other hand formed a bowl to wash the contents, rotating his cupped hands in the slower moving water to one side of the platform of rock.

He repeated the process, allowing the lighter stones to escape and the heavier, more dense ones to remain in his palm. The sun was now beating down on his back and the water that enveloped his hands was cold by comparison. With a final rotation, he opened his hands and deposited the contents onto the flat surface of the rock. The river continued to provide a gentle stream of water that trickled across the stones to remove a few more grains of the lighter grit.

He knelt in front of the slumped pile and, probing again with his fingers, he picked out the larger uninteresting stones and dropped them back into the river. A sudden bright flash of colour sparkled in the intense sunlight, and he extracted a couple of surprisingly good, albeit small, blue sapphires, together with a red and a yellow stone that he recognised also to be sapphires. He quickly washed each of the little gems and placed them in his pouch.

As he had felt some larger pieces of stone slightly deeper, he returned to the hole for one last rummage. He thrust his hand down until his shoulder was at the rim, his long, curly, black hair trailing in the cold water. Gradually, he lifted his body to withdraw a handful of larger sized material that was surrounded by a mass of fine detritus. Because of the size of these stones, for which he held no great expectations, suspecting them also to be worthless, he placed the soggy mass on the wet surface of the rock, rather than washing them through his fingers.

He splashed them roughly with water, but then he paused. Slowly, he leant forward and looked more closely before rolling one of the largest stones over and rinsing it in the water of the pool.

Then he took another, and another, and yet another until he had lined up four stones to stand apart from all the debris that was gradually dissipating back into the flowing river. There were two large stones, one medium size and one smaller; all of which had a unique hue, quite different to those already collected. The luminescent yellow colour, with clear hints of a light orange, were partially obscured by a harder sheath of stone that was wrapped around them. Their inherent beauty was nonetheless obvious.

They were large.

By any standard, they were very large.

With a shaking hand, the young man carefully washed each individual stone once again, scratching at the enveloping sheath to try to reveal more of the underlying gem. He held each up to the sun in turn. Even in their rough form they glowed like the petals of the lotus flower, and suddenly he understood the description applied to the Padparadscha sapphire.

Sitting cross legged before his find, he furtively looked around to see if anyone had been a witness to his discovery.

He was alone.

The sound of the river enveloped him as he sat motionless on the rocks. He was transfixed by the beauty of what he had found.

These were extremely rare stones.

Of an exceptional size.

And highly prized.

Suddenly Randul's simple life had become more complicated.

Chapter 2

Stephen Silchester closed his book and leant back against the headrest, exhausted. The chilled glass of champagne stood untouched by his hand, and he dozed as the Sri Lanka Airlines flight from Heathrow to Colombo's Bandaranaike International Airport settled at its cruising altitude.

The last few weeks had been crazy, leaving him drained of energy. This was the first occasion that he had had some time to himself, to have the opportunity to reflect on what was in prospect for him over the coming months. He had only entered the competition as a bit of fun. A joke with the lads and lasses in the kitchen where he was an under-chef. However, as the process continued Stephen found himself becoming increasingly competitive with a growing desire to prove himself, if not win.

Chef Chitterbaya ran and owned the restaurant at which Stephen worked and initially he was sceptical that Stephen would actually get further than the first couple of rounds. But as he swept into the semi-finals, Chef started to take the whole thing rather more seriously. He privately tutored his protege on some dishes that he thought would impress the judges, as well as the celebrity diners who were brought in to give the new programme format appeal to the young. Gradually, with each week's success, Stephen found that his own celebrity status began to expand, and Rane Chitterbaya realised that he had an asset that was bringing custom into his establishment like never before. Of course, Stephen was unable to make any personal appearances at the restaurant during the series under the rules of the competition, but this did not stop Rane using his employee's newfound fame to his advantage.

The final had been a challenge that Stephen simultaneously hated and enjoyed. The strain of preparing his signature dishes was intense but receiving unanimous acclaim for each one gave him a buzz of immense satisfaction. The glare of the studio lights, the constant delays for a new shot to be set up, or a retake, was irritating but as this was all a new experience for the young chef, his enthusiasm and drive was maintained by both ambition and adrenaline. The last show was televised live which was a further challenge, but when the diners had completed their tasting and he stood nervously before them, he felt the glow of achievement overwhelm him as they each gave universal approbation as to taste, texture, colour and presentation.

Thankfully the decision as to the eventual winner was down to the expert presenters and their guest diners rather than a public vote – a method that had applied in all the earlier rounds. If the public had been the arbiters of culinary excellence against flamboyance, then there was no doubt that the cross-dressed Armand, the darling of a huge social media campaign, would have stolen his crown.

As Stephen relaxed into the business class luxury of his surroundings, he thought of what the future held in store for him. The principal prize was more than he could have hoped to achieve at this stage of his career. He had already shown himself to be a very competent, if not talented, pupil of Chef Rane - permission had been given for Stephen to use Chef's first name following his success in the competition. However, he would never have been able to attain the status of proprietor of his own restaurant for some years to come. By defeating Armand and the others, Stephen now found himself with not only a cash prize of fifty thousand pounds in his bank but, more importantly, the opportunity to demonstrate whether he could succeed in opening and running a restaurant in premises, sponsored for a year by the television company, in a prime location on Brook Street in Mayfair, London.

Stephen had clear ideas as to how he wanted the restaurant fitted out. The television company had their own agenda and insisted that he was assisted by a celebrity interior designer who was desperate to kick-start his own fading career. This prima donna had attempted to veto all of Stephen's design proposals in favour of his own garish Essex style. When Stephen flatly refused to endorse his vision, the guest designer initially took umbrage and then, after a short period of sulking, managed to convince the producers that it was he who should rightfully claim the credit for being the inspiration behind Stephen's original concept. It was a battle Stephen was happy to lose in order to win the war.

While the works were now well in hand, they would take some months to complete. In the interim, as the final part of his prize, the television company was sending Stephen on a fact-finding trip to a destination of his choice to collect ideas for a new cookery programme, hopefully to be accompanied by a book, that would be televised later in the year at his new restaurant.

Hence, Stephen was now on his way to Sri Lanka, paid for by a well-known national travel agency that had been one of the sponsors of the television show, on a voyage of culinary exploration to discover some original dishes for the Grand Opening of 'The Sauceror's Apprentice' restaurant at the end of the year. Sadly, the name was not Stephen's. He had heard it used by the daughter of a friend of his parents, adopted it and, taking his cue from the designer, claimed it as his own.

The only slight downside for Stephen to the whole trip was that a TV crew was due to join him towards the end of his time in Sri Lanka. They wanted to film one programme on location as a resume of the series. Stephen could live with that. At least he would have a couple of weeks on his own to get over the whirlwind of the last few months.

Stephen had left London as a TV celebrity. It had required Armand publicly and effusively to endorse the result of the competition, declaring Stephen as a worthy winner and a dear friend. The condition placed on such approbation, quietly discussed behind closed doors at the TV company's offices, was a position in Stephen's new kitchen. Stephen was more than happy to agree, particularly as Armand was a master pâtissier, a discipline that Stephen had never been terribly interested in. The television company executives were delighted with the unexpected arrangement that endorsed its recently adopted 'diversity and inclusivity' policies while simultaneously ensuring an enthusiastic LGBT+ audience.

So now, after all the furore of the past few weeks, Stephen welcomed a return to a short period of relative obscurity. He intended to use the time to concentrate on the task of finding some original ethnic Sri Lankan dishes that he could adapt into his own style. His ambition? To rival the creations of his mentor Rane or, better still, to outshine those of his erstwhile master. Stephen knew that this was a tall order. To earn one Michelin star was good and to hold two was exceptional. Rane held three.

Stephen was flattered that Rane treated him as his friend, but not his equal - yet.

Chapter 3

For most of the residents of Kandy, the day had yet to start. The pollution of the previous day had been washed away overnight by the monsoon rains. At this time of the morning the narrow street off Peradeniya Road was travelled by few. One of those was a limping figure, hunched and wrapped in an oversized raincoat with the collar turned up. He was in keeping with his surroundings, drab and unremarkable. That was how he liked it, but still he maintained a shrouded vigilance that belied his scruffy demeanour. It was a habit of which he could not rid himself. Consequently, he took furtive looks behind him every so often, stretching his neck round so that his one good eye could fully survey the whole length of the road to check if he was being observed or followed. His other eye was absent from its mutilated socket inside a faded black eyepatch. The dirty elastic that held it tightly in place cut a ditch into the soft flesh around his skull.

Never believe you are ever alone.

Advice that had remained with him ever since…

He pulled out the keys from his pocket and unlocked the rickety door that gave less than secure protection to his domain. When he flicked the switch to turn on the lights, nothing happened. He cursed under his breath, unsure if his irritation was directed at the failing electricity authorities or the ancient and inadequate wiring within his premises. He shut and relocked the door behind him. Purely by virtue of the regularity of the fault and his familiarity with the layout of the interior, he deftly moved through the shop to the cupboard clinging high up on the wall in the rear room. He randomly pushed the grubby white china fuses into their seating and then turned the main switch swiftly off and then on again. A small flash momentarily lit his disfigured face and then the fuse board buzzed ominously before the room was filled with a dull light. He hesitated by the fuses in anticipation of the system blowing once again. After a short while he was satisfied that the electricity supply was secure for the time being and closed the door to the flimsy cupboard. It did not fit in the frame properly and so remained jammed partially open.

Ziyad surveyed his emporium with disgust. The previous day he had left the shop early to meet with some of his business associates, namely a selection of the many drivers who ferried the tourists to, from and around Kandy. These visitors were the life blood of his business, arriving in their hoards to purchase bejewelled gifts for their loved ones. It was these that Ziyad preyed upon from his small premises behind one of the main thoroughfares.

To succeed, however, he had to regularly remind the drivers of the excellent rates of commission that they could earn in exchange for guiding their charges into his emporium. The meeting had proved to be very productive, not least because he was able to out manoeuvre one of his main competitors who, he recently learnt, had taken an expensive shop in one of the main retail centres in Kandy. Consequently, his competitor's margins were suffering, but such was the price of respectability. This was all to the advantage of Ziyad. His modest shop suited his purposes well, quirky enough to amuse and intrigue the tourists but sufficiently dilapidated to maintain a low profile and thereby not garner the attention of the authorities. His was in a cut-throat industry and as far as he was concerned, the lower his overheads the better.

However, this morning, Ziyad looked around his shop with annoyance. Obviously his assistant had used his employer's early departure as an excuse to slope off before the formal close of business, rather than complete the necessary tidying and preparations for the following day.

He would deal with the idle boy later.

In the meantime, muttering all the while, he hung up his raincoat and busied himself sweeping floors and dusting countertops, finishing off by washing the accumulated grime and dust that daily clung to the glazing of the simple shop front. As he completed his chores, or more accurately, his assistant's chores, the sun rose from behind the hills that surrounded Kandy, lightening the dark shadows that made the street slightly forbidding. Ziyad, with a final flourish of his cloth, removed the last few remaining smears on the glass that were highlighted by its weak rays.

Only when finally satisfied that all was ready did he retreat back into the shop. He dumped the cleaning materials into a pile on the floor to emphasise to his assistant, when he eventually arrived, his displeasure at the heinous failure to attend to his allotted duties.

In the rear of the shop, behind the sales area, in the room containing the erratic fuse-board was a huge, antediluvian steel safe that was concreted and bolted to the floor. It dominated one wall of the room and on the many internal shelves lay small boxes and trays covered with velvet cloths. A battered cash box was to be found on the bottom shelf above two locked drawers that were built into the body of the safe. At the top, well above Ziyad's eye line, was a narrow shelf on which a lightly oiled pistol was stowed, wrapped in a grimy chamois leather cloth. It lay there fully loaded, but it had not seen the light of day, let alone been fired, for many years. It was Ziyad's insurance policy against unexpected or unwelcome visitors. Beneath this shelf, splayed diagonally across the face of the lower section of the safe was a stout baseball bat. Ziyad ignored the former and removed the latter which he placed against the side of the safe. This was protection against more local threats which never really materialised. It was there, just in case.

He started to remove the numerous slim boxes stored in the interior, stacking them onto a stout table that stood to one side of the safe. The external door to the shop suddenly rattled. Ziyad looked up at the clock hanging on the wall, its glass face cracked and, as if deaf to the commotion outside, returned to the job at hand. He knew that the arrival was his lazy assistant who would rue the previous evening's lax behaviour. Ziyad was going to make sure that the boy regretted his decision to escape early.

Beyond the rear room, accessed from a mean side corridor, was an even more unpleasant alley running down the back of all the buildings that fronted the street. At the end of this alley was a communal latrine that was used by all the local businesses and some residents, together with any passing visitors desperate enough to have no alternative but to enter its foetid portal. Ziyad never used it, preferring to take a short walk to one of the many new boutique hotels that regularly opened in the vicinity. The latrine was infrequently, if ever, cleaned as, not surprisingly, everyone shunned the unpleasant responsibility.

But not today.

Today it would be spotless, and Ziyad knew exactly who was going to do it.

After a few minutes and upon hearing a persistent, but less vigorous, tapping on the glass of the front door, Ziyad paused from his task and hobbled across the shop floor with his keys in his hand. He unlocked the door and swung it open without uttering a word of greeting. Turning on the spot, he retraced his steps to resume the unpacking of the safe, silently pointing as he passed to the discarded pile of cleaning materials on the floor.

The boy, who was really a young man of around twenty, scuttled busily around the shop, now realising with dread that his employer had discovered his misjudged absence and had already completed the tasks that he was meant to perform before he left the previous evening.

Aloka, for that was the name of the 'boy', had had a date yesterday evening and he did not want to be late. He quietly collected up the cleaning materials and hesitantly advanced to the doorway of the storeroom. Once again, he tried to offer a cheery good morning to his employer. The older man did not cease from what he was doing as he acidly reprimanded his assistant.

"You are an idle, useless boy, Aloka. I leave you in charge of my shop and you betray my trust."

Aloka looked down at the floor. He knew his master would be unforgiving and certainly unsympathetic to any affairs of the heart.

"When you have put all that away," he nodded towards the various items in Aloka's arms, "and we have completed the displays, you will go and clean the latrine."

Aloka's face fell, and he started to protest but Ziyad would not hear another word.

"I want to be able to eat my supper in there when you have finished – not that I have any intention of doing so."

The young man's shoulders slumped. He knew that during the day the latrine was frequented by many passers-by, undeterred by its state but relieved that it was there as such facilities were few and far between in this older part of the town. His attempts to clean the place would be constantly interrupted by visitors, negating upon their departure any of his efforts prior to their arrival.

The shadows in the street continued to shorten and the two men silently transferred the contents of the velvet lined boxes into the window, gradually building a sparking display of corundum, sapphires, rubies, emeralds, garnets, spinels, tourmaline and other precious and semi-precious stones. These were laid out on black velvet cushions and mats, whilst on the upper shelves of the shop window were placed trays of bracelets, necklaces and rings. Bright yellow and white gold flashed behind the glass frontage, enticing the tourists to enter and challenging them to find a bargain.

Remaining locked in the bottom drawers of the safe were the more expensive items that were reserved for 'special' customers and sold at private viewings arranged for after the formal closing time. Frequently, when Aloka had left having correctly completing his chores, Ziyad's day would continue. It was then that he met with wealthier buyers, or those who wanted to quietly and legitimately sell illegitimately obtained gems and gold, whether through illegal mining or purloined from careless tourists who fell foul of the manual dexterity of artful pickpockets or conmen who were as prevalent in Kandy as in any other town or city.

Ziyad limped outside his shop and viewed the window display with his ever-critical eye. Aloka stood inside ready at the whim of his employer to make any infinitesimal alterations to the juxtaposition of the glittering wares. He was in no hurry for Ziyad to conclude his inspection. The longer these final detailed movements took, the longer he could postpone the unpleasant task that had been assigned to him.

Finally satisfied, Ziyad nodded his head at Aloka and returned to the interior of the shop. The clock showed the time to be 7:45am and, as he did at this time every morning, Ziyad went and put a blackened pot onto the small, even blacker gas ring to heat up the first of his many cups of strong, acrid coffee that he would drink each day. Aloka was not offered any refreshment, he never was. Nevertheless, he hesitated in the shop, trying to appear busy. From the back room Ziyad coughed loudly, clearing the phlegm from his throat that also told Aloka that he had a task to perform. Resignedly, Aloka slouched past where Ziyad was preparing his refreshment and disappeared down the corridor, collecting a cheap plastic bucket and threadbare mop from outside the rear door of the shop. He knew that it was the worst time of the day to start his penance, but his employer was impervious to any negotiation that might defer or make the task easier.

His worst fears were confirmed when he turned into the rancid alley and saw the short queue outside the latrine. Today was going to be both very long and very disagreeable.

Ziyad quietly took his cup of coffee into the shop and sat behind the counter on a tall metal stool. This was a time for quiet reflection. There would be no customers until later when those tourists who were in town emerged from their hotels and guesthouses. Recently all businesses had struggled because of the widespread civil unrest and Ziyad feared that the cease-fire was looking increasingly precarious.

Chapter 4

Randul sat out on his veranda, leaning back on an old Windsor backed chair thinking, his hands stretched across the back of his head. On the small, round, metal framed table in front of him stood an untouched glass of coconut water and five small, neatly formed piles of stones. Most were predominantly blue but interspersed with some yellow and red. Each pile had been sorted into differing sizes and depth of colour. These little stacks of gems alone were worthy of anyone's attention, but Randul's concentration remained on the four stones that were lined up in order of size, the smallest to the left, the largest on the right.

Without thinking, he took a piece of betel leaf, covered the surface with a veneer of bright, white, lime paste and placed a thin slice of areca nut in the centre. Carefully, he folded the edges of the leaf around the areca nut and then slid the small parcel into his mouth. He chewed rhythmically.

It took only a short time for the effect to kick in, and gradually a sense of calm and wellbeing settled over him. Any worries that he had about the future of the stones faded and the benign beauty of the day unfolded around him.

He rocked gently backwards and forwards, balancing on the two rear spindly legs of the chair, gradually rolling more to the fore until the chair settled and creaked softly under his transferred weight. Now leaning forward, his elbows balanced on his knees, his face held in his hands, his eyes almost level with the surface of the table, he stared at his collection. How, and why, had he allowed his hoard of raw gems to reach the volume that now lay before him? The smaller coloured stones that shone out from behind the four giants, despite their own undoubted beauty, were not the problem.

No, the real issue was the four larger stones. As they caught the light, Randul was bewitched by the colour of the fiery shadows that danced on the surface of the rust pitted tabletop, like the colouring of the lotus flower or a morning sunrise. He was mesmerised by their beauty despite their coarse exterior.

To the rear of these exceptional stones were two yellow stones, each about the size of his thumb nail. They appeared almost insignificant in the presence of the four titans, but each of these yellow stones was impressive in its own right. He pushed them gently to one side, not to dismiss them, but to allow the purity of the sunlight that penetrated the four suspected Padparadscha to spread across the table surface.

To his certain knowledge, such a unique, and potentially valuable haul had never been officially reported, and this presented him with his current dilemma. If his suspicions were correct, and these four uncut stones were Padparadscha, then how was he to sell them? To the right people, each was a potentially fabulously valuable jewel. So how would he benefit without drawing attention to either himself or the location where he had found them?

Randul, as a Veddah tribesman, knew the forest better than most, including areas that were remote from individual villages and remained inaccessible without some considerable effort. One case in point was the river bend where Randul's father had shown him the secrets of the rock holes. He did not wish to relinquish his possession of a spot that held so many fond memories of his father to some avaricious corporate prospector.

It was a place of retreat, a place of tranquillity and relaxation. As a boy, Randul would sneak away alone just to lie quietly on the rocks and watch the myriad of brightly coloured birds that came and drank or washed in the cool refreshing water. It was here that he had seen green-billed coucal, white headed starling, ashy-headed babbler and the broad-billed roller. On one memorable occasion, he had been frozen to the spot as a young leopard, so rarely seen in the forest now, came to drink at the water's edge. It had looked up and stared into Randul's eyes, fixed the child with a hypnotic stare, measuring the risk that the young boy posed, before lowering its head once again to drink some more. Randul had never seen or experienced anything like it, and probably never would again. The memory of the beauty and grace of the animal remained with him into adulthood, together with the trust that the leopard had placed in him.

For some of the few remaining indigenous families, gemming was more than a pastime and even though their efforts yielded little more than scraps of stone, this supplemented their meagre incomes. The authorities turned a blind eye to such small, chance discoveries because they had limited intrinsic value.

Their finds would be accumulated over time and then taken to an intermediary in their village or a neighbouring village. There they were paid a pittance for each small, illegal haul while the local dealer made a slightly greater profit from sales to the larger dealers in Kandy or Ratnapura. The majority of the stones found were of little use for jewellery most being ground down for commercial or industrial purposes.

If a stone of any real quality was found that had any genuine value, then the finder did have the opportunity to go to the National Gem and Jewellery Authority and surrender the stone in exchange for sixty percent of the market value.

Sixty percent of what?

This governmental body had complete control over the supply of stones and thereby protected the market values, but like so many official bodies there were rumours that it was subject to corrupt practices by some of those who administered the rules. If Randul chose to avoid those rules and was caught trying to sell his stones on the black market through illegitimate dealers, then he faced the immediate confiscation of his stones and a hefty fine, or even imprisonment.

In normal circumstances, the Veddah would not count wealth in terms of material belongings. Randul still respected and honoured the traditional ways of life, but he was also an educated man. With knowledge comes failings and weaknesses to which a mere human being is so fallible. When he had to return home to nurse his dying father, he developed a frustration at not having had the opportunity to complete his research at Colombo University, or fully exploit the resources that would have been available to him. Randul sometimes wondered if they would let him return. But in his heart he knew that the price of that would be to surrender his life in the jungle. Here was the bountiful source of all his raw materials, the larder that he lived in still had further delights to impart, exotica yet to be discovered. To return to a polluted urban environment was not a realistic, or appealing, option.

It was not as if he relied on his foraging and research to earn him a living. He managed to survive adequately off the modest income he received from the Forestry Department and the tips he was given as a guide and lecturer by the wealthy overseas tourists and academics who came to visit the nature reserve. By virtue of his qualifications from the university and his own secretive research that he undertook in the privacy of his home laboratory, his expertise and knowledge meant that he had become a well-respected and consulted expert of the flora and fauna of the local area.

Any little illicit gemming was merely a light-hearted diversion from his more important academic studies. He had continued to expand his research into a far wider range of plant material sourced from both the immediate forest as well as the other equally remote areas of Sri Lanka. His discoveries, having both culinary and medicinal uses (and some with unexpected properties) were unpublished and so unknown to anyone but himself. At times, this had taken him into areas that he had not expected and produced results that might not be wholly acceptable to his peers should they become aware of them.

Each revelation fascinated Randul and was written up meticulously in his journals that were stacked in chronological order on a shelf in his laboratory. The occasional bit of practical research was undertaken with the unknowing cooperation of an acquaintance who ran a small guest house in Kandy, the results also being carefully annotated in his journal and retained for future reference.

Notwithstanding the fact that Randul would normally eschew material wealth, he had to acknowledge the beneficial effect the four Padparadscha would have on his private research.

While he was far from being an expert, like everyone, Randul had heard about the existence of the mythical Padparadscha stones. His father had searched for one all his life, but without success. Now, the myth was a reality. Here he was with not one, but four – all extremely rare, all highly sought-after, the largest having the potential of being the most valuable sapphire in the world.

If his suspicions were correct, then each one was worth far more than the local 'under-the counter' gem dealer was able either to handle or keep secret from the ever-vigilant ears and eyes of the National Gem and Jewellery Authority. It was not an unpleasant problem to have, but it was a problem, nonetheless.

Whatever the outcome, Randul was fairly confident that the treasures lying in front of him on the rusty surface of the table had the potential to radically alter his life.

Little did he know just how unexpectantly radical that change was to be.

Randul carefully swept up the stones and placed each of the graded piles into separate small chamois leather pouches, while the two larger yellow stones and the four Padparadscha he placed into a single, larger pouch. It bulged and the draw strings around its circumference were stretched to their limit. He weighed it carelessly in his hand as he entered the bungalow and crossed to the corner of the kitchen area where he eased up a floorboard. A void had been created beneath and he stashed all the bags into a box constructed beneath the flooring. Standing on the replaced board, he bounced lightly up and down to ensure that it was firmly back in place.

His improvised safe was almost full, and he knew that he was going to have to dispose of some of his accumulated gems soon, or else find a more sensible location to store them. The usual local village dealer was not a feasible option as village gossip would inevitably travel beyond the local population to other, less scrupulous opportunists who would start to become curious.

An alternative had to be found.

Chapter 5

Ziyad locked up his shop, darkness having crept back into the street, the large moon casting an eerie blue light over his surroundings. All in all, it had been a good day with a constant stream of tourists coming to buy his wares. His meeting the previous evening with the drivers had paid off handsomely, even though there had not been any particularly momentous sales. However, each small purchase by a visitor added to Ziyad's not inconsiderable fortune that he had amassed over the years since he had arrived in Sri Lanka.

To look at the man who turned from the door of his modest premises and limped down the street, one could be forgiven for thinking that he was just a poor shopkeeper returning to his simple home somewhere in the shabbier suburbs of Kandy.

That would be a mistake.

Once Ziyad had moved out from the immediate environs of his shop and hobbled along the busy main thoroughfare, ignored by the tourists eagerly searching for restaurants and bars for sustenance and refreshment, he surreptitiously slipped into a side alley. There, in the shadows, he found the taxi that was waiting patiently for him, as it did most evenings. Slumping into the back seat, Ziyad closed his eyes and tried to ignore the dull ache that settled in his damaged left leg. He could not wait to take off the poorly fitting prosthetic foot and replace it with the much more comfortable one that awaited him at his home.

The taxi turned away from the city centre, the road climbing up towards a viewpoint that looked across Kandy Lake towards the Temple of the Sacred Tooth. The humidity was high and the surface of the lake still, reflecting the lights from the surrounding buildings on its limpid surface. Earlier the storks had wheeled overhead before they roosted for the night in the overcrowded trees that grew along the edge of the lake. The sound of disputes for the best spots continued to echo up into the dusky sky.

The driver said nothing, knowing that any trite conversation was not appreciated by his weary passenger. That was fine by him, as was the fact that he would receive no payment for the journey, or the one that he did every morning at six thirty when he returned The Arab to the same kerbside in the same backstreet of Kandy.

Why?

Because his passenger owned this taxi, and the new Mercedes was air conditioned, comfortable and gave the driver an edge over his competitors, most of whom drove less salubrious Toyotas. The driver plied for the lucrative trade from the travel companies that wanted reliable and safe passage for their clientele. With the reduction in the number of visitors due to the civil war he needed that competitive edge.

The alternate routes that the passenger insisted the driver take on each journey remained a secret between the two of them, which was no problem if it preserved the continued patronage of Ziyad. It was a symbiotic relationship that the driver was not about to upset.

The distance to be travelled was not far, but the roads together with the erratic driving, particularly at night, meant that what should take fifteen or twenty minutes invariable took considerably longer. Tonight proved to be no exception but eventually the car pulled up at a grand entrance protected by ornate metal gates hung on solid, white painted piers that stood either side of a paved drive. Cast iron carriage lights hung from curlicued brackets, each shining a guarded welcome along the drive that curved such as to place the house out of sight from prying eyes.

"Do you want me to drive in, sir?"

"No. Stop here," Ziyad commanded. He shuffled forward on his seat in order to get his balance before attempting as dignified an exit as possible from the vehicle. As always, he took the opportunity to check around for any lurking individuals, unaware that his driver had already performed his own inspection.

Before he had the opportunity to reach out for the doorhandle, the driver had appeared at the side of the car and whisked the door open. He offered a hand to give assistance, but it was rejected, as it was at the end of every journey. Ziyad scrambled out and carefully surveyed his surroundings again before moving away from the car.

The driver closed the door and returned to his seat. He gently pulled away, slowly rolling down the deserted road, but with his eyes constantly watching the furtive figure as it receded in the rear-view mirror.

Satisfied that there was no one taking any interest in him, Ziyad took a fob from his pocket and held it against the face of the keypad on one of the piers. The lock clicked and the motor whirred as the metal gates shuddered into motion. With one final check, Ziyad slipped quickly through them. The driver watched him enter his property and, when he was satisfied that his client was safely home, accelerated away to his next more lucrative pick up.

Ziyad did not proceed immediately along the drive but paused and waved his fob back over an inner control panel. The whirring motor stopped, the heavy gates shuddered on their hinges with the sudden interruption of their progress, and then slowly returned to their original closed position, the automatic locks clicking securely into place once again. Just by way of a final reassurance, Ziyad rattled the gates and only then did he turn to trudge up the drive.

After a refreshing shower and a change of clothes, Ziyad sat on the edge of the bed and massaged the chafed flesh at the end of his leg. He applied the soothing cream that he had delivered each month from the United Kingdom. There was no need to continue to suffer the increasing discomfort from the worn and decrepit prosthetic foot supplied to him all those years ago. Over the last few months, he had increasingly considered whether he should dispose of his alter ego. But he fretted that the takings of the poor, disabled immigrant gems dealer who scraped a meagre living from his modest shop would be adversely affected if he resorted to wearing a more comfortable foot. He suspected probably not, but he would welcome easing his exaggerated limp and his propensity to wear the scruffy mantle of poverty.

He had become comfortable with how his customers perceived him, particularly those from the Western world. Most seemed to take pity on him and assume that, as a disabled person, his suffering imbued upon him an honesty that was unimpeachable. To avoid their own embarrassment, they would try to avert their gaze from his empty and scarred eye socket that he kept just visible beneath a tattered black eye patch. A patch that was now replaced with a much more stylish, if not rakish substitute. The facial scar-tissue also served to discourage any real attempts by the tourists to barter on price, despite the tacit encouragement to do so from their tour guides - or from the pages of their Lonely Planet.

Once back in their comfortable hotels, over an iced glass of gin and tonic, they would convince themselves as to the reasons for their unwillingness to take advantage. "Look, the man's a cripple with one eye," they would say. "He's doing his best to make a living to support his family. It would be taking advantage to haggle with the poor fellow."

But who was taking advantage of who?

Ziyad had no such scruples. He prided himself on the fact that he nearly always obtained prices for his jewellery and gems that far surpassed their intrinsic value. Naturally, most dealers in the city would make such a claim, but Ziyad exploited his situation with consummate ease and guile. He provided tourists with a warm glow, a sense that they had done their bit in making the Third World a better place for at least one of its inhabitants. While they were aware that they would never get any real bargains from whichever dealer they bought from, their consciences were invigorated when striking a deal with Ziyad. They left with a self-congratulatory grin as they waved away, or ignored, the crowd of desperate street urchins who held out their grubby hands for alms or sought to sell their own pathetic curios.

Equally, Ziyad was satisfied that he had never paid over the odds for any item that the rural peasantry had offered to him. He managed always to convince them that his price was the best and his discretion absolute. The latter was both crucial and perfectly true. He wanted to ensure that a constant supply of raw materials continued to flow into his shop and that would only be achieved if the simple fools implicitly trusted in his silence. The discount on any true market value was begrudgingly accepted by most in exchange for the surety that a corrupt government official or ambitious police officer was not going to come knocking on their door.

Of course, there was always the odd young hotshot who thought he could outwit Ziyad or tried to pursue too hard a trade. Ziyad had no qualms about letting such an opportunist temporarily pass him by. If he desired the merchandise that was being offered to him, a brief word to one or other of his contacts in the police usually brought the welp to heel, and the item would be his via the conveniently diligent law officer. After all, in accepting the discount, it had to be appreciated that Ziyad also had expenses that he needed to cover in order to keep the authorities from his own door.

Ziyad rose from the bed and gingerly placed his weight on his professionally fitted prosthetic foot, wincing slightly before dismissing the discomfort as the price to be paid for wealth and success. He tentatively walked from his bedroom onto the wide landing, his gait much more even than when wearing his "business" foot. Leaning against the balustrade, he looked across the open courtyard that dominated the middle of the house and felt a heightened sense of self-satisfied contentment at what he had achieved in his adopted country.

A broad staircase curved down into the cool courtyard, the focal point being a small fountain at its heart, breaking the silence with a soft babbling sound, the crystal-clear water flowing from the stone bowl to splash into a shallow pool below. Dark mahogany double-doors to the rear of the courtyard opened into a vast living room beyond which was a wide terrace incorporating an infinity pool. The water surface was as smooth as glass, lying flush with its marble surround. The land dropped steeply away from the edge of the pool, giving a spectacular view over verdant forest, while deep in the canyon below could be heard the roar of a river.

The division between the interior of the house and the external terrace comprised of a full height glass sectioned partition. With the aid of invisible motors, each giant panel moved aside and disappeared into the wall on both sides of the opening to combine both spaces into one. During the height of the summer, shade was provided by a deep, overhanging roof supported on tall, tapering columns, the whole structure protecting both the room and the terrace from the full heat of the afternoon sun. All around the terrace were mock Victorian gas lights, their flames flickering in the breeze.

Any guest suddenly dropping into the house would be forgiven for thinking that this chic villa was in the south of France rather than on the grimy outskirts of Kandy.

Ziyad descended gingerly down the stairs and walked over to an inlaid antique cabinet standing to one side of the drawing room. A fresh jug of iced water and sparkling cut glass tumblers had been placed on a silver tray to await his arrival. He took one of the glasses and opened the silk panelled doors that concealed the cabinet's true purpose. Pouring a heavy measure of his favourite malt whisky from a square decanter, he added an equal measure of water from the jug. Ziyad lifted the tumbler to his nose and inhaled deeply to appreciate the vapour that rose from the surface of the liquor. Satisfied, he took a delicate sip of the contents and exhaled, his shoulders sloughing off the trials of the day.

"Where are my children to greet me from my day's labours?"

Despite appearing to be speaking to an empty room, a woman's voice answered from beyond the open wall of glass. "Ameesha is with friends in town. As for Thinuka, you won't be surprised to hear that I've not seen him all day. Will your wife's greeting suffice?"

Ziyad sauntered out onto the terrace and bent over the slim figure reclining on a chaise-longue, dressed in jogging bottoms and a soft cashmere V-necked jumper. He kissed her forehead and slumped into the chair next to her.

His wife continued to read the glossy magazine that updated her with celebrity gossip from around the world. He watched her and, despite his disapproval of her adopting any Westernised name, let alone Honey, when they arrived in Sri Lanka, he maintained an infatuation for her. She had acquired a self-confident elegance that replaced the rough, rural manners of the shy, young village girl he had married when they started out on their life together. With the passing years she had honed her sophisticated airs while simultaneously retaining and toning her curvaceous figure, albeit with the assistance of the private gym he had installed and, at Ziyad's insistence, a female personal trainer who visited her three times a week.

As part of her regime, Honey maintained an almost obsessive routine in the swimming pool. As far as she was concerned, the pool was there as an adjunct to her fitness rather than an indulgence to be enjoyed. The rest of the family knew better than to be in the vicinity of the water at the time of her regular twice daily sessions. Honey expected exclusive possession, not least because her arrival, exercise and departure was undertaken naked. During this time, she would zealously drive her body up and down the twenty-five-metre length until the required distance had been accomplished. Afterwards, she would do several yoga stretches on the terrace before vacating the area as peremptorily as she had arrived for a long shower, to do her hair (unless it was a day for her hairdresser to call), apply her make-up and elegantly clothe herself.

Since the children had grown up, Ziyad had found himself using the pool less and less, although if he was at home, he would always secretly watch Honey take her swim. He suspected that she knew he was there as on those occasions she invariably assumed ever more provocative poses as part of her regular stretches. There for him to see but increasingly rarely to touch.

He had enjoyed splashing around with Thinuka and Ameesha when they were little, so long as he remained within his depth. Despite his own inability to swim, there was a sense of fulfilment as he watched his children become more confident and proficient in the water. Inevitably, over time that proficiency grew to a point that far exceeded his own deficient aquatic abilities and so, gradually, he withdrew from any attempts to entertain, amuse - or compete with them in the water.

To be seen as displaying a weakness in anything that he did was unacceptable to Ziyad, even if a weakness was at the hands of his children - especially if it was at the hands of his children. Consequently, he concentrated his efforts on identifying the next challenge at which he might excel over and above the talents of his children.

The same approach applied in his business dealings – losing was not an option and on the very rare occasions when such a defeat was experienced, he would become so maddened that, until his rage had assuaged, all around him knew that Ziyad was to be avoided.

"When are we eating?"

Honey did not stop reading her magazine or raise her eyes from the page to acknowledge her husband's question. She merely replied casually, "I've eaten. Why don't you ask Marie to get you something?"

Ziyad rose from his chair, irritated that, yet again, she should have chosen to dine early without waiting for him. Her apparent lack of concern as to what he considered to be her basic marital duties had long irked him, but he had avoided any form of confrontation. He had no intention of involving himself in the domestic arrangements of the house or the female members of his staff. That was a women's task.

"I shall be in my study," he announced tersely. "Tell Marie I will eat in an hour." He wavered for just a moment to be sure that his displeasure had registered with his wife before returning to the cabinet and taking the decanter of whisky with him.

On his departure Honey infinitesimally raised one eyebrow, but still her attention did not waiver from the page that she was not reading. Her mobile phone remained where she had hidden it, between the soft cushion and her toned thigh. The message that she had received just as her husband had appeared on the terrace still awaited a response.

Ziyad stumped across the central courtyard and opened a door to his study at the front of the house. He replenished his glass before setting the decanter within easy reach on his desk. The room he had entered was not lavishly furnished or in the style of the remainder of the house. One might have expected a gentlemen's study, but this room was more akin to a commercial office. It was austere, with a functional desk and cabinets, all having lockable drawers, together with a sophisticated CCTV system and a range of electronic communication equipment that was ahead of its time and served Ziyad's business needs rather than his aesthetic tastes.

His study was like his marriage. Functional. Any outward show of extravagance or pleasure was reserved for external perceptions. Ziyad's physical needs were satisfied by his mistress who was housed at his expense in a comfortable apartment in an affluent area of the city. His wife did not complain because he was confident that she did not know of the liaison. In fact, it had never occurred to him that she might either know or complain. He had provided her with a lifestyle that she would never have imagined. Had she remained in their homeland she would have suffered the deprivations that existed under corrupt, puppet dictators and uncaring coalition forces.

Not that he had any great affinity with the rebel militia that he had been compelled to join at an early age. He knew no better. However, in all the chaos of invasion, defeat and counter insurgence, escaping from the clutches of his rebel masters had not proved to be so difficult. It had been relatively simple to hoodwink all those foreign Samaritans who flooded into his country with their liberal ideals, and who bent over backwards to identify and free those whom they considered by their western values to be oppressed and persecuted.

With so many people dispossessed, transient and impoverished, both morally and physically, no one could reliably substantiate what was true and what was false. Ziyad managed to fabricate a plausible story which was as impossible to verify as it was to prove, but due to the confusion that existed throughout his country the surrounding nations were incapable of resisting the flood of refugees fleeing from the conflict.

Ziyad had no intention of staying either impoverished or destitute, deciding that a future in another land was much more appealing. But he needed a good dowery for his new life. Gradually over several years he ingratiated himself with the precarious leadership of the rebels where, recognising his innate financial skills, he became their trusted financial advisor. This had made him privy to the enormous sums of clandestine fiscal support that had been flowing into the rebels' accounts from sympathetic foreign governments and corporations, eager to establish an influential foothold with what they saw as the inevitability of a rebel victory. This gave Ziyad the opportunity to regularly and surreptitiously redistribute a small percentage of this officially non-existent monetary support into various secret personal accounts that he had created beyond the grasp of the vicarious owners of the money.

Of course, these misappropriations did mean that if discovered he was in danger of becoming a dead advisor. Without admitting as to the true reason why his former rebel comrades and their defrauded paymasters would be pleased to see him dead, the task of proving that he and his family were in real danger and deserving of refugee status was undeniable.

While it seemed that most of his fellow refugees wanted to go to the UK, US or Europe, Ziyad was very content to disappear to a not so obvious alternative. As he secretly built up his fraudulently acquired financial empire, he was unaware that some of the hierarchy within the rebels were beginning to piece together his activities. Fortunately, he was simultaneously formulating his own plans to secure a safe future for him and his family. He had identified Sri Lanka as a relatively peaceful country, before it descended into its own civil war, and was delighted to discover that they were prepared to take a limited number of refugees as part of their foreign policy.

He changed his name and started to work as a trainee for a respected gem dealer in Ratnapura. He discovered that he had a talent for the trade and gradually became proficient and confident enough to break away and open his own business in Kandy. This provided him with an excellent front that, over several years, enabled him to efficiently launder the stolen rebel money without any undue scrutiny or problems. Doing business locally was not so very different to what he had been used to at home, save that there was slightly more subtlety and subterfuge in corrupting those who wished to appear incorruptible.

Ziyad had already worked successfully for his rebel paymasters in the western investment markets and had learnt all about the different sectors of the financial markets. He created a web of companies and exploited a wide range of investment vehicles to protect and grow the proceeds of his fraud, as well as the ever-increasing trading profits from his own legitimate jewellery business. His single-minded diligence and inherent business acumen resulted in the creation of a substantial personal fortune held through a diverse portfolio of equities, bonds, private equity and real estate. He trusted no-one and maintained as clean a record as was possible in Sri Lanka by promptly paying all his taxes and dues while simultaneously making modest contributions to certain important worthy causes. These primarily consisted of several senior members of government and the appropriate regional officials, as well as a few senior police officers.

The downside to his success was that he had had to disclose to Honey the true reason for them having to flee their homeland and adopt a new identity. Simultaneously, he insisted that she should not exhibit any conspicuous behaviour that might draw attention to themselves. Ziyad tried to keep the true extent of his wealth a secret from her, but she knew that they had considerable resources and found it difficult to resist the temptation to spend money rashly. Despite the constant warnings that discovery of their real identity by certain parties would not be in their best interests, Honey was unable to contain her extravagant lifestyle. So far Ziyad had managed to limit her more lavish demands, but it was becoming increasingly difficult as time passed, and they became more remote from their previous life.

When Ziyad and Honey fled, their children had been too young to appreciate the dangers that they were in. But now they were entering adulthood, his ability to control their behaviour and public profile was much more of a problem. They were not aware of the continuing risks that Ziyad and, consequently, they faced.

Why should they?

Their safe, cossetted upbringing had been one of considerable luxury. A mistake in hindsight, and to compensate for the constant warnings of an inexplicable fate that they could neither see nor understand, he showered his family with gifts and extravagances that they came to accept as necessities. There was no rational explanation for such largesse, which his children accepted like the spoilt children they were. Ziyad had hoped that his generosity would distract them from any overtly extreme behaviour. He used the civil war that was plaguing Sri Lanka as an excuse for his overly zealous attitude to their safety and security, while he continued to conceal from them the true source of the family wealth.

Ziyad settled himself in front of his twin computer screens, the screen to his left constantly flickering as the display updated the latest global share prices and automatically calculated the impact on his portfolio of investments. He looked at one of the five digital clocks that showed the local Sri Lankan time (22:00) and the corresponding times in the Cayman Islands (12:30), London (16:30), New York (12:30) and Sydney (03:30).

It was time.

He turned to the second screen and clicked into the pre-arranged meeting with his bankers in the Cayman Islands.

There was not a huge amount to discuss, most of the important decisions having already been made, but Ziyad still preferred to check that his detailed instructions had been followed. He flipped his attention back to the first screen and pulled up a research paper on the London commercial property market to remind himself of the forecasts that the analysts had made for the next twelve months. He had read the piece the previous evening and compared it to the reports from other advisors. He treated the reports with caution as they had been produced by property advisors who had a vested interest in their agency business brokering transactions. To deflate the market would be bad for business so the general tone was positive and encouraging for investors to sink further funds into the London market – oh, and by the way, they were the people to help you to do so.

The second screen went blank and then a fuzzy image rolled briefly before splitting to reveal two smartly dressed individuals in their dark grey suits, white shirts and bright, perfectly knotted ties. The older one had a shock of grey hair that was too long for his age, but perfectly combed back over his scalp and held in place by a mixture of hair oil and an elasticated band at the back of his head to produce a lank ponytail. The other was considerably younger and sported a couple of days growth of downy stubble that was, no doubt, considered in his circles to be hip. Ziyad thought that it made him appear unwashed and unprofessional. However, that aside, they were diligent and good at their job, so long as Ziyad kept them on a short rein.

Simultaneously, both men greeted Ziyad with a formality that he had insisted that all his advisors adopted when speaking to him. He wanted a feeling of superiority as he considered them all to be necessary parasites that the wealthy had to endure in order to maintain and expand their wealth successfully. For the exorbitant fees that he was paying them, Ziyad expected to be able to call upon any of his advisors at any hour of the day or night and still receive an instant and attentive service.

"UK Retail still looks incredibly weak at present," said the younger of the suits.

"Maybe, but as the yields are higher than they've been for quite a while it seems to me to be the right moment to get back into the sector. I view the misfortunes of others as opportunities for me." Ziyad liked to adopt a counter-cyclical approach to his property investment strategy, buying cheaply whatever is out of favour and waiting until the lemmings came to their senses.

"Well, I know that the Mayfair location is prime, but we were still fortunate to secure that unexpected letting to the TV company, even though it's only guaranteed for a year's duration. At least there'll be some income rather than a lengthy void," the older suit remarked.

"Remember, gentlemen, this is but a small part of my overall real estate portfolio. The industrials across the rest of the UK will off-set any small blemish to performance from the Mayfair building, as will the other European and US assets. In addition, the residential units, with a little judicious investment, will provide some excellent capital growth even allowing for the fact that the net initial yield is not that attractive."

In unison, the two bankers nodded sagely at the wisdom of their client.

Ziyad had no time for sycophants and moved swiftly on, "I assume that you've made all the necessary arrangements, as I instructed, and the money will be with my London solicitors in time?"

"Yes, sir, it's all in hand. The quoted investments have been liquidated from the Emerald portfolio; you made a nice little profit from the short term hold even allowing for the transaction costs. The market is so volatile, the timing was everything, and we seem to have hit it on the button."

Ziyad grimaced at the use of the collective pronoun. If he remembered correctly, the suits had not been at all in favour of risking a few days' exposure to the US stock market, but here they were, quick to claim the initiative for themselves. Ziyad suppressed his desire to argue the point and consequently ignored the comment.

The younger suit was looking away from his camera, and hence Ziyad, to study a spreadsheet showing all Ziyad's portfolios – or those about which he had first-hand knowledge - including the recently liquidated Emerald Portfolio. He was eager to confirm their other recent successes and started to report on overall performance, but Ziyad was well versed with his returns and did not need any unnecessary self-congratulatory preening from these over-paid peacocks.

Ziyad spoke across the younger banker, "Please do not delay. Make sure the transfer of the whole sum is completed and in my solicitor's Client Account as soon as possible. And don't forget to use the correct reference this time."

The bankers inwardly smarted at the pointed reminder of a rare error perpetrated some years ago, but never to be forgotten by their client.

"You're not going to take any debt on this one?" The disappointment in the young suit's voice was clear for all to hear and the older man flashed a look of warning to the impetuous youth.

Ziyad bridled in his chair as this had been discussed and dismissed at a previous conversation. He did not expect to have to go over the matter again.

"I said no before, and I still say not" The exasperation in Ziyad's voice was unmistakable, even to thick skinned bankers. "Please don't try, yet again, to convince me otherwise. You earn enough fees from me already so," he paused to recall the epithet correctly, "don't look a gift horse in the mouth."

The tone was sufficiently cool to silence the two men before the elder suit concluded the discussion with the obligatory, "Is there anything else we can do for you or that you require of the bank, sir?"

"Only confirmation that you have successfully completed my instructions." Ziyad took another sip of his whisky and stared silently at the suits who looked uncomfortable. Before they could say anything further, Ziyad reached forward and cut the connection and the unhappy couple instantly disappeared from his desk.

Ziyad sat back and savoured his Scotch as he waited for the screen to buzz once again. He lugubriously stretched his arm forward and, with the edge of the whisky glass at his lip, he pressed the requisite keys on his keyboard to join the second prearranged online meeting.

This time a young woman appeared on the screen. She was wearing designer glasses and an expensively cut suit. Her hair was piled on the top of her head and a wedding ring flashed from her finger as she adjusted the camera angle on her computer.

She greeted Ziyad with a friendly smile and slightly less formality than the bankers. Ziyad liked this smart young woman. He admired her intellect and her air of efficient professionalism. He also found her very pleasant to the eye and were he a younger man, well, who knows?

"I've just spoken to Monty and his young sidekick, whose name I can never remember…"

"Justin" the young woman interjected.

"Yes, Justin, and the bank should have transferred funds to you. If you haven't received them yet, then you should do so at any moment," he announced between sips. The whisky was producing the usual soft, pleasantly muzzy feeling in his head. "I've read your title report, very thorough if I may say so. I'd like you to proceed as we previously discussed. The Agreement for Lease to the television company is complete?"

The woman checked her notes. "Yes, this morning. We've also submitted a request for a licence from the freeholder consenting to the alterations for the fitting out of the unit to the tenant's specification. The work has started, as agreed, and I have spoken to the freeholder who has assured me that there will be no problems."

That was what Ziyad liked about this woman, things were thought through and executed without constant reference back to him.

"Does it have the necessary planning consent?" he asked, knowing what the answer was likely to be.

"Yes."

"Good." Another sip of whisky was taken before Ziyad continued, "And there are no problems with the authorities over the money?"

"Not that we're aware of. We've been through the source of your funds and all the requirements have been dealt with satisfactorily."

"Excellent. Can you just confirm exactly how many flats are above the restaurant, and how many are vacant? I want you to get the interior designers in there as quickly as possible so we can get them relet." The appointment of his interior designer was beyond her usual remit to clients, but the solicitor nodded her assent. For the income she earnt from this client she was happy to stretch her professional role.

"There are seventy-two flats in total, fourteen are vacant and eleven of those require refurbishment." Ziyad so enjoyed working with this young woman who had all the facts at her fingertips and concisely provided the information he needed, not to mention that she had an attractive, open face and, from what he could see on screen, a good figure.

"I believe one of them is on the top floor, I want that to be…"

"Ah, the funds have just arrived in our Client Account", the lawyer interrupted Ziyad in a matter-of-fact manner. He did not object. He was relaxed in her company. An email notification pinged onto his machine from the bankers also confirming the transfer of funds.

"Good. In that case I'll leave you to do all the necessary and I look forward to hearing that the purchase has been successfully completed. Thank you for your assistance."

Ziyad suddenly had an after-thought, "What's the name of the restaurant that's taking the ground floor?"

The solicitor hesitated and looked at the papers on her desk, "The Sauceror's Apprentice. Sauceror is spelt…"

"It's OK. I've worked it out. We might have dinner there when I am next in London?"

The solicitor wondered if 'we' referred to her alone or with his family but did not seek clarification. She would deal with that problem if, and when, it arose. Ziyad waited for a reaction and when none was forthcoming, he thanked her politely for her assistance.

"You're very welcome." The lawyer leant forward and Ziyad's screen went blank again.

He picked up his glass once more, realised that it was empty and refilled it with another hefty measure from the now almost empty decanter. Ziyad leant back in his chair and smiled contentedly to himself. It had been a good day.

The smile evaporated as a more domestic question entered his befuddled brain.

'Where is that damn son of mine?'

Ziyad rose somewhat unsteadily from his desk. He sauntered, decanter swinging from one hand and his empty glass in the other, towards the dining room to see what was awaiting him for his solitary supper.

Chapter 6

The ancient bus roared along the street spewing out a cloud of black fumes from its exhaust pipe. The driver was impervious to the traffic around him, expecting every other road user to get out of his path. Braking hard and swerving across the carriageway, he narrowly missed a tuk-tuk loaded with a family of six and all their wares.

Randul was thrown against the withered old man who sat next to him. He did not flinch, his creased face like worn leather, ageing him beyond his allotted years. Randul noted that he was dressed in a traditional sarong and a well-worn white Ralph Lauren polo shirt. An ensemble that Randul assumed to be his one set of smart clothes, worn each week specifically for his trip into town for the market. No doubt he would meet up with the other senior members of local families in one of the many coffee houses and while away the time either reminiscing or playing fiercely competitive games of carrom or peralikatuma.

They had chatted desultorily throughout the long journey, the old man lecturing Randul on what he saw as the destruction of his country by the Tamil Tigers, the corruption that was visible to all but denied by those in authority, the general migration of the young into towns and cities from the rural villages, the increasing lack of respect for their elders and various other woes that seemed to afflict the elderly as they reflected on modern life. No doubt, one day, Randul would chunter in a similar vein against the iniquities of the government and the unstoppable march of progress.

At Randul's feet, but with the shoulder strap held tightly in his grip, was an old canvas knapsack that contained all that he needed for his brief stay. A change of clothes, a small wash bag, his precious journal and, of course, the leather pouch that held just a small selection from his collection of rough gemstones. He had included two of the smaller Padparadscha stones with a view to testing the water with his chosen dealer to ascertain what price they might command.

Randul had been remiss in allowing his regular discoveries from the river to build up. In fact, it was only when he removed his complete collection from under the floorboard in his kitchen that he realised how much he had amassed. He had not bothered recently to take them to the local village dealers because he had been absorbed with his work in his laboratory. His relatively solitary and simple lifestyle meant that he had little need for the additional funds that regular small sales might provide.

When he had got around to sorting the collection, he worried that he might have to break the two largest Padparadscha stones into smaller segments in order to surreptitiously slip them onto the open market.

That would have been a shame.

After he had found the Padparadscha stones, he had used the Forestry Department's internet to look up the size of the world's largest stone. He discovered that it was an oval cut 'Pad' of just over one hundred carats, and it sat in a museum in New York.

At nought point two grammes to a carat, he calculated that the New York stone would weigh around twenty grammes. It made his stomach turn when he realised this and, upon returning to his bungalow, he had weighed the largest of his own uncut stones.

The largest was just in excess of one hundred and twenty grammes! Admittedly, this was the raw, uncut weight, but even so. Allowing for a maximum wastage of seventy percent to produce a finished oval cut gem, the resultant jewel would weigh approximately thirty-six grammes, possibly more if the wastage was less.

One hundred and eighty carats!

Randul could hardly believe it. His was almost double the size of the New York Padparadscha! He had then quickly weighed the others.

Using the same calculations, he concluded that if his four rough Padparadscha stones were cut and polished into oval gems then he would be the owner of one of the greatest collections of Padparadscha gems in the world. He jotted down in his journal the results of his calculations.

Gross weight – grammes	Cut weight – carats (70% wastage)
121	181.5
87	130.5
52	78
16	24

A grand total of just over four hundred and fourteen carats!

Randul had no way of working out the true value of his stones as he was not qualified to assess the quality of the underlying gems. This would have an impact on value, and on this matter, he had to trust the dealer that he chose to be relatively honest with him.

The table in his Journal merely emphasised to him the fact that there was not the remotest possibility of getting any of the local village dealers to contemplate taking even the smallest stone, let alone four, without full certification and authentication. And there lay the problem – provenance.

Even the most unscrupulous dealers would not be willing to expose themselves to the inevitable publicity that such a clutch of stones would garner should their existence become known to the world market. Undoubtedly, the potential availability of such a collection would elicit global interest amongst the mega-rich. Randul assumed that it would be inevitable that any sale would be in the gift of one of the major auction houses in London, Geneva or New York. However, long before it reached any saleroom, the Sri Lankan National Gem and Jewellery Authority would confiscate the stones and Randul would be in line for that substantial fine or custodial sentence.

This was not a situation that he wished to find himself in.

One alternative option was a private sale to a person who was willing to deal outside the realm of the accepted market and who had the funds to make the jewels disappear from public view. There were such people, but Randul did not know who they were or how he could contact them. The discount for the lack of the required provenance would be substantial. He guessed that any such discount could be largely offset by the extra premium a private collector would pay for the opportunity to acquire such uniquely sized jewels away from prying eyes. However, Randul had no access to such high-net-worth individuals and knew that, again, he would have to rely upon others if he was to successfully sell even the smallest of his stones.

The bus rattled into the Kandy bus stand at the end of its journey and people started to gather their belongings for disembarkation. With a formal bow, the old man bid Randul farewell and shuffled off to join a much younger woman who was seated towards the front of the bus. After initially fussing over him, she guided him down the steps onto the dusty street.

Randul remained seated to allow the bus to empty before picking up his bag and swinging it over his shoulder. He politely thanked the driver who looked askance that anyone, let alone a Veddah, would bother, but smiled broadly when he realised that the gratitude was genuine.

After such a long journey, Randul was badly in need of a refreshing cup of tea. He stopped outside a small café where he could sit down and recover from the heat and noise of the bus, while watching the hustle and bustle of people in the busy street. A young waitress with bare feet and dressed in a smart blouse and long skirt approached him as he hovered by a vacant table. At her bidding, he sat down and placed his order. His bag was carefully positioned on the ground between his feet, still with the shoulder strap held fast in his hand.

Randul used to enjoy the rare trips he made into Kandy but on this occasion, he felt conspicuous and more than a little vulnerable. Every so often a small gaggle of tourists passed his table, their attire and accessories making them easily recognisable as strangers in town. Randul had rejected traditional tribal dress and opted to wear his work clothes. They were less distinctive and would attract less attention. The tourists gave him no more than a cursory glance, although the girls admired the almond-eyed young native with his slim build, wild hair and ready smile.

He slowly drank his tea and tried to decide upon the best approach to his chosen dealer.

Randul had listened to the conversations of other guides and villagers who regularly traded their own small finds. On each occasion, he made a careful note in his Journal of the various names of those who were considered safe to approach. An amiable villain was acceptable, but a violent criminal was to be avoided at all costs – and there were plenty of those around. There was one name that was mentioned by a couple of people, a man referred to as 'The Arab'. Randul understood from those that he trusted, without giving any hint as to why he was interested, that while The Arab negotiated a hard price, he had a reputation for absolute discretion and was relatively 'honest' – or as honest as might be expected.

Randul had carefully selected a few stones that he was willing to sell in order to gain some idea of the integrity of the man. He knew the address but wanted to avoid visiting the Arab's shop during the busy time of the day and so Randul intended to wait until the shop was quieter.

He finished his tea and paid the young girl, before strolling down towards Kandy Lake past the Colombo Stock Exchange building. The Temple of the Sacred Tooth stood in the distance, a constant stream of tourists moving along the pathway leading to the ticket offices. He turned right and walked along the edge of the lake, marvelling at its scale and length – all hand dug for the benefit of a former ruler. The trees provided shade for a group of old men who were discussing the latest news on the civil war. The December 2000 ceasefire was looking unlikely to hold and opinions were varied as to what the government should do. Randul looked to see if his companion from the bus had settled down with the group, but he was nowhere to be seen.

Randul started the climb up through the Royal Palace Park into the tangle of streets that overlooked the Temple and the lake before it. He intended to check in to the small guest house that he used whenever he came to Kandy. It had clean rooms and provided a very acceptable supper for its guests at a modest price. He knew the owner and whenever he stayed, he always tried to bring a small sample of something that he had foraged from the forest or that he had been experimenting with in his small home laboratory. These offerings were always well received as Randul invariably tried to include something new or unusual. This visit would be no exception and Randul was excited to see if the other residents experienced a more interesting evening meal than might otherwise have been the case. Despite the occasional contribution that Randul might make, the standard of the food served at the guest house was probably some of the best Kandy had to offer. However, he always liked to set himself the challenge of adding something a little special that gave an extra piquancy to the fare.

It was not somewhere that any unknowing tourist would venture. However, had they been courageous enough to pass through the rather drab and uninviting entrance, they would have been assured of a genial welcome from the family that owned and ran the unassuming premises. The husband was the chef, entirely self-taught having cooked for most of his adult life, while his wife and daughters provided front of house and general duties. His wife additionally handled all the finances with great diligence and aptitude, her husband having no great interest in such things. He concentrated on his cooking, tending the myriad of bubbling pots balanced precariously on the multitude of gas rings that turned his small kitchen into a furnace.

The arrival of Randul was greeted with the usual expectant excitement and the husband quickly emerged from his hellishly hot workplace to hurriedly greet his guest with a formal bow and a cheery, 'Ayabowen'. But it was obvious that he was impatient to see what delicacies Randul had brought for him. Randul laid out a modest selection of exotic spices for his host to inspect. In the markets of Kandy the chef had access to a wide selection of everyday herbs and spices, but Randul always foraged for items that were a little more out of the ordinary and beyond the expertise of less knowledgeable or adventurous foragers.

A few passing guests lingered to listen to Randul expound as to the purpose of each in either cooking or medicine. As always, the chef listened carefully to the narrative and noted any suggestions as to the use, taste or texture of each little colourful pile of powder or gnarled root. When Randul paused, the cook chose an item to sample, his face either lighting up with delight or wrinkling in contemplation as to how he might use the ingredient to its best advantage.

After the initial inspection had been completed, the chef showed a slight sense of anti-climax. While interesting, the delicacies provided were unexceptional, or unexceptional in terms of Randul's usual standards. Randul detected the silent disappointment and dug in his bag to extract from its depths his final offering - a small twist of paper. The tiny package was carefully held in the palm of Randul's hand and he opened it to reveal a coarse, pale reddish-brown powder

The chef's brow furrowed, and he leant forward to sniff for any aroma arising from the sample.

There was none.

Next, he went to stick a slender finger into the precipitate to take a tasting. Randul quickly withdrew the paper twist, leaving the chef's hand hovering in mid-air. He huffed in frustration and Randul swiftly explained the reason for his action.

"You will only need a grain or two. If you use more, you will not taste anything for the next couple of days. Be sure to blend it with some curd or vegetable kottu but use it very, very sparingly."

The chef looked at Randul with a sceptical sideways glance, unsure as to whether it was necessary to heed the warning. Experience should have told him by now that this Veddah was passionate about his foraging, and he did not make facetious comments regarding any of the produce that he brought. The chef wiped the end of his finger on his turmeric-stained apron and, with great precision picked out between his fingertip and thumb a single small grain of the powder. Very cautiously, he touched his tongue against the grain, lips pursed, and waited. Initially, there was no sign of any perceptible impact on his taste buds. Then, suddenly, his head rocked back, and his eyes opened wide. His wife looked on with some concern until an expression of sheer delight spread across his face.

The chef was experiencing a moment of ecstasy.

"This is wonderful. Out of this world. A gift from the Gods." The chef kept extolling the virtues of the little grain and Randul was delighted.

He had worked many late nights to perfect the powder and tonight he was hoping to see its effects on those who would dine at the guest house. Once the chef had calmed down, he asked, "Mr Randul, what is this?"

Randul could not help smiling as the chef immediately realised that it was foolish to seek any information as to the source, content or method of extraction of any of the special surprises that his guest so generously delivered.

"This time, Mr Randul, you have excelled even your exacting standards. This is pure magic, pure alchemy."

"Thank you, Rajid. Your praise is appreciated. Now it is up to you to use your own magic and create an appropriate dish for its use."

Randul continued to watch the cook as his eyes glazed slightly and a benign grin bathed his face. The creases around his eyes relaxed and the sallow skin took on a radiance that had been lacking after years in the heat and steam of his kitchen. The effect of the powder was as successful as ever Randul could have hoped. He cocked his head to one side as he witnessed the continuing euphoria on the chef's face. Their eyes met conspiratorially and then they both broke into raucous laughter.

The chef's wife watched in bemusement and tried to take her own grain, but her husband swiftly snatched the paper from her reach and retwisted the top to seal in the valuable ingredient. He swept up the remaining items on the table and hurried back down the corridor that led to his kitchen.

"I need to think," he muttered as he receded from sight, and then, in a quieter voice, he repeated to himself, "I need to think."

As he disappeared through the battered swing-door, he called out over his shoulder, "You will be eating with us tonight, Mr Randul?"

"I wouldn't miss it for the world."

The door closed behind him without listening to Randul's respond. His wife turned to Randul and shrugged her shoulders. "I will not see him again until this evening."

A disembodied voice shouted something inaudible from behind the closed kitchen door and his wife called to one of her daughters to go and see what he wanted. She returned her attention to Randul but made no attempt to fill in the register. She merely handed over a large, old-fashioned key to a padlock.

"We've given you your usual room."

As Randul took his key she adds, "Whenever you come here, you always set him a challenge."

"Whenever I set him a challenge, he rises to it," Randul replied. The wife nodded her agreement and returned to more mundane matters requiring her attention. With a grin, Randul turned and walked across the courtyard to climb the worn stone steps to the first floor.

A landing encircled and overlooked the open courtyard that served as reception and, later, the dining room. There was a dark stained, timber balustrade, and the floor was covered with a mosaic of brightly coloured rugs of various designs.

Each door off the landing had a faded number painted onto the upper panel, seemingly in no logical numerical order. Randul knew exactly where he was going, the confusingly random distribution of room numbers irrelevant to him. His room was to the rear of the hotel, and he noisily unlocked the ancient padlock and pulled apart the simple metal hasp that secured the door.

The interior was simply furnished having a metal-framed single bed with a bedside cabinet on which stood a lamp with a bare bulb and no shade. Next to the closed window that overlooked the street was a high-backed rattan chair and a small round metal table. Randul liked this room because he could hear the traffic and sit and watch the comings and goings of the people who busied themselves on the street below. It was in complete contrast to the peaceful, solitary life that he led in the forest. In some respects, it was cathartic, the frenetic change being exciting, but only for short periods.

To open the window, he gently but forcibly hit the side of the swollen wooden sash with the heel of his hand, while simultaneously lifting the semi-circular brass handle that was screwed to its lower edge. It was always the same, the owners never having been the most diligent about attending to the everyday maintenance of the building.

He could hear that the traffic was heavy in the busy road below and, as the window banged open, this was reinforced by a waft of diesel fumes that was sucked into the room by the thin billowing curtains. The toxic smell mingled with smoke from the embers of the many small fires that had been set earlier in the day to burn the rubbish and clear the streets of litter. Randul looked up to the hills that formed the bowl in which the city lay, trapping the pollution that would only be dispersed when a welcome breeze blew in. The humidity was high and the air stagnant, so the likelihood of immediate relief was doubtful.

Turning away from the chaos below, Randul sat down on the wicker chair and took out his journal and a pencil from his canvas bag. He made some brief notes, logging the date and time he gave the powder to the chef and the initial reaction that had been observed. He would complete more comprehensive notes later that evening, following dinner.

He crossed to the bed and flopped down onto the thin mattress with his journal balanced on his chest. Turning back through the pages, he started to read but before too long his eyelids slid closed and he fell into a deep sleep.

Randul awoke with a start and looked at his watch. The afternoon light was fading fast, and he cursed as he leapt up from the bed and rummaged in his backpack. The leather pouch had worked its way to the bottom and in his haste to extract it, he scattered his clean clothes over the bed, some of which fell to the floor. He hurriedly collected them up and tossed them back into a crumpled heap before extracting the pouch containing the stones. He weighed it in his hand as if to assess whether any of the gems were missing before realising that the bulging pouch was too big to stuff into his trouser pocket. He tipped the last of his meagre belongings onto the bed and put the soft leather bag back into his now empty knapsack.

It was almost 6:00pm and he was not entirely sure when The Arab would close his shop for the day. Some remained open late into the evening, but the gem stores varied. He regretted not having located the premises earlier instead of falling asleep.

Randul did not like surprises or to be unprepared.

He hurried out of the guest house to the surprise of his hostess who called out that dinner was to be served at 8:00pm. Randul waved a hand in acknowledgement and walked swiftly out under the arched entrance in the direction that he believed the shop owned by the Arab was located.

Chapter 7

Ziyad was seated on his stool, with yet another astringent cup of coffee cradled in his hands. He was eagerly awaiting the return of the young American couple who had visited his shop earlier in the day. He felt confident that they would do so as he had flattered them and cajoled them into showing a strong interest in purchasing an engagement ring from one of his more expensive ranges. This warranted a degree of privacy, so he had suggested that as 'special clients' they should return to see him at the end of the day, shortly before he closed. He would then be able to give them his undivided attention.

Ziyad knew that it was always a risk allowing a rich customer out of the door, but after years of experience he recognised when to employ such a tactic in the certainty that it would yield greater rewards. As he had anticipated, the young man was flattered both to be accorded the enhanced 'special client' status and to be given the opportunity for a private, after-hours viewing of what he hoped would be something exceptional and unique.

Despite Ziyad's obvious disabilities, the Texan quietly respected his entrepreneurial spirit. As a cripple, this broken individual was trying to make the best of a hard life, to earn an honest living in order to feed and clothe his family in the American way, and such enterprise was to be admired. It never occurred to him that Ziyad might have been directly or indirectly responsible for inflicting horrific life changing injuries or even facilitating the death of many of his fellow American servicemen.

His fiancée had gazed adoringly at Brad, but Ziyad saw the truth. She was seduced far more by the sight of the jewels that had been laid out before her, and the prospect of better yet to come. In her mind's eye she was already posing for photos in that revealingly low cut, black dress that she had packed. She could then post the pictures to her slowly improving number of global followers on the new social media thingy. But, more importantly, her coterie of girlfriends in Austin would enviously note the large, bejewelled engagement ring on her finger, together with any other sparkling embellishments that Brad might generously bestow on to her body.

She knew that Brad, or more particularly his dad, could easily afford any of the baubles that this poor, dear man might bring out from the depths of his grubby little shop. Similarly to Brad, she viewed their patronage as helping the miserable wretch to provide for his own impoverished family. In fact, she had decided that on her return to the shop she would ask the old man if she could take a selfie with him to show everyone what a fine thing it was that she and Brad were doing for the people of the Third World.

Ziyad had restrained himself from rubbing his hands together with joy when they had eagerly agreed to resume their conversation later in the day. Innocently asking for the name of the hotel they were staying in, he noted that it was very much at the luxury end of those available in Kandy. Ziyad would attend at their hotel should they have a change of heart about returning and so he regarded this information as his guarantee of their custom.

He relished the opportunity to gently guide them towards a few more extravagant purchases, in addition to the matching earrings and necklace that he had already sold to them.

Ziyad impatiently watched the hands of the clock as they eased towards the appointed 6:15 meeting. The shop was quiet. Aloka had been dismissed for the day and the feeling of anticipation was a delight, filling Ziyad with an adrenalin enriched sense of wellbeing. He loved the haggling. The pathetic downward turn of the mouth. The stumble as he moves uncomfortably from behind his counter. The pleading look from his one perfect but watery eye. The move with shaking fingers to straighten the shabby patch over the other eye, just to remind them of all his disabilities. As they left, his clients would shake Ziyad's hand and quietly congratulate themselves on beating him down to a price that still far exceeded anything that he might achieve from any half-knowledgeable customer.

He sat with his coffee and the hint of a self-satisfied smile on his face, until his thoughts were dispelled by the door to his shop bursting open. An unexpected, local man breathlessly rushed in. Ziyad muttered an incoherent blasphemy at his carelessness for not having locked the door after Aloka had left. He immediately leapt up from his stool.

"We are closed!" he snapped. "Go away!" He slammed his cup down on the counter and the hot coffee scalded his hand as it slopped over the rim. Ziyad swore again and mopped his hand with a dirty handkerchief that he had hastily pulled from his pocket.

Randul stopped on the threshold and was unsure whether to proceed or retreat. Ziyad hobbled from around his counter and waved his hand at the dark skinned, wild eyed, young ruffian as if to sweep him from the premises. He looked quickly out into the street beyond his uninvited visitor and was relieved that the young Americans were nowhere to be seen.

Randul felt uncomfortable at the terse dismissal but pushed ahead regardless. "I wonder if you'd look at some stones I have?"

Ziyad looked at the tribesman with undisguised contempt.

"Not now, boy. I'm expecting some clients at any moment. We're closed"

Randal, having started was not to be deflected.

"I just need you to let me know if they're any good and whether you'd like to purchase them? I am told that you give a fair price."

The young man had clearly spoken to the wrong person, but Ziyad could not resist a quick deal with this naive youth who was in such a rush. Any vendor in a hurry was always a virtue for Ziyad. He checked the street once again and ushered Randul into the shop closing the door behind him and turning the key in the dry lock.

"I don't have much time. I've important clients arriving at any moment," Ziyad repeated, undertaking one more visual check of the street outside. "And when they do come you must be gone." Having laid out his terms, he waited to see what Randul would do. Impatience got the better of Ziyad.

"Well? What've you got for me?"

Randul took off his backpack and retrieved the leather pouch from inside. Ziyad returned to his stool and mopped up the remaining spilt coffee with a tissue from a box under the counter. As he did so, he surreptitiously watched the young man. From his appearance, the tousled black hair, the full beard and the reddened gums from chewing betel, Ziyad had him marked as a Veddah almost immediately. Admittedly, he was not dressed as a Veddah, his clothes were those of a forestry guide. But in contrast to the weary demeanour of the usual rural chancers who entered his shop to trade, this one had alert eyes that signalled to Ziyad increased levels of adrenaline rather than betel. Ziyad had come across theses aboriginal tribesmen before and he was always slightly wary of them. He judged them to be naturally wily and not to be underestimated when not under the influence of alcohol, the betel or some other stimulant, in which event they became volatile and highly unpredictable.

Ziyad did not hold out any great expectations as to what this one would have to offer until Randul carefully shook out onto the counter a small number of light blue sapphires. Even to an untrained eye, and Ziyad had one of the sharpest eyes in the business, it was clear that these were stones of quality, despite their modest size. Randul had carefully held back the two larger stones within the base of the pouch, secured between his finger and thumb. He wanted to see what the Arab would say about his initial offering first. If the price was derisory then he would pack up and try elsewhere, but he had to start somewhere.

Through years of practice, Ziyad maintained a stern face and showed neither admiration nor overt interest. He curled his top lip and wrinkling his nose as he looked down at the collection.

"Well, they are very small and do not seem to be of any great quality."

He pushed the little pile of stones around with his forefinger in a desultory manner as if trying to find something of value. Exhaling hoarsely, Ziyad made his initial offer without apparently intending to inspect them in any more detail. Randul was not to be taken in by the implied disinterest and went to put the stones back in his pouch. Ziyad stayed his hand as it advanced across the counter towards the stones. It was apparent that this Veddah understood the rules of the game and was not to be so easily fooled.

"Wait. Let's not be hasty. Let me take a closer look." Ziyad took his eyeglass from beneath the counter and pushed it into the socket of his good eye. He re-examined the specimens and as he did so, he innocently enquired, "Have you come far?"

Randul had no intention of giving the Arab any more information than was absolutely necessary at this juncture.

"Far enough."

Ziyad studied the offered gems closely for the first time, confirming his initial conclusion that they were actually rather fine. The clarity and the intermediate level of blue, neither too dark nor too pale, made this little collection of some value to a competent jeweller. He looked up at Randul, his one eye magnified through the eyeglass giving him a comically malevolent air. Holding the younger man's gaze, still trying to sum him up, he conceded,

"Mmm, well on closer inspection they are a little better than I had initially thought. Let me put them on the scales."

He turned and took a set of brass balance scales from the shelf behind him, electronic scales having never suited Ziyad's method of doing business. He placed some of the larger stones individually on the pan and then replaced them with the remainder.

"You have a total of around eight carats of assorted bits and pieces. They won't yield much once cut." He maintained his air of indifference, but Ziyad was becoming increasingly intrigued by the young tribesman. Obviously, the stones weighed heavier than he had quoted. The thin strip of copper attached to the underside of the balance pan on which the counterweights had been carefully placed skewed the weight to Ziyad's advantage.

The colour of each stone was enhanced by the reflected light from the polished brass pan. These were undoubtedly small but handsome stones and Ziyad wanted them. He was still unsure if his seller was aware of their true worth, but increasingly felt that he was not stupid, or as trusting as he might be trying to appear.

"Where did you find these?" Ziyad's enquiry was made without looking up, but the casual nature of the questioning was not going to trick Randul.

"In a river."

"Which river?"

"Near my home."

Ziyad thought for a moment. The response was evasive and of little help to him. There were still many areas of Sri Lanka where the remaining Veddah resided.

"Do you have any more?" Ziyad had seen the palming of the remaining contents of the pouch and suspected that the best was yet to come.

Randul did not answer immediately. He was undecided as to whether the Arab was to be trusted, let alone made a confidant. His strategy had been to assess the man by the price he was prepared to offer for these pretty shards of stone. If acceptable, he might then move on to the main purpose of his visit. It was a cat and mouse negotiation, and he would have preferred more time to deliberate and weigh up his options.

"I might have, but we need to strike a deal on these before we discuss anything else."

Ziyad was processing the information that the Veddah had given him, which was not much. It was clear that he had been shown a taster of what this young man had to offer and he was becoming more interested in discovering the Veddah's source.

What lay on the counter before him were small, but they were good. With expert cutting and polishing, they could be made into highly marketable jewellery. If there were any more, then he wanted to see them. If he was to be denied that opportunity, then he might still find it advantageous to strike up a relationship with the stranger. Such an arrangement, he convinced himself, might be in both their longer-term interests.

Ziyad had come to a decision.

"Bearing in mind that I must assume that these are not legitimately obtained," he paused to see if Randul reacted, but the expression of the tribesman remained unaltered. He continued, "And the fact that the authorities do not encourage illegitimate mining; the price must reflect the risks to me."

"True, but I could go to the NGJA and they would pay me sixty percent of market value for a chance find. No questions asked."

Ziyad turned his face slightly to focus his good eye on the man. Had he misjudged or underestimated the nature of the man he was dealing with? He gave his response in a slow and deliberate manner, as if lecturing a child.

"You are quite correct, for the odd chance find. But you have more than might be picked up from a quick swim in a rock pool." Ziyad hoped his assumption would elicit a reaction, but still nothing. He continued, lowering the tone of his voice further. "They would not look kindly on such a fraudulent claim." Ziyad paused to assess whether his words were having any effect on the Veddah, and on still seeing nothing pressed on.

"Confiscation, large fines, possibly even imprisonment. Are you willing to risk such things?"

Randul did not flinch.

"I understand that." Randul held the pouch loosely in one hand and Ziyad could not stop his eye watching it.

"You have always been well respected and considered fair, although not overly generous, to those who supply you with special items. It seems that I must rely upon your discretion, as you must rely upon mine."

"It appears that you have researched into my reputation, but what guarantees do I have that you are as discreet as I am believed to be?"

The young Veddah gave a broad, disarming smile, his teeth white against his reddened gums that now clearly displaying the effects of the betel.

"You don't."

Ziyad slumped back onto his stool in an overt display of disappointment.

"You will have to rely upon my word," Randul said. For the first time he felt that he might have the upper hand in the negotiation. He dangled the pouch tantalisingly before Ziyad, the weight of the remaining stones obvious.

"I suspect that you might already feel a compulsion to work with me, at least for a while."

Ziyad recoiled in surprise at the boy's insightfulness, verging on impudence.

"Why on earth would I want to do that?" For some inexplicable reason, Ziyad was almost beginning to like this young man and now he was determined to discover what more he might have in that damn bag. He raised his eyebrows to signal that he was waiting for Randul to reveal more details.

Randul took a deep breath.

"Do you get many Padparadscha sapphires passing through your shop?"

Ziyad froze momentarily, his heart giving an involuntary lurch, before quickly recovering. He tried to hide his shock by taking a sip of the dregs that remained of his cold coffee. He adjusted his position on his stool.

"As you are obviously aware, they are highly sought after and extremely rare. Do you have one?"

"Maybe. How would I know? You are the expert." Randul grinned impishly and knew that he had hooked Ziyad whose eye sparkled with greed.

"Can I see?" Ziyad leant forward over the counter nodding his head towards the bag to encourage the Veddah to reveal the contents.

"Not now." Randul flicked his wrist to swing the pouch in a circle to land in the palm of his hand. His long slender fingers closed around the stones within. For a second time, Ziyad slumped back onto his stool in frustration.

"Let's reach an agreement as to the price that you'll pay me for what is already in your balance."

Ziyad stared down at the pale blue stones again and made a rashly generous offer that ran contrary to his better judgement. He hoped that it would ensure that this intriguing young savage would take him into his confidence. Randul extended his hand in the style of a westerner to apparently seal the agreement, an action wholly inconsistent with both of their ethnic origins.

Confused, Ziyad wondered, once again, if he had made a terrible error of judgement. He hesitantly took the Veddah's hand and gave it a perfunctory shake. He removed the pan from the scales and tipped the contents into a small plastic bag that had miraculously appeared in his other hand. The top of the bag was sealed in one quick movement, and Ziyad went to place the stones beneath the counter, out of sight. However, Randul, with lightning speed, caught his wrist and held it with a strength that both surprised and hurt. Ziyad winced with pain and looked affronted but allowed the plastic bag to drop back onto the counter, the stones clinking together as they settled.

No words were spoken but the intent was clear. Ziyad nodded a submission to the Veddah, who released his grip.

"Wait here." Ziyad said and he scuttled back into the rear room before returning with a battered petty cash box. He carefully unlocked the lid and counted out the agreed sum. He handed the notes over to Randul, while simultaneously taking possession of the bag of stones. For a moment both men held the notes between them, eye contact being maintained until Ziyad released them.

"What is your name?" Ziyad asked. "How can I contact you?"

"You can't. I will be in touch with you."

"But what about the Padpa....?"

The door to the shop clattered as the two young American sweethearts noisily tried to enter the shop but found their way barred. They stopped and peered in through the glass, giggling like excited children on a school outing.

"You must go," Ziyad urgently said. "Come back to see me tomorrow." Ziyad stumbled from behind his counter and took Randul's arm to usher him from the shop. In his haste to eject the Veddah, he had left the almost empty petty cash tin on top of the counter. Conflicted between welcoming his returning customers and protecting his cash, Ziyad dithered before releasing his grip and hurrying back. He grabbed the tin box and quickly returned it to the safe. He was flustered. The revelation by the Veddah that he might have a Padparadscha had caused Ziyad to momentarily forget all about his appointment with the Americans.

Ziyad could move with considerable speed when required, despite his disability. He shoved Randul across the shop and swiftly unlocked the door before opening his arms in an effusive greeting to his next customers.

The Americans spoke as one, gushing their apologies to Ziyad for being so late for their appointment. Brad looked from Ziyad to Randul and back again.

"If it isn't convenient or we've disturbed you, we can always come back tomorrow."

Ziyad could not allow that. He had already permitted them to slip away once, and any further delay in taking their money was inconceivable.

But was he wise in letting the Veddah escape? It was all too perplexing. Ziyad even questioned whether he was losing his touch. Pushing the self-doubt from his mind, he ushered the Americans in through the door.

"No, please, come on in. We have just finished anyway." Ziyad raised his eyebrows at Randul for his acknowledgment that the meeting was concluded...for the present.

Randul took hold of the door handle as the Americans slid into the shop. As she brushed unnecessarily close to Randul, the girl stared approvingly at the striking young man who was about to depart. He was almost as tall as Brad but looked lithe and fit without any signs of the band of fat that had started to appear around her fiancé's waist.

To Ziyad, Randul said, "I'll be back to see you again, soon."

The American was surprised to hear him speak to Ziyad in precise English. Randul smiled warmly down at the young woman, and she bashfully flushed as she pressed her way passed him in the doorway.

"I shall look forward to it," Ziyad replied and gave a small nod, his lips pursed together as he speculated as to whether he had backed the wrong horse in releasing the Veddah in favour of the Americans.

Chapter 8

Stephen had seen enough Temples and stupas to satisfy his cultural curiosity for some years to come. The Ibbankatuwa megalithic burial site was fascinating and the Dambulla cave temples beautiful and serene. The majesty of Sigiriya was awe inspiring. He had climbed up the rickety staircases and paused at the Lion's Paw before completing his ascent to the very top, unaware that the descent was far scarier than the ascent.

All this had been magnificent and exhilarating, but his appetite for yet more tourist destinations was waning. The hotels that he had been booked into were luxurious and his treatment by staff and management exemplary. All this had been arranged by the travel company that had been one of the sponsors of the television show. Initially this had been an enjoyable extravagance, but Stephen was impatient to pursue the real reason for his trip.

Having been catapulted into the realms of a minor celebrity, Stephen wondered whether he would be old news by the time he returned to the UK. The new world in which he found himself was transitory, and so fickle. The marketing team at the TV company had decided to use something called SixDegrees, a social media platform, but Stephen had no idea what this was or how it worked, and frankly was not interested. It was probably a fad that would pass.

They also asked him to contribute to a thing called a blog but again, Stephen had to rely on the nerds in London to run this for him. He just sent emails with photos attached which he assumed they used.

The newspapers and gossip columns were the main areas that had to be kept informed as to his activities, but without an attractive young woman at his side, they quickly tired of the story. Stephen was only too aware that the faster you rose in the public consciousness, the greater the target you became for newspaper editors who at a whim could bring you crashing down to earth. Perhaps this new social media thing would restore a degree of balance and stop the newspapers acting so vindictively towards those who they deemed unworthy of their support.

He knew that he was going to have to rely on the assurances of the television company that they would continue to maintain a positive media profile during his absence, and ramp this up on his return from Sri Lanka to open his new London restaurant. The possible cookery programme was dependent upon the success of the restaurant. And then - perhaps a book? Already he was thinking about a further series incorporating travel themed cookery programmes, but quickly realised that this was covered by Stein, the Hairy Bikers and most of the other celebrity chefs. He needed to find something unique but at present ideas escaped him.

The immediate future looked bright, and so he was keen to get back to his first love and create some new dishes that would put his embryonic restaurant on the map as *the* place to dine in London. As far as he was concerned the enforced cultural element of his trip was at an end.

He had visited several restaurants and cafes that he was assured served traditional Sri Lanka fare, but all had so far proved to be disappointing. The food that he tasted was good, even wonderful on some occasions, but to date nothing had set it apart from any other exemplary forms of cooking. He was desperate to find something out of the ordinary and had consulted the overly anxious Celia, the sponsoring travel company's local representative. Unfortunately, her main preoccupation was to ensure that the regular reports she submitted to the TV executives reflected well on her and her employer.

Celia was thirty something, the public school educated daughter of a doting father who did something important in the City of London. Home was a large 1930s house outside Guildford set in a few acres with a swimming pool, grazing for ponies, a tennis court, five car garage and many other accoutrements that any well-bred young lady might expect. Most of her social circle had drifted into various companies akin to her father's and were either married or living with partners in the more affluent suburbs of London. She was considered a rebel for having chosen to travel, albeit that she had done so in the absence of any suitable offers of employment from PR companies - despite Daddy having used his best efforts to slot her into the profession through his contacts.

That is not to say that she was not a pleasant, attractive, well spoken, young lady. She just lacked any imagination or intellect. Fortunately, her mother had unexpectantly met an old school friend while at Royal Ascot who was in the process of setting up a travel company that fashioned extremely expensive tailor-made tours for a 'discerning clientele'. Celia was persuaded to join the company on the basis that her parents were no longer prepared to sponsor her expensive globetrotting tastes, it being far cheaper for Daddy to invest some private equity into his wife's friend's new venture.

Celia was offered the opportunity to chaperone the winner of the cookery competition on a trip to Sri Lanka on the strict understanding that she would ensure that her employer gained as much positive exposure as possible. There was the added advantage for the proprietor of the company that Celia's absence would limit her interface with the more important clients at home. Unfortunately, as Stephen had discovered, Celia lacked initiative or original thought, both having apparently been expunged from her brain through the years of facile trips paid for by her desperately indulgent father and organised by her overly protective mother. In summary, she was a cossetted vacationer whose requirements were expensive and whose adventurous experiences manufactured. If the hotels were luxurious, with all the creature comforts, any overt exposure to poverty made invisible and all discomforts eliminated, then Celia was very content. She had no desire to experience the less well-trodden routes faced by more hardened travellers for whom such trips were created for the very purpose of absorbing new cultures, embracing physical challenges and experiencing true adventures.

As a result, Stephen had nothing in common with her and did not care much for her privileged upbringing and the patronising attitude she displayed towards him.

Stephen had awoken that morning refreshed by a deep sleep and was excited at his decision of the previous evening to strike out independently from his driver and the ever-present Celia, who constantly and irritatingly hovered around him like a moth about a flame. When, over a nightcap, he told her of his intentions she looked horrified, desperately cautioning against any such proposition.

To add to her woes, she was furious to discover that prior to retiring to his room for the night, Stephen had requested that the hotel reception arrange for him to have a hire car for the next few days. Her irritation was primarily directed at the hotel staff for not having consulted with her before making the arrangements. On top of that she had to deal with an angry company driver who was offended, thinking that Stephen was unhappy with his driving, and consequently refused to ferry Celia around as she had become accustomed.

Celia was reaching a level of stress beyond her capacity, and she became increasingly fretful that she might lose a high-profile client in some horrendous traffic accident.

That would spice up the media coverage.

However, despite her best efforts to dissuade him, Stephen remained adamant.

As he emerged from the hotel after breakfast, Celia was at his shoulder still trying to persuade him to change his mind. A small white Toyota was waiting for him at the bottom of the entrance steps, all the paperwork, such as it was, having been completed before Stephen sat down to egg hoppers and some rather fine seeni sambal, all washed down with a refreshing glass or two of wood-apple juice. He had chatted to the young chef who had prepared the cup shaped pancake hoppers, with two eggs perfectly cooked in its base, to get the recipe together with that of the caramelised onion. He made some notes as he ate believing that the hoppers could be used to better advantage on his menu.

It was clear from the reaction of the concierge at the front desk that their guests did not usually use hire cars to travel around the island, preferring to use the services of professional drivers. It could be due to the reputation (one that Celia had vividly and repeatedly conveyed to Stephen) of the almost suicidal driving that most of the otherwise placid Sri Lankan population seemed to adopt once seated behind the wheel of a vehicle – any vehicle. However, Stephen had been to India and in comparison, the local driving in Sri Lanka seemed to him to be a lot less scary.

He had studied his map and had already decided that he would travel towards Kandy, incorporating a good walk on the way in the curiously named Knuckles Range to clear his head. He would then go into Kandy, with no real idea where he might stay overnight, intending to mooch around the town before returning the following day to a relieved Celia.

He was relishing the short period of freedom that he was awarding himself.

Celia followed in his wake babbling about the dangers of driving after dark and the rules and customs that he must follow. He politely thanked her for her concern and climbed into the vehicle. She was still talking when he pulled away to start his journey. As the dust obscured the back of the departing car it suddenly dawned on Celia that, in her panic to discourage Stephen, she had not elicited from him where he was going or for how long.

She had lost her client, hopefully temporarily. Head Office was not going to be pleased.

Stephen quickly became accustomed to both the car and the traffic, finding the solitude a welcome break from the busy itinerary that had been set by the travel company. Now he had the delightful prospect of a day or so to himself doing whatsoever he desired. He had seen from his guidebook and the map lying on the seat next to him that the Knuckles area was high country with numerous challenging walks. While these were popular tourist areas, he hoped that he would be able to explore them on his own terms. He relished the opportunity to meet and talk to any local people that he randomly met, hopefully tasting their food, hearing their stories and experiencing their environment. Stephen liked meeting people - you could not go into the leisure industry, particularly the restaurant trade, without having a strong empathy with your customers and their expectations.

The drive was slow, and he had to consult his map at frequent intervals. He stopped at roadside stalls and, for just a couple of rupees, revived himself with the fresh king coconut juice. He watched in awe as the machete wielding stallholder cleaved the nut in half, handing Stephen one side for him to scoop out the immature jelly-like flesh. The flavours from such jungle-fresh produce were superb and Stephen stopped at more stalls than was necessary to taste the differing snacks that were arranged on the randomly constructed kiosks that dotted the roadside.

There were rickety tables with awnings draped over them that sold fresh fish, as well as others that offered a variety of carefully displayed seasonal fruit and vegetables. Stephen was forced to stop again and again to chat to whoever was tending the stall, whether that be local women, elderly men or small children. With the use of gesticulation and mime, the conversations were both amusing, friendly and informative. After each one, Stephen sat in his car for a moment to jot down what he had learnt in a dog-eared notebook.

What was becoming increasingly clear to Stephen was that he had seriously underestimated how long his foray into the countryside was going to take. It was late afternoon and he had not even got into the Knuckles range. Already he had decided that he would have to add at least one day on to his short period of independence. Most of the day had slipped away and the sun was well below its zenith. Soon dusk would cast a veil across the hills and Stephen intended to heed the advice he had received not to drive after dark.

The road came to a T-junction and his map told him that left would take him into the Knuckles and right headed for Kandy. He looked at his map one last time before he turned right towards Kandy. He would have to reverse his plans and explore the Knuckles after a day in Kandy.

The peace and fresh air of the countryside was banished on arrival in the city of Kandy. A chaotic jumble of streets greeted him, all much busier than any he had encountered elsewhere during his first day. He needed to maintain concentration as people and animals wandered across the road, tuk-tuks sliced their way across his path and bicycles wobbled through the melee of vehicles that had surrounded him. The road widened to form an irregular square that Stephen hoped was close to the centre of town. Vehicles were randomly parked along one side, the far side, and he cautiously edged his way across the unyielding flow of traffic to a cacophony of horns. Whether these were directed at him or just part of the general commotion seemed immaterial. He anxiously searched for a parking space while continuously having to avoid the mechanised chaos that swirled around him. All he wanted at this stage was somewhere he could abandon the car for the night.

Fortunately, as he moved slowly along the centre of the carriageway, across from the line of parked vehicles, he spotted the back of a battered Nissan truck. Black smoke belched out from its low-slung exhaust that was held in place with what appeared to be a cable tie. The driver reversed to get a clear run into the traffic and, with a couple of uncontrolled lurches, careered into the approaching vehicles that swerved either side to avoid his sudden appearance.

Stephen shot forward through the confusion to bag his space. The sudden change of speed from a dawdle to a sprint, and then to a sudden stop in order to parallel-park, resulted in mayhem behind him. Initially everyone had followed his lead and accelerated forward but as he stopped and swiftly engaged reverse gear, there was a desperate exodus from the vicinity of his rear bumper into the opposing stream of vehicles. Everyone came to a noisy, gridlocked impasse. Stephen waved his hand generally in thanks to all the confused drivers around him as he finally slid into the vacated space.

With considerable relief, he turned off the engine and sat for a moment observing the traffic around him as it extricated itself to restore some form of order. A stream of pedestrians drifted past him, some on and some off the rough path that served as a pavement. He realised that it was a miracle that he had completed the manoeuvre without mishap.

He grabbed the small holdall that he had thrown onto the rear seat and stiffly extricated himself from the small car, stretching his large frame as he emerged. Locking the doors, he swung the holdall over his shoulder to go and find somewhere to stay. There were several hotels available to him, and he chose one at random quite near the centre of town. The receptionist had no trouble in taking in an unexpected guest, booking him into a simple but comfortable room.

Stephen put his bag on the bed and intended to study his map when he realised that he had left it on the passenger seat of the car. He meticulously unpacked his bag, placing his belongings either in drawers or on the washstand, even though the duration of his stay was to be only one night. Satisfied that everything was correctly stowed, he retraced his steps back to the hotel foyer and then down the street to the parked Toyota.

The traffic had died down slightly but there was still a large number of people milling around the street. Many of the shops seemed to be selling jewellery; each window stacked with glittering wares to tempt in the tourists. Stephen had no interest in such baubles but was fascinated by the number of couples who stood outside gawping at what was available, before probably entering to buy something unaffordable.

The parking area had emptied slightly, the Toyota having spaces available both back and front. He retrieved his map and guidebook before relocking the car. Not knowing anything about Kandy, he had been wondering where he might eat that night. The hotel menu included in the information pack in his room had been long, corporate and uninspiring. He was tired of unoriginal food that attempted to cater for the global traveller and consequently failed, as far as he could discern, to reflect any Sri Lankan, Asian or European culinary skills. He leant on the bonnet of the car and studied his guidebook, the map laid out next to him, seeking inspiration but finding none.

"Are you lost, sir?"

Stephen looked up from the map and saw before him a tall, dark skinned but relatively smartly dressed, young Sri Lankan with a bag over his shoulder. Stephen was being studied with what appeared to be an earnest concern. He carefully folded his map and smiled as he stood up from the bonnet of the car.

"No. Not lost," Stephen replied. Without thinking, he added, "I was looking for somewhere good to eat."

The man nodded as if he appreciated Stephen's dilemma.

"It is never easy in a strange town." The man came forward to stand next to Stephen and was his measure for height at just over six foot. Stephen had not seen many tall locals and his stature made him an imposing figure. He had a tousled head of jet-black, shoulder length hair, together with a full beard. His eyes sparkled when he smiled, the smile revealing a thin margin of red colouration to his gums where they met his white, perfectly aligned teeth.

"I fear the tourist hotels are never quite up to providing the best that my country has to offer." He had a confidently casual manner. His English was quirkily exact, the accent noticeable but the enunciation remarkably clear. If he had met him in London, Stephen would have put him down as the product of a minor English Public School education, much like his. There were always one or two foreign students whose parents wanted to give their offspring an English veneer. Stephen doubted if the man before him was one of those, although he had obviously had a good formal schooling. Above all, there was an open friendliness to his face.

"If I may ask, what do you like eating?" The young man crooked his head to one side to await Stephen's response.

"I'm very open, but I do want to try to find some real Sri Lankan cuisine, not a touristy version of what they think we want to eat." Stephen held back being too precise as to why he wanted this authentic experience, but realised, perhaps too late, that his comment might be taken as a slur on Sri Lankan hospitality. He need not have worried as the young man chuckled.

"You sound like a, how do you say it…a foodster?"

It was Stephen's turn to laugh as he corrected him, "I think you mean a 'Foodie'."

"Ah, yes, a Foodie. Is that what you are, Sir? Perhaps a critic for The Times newspaper in London?"

"No, nothing like that. I'm Stephen, by the way." He extended his hand, but Randul ignored it and put his palms together, the fingertips just beneath his chin, and bowed his head in a formal greeting.

"Ayubowan, Stephen."

Stephen immediately withdrew his hand and followed suit.

"Ayubowan. And you are?"

"Randul Ranatunga at your service."

"Ayubowan, Randul…" he struggled pronouncing the surname, "Ranatunga." Stephen bowed once again and then paused a moment in thought.

"Are you related to your Lions captain, Dimuth Ranatunga?"

Randul burst out laughing, the sound infectious, causing Stephen to guffaw, unsure if this was partly in embarrassment at the stupidity of his question.

"I am afraid not. I wish I could claim kinship, then I might get some tickets to the match. Are you keen on the cricket, Stephen? Is that why you are here?" Before Stephen could reply, Randul added, "Perhaps, you are part of your English Barmy Army?"

"No. No. Nothing like that. Although, at home I do follow the cricket, and I know that all Sri Lankan's love their cricket."

"Oh, yes. Apparently, we are all cricket mad. But not me. I have little time for such things."

The conversation seemed so natural, as if they were two friends meeting again. Stephen had entirely let down his guard as a foreigner in a strange country, prey to the guiles of the local charlatans and crooks. Randul did not strike Stephen as anything other than a helpful local resident seeking to assist a guest in his country.

"If I may ask again, Stephen? Why do you seek out authentic Sri Lankan food. Are you sure you are not a...," Randul hesitated and then remembered the correct word, "a foodie?"

"Not exactly. I'm a chef." The title sounded good to Stephen. Not commis-chef, under-chef or assistant chef, just Chef. It was the first time that anyone had asked Stephen what he did since the competition had finished, and certainly the first time he had formally described himself to anyone as such.

"So, are you a famous chef in London?"

"No. But I did train under a famous chef. Have you heard of Rane Chitterbaya?"

Randul looked puzzled and shook his head.

"Well, he is an award-winning chef in London and that is where I trained." Stephen then briefly recounted the events of the past few weeks culminating in his arrival in Sri Lanka. Randul became increasingly engaged with the story, interrupting to ask questions about the programme, its filming and Stephen's use of ingredients. Finally, upon hearing that Stephen had won the competition, Randul expressed his delight with a loud and enthusiastic clapping of his hands. A couple of passers-by turned to see what the excitement was before moving on.

"So, you *are* a famous chef, yes?"

"Not yet. But I hope to be one day." Stephen was curious at Randul's persistent enquiries regarding his style of cooking, the ingredients he used and where he cooked. On his part, Randul could barely contain his glee at finding his famous, celebrity chef.

"But you have been on television. You won the competition. So, you are famous man." Randul clapped Stephen on the shoulder, and then looked self-conscious at his familiarity towards a stranger.

It was then that Randul had a splendid idea.

"Tonight, you must come to where I am staying. It is nothing grand, but the cook is my friend, and his food is very traditional, sometimes a bit special. You can come?" Randul looked with excited expectation at his new acquaintance.

Stephen thought for only a couple seconds before he smiled appreciatively at Randul and said, "I would be delighted. Where are you staying?"

"No. It is simplest if I come and collect you later at your hotel. Where are you in?"

Stephen gave Randul the name of his hotel and pointed up the street in its general direction. Randul confirmed that he knew it and agreed that he would come at seven thirty to take Stephen to his lodging house.

"We can walk. It will only take a few minutes."

"That sounds great. I'll see you later then." Stephen slapped the redundant folded map against the palm of his hand and Randul walked off with long, flowing steps, waving over his shoulder.

Having a little time to kill, Stephen decided he would go and try to find the lake and the Temple of the Sacred Tooth before returning to his hotel to freshen up prior to dinner with his newfound friend, Randul.

Upon him entering his hotel, one of the two receptionists seated behind the desk in the foyer immediately rose and attracted his attention, informing him that an anxious Miss Celia had left numerous messages for him to ring her. The other receptionist smiled knowingly, suspecting some love interest in the best traditions of any of her favourite Bollywood films that she adored so much. Stephen, resigned to the fact that he had been found, unenthusiastically thanked the girl for the message, took his key and entered the lift.

Even the exertion from his modest early evening exercise, notwithstanding the benefits of the cool air-conditioned environment, exhausted him more than he had expected. Stephen made a mental promise to himself that, when he got back to London, he would start an exercise regime to lose some of his excess weight. He had not been aware of the extra pounds he was carrying, but as he entered his room, and looked in the mirror it was clear that some urgent work was needed.

He flopped onto his bed and, checking his watch, saw that he still had a few minutes before he needed to shower and change for dinner. Stephen closed his eyes, but no sooner had he done so than the telephone beside his bed rang. He rolled over and picked up the receiver. Before he had a chance to give his name, the piercing voice of an excitable Celia exploded into his ear.

"Thank God you're there!"

Stephen sat up and held the receiver away from his ear,

"What's up?"

"Where the hell are you? I mean, I now know where you are, but where have you been?" Celia snapped, entirely forgetting that Stephen was her valued client. "I've been trying to get hold of you all afternoon. Are you alright? Have you had an accident?" The agitated voice irritated Stephen. He was tired, hot and did not need an overbearing nursemaid monitoring his every move.

"Celia, calm down. I'm fine. Now, why are you calling me?"

"Why?" The woman sounded both incredulous and hurt that her professional concern was being scorned. "Do you realise how dangerous the roads are to drive on? Then you wander off God-knows-where without a guide into wild country. I mean…of course, I have concerns for you. It's my job to have concerns for you. Do you realise what a hell of a job I've had trying to track you down? Do you know how many hotels I've had my team ring just to find you? The company has responsibilities you know. You can't just…."

"Hang on, Celia." Stephen stiffly cut off Celia in mid-stream. "I'm a big boy and can perfectly well look after myself." He paused before adding, "Thank you."

There was silence for a moment at the other end of the telephone as Celia collected her emotions, the relief of finding him in one piece easing her fears, slightly.

"I'm sorry. It is just that we…" the speed and pitch of her voice started to rise again, and so Stephen had to interrupt her once more.

"Celia, I can assure you that I'm fine. I have had a wonderful day and so, please, do not spoil it."

Another silence.

"Celia?"

There was a long intake of breath from the other end of the line as if the voice was trying to regain some composure. After a brief interval, she spoke more calmly.

"Why did you choose that hotel? We could have got you a room at a much better one. There's no spa or wellness facilities there, and the food is not much to write home about either." Stephen noted that Celia's travel imperatives were far removed from his own.

"This one is fine. As for the food, it doesn't matter because I'll be eating out this evening."

"Where are you going?" The tone of the question was a lot sharper than she had intended, so she followed it up softly, "Can I make you a booking? We know of one or two suitable places." The tension in her voice was barely controlled.

"No, thanks. I met a young guy on the street who is taking me to an authentic local place in town that he recommends."

"What!" The volume had risen again and was tinged once more with fear. "What guy? How did you meet him? You must be careful." Celia's warnings were cut short yet again.

"Celia, I can make my own judgements. This guy is very charming, and I trust him. As it happens, I like him."

"Oh, God. Please do be careful. I know that you are an adult and all that, but please consider how it will look for me if anything happens to you." Celia's voice had turned from concern for the well-being of Stephen as a client, to concern for her own position with her employer should her celebrity client get himself into any trouble. What if he was kidnapped, or worse, murdered on her watch? How would she explain that to the media and TV crew that was due to fly in any day? Increasingly bizarre scenarios whirled around in her imagination, all resulting in the same conclusion – the loss of her job. What would her father say?

"Will you promise to ring me when you get back from dinner? Please?"

Stephen sighed and agreed to let Celia know when he was back.

"Anytime. It doesn't matter if it's late. Just ring me."

"OK, Celia." Stephen made his voice sound overly weary, "We will speak later, I've got to get ready. Bye."

Stephen replaced the receiver without waiting for any response and got up to take a shower, irritated that his free time had been invaded by this ridiculous young woman. There had to be some pyrrhic penalty for her meddling, and he had already decided that the price would be another day or two on his own exploring the island. He knew that the TV crew were due soon but, if necessary, they would just have to wait for him. Celia would probably have a heart attack, but she would have to cope without knowing his every movement. It would do her good, he thought with a wry grin, as he dried himself off.

The telephone rang again, and he swore in anticipation of Celia making yet further impositions on his time.

"What do you want now?" he snapped.

"I am sorry, sir?" The receptionist sounded confused. Stephen immediately apologised and the girl on the other end persevered, "Your guest has arrived, and he is waiting for you in the foyer bar. He says that he knows he is slightly early."

Embarrassed at his own error, Stephen softly apologised once again to the receptionist, and told her that he would be down in a few minutes.

Quickly dressing in a loose fitting, collarless white shirt, linen trousers and espadrilles, Stephen placed his wallet in his back pocket and strode down to reception to meet Randul.

Chapter 9

Randul was seated at a low table in the foyer bar, looking relaxed with his legs crossed and reading a magazine. He jumped up at the arrival of Stephen and the two men formally bowed to each other, as had become their custom. Stephen looked his friend up and down and admired his high-collared, long-sleeved shirt, buttoned to the neck with the yolk cross stitched in contrasting colours. His trousers were loose fitting, gathered slightly at the ankles with soft leather sandals on his feet. Even though the temperature had moderated slightly, Stephen still showed the effects of the dissipating heat of the day while Randul looked cool and composed. The English summer clothes that he had brought with him weighed heavily on his body, the cheap material stifling the circulation of air around his skin.

For a moment the two men stood looking at each other awkwardly until Stephen broke the spell and offered Randul a drink. This was politely rejected on the grounds that he was keen to get to the guest house for supper.

As they walked along the dusty street, Randul and Stephen chatted like old friends. Stephen quizzed him about his life and Randul recounted to Stephen his time at university, his job as a guide and his passion for foraging in the forest. At this, Stephen pricked up his ears and pressed him further about what he found and how it was used locally.

Randul was delighted to find someone who was interested in his pursuit for new ingredients and who seemed to appreciate the subtlety of blending different tastes and the effects that freshly foraged produce could bring to a dish. Perhaps unsurprisingly, Randul discovered that his guest had just as deep an understanding of the skills necessary to bring out the best of these ingredients when cooking with them. Even Ranjid, the chef at the establishment he was taking Stephen to, was not as knowledgeable as the man who strode beside him, almost matching him pace for pace.

Randul had an easy, long, loping gait while the less fit and considerably heavier, Stephen puffed alongside. While unwilling to show that either his bulk or lack of fitness impeded his ability to keep up with his young friend, he was beginning to hope that they did not have too much further to go.

So deep was their discussion that Stephen did not really take in the route that they were following or the direction they were travelling. He did not notice that the buildings around him had become more dilapidated and the locale increasingly jaded. The streets were not as well metalled, and the pavements, such as they were, slumped and melded into the carriageway. What Stephen did appreciate, unlike when he was in India, was the lack of rubbish. Most seemed to have been cleared into small piles at the end of the day, to be burnt in the morning on fires that would heat up water or cook the first meal of the day.

The road that they were on was still busy more with people, bicycles, scooters and Tuk-Tuks than motor cars and trucks. If he had been aware or considered his situation, then this was probably not an area that Celia would feel at all comfortable about him entering. But Stephen was happily oblivious to his surroundings, enjoying both the company and the conversation of his animated friend.

Randul suddenly stopped outside a scruffy, unassuming door with most of the paint bleached and peeled from its surface by the sun. Two decrepit carriage lamps hung lopsidedly from the wall either side of the entrance, one was lit, the other blank, the glass to the front cracked but not broken. The door was slightly ajar. A yellow light flickered from within, and the murmur of male voices in lively conversation escaped into the street. Both were tempting them to open the door and enter the building.

Stephen stood back and looked up at the facade to see if there was any signage. He could just make out some feint wording that looked like 'Karma Guest House', the lettering almost invisible in the cracked plaster and faded paint on the wall above the door. He heard Celia's cautionary voice in his head urging him not to enter, but he banished her quickly from his mind. Randul smiled a welcome as he pushed on the door and extended his arm to usher Stephen through, into the premises.

As he entered, he saw what he assumed to be the original gateway to the property. There was a vaulted roof but the thick timber doors that once hung on the rough cast iron pegs inset into the wall on either side were missing. In turn, this gateway unexpectantly opened into a pretty, brightly lit courtyard filled with exotic plants and the sound of running water. Several doors led off this area while above, overlooking the spot where Randul and Stephen stood, were long balconies giving access to the upper rooms. Over their heads was nothing but an inky-dark sky, framed by the high walls, with a million stars that formed a canopy to the courtyard below.

In the middle of the courtyard stood a large, metal fire bowl that crackled and spat as the flames consumed the course, gnarled wood, a thin stream of smoke spiralling vertically into the still night sky. The lights from the balconies cast eerie shadows down onto the floor below and a small water feature splashed to one side. A single, large communal table surrounded the fire bowl on three sides, the latter being the focal point for both the space and the diners. As yet, no-one was seated, but small groups of men stood around chatting with drinks of fruit juice or water. A few took nothing more than a passing interest in the new arrivals and the conversation did not miss a beat. A girl, no older than eight or nine, materialised at Stephen's elbow with a tray holding two glasses of juice. He smiled at her and thanked her as he took one of the glasses. She kept her eyes averted and did not look at his face but merely melted away with the now empty tray.

"Most of these fellows are businessmen from the north, some gem dealers looking for a bargain or traders having delivered their wares for sale in the many shops or in the shopping mall near the Temple. They stay a night or two before returning to their homes. It gives them a break from their wives, and their wives a break from them."

Stephen was not sure if this last statement was factual or meant as a joke. Randul grinned, waggled his head from side to side and wiggled his thick eyebrows up and down. Stephen laughed at the comedic cliche that his friend had demonstrated so wonderfully. He thought about the comment and suddenly it occurred to him that Randul might be referring to these men using the premises on their trip as a brothel. He quickly glanced around but there were no women anywhere to be seen. He did not like to ask Randul where the women were as this might insult his host or add to any misguided dread that was already formulating in his mind. Briefly, Celia returned to castigate him for his stupidity at being lured into a house of despair.

Randul detected that Stephen might have misconstrued what he had just said.

"This is a guest house for men only. It provides simple inexpensive accommodation. Some of those here may obtain a receipt on the stationary of a top hotel in the city and make a claim for a much larger bill from their employers, or the tax authorities. Others, mainly those who work for themselves, will merely be grateful for clean, inexpensive lodgings and a good evening meal. And truth be known, it is the latter that they all come for. The food. This is somewhere that we jealously guard from the greedy eyes of the foreign tour operators and their scouts who seek ever more genuine experiences for their clients. Each place that is found by them, is destroyed by them. Either success goes to the owner's head or the pressure of the demands made by the tourists break the will of an honest proprietor. However, there is always a charlatan waiting in the shadows to pick up the pieces, to take over these once revered places, and to make a quick profit before the egg that lays the golden goose dies."

Stephen chose not to correct the back-to-front metaphor but did find it difficult to stifle his laughter. He quickly sought to mask his amusement with what he hoped was an expression of sympathy for Randul's summary of the impact of foreign travel on any haven. Stephen tried to defend the traveller by pointing out that any adverse effects that global travel may have on the authenticity of a culture is counter balanced, to a degree, by the economic benefits. Randul's head flopped to one side, and he looked at Stephen with deep scepticism.

"Money does not compensate for the fact that ultimately the very authenticity that they seek is destroyed, for them and for us."

Before Stephen could respond a gong sounded and the conversation subsided as the various groups of men wandered over to the table and randomly took a seat on the long benches down each side. Stephen took his lead from Randul and sat on what looked like a thick, intricately embroidered mat laid across the bench.

A large, bearded man with an untidy turban wrapped around his head and wearing a cream-coloured robe, tied with a cord around his expansive waist, squeezed himself between the bench seat and the table. He nodded a silent, curt greeting to Stephen, gave Randul a long look as if trying to work out what business he might be in, before turning to his neighbour to resume his gravel-voiced conversation in a language that sounded both harsh and argumentative. Stephen was unable to see past his bulk to identify the other man and so reverted his attention to Randul.

After a minute or two all the guests were settled, and Stephen noticed that there was not a vacant space to be seen. Hopefully he would be able to fill his restaurant as successfully. As if in response to a silent cue, youths and children of various ages emerged from a side door, each carrying a wide selection of dishes in small stainless-steel bowls. Each one was placed along the table in easy reach of the diners so that they could help themselves. Stephen looked around and saw dhal, fish and beetroot curries, vegetarian kottu, salted fish, various sambals and what looked like a sort of pennywort salad. Bowls of red Sri Lankan rice were dotted between these dishes and, almost as one, the guests leant forward and started to attack the food.

Stephen wavered, taking a morsel from each dish in an attempt to identify individual flavours before it was snatched away by his fellow diners and spooned into the bowls that were laid in front of everyone. As a dish was emptied, a replacement miraculously appeared to take its place. Unable to take notes, Stephen dived in, and the volume of the conversation rose and then subsided as mouths were filled with succulent, spice infused food.

There was little refinement to the art of eating. Food was piled into the bowls over a bed of rice and then, using the right hand, blended into a paste. Randul saw Stephen watching the process and explained.

"The food might be cooked separately but the overall taste is only truly appreciated by mixing the individual items together, so that all the flavours react with each other. Like a chemical reaction."

Stephen was delighted to adopt the local custom, although he found that it was not as easy as he might have expected. Food dropped down his shirt and onto his trousers, but no one appeared to notice, or care. Randul chatted throughout the meal, describing the ingredients, their effect on each other and methods used to prepare or cook them. Stephen listened intently, cursing himself for not having brought along his scruffy notepad and pen to jot down all the information that was being imparted to him.

Some dishes he was very conversant with, but others were new, or had elements of flavours that were unfamiliar to him. He paced himself, only too aware how fast he could become sated with the differing flavours and textures that were imbued into each different element of the meal. Stephen was having to use every ounce of his analytical skills to identify all the ingredients, and on numerous occasions he had to admit defeat. Randul assisted him as much as possible but enjoyed observing the frustration the famous English Chef was experiencing in his new environment.

Randul passed him a couple of bowls and told him that he was particularly interested in his reaction, seeking Stephen's professional opinion on each. Stephen saw this for what it was - a test. From their conversation earlier, he knew that Randul had supplied the proprietor in the kitchen with several of his foraged spices and herbs. He took each dish in turn, resisting the temptation to mix them together as he had previously been shown.

The first he tasted was a vegetarian kottu, shredded giant paratha forming the base but with a selection of vegetables and herbs that Stephen was easily able to identify. As he named each one in English, Randul nodded and gave the local name in response. But underlying all the flavours that fronted the dish was a blend of subtler fragrances and tastes that still eluded Stephen. He tried the food repeatedly and while the various receptors on his tongue fought for supremacy, ultimately each had to accept defeat and admit that there was no record in his memory of any of the concealed ingredients that he was being pressed to identify. The overall effect was a joy, like nothing else that he had experience before.

The second dish that Randul gave him was a jackfruit curry that he called a polos curry. On this occasion, the combination of flavours confused Stephen, and the more he tried to identify individual constituents the more perplexed and frustrated he became. However, what was apparent every time he returned to a particular dish was that the combination of flavours seemed to change on his tongue. The overall experience was one of sensory confusion mixed with sublime delight. Each mouthful gave him a hint of his most favourite flavours that were then combined or adapted by these unidentifiable trances of one or more secret ingredients. With each spoonful, the blend of flavours changed.

Eventually, his palate and tastebuds became completely bewildered and disorientated and Stephen had to admit defeat. Randul gave a delighted chortle and said that he would make some suggestions and Stephen could try the dishes again. Stephen agreed, unsure as to how the game would turn out.

"Is there a hint of Mango?" Randul asked and waited as Stephen looked from one dish to the other.

"Which one?"

"You choose."

Stephen cautiously took the polo curry and smelt the contents. He immediately detected a hint of the sweet aroma of ripe mango. He dipped a finger into the sauce and licked it with the edge of his tongue. Now the flavour was unmistakeable, but he was convinced that, despite his best efforts, it had not been identifiable when he initially tasted some of the dish.

"How on earth…?" Stephen did not complete his sentence, eager to try again.

Randul thought for a moment.

"Goat".

"Don't be ridiculous. These are vegetarian curries and surely the chef would not use any animal stock?"

Randul turned down the corners of his mouth, lifted his eyebrows and shrugged his shoulders as if to say, 'Try it. See for yourself'.

Stephen took up the kottu that he knew to be wholly vegetarian based, disbelief written all over his face. He smelt the contents and after just one small sniff his head suddenly jerked back in surprise. He approached the dish again using his nose to draw in the smells that emanated from the food. He could hardly believe his senses and looked across at Randul in stupefaction. His host was leaning back slightly, a complacent grin across his face, enthralled at Stephen's incredulity.

Stephen used a different finger, as if that would alter the result, and scooped some of the food into his mouth. There was no doubt in his mind that there was the distinctly gamey flavour of goat in the depths of the other herbs and spices. Confused, Stephen turned to the large man who sat deep in conversation and tapped him on the shoulder. The man turned lugubriously to face Stephen; his expression questioning but also tinged with a hint of irritation at having had his discourse interrupted.

"Excuse me? Do you speak English?" Stephen enquired.

"Of course. A bit." The man said with a heavy accent that Stephen could just understand but not place. Turning back to his companion, the bearded man sought to resume his conversation with his companion as if that was the end of the exchange. Stephen persevered by tapping him on the shoulder again.

"I'm sorry to disturb you, but would you be kind enough to do something for me?"

The man sighed deeply as if humouring the Englishman and nodded his head.

"Can you tell me what flavour you liked most when you ate that dish?" Stephen pointed down to an almost empty bowl that lay in front of both men. The second man watched with curiosity as the big man took a small piece of pita bread and dipped it into the remaining liquid. He lifted it, the juices dripping a path across the tablecloth before he slid it into his mouth, whereupon the second man followed suit, intrigued at what the stranger was up to.

"Well?"

Both men considered their answer and simultaneously contradicted each other.

"Woodapple."

"Cinnamon."

They looked at each other and then started to debate the flavours, trying to convince the other that his taste buds were mistaken. Stephen listened for a while as the conversation became more strident before he quelled their debate with another question.

"Can either of you taste any coffee?"

Both men laughed loudly and then, realising that Stephen was serious, tasted the dish again. A look of bewilderment covered their faces as they licked their lips and looked down at the dish again.

"What is this? Some sort of magic?" The second man asked. Stephen suddenly realised that he was witnessing something extraordinary and did not want to pursue the discussion any further.

"No. No. You're quite right. I'm sorry, but my friend and I were not sure what flavours I was detecting and wanted a second opinion. Please, don't let me disturb you any further."

The two men held Stephen's gaze momentarily and then, turning away from Stephen, leant towards each other and had a whispered exchange about the strange Englishman.

"How's that possible?" Stephen asked Randul. "They both tasted different flavours until I suggested coffee, and then they both accepted that that flavour was also present." Stephen scratched his head and waited for an answer from his host.

Randul was reticent to say more but could not avoid the self-satisfied expression that spread across his face. Stephen found what he interpreted as arrogance, mildly irritating before asking Randul where the chef was and whether he could meet him.

He wanted to congratulate him for creating one of the best, and most curious, meals that Stephen had ever experienced. As a fellow chef on a quest for the original, Stephen was becoming increasingly animated. He desperately wanted to make notes, terrified that he would forget or overlook some detail if he had to wait until he returned to his hotel. Was the culinary genius behind the kitchen door, or sitting next to him? How was the suggestion of a flavour transferred into a subliminal desire by each diner to taste that flavour? How was it possible for the suggestion of a taste to materialise in their mouth? Was it a hallucinatory drug or magic, as suggested by the stranger seated alongside?

Simply, Stephen could not understand what he had just witnessed in this simple guest house dining room. Perhaps none of the diners had appreciated exactly what they were eating or exchanged opinions as to the flavours that were the essence of their meal. Perhaps they never considered how the same dish could metamorphose into their own individual choice of flavours. The quality and quantity of the food was very satisfying, and that was all that they needed. They were not here to critique the dishes; they were here to eat. What they ate was, so it appeared, immaterial so long as it satisfied both their tastes and their appetites.

To Stephen, this was culinary alchemy the like of which he had never come across before.

This was his Nirvana. If he could produce this chameleon-like cuisine for his London clientele, he would be made. At that moment, he knew that he had found an exceptional basis for a unique menu.

His menu.

A menu the like of which had never been offered by any of the great chefs – save for this one modest Sri Lankan cook in a simple guest house on the outskirts of

Kandy. Not even his mentor, the great Rane Chitterbaya, would be able to replicate such a masterpiece.

Stephen bombarded Randul with a multitude of questions which were constantly parried whenever he tried to delve into the very essence of a product, or a procedure. What had transformed these everyday fresh, local ingredients into something beyond Stephen's wildest imaginings?

Randul always remained polite, but unforthcoming in divulging any specific details. Despite ever more fevered attempts by Stephen to extract information, Randul would not expand on either the precise source of the foraged ingredients, or the exact processes by which he converted them into the additives that the local chef had so successfully utilised in his dishes.

After a while, the young Sri Lankan became impatient and held up his hand to stem the inquisition. However, Stephen had started to appreciate that the chef was the instrument of delivery, while Randul was the ringmaster. His desire to accompany Randul on one of his foraging trips became a priority for him.

Whatever else Stephen might have been planning for the next day was immediately shelved in favour of the meeting. In fact, the more Stephen thought about the prospect, the more he started to formulate a more radical change to his plans. Perhaps he could persuade Randul to allow him to spend a few days with both him and Ranjid, to observe the chef at work and join Randul on his foraging sorties into the forest.

"You've got to tell me. Where do you source your ingredients?" Stephen persisted.

Randul felt no compulsion to reveal to the Englishman where he foraged and so gave as bland an answer as he could.

"From the forest. I, or rather we, the Veddah people, are granted special permission by the Forestry Department to forage and use whatever we might find. Since I left Colombo University, I have continued privately to study the flora and fauna throughout the island and have found some things that have some unique properties."

"Who are the Veddah people?" Stephen asked. Randul suddenly felt on safer ground and happily recounted the history of his people.

"We are the original people of Sri Lanka. A tribe if you like. We are given special rights over our ancient hunting grounds. While most of my people have not bothered to continue, I have chosen to follow the ways of my forefathers." Randul drew himself up to his full height to emphasise the strong sense of pride he retained in his traditional lifestyle and heritage.

Stephen looked at the young tribesman with a renewed respect. This was no uncultivated heathen guiding tourists for lack of any other opportunity in life. This was a well-educated individual who had spent his short life utilising the knowledge of his forefathers and melded it with academically based research. The result appeared to be the discovery of a wide variety of natural and processed ingredients that could possibly revolutionise the culinary world.

Stephen's culinary world.

If Randul thought that his simple explanation would satisfy Stephen, he was wrong. Stephen's mind was working at maximum intensity, trying to find a way to extract as much as he could from his friend.

"Why have you not marketed your discoveries. They could be very valuable."

Randul was becoming weary and sat down on the bench next to Stephen. Unseen by Stephen, the chef, Ranjid, wandered out of his kitchen and disappeared into the body of the building while his wife crossed the courtyard to a desk and, with head bent, proceeded to sort out her paperwork.

Randul took from his pocket a small metal tin and opened it to reveal slices of areca nut as well as betel leaf and folded silver-foil. Stephen watched as he studiously created a small green parcel out of the contents of the tin and slid it into his mouth.

"What is that?" Stephen asked.

"Betel." Randul chewed solemnly, the areca nut slowly releasing its warmth, imbuing a sense of well-being that slowly engulfed him, a gentle euphoria that Randul welcomed.

He looked down at the tin lying under his fingers. The corners of his mouth turned down slightly at the bitter taste of the betel and lime slurry. He spoke slowly, his voice slightly lower as his vocal cords softened into repose.

Against his better judgement, he knew inwardly that he was going to take his new acquaintance into his confidence. It would be cautious and measured, but the course of the evening seemed to him to be predestined.

"You have to understand, the forest is a very special place. It is a Deity, and as such it must be revered, treated with honour and respect. It is the preserve of future generations of all our tribes. Thankfully, commercial exploitation through forestry and mining have been substantially reduced, but not stopped. Corruption will never allow it to stop, but we must try to protect what we can. We are the forests' guardians for our children, and their children. I do not want to be the cause of any renewed exploitation that would destroy forever such a fragile ecosystem." Randul remained stationary and the room had become very quiet. Stephen listened spellbound as Randul took a deep breath.

"Every so often I do bring Ranjid, here, a sample of my work, and his kitchen and his guests are the perfect testing ground. Sometimes what I bring is successful, and sometimes they are not so good. Tonight, they were successful."

"I would second that." Stephen was silent for a moment, watching his friend, admiring his smooth complexion and his almond eyes that were now slightly glazed as the betel juice was absorbed into his body.

Ranjid's wife had been half listening to the exchange and saw the change in Randul's mood. She did not approve of the use of betel but was fond of the Veddah and so allowed an exception in his case, so long as he was discreet. She had no idea what was being said between the two, serious young-men, but she detected a growing bond that had emerged as the evening progressed. A woman's intuition. She watched, knowing that she should get back to more pressing matters that required her attention, but fascinated by the emotional intensity that emanated between her two guests.

Stephen reluctantly stood, realising the lateness of the hour, and turned to her, effusively thanking her and her absent husband for their hospitality and the most extraordinary culinary experience of his life. The tone of his voice was sufficient not to need any translation and she bowed before telling Randul that they were both welcome to return at any time.

There was a blizzard of conflicting thoughts that put Stephen in as much of a trance as that currently being enjoyed by the Veddah. Suddenly Randul seemed to notice that the room was empty and focussed on his guest with red rimmed eyes that shone beneath thick curling eyelashes.

"Is there any chance we could meet tomorrow to talk about your work?" Stephen pleaded softly. "I really would love to come with you on one of your foraging trips?"

Randul sat, his head turned upwards towards Stephen, and found his resolve was weakening further. They were kindred spirits; he felt an empathy with Stephen and his quest for the exceptional and he valued the deference that his foreign guest had shown towards Randul's tribal traditions and beliefs.

Their hostess watched silently, her head bowed, her eyes shaded beneath her brow. A knowing smile hovered on her lips; the two boys voices were hardly audible as they spoke softly together.

"I don't want to desecrate or commercialise any of the places that you go," Stephen said, "or the forest generally. I merely want to understand more of what you do. How you prepare your ingredients, how Ranjid uses them to produce dishes such as we had tonight. Nothing more, I promise."

Stephen immediately recognised that he had made a promise that he could not keep.

Randul chewed slowly, an uncertain anxiety hovering over him. He needed time to weigh up his conflicting emotions but fate had cast her die.

"If you wish. We will meet tomorrow."

Stephen was delighted, but Randul held up his hand to stop Stephen from expressing any over effusive thanks.

"However, I have some business to attend to first thing. So we will meet late morning."

"I'll be waiting for you. At my hotel?"

Relieved and excited, Stephen left the guest house with Randul, his pace spurred on by his desire to get back swiftly to his hotel. He tried to remember all that he had learnt and experienced in order to write it down before it slipped from his memory.

Randul had insisted that he escort Stephen back to the main road and both men walked in silence, each surrounded by their own private thoughts. When they reached the main thoroughfare and Randul had pointed out to Stephen where his hotel was located, they hesitated as they faced each other. Stephen was unsure how to leave his friend, although he had a strong desire to put his arms around Randul and hug him. He resisted and the tribesman offered the traditional bow, before he turned and, with a relaxed gait, walked away back down the side street.

Stephen watched the receding figure, willing him to look back and wave, until he disappeared around the corner.

Chapter 10

Light was spilling out from the shop on to the dour street, the darkness of night banished to the shadows. Ziyad was inside still revelling in the success of his sale the previous evening to Brad and his fiancé. Even by his standards, he had achieved some remarkable prices for the set of matching earrings, necklace and bracelet that were inset with some flashy, but otherwise unremarkable heat-treated sapphires. Admittedly, had they been untreated then the price paid would have been about right, but these were not. The use of beryllium to enhance the colour was also a fact that Ziyad had overlooked.

They should have asked.

As a licenced gem dealer, he would have been duty bound to inform them of the fact. What the happy couple were ignorant of was the unpalatable fact that any reputable, high-class dealer would eschew a heated, beryllium treated sapphire, and the price would reflect this accordingly. Ziyad briefly considered their disappointment when they had an insurance valuation undertaken upon their return to Texas, but by then it would be too late. There was little chance of any comeback.

However, the diamond and sapphire engagement ring had been Ziyad's masterpiece. Brad was almost physically seduced in the shop by his bride-to-be. She had instantly fallen in love with the brightly sparkling stones as opposed to enquiring after the attributes of the jewels and the purity of the white gold.

Apparently Ziyad was reticent to sell such a 'special' piece. He was holding it for an Arab prince who was to gift it to his third bride. The greater the difficulties Ziyad presented, the greater was the challenge to Brad to purchase the piece for his own bride. The price escalated to encourage Ziyad to disappoint the prince. This was one contest that the Texan was not going to lose. Reluctantly, but emphasising his fear of the wrath that would rain down on him from the mythical prince, Ziyad relented and agreed a price, 'because you are such a lovely couple'.

Yesterday had been a very profitable day, even allowing for the rather fulsome price that Ziyad had paid to the unexpected young Veddah for the small collection of blue sapphires earlier that day. Now he could only hope that his generosity would bear fruit. It was the mention of a Padparadscha that had grabbed Ziyad's attention, as he suspected the young man thought it might. No gem dealer the world over would fail to be excited at the prospect of acquiring a Padparadscha sapphire. These were the rarest of sapphires, found in only a few places in the world, Sri Lanka being one of them. To be the owner of just one such stone would be the pinnacle of any dealer's career. Depending on quality, each carat, unheated, could command upwards from three hundred to four thousand US dollars. If the Pad was of an exceptional size, then the owner could dictate their own price.

Ziyad was only too well aware that recently there had been a surge in demand, particularly from India. This had outstripped supply and so prices remained very strong. As with the more common sapphires, the top prices were obtained for natural, untreated stones. Any wastage from cutting would be kept to a minimum to ensure that as much of the weight as possible was retained, while emphasising the clarity and revealing the delicate lotus-blossom hue to its best advantage. The mounting of such a jewel was usually undertaken in white gold or platinum and in many cases the central stone was surrounded with diamonds or white sapphires. The effect was stunning and in all his years, Ziyad had only ever seen one very modest example. He had dreamed of one day going to the American Museum of Natural History in New York to see what was reputed to be the largest Padparadscha, weighing in at an incredible 100.18 carats.

Ziyad hoped above all else that the Veddah would return swiftly and that his gem was the real thing and not an enhancement or, worse still, an imitation. He accepted the inevitability that it would never match that held in New York, but ten or twenty carats would be a dream come true.

The previous evening, over yet another solitary scratch dinner, he had allowed his imagination to run ahead of itself. He fantasised seeing a huge stone being extracted from the tribesman's bag, Ziyad negotiating a modest price for the vast gem and then making a world-famous sale. The wish was dispelled by the realisation that his sudden exposure to the media was not something that would be sensible for a man in Ziyad's position. But if he owned such a jewel, he was sure that he could find a way to avoid becoming the most famous jewel dealer in the world. Perhaps he would keep it, take it out of an evening and admire it over a glass of the finest malt whisky.

Perfection, pure perfection.

However, sadly in the real world it was equally possible that what the young man had was nothing more than a false gem, deceivingly good when in water but worthless when dry.

Ziyad had drunk two cups of coffee already that morning and was contemplating a third when the door was shaken tentatively against its lock. His face clearly visible by the light that shone through the glazed door, Randul stood outside with his hand up to the glass trying to see if anyone was inside.

He tried the door once more as Ziyad waved his hand in what he hoped appeared to be a friendly greeting. A shiver of excitement slithering down his spine, and he dismounted from his stool to open the door for his client.

"I did not expect you back quite so soon, or so early. Salam Alaikum," Ziyad greeted his visitor and extended his arm to usher Randul into his lair. Randul put his hands together and bowed in local greeting.

"Ayabowan."

The shop smelt of a mixture of burnt coffee and sickly-sweet eau de cologne. Randul wrinkled his nose.

"I wanted to catch you early, before you became busy."

"Yes, of course you did. Perfectly understandable. Now, I am fascinated. What have you got for me to see?" Ziyad walked swiftly to his usual position behind the counter and stood facing Randul. It was of no surprise to Ziyad that such a transaction would be conducted in the twilight hours.

Randul opened his bag and Ziyad saw the chamois leather pouch from the previous evening. It sat on the top of carefully folded clothes. Randul placed the knapsack on the floor and held the pouch by its draw strings.

"I have a couple of rough stones that I suspect may be Padparadscha sapphires." He paused for effect, allowing Ziyad the opportunity to experience a wave of anticipation.

"Well, let's see, shall we?" Ziyad held out his hand and noticed that his fingers were quivering. Despite his best efforts he was unable to bring them under control.

Randul had already noticed his eagerness. He felt into the bottom of the soft pouch and took the smaller stone out between finger and thumb. He placed it carefully onto Ziyad's outstretched hand.

Ziyad inspected it and then slowly fixed the eyeglass into the socket of his sound eye. The stone rolled off his palm onto a piece of black velvet that lay on the counter. Not a sound was to be heard from the interior of the shop as Ziyad slowly lowered his head directly over the sapphire and brought it into focus.

He could feel his intestines contract and he had to consciously clench his bowels for fear of soiling himself. After thirty seconds in absolute and motionless silence, Ziyad straightened and removed the eyeglass, placing it carefully on the glass top of the counter. He picked up the jewel and held it to the light, gently rolling it between finger and thumb.

"Very pretty," was all he could say, and he repeated it several times. Eventually he focused his eye on Randul, thinking hard as to whether this prospector was truly aware of what he had brought to the dealer. He suspected that he was more knowledgeable than he was making out and so decided upon another approach.

"Can I see your artisanal mining licence?" He watched Randul very carefully and it was all that Randul could do to keep his facial expression unchanged. He had been expecting this and was prepared.

"The mine is in my father's name as is the licence. He is not here with me, but I wanted someone trustworthy to verify the find." The statement was perfectly true, to the extent that Randul's father did once have a licence, and he was not here with Randul. Unfortunately, the licence only lasted for two years and had long since expired, as had his father.

"Mmmm. I see." Ziyad was reluctant to dismiss the boy, for that is how he saw Randul, or do anything that might result in him taking fright and walking out. The stress he suddenly felt was like nothing he had ever experienced before. Ziyad was walking a tightrope.

He wanted that stone.

Oh, how he wanted that stone.

"May I see the other one?"

Randul delved back into the bag and hesitated before removing the larger stone. Ziyad assumed that this one was going to disappoint and relaxed somewhat. However, when the gem was revealed and Ziyad saw the size, he could not stop the automatic, sharp inhalation of coffee steeped breath. Randul carefully placed it onto the velvet as if it would shatter. Ziyad breathed out slowly and with as much control as he could muster. He made no move to pick up the stone but just stood and gazed at it. The silence cocooned them, heavy in expectation.

Ziyad walked over to the door to the street, locked it and rattled it to check that it was secure before returning. Without taking his eye of the gem he distractedly took a sip of cold coffee dregs before delicately undertaking his inspection of the new offering.

Methodically, he surveyed the stone from all angles and then pulled out his scales from beneath the counter. In deep concentration, he weighed each stone, handling them reverentially. On each occasion he placed the individual weights onto the brass pan and paused until a perfect balance between stone and weights had been achieved. Ziyad returned each stone to the centre of the velvet cloth.

Once again, he bent down behind the counter and took out a small, dog-eared pad and, with a stub of a pencil, noted down the weights. He casually placed a hand over the page, but Randul had already added up the counterweights and also read the scrawled figures.

Thirteen grammes and forty-nine grammes!

Randul tutted and before Ziyad could react he had snatched the stones back into his possession. Ziyad protested as Randul picked up the pan on which the weights had been placed and turned it upside down. The tarnished strip of copper was clearly visible.

"That is not a good start to our relationship," Randul said as he handed the pan back to its owner. Ziyad looked abashed and resented the fact that Randul had so easily exposed his dishonesty.

"It weighs three grammes light, I know that." Ziyad tried to undo what had been done, "But I only resort to applying it when I have to, and I accept that now is not the time."

Randul was not convinced, and his face showed it. He was about to walk.

"I apologise. I made a mistake. Please forgive me." Ziyad was desperate and genuine in his grovelling apology. As if by way of reparation, the rattled Arab made a quick calculation. Even if there was a maximum of seventy percent wastage (and on seeing the stones he felt that he could get that down to fifty-five, at worst sixty percent) it meant that the two stones had an unbelievable net weight of twenty-four and seventy-eight carats, respectively.

The Arab had to control his breathing and felt a light headedness that almost took his legs from under him. He sat heavily on his stool. Neither man spoke, Randul watching Ziyad and Ziyad's eye focused on the clenched fist now holding the two gems. A seed of avarice burst in the heart of Ziyad, germination manifesting itself as a sudden deep and spiteful loathing for this ignorant savage who held in his hand two of the most precious things that Ziyad had ever seen, and now violently coveted.

If the boy drove a hard bargain, Ziyad knew that he could just afford to buy the smaller stone, even at his prices. The battered cash tin that lay in the safe had been bolstered by the Americans but was going to be short by a few thousand dollars – and Ziyad was certain that the Veddah would want rupees, of which he had but few.

Ziyad wanted them both – and anything less was unacceptable. A bubble of bile rose in Ziyad's throat, and he gagged, coughed and wiped his mouth with a soiled handkerchief. Randul watched implacably as the Arab fought to suppress a sense of panic.

"Excuse me, I need some water." Ziyad scuttled into the back room. He needed time.

His first thought was what else might the savage have hidden away? Ziyad's years of experience and intuition told him that it was possible that these two, albeit exceptional, stones might not be the only gems held by this heathen. If this was the entirety of his find then, surely, he would be more open, more willing to quickly sell both stones. But there was no urgency shown by the boy. Perhaps there was another dealer with whom Ziyad was being placed in competition? Ziyad would have to realise some cash, a lot of cash, if he was going to be able to acquire both stones. Not impossible, but it would take a day or two. But what if there were more? Other better stones? He needed to know.

Ziyad returned sipping from a plastic bottle half full of water, the tin cash box in his other hand. Once seated he glared at the Veddah.

"How are we to do this?"

"Make me an offer."

Ziyad waited and then asked,

"Do you have any more?" He watched intently for any flicker of deceit and was gratified to see Randul flush slightly.

"Well?"

"Let's deal with these first." Randul held his closed hand in front of Ziyad's face as if tempting him, which he was.

"Very well. The small stone is reasonable, not good, but reasonable."

Randul listened and nodded his head, nothing that was said was unexpected. Ziyad continued,

"The larger one is better; in fact, it is rather good." Ziyad saw no point in trying to score points, he was playing the longer game. Randul nodded again.

"You could go to the Authorities and get, maybe, sixty percent of their assessment of market value – if, that is, they deemed them to be mere chance finds. Of course, they will ask questions, want to know where they were found and in what circumstances." Ziyad maintained eye contact with Randul throughout the conversation.

"I get the impression that you do not want that?" It was a rhetorical question and Ziyad pressed on. "If I match that sixty percent without questions that would seem to be a very generous offer."

Randul smiled.

"It depends on what your assessment of open market value is going to be, and what wastage you estimate to produce a quality jewel. You have the advantage of me on such matters."

It was Ziyad's turn to nod as he rubbed his stubbly chin and thought swiftly. He had just about enough cash to buy the small stone but did not have sufficient to buy the larger.

These negotiations were going to be more tortuous that he had expected. The bile refluxed into his throat, and he took another sip of water. He was nervous. He was never nervous in negotiations. He always had the upper hand. But not this time. This was a bloody savage, but a savage with two Padparadscha, perhaps more.

So beautiful, so beguiling and so powerful in their hold over him.

*

The spring in his step and the smile that was spread across Randul's face was sufficient to make passers-by turn to watch the young man who strode so confidently down the street. The backpack was slung insouciantly across his shoulder as he entered the hotel and asked at reception for Mr Silchester. The young female receptionist admired the handsome new arrival as she telephoned up to Stephen's room. Randul turned to survey his surroundings and contemplated booking a night at the hotel but dismissed the notion as extravagant and unnecessary. The larger stone remained in the chamois pouch at the top of his backpack.

At that very same moment the smaller stone was being greedily stored away in the safe in Ziyad's shop. The Arab was disappointed not to have been able to acquire both stones but the cost of just this one had been enough to clear him out of all the cash that he held in his safe, and in his wallet.

But he had designs on the second, larger stone.

Provenance was everything in the gem market and Ziyad was the key to Randul legitimising his stones. It became increasingly clear during his negotiations with Randul that the boy had more of these exquisite pieces of rock. However, he would need the cooperation of a dealer such as Ziyad to provide the necessary certification.

Ziyad had repeatedly tried to coax from Randul the details of where he had found the stones, but all to no avail. The smooth surfaces immediately confirmed what little Randul had told Ziyad, that they were sourced from a river. Which one of hundreds of rivers and streams that ran through the forest only Randul knew. The man was a Veddah, from his dark skin and wild features that fact was in no doubt. He was not clothed in tribal attire and that told Ziyad that he was probably crudely educated, which increasingly was becoming the norm as they had the benefit of heavily subsidised education. The government worked on the principle that by slowly educating and integrating them within the rest of Sri Lankan society, the tribe would eventually be erased from their ancestral homelands and independent lifestyle.

Throughout their business dealings, the savage had remained very cautious, and it was clear to Ziyad that the Veddah did not trust him. Ziyad chuckled to himself, the boy was a good judge of character. He had given nothing away to Ziyad as to the source of the stones which meant that he would have to resort other methods.

At that precise moment, the instrument of his choice walked into the shop.

Thinuka was not the brightest of sons, but Ziyad was forgiving of most of his failings since he was his firstborn – and he was a son. The son that he had always desired and who had been so difficult to conceive with his wife.

Yes, he was a feckless, free spending, callow, young bachelor, who was a constant drain on Ziyad's hard earned resources. Thinuka's liberal consumption of alcohol, however, was something that Ziyad found hard to accept, even though he knew that this was hypocritical bearing in mind his own love for his malt whisky. But his consumption was in private, whereas Thinuka seemed to revel in public displays of intoxication.

Whether the young fool had succumbed to anything more toxic, Ziyad remained in ignorance. On religious grounds, Ziyad's ferocious father had never permitted any alcohol into the house and, therefore, in his youth, Ziyad was ignorant as to its effects. It was only when he was much older, and the life and influence of his father had departed, that he discovered the delights of a good, mature malt whisky and he yielded to temptation. No other form of alcohol, just his beloved malt.

But his son was young, as Ziyad had once been. He could not bring himself to repeat the same zealous strictures on his son that his father had imposed on him. Surely a father could be forgiven for indulging his only son. In return, Thinuka was passionately devoted to his father, reciprocated in full by his father.

Thinuka was smartly dressed in an expensive western style suit, a freshly pressed white shirt, and carefully polished loafers on his bare feet. The shirt was open at the neck to show off a thick gold chain hanging loosely around his neck and his index finger sported a chunky gold ring that Ziyad had given him when he reached twenty-one. His complexion was clear and his eyes sparkling with untold mischief, all of which made Thinuka an attractive and popular man about town.

However, this morning, despite his perfect attire, he looked crumpled, tired and slightly hung-over. He crossed the floor of the shop and gave his father a kiss on his forehead before giving him a hug.

"Good morning, Baba." They parted and Ziyad could not miss a strong smell of alcohol on his stale breath. He moved towards his gas ring to put on a fresh pot of strong coffee.

"You look like you need a good Baba brew, my son."

"I do. I do." Thinuka took his father's seat on the stool and ran his hands through his thick, oiled hair. From the back of the shop, Ziyad asked,

"I didn't hear you come home last night?" The intonation was one of gentle chastisement and Ziyad knew that the answer would be noncommittal, if not an outright lie.

"I stayed with friends; we had a bit of a party last night."

Ziyad replied with his usual, "Mmmm."

This was the noise he made for customers whenever he wanted time to think before making a mischievous request, quoting an outrageous price or an unwelcome offer.

"Right, well forget the partying for a moment. I want you to do something important for me."

Thinuka was relieved that Baba had not sought to pursue his enquiries into his activities of the previous evening. In truth, some of it was a bit of a blur and, in any event, it would be too embarrassing to discuss or relate to his father. All he knew was that the party he had inveigled his way into had involved the consumption of large quantities of liquor and the smoking of some high-quality hashish. He had struck up a friendship with a striking French girl from Toulouse who had subsequently proved to have a healthy and unrelenting stamina for some energetic sexual experimentation. She demanded his attentions four or five times during the night. Hence, he was shattered and somewhat relieved at her early departure from the hotel to travel to the North of the island. Another night of such extreme exertion would have wiped him out for a week.

His father returned with the caustic flavoured coffee and placed the grimy cup before the exhausted Thinuka. In his other hand he held a small package.

"I have done some interesting business this morning."

"Already. It's early, even for you, Baba." Thinuka sipped the scalding coffee and looked questioningly at his father, eager to learn what profit had been made. Baba always made a handsome profit; it was just a question of how handsome. Gathering from the smug glint in his eye, this had been a very good return.

Thinuka had watched his father at his work as a child and inherited the family interest in all that glitters and sparkles. His own eye for a quality gem with an appropriate concentration of colour and clarity was almost as proficient as his father's. In fact, with some considerable pride, Ziyad thought that his son was possibly more astute than he was as to what constituted a good stone. He just needed to acquire the necessary skills and negotiating guile that was Ziyad's overarching strength. If he would just concentrate on commercial matters instead of spending his time gadding about town, Ziyad was confident that that attribute would emerge.

What Thinuka might lack in negotiating ability he compensated for in greed. A greed that verged on the obsessive and was equal to that of his father. They were two of a kind in that regard. If he set his mind on something that would yield him a profit, then nothing would divert him from contriving a strategy that would be to his fiduciary advantage.

Ziyad laid the small parcel on the velvet cloth and asked Thinuka what he thought of his latest acquisition. His son placed his cup next to the package and gently unwrapped the cloth from around the inch long stone. As soon as he saw it, he looked up into his father's eye that was glistening with excitement.

"Baba, is it real? Natural? Unheated?" He picked up the uncut stone and held it to the light. Amazement flooded across his face, but he was uncertain as to whether what he held was truly what he suspected.

"Is it what I think it is? Is it really a Padparadscha?"

"It most certainly is, untreated and unheated. As natural as you will ever find. I have never seen one like this before, not as pure or as fine a colour. The clarity, even in its raw state is indescribable. As far as I can detect there's not an occlusion to be seen." Ziyad watched as his son turned the stone over and over, examining it from every angle. Thinuka was imagining how each facet might be cut onto the stone with the minimum of wastage to create one of the great jewels of the world, and it was theirs.

"What's it worth?"

Ziyad loved his son more than anything else in the world, including his daughter and, perhaps, even his wife. Despite this, he was painfully aware that Thinuka was easily tempted into the transgression of boasting to impress his peers or excite the female tourists seeking a holiday adventure.

"That is hardly the point with a stone of this quality. Is it not the most beautiful thing you have ever seen?"

Thinuka was still preoccupied with the value and was labouring to undertake a mental calculation similar to the one that Randul had completed in a millisecond. It was taking him much longer this morning, but the estimated result was none the less stunning.

"Where did you get it? Are there more?"

Ziyad recounted the events of the previous evening and that morning.

"I know that there is at least one more. But there may well be others, possibly even better."

Thinuka let out a long whistle and had entirely forgotten his hangover or the cooling coffee on the counter.

"Have you seen the other one?"

"I have." Ziyad could not contain his excitement, "It's huge and as clean as this one, if not even better."

"How huge?" Thinuka was now fully alert and took a gulp of coffee. Ziyad told him the weight. Thinuka sat motionless, looked at the stone again and then stared lovingly at his father, his resourceful Baba.

"How are we going to get them?"

Ziyad gave his son a sly grin.

"Well, my resourceful son, that will depend upon a little task that I would like you to perform for me."

"Of course, Baba. Anything."

Ziyad outlined the proposed assignment for his son who quietly relished the idea of undertaking a secret mission on behalf of Baba, particularly as the cause was so appealing. An opportunity to take up the mantle of his film idol, Sunny Deol, or perhaps James Bond.

After recounting the limited information that he had managed to extract from Randul, and having satisfied himself that Thinuka had grasped what was expected of him, Ziyad passed to his son a small bundle of crumpled bank notes, the last of the cash resources currently available to Ziyad.

"This is for any legitimate expenses that you might have to incur."

Thinuka was still gazing at the gem.

"Listen to me!" Ziyad roughly squeezed Thinuka's chin between finger and thumb. He pulled his son's head away from the stone to face him, so that had had his undivided attention.

"This isn't for squandering in the hotel bars." Ziyad affectionately clipped the top of Thinuka's head with the palm of his other hand. Thinuka hated the way his father still treated him like a kid and quickly reset his ruffled hair, giving his father a peevish scowl.

"Where is your car?" Ziyad asked, ignoring the petulance. Thinuka had to think for a moment as to where exactly he had left it. Having recalled its location, Ziyad instructed him to go and get it and to park it close to the bus station.

"The man I acquired this from," Ziyad pointed to the stone dramatically, "is a Veddah and so I doubt he drove himself into Kandy." Thinuka sneered at the prospect of dealing with a savage but accepted his father's assumption as probably correct. He understood that Veddah tribesmen did not believe in possessions that did not serve a useful purpose in life. A car would not take priority over a long-handled hunting axe, a strong bow and a quiver of straight arrows or a bundle of thin wired snares. Ziyad continued with his instructions.

"It is possible that he has another dealer interested so hang around and see if he meets anyone and follow him. Try to find out where he comes from, and we can then study some maps for suitable rivers." His father grinned conspiratorially before tightly embracing his son. He released him and slapped him on the back to denote that he was dismissed and should be on his way.

Thinuka was happy that his father had trusted him in such a delicate task and eagerly departed on his exciting mission.

"Where will I find him?"

"I would try the tourist hotels first. Now, what are you waiting for?"

When he reached the door, Thinuka paused once again and turned back, taking a couple of steps towards the back of the shop. Ziyad was carefully rewrapping the stone and looked up.

"What's the problem?"

"No problem. Just, what does this Veddah chappie look like."

Ziyad looked vexed at what he saw as a stupid question.

"He's a Veddah. You know, a Veddah. They all look the same. Dark skin, wild hair, bushy beard. Taller than most but, you know, he's a Veddah."

Thinuka shrugged his shoulders and conjured up a picture in his mind's eye that was some way short of Randul's true appearance. He continued in the direction of the vault.

"Where are you going now?"

"Er, I need the toilet," he lied.

"I wouldn't use the one out there," Ziyad nodded his head in the direction of the rear latrine, "even though Aloka cleaned it. Wait until you can get to a hotel, if I were you." Thinuka thought for a moment and then shrugged his shoulders again.

"When needs must. Do you want me to put that back in the safe for you?" He pointed to the package on the counter.

Ziyad bobbed his head to one side and raised an eyebrow, "I think I can manage. Now, you get along."

Thinuka shrugged for the third time and went through the door into the back of the shop, quickly checking whether his father was watching him. Ziyad continued to tidy the countertop and once satisfied that all was ready for the day's trading, took the wrapped stone and followed in his son's footsteps to place the gem securely into the safe.

As he entered the vaulted room, Thinuka was just leaving down the narrow corridor towards the rear exit.

"Come on, boy! What are you dillydallying about here for?"

Thinuka muttered something inaudible and scuttled out of the rear door into the alley. Ziyad shook his head from side to side in despair at the fact that his son was obviously still suffering from the hangover. He would have to speak to him about his excesses in the evening when he got home.

Ziyad noted that in his excitement to show Thinuka his new acquisition he had failed to close the safe and had left the door slightly ajar. He chastised himself for his carelessness, pulled the door fully open and carefully stowed the gem in one of the lockable drawers that sat below the lowest shelf.

Despite its strength and impregnability, Ziyad wondered if he was wise to leave the jewel in the shop unattended. It would be better if someone stayed and guarded it overnight. He fussed around inside the safe tidying things unnecessarily before he pushed the heavy door shut and locked it.

When he returned to the shop, a flustered Aloka was standing just inside the front door. He was late yet again and had tried to silently slip in but had been caught in the act. Ziyad tutted and noted his assistance's flushed face and tearful eyes. Before he could say anything, he heard the back door squeak as it was slowly opened. Ziyad spun round and hurtled across the floor with unexpected speed towards the safe, only to find Thinuka riffling through the clutter on the side table. Guiltily he looked up at his father.

"What are you doing, boy? What is wrong with you today. Get going. Now!"

"I forgot my keys." He said lamely and tossed the bunch of car keys into the air as if to confirm his story. He glanced quickly past his father's right shoulder into the shop where Aloka was forlornly standing and, on seeing Thinuka, his cheeks flushed. Their exchange in the street outside just a few minutes ago had been brief, and Thinuka cruel.

"What are your keys doing there?" Ziyad asked in exasperation.

Thinuka did not wait to give an answer, merely waving a hand and disappeared down the corridor once again. Ziyad was bemused at his son's erratic behaviour. He moved to his stool behind the counter as the departing Thinuka slammed shut the back door for the final time.

Aloka flinched and was obviously expecting a tongue lashing for his tardiness. However, Ziyad's mind was on other matters that needed his attention. He gazed at Aloka with an almost paternal benevolence that was far more unsettling for his distraught assistant.

"Ah, Aloka, my boy. Are you doing anything tonight?" In truth, Ziyad was not in the least bit interested if Aloka was doing anything or not.

"I have an important, albeit modest task for you."

Chapter 11

A uniformed waiter attentively approached the local man who sat alone at a low table in the centre of the foyer. His advance was not with any intention of taking an order. He recognised the uniform, merely a local guide waiting for a guest. However, it was hotel policy that no guides, and certainly not Veddah guides, should wait for their clients in the hotel foyer. He should be waiting outside the front entrance like the others.

As he approached, a relaxed Randul smiled up at him and, forestalling any form of reprimand, politely requested, in English, a pot of tea. The waiter was taken aback and Randul was amused at his obvious surprise. The intended dismissal from the foyer was itself dismissed from the waiter's mind and he demurely took the order and returned to his station. Randul had already decided that he would leave him a generous tip when he departed. He could afford to.

Relaxed, with more money in his bag than he had ever had in his life, Randul looked confidently around the foyer with a renewed interest. Hotels such as this had been built for wealthy foreign visitors and only the higher echelons of Sri Lankan society got beyond the automatic entrance doors. Locals such as Randul rarely sat at the carefully laid tables with their floral embellishments and crisp white napkins. They came in as staff, entering through a discreet rear door to work behind the scenes, invisibly ensuring that the opulence afforded to the guests was maintained to the correct standard.

Randul had left his guest house early, having slept badly, fretting about his next meeting with The Arab. Having successfully completed that task, his worries revolved now around his uncharacteristic candour of the previous evening. Revelations to a total stranger about his life, his foraging and his research. He had spent since before dawn walking aimlessly around the streets of Kandy thinking hard about all that had transpired over the previous twenty-four hours. His negotiation and sale to The Arab of one Padparadscha, the chance meeting with Stephen, the supper at the guest house and the persistent curiosity of his guest.

Randul acknowledged that there was an undoubted affinity between himself and the Englishman. Perhaps this was partly explained by their common interest in gastronomy but there was something else. Something indefinable that afforded a sense of ease between the two men. Randul was not a social being, preferring his own company in the forest, working in his laboratory, guiding the foreign tourists with an indifference spawned from familiarity and repetition. He only worked in order to provide the funds to continue his private research, but now that might change. He had already obtained sufficient cash from the Arab to keep him going for some months, if not years, and the prospect of throwing in his job had become a reality.

The waiter returned carrying a silver tray with all the accoutrements for serving a cup of tea. He carefully placed it on the low table in front of Randul and asked if he would like him to pour it for him. Randul nodded and then noticed a plate of sugared shortbread biscuits.

"I didn't order any biscuits."

The waiter suppressed any brief sense of superiority that he might have enjoyed as a result of the local man's naivety as to the norms within such establishments.

"They are complimentary, sir," he continued to set the porcelain cup before adding, as if clarifying his statement to a small child, "They come free with the tea."

With carefully manicured hands, he poured the black tea into the thin china cup. Randul remained silent, feeling slightly foolish. The waiter carefully positioned the cup in front of Randul and, picking up a small jug with a pattern matching that of the cup, asked,

"Milk, Sir?"

"Milk? No, thank you."

"Will that be all, Sir?"

"Yes. Thank you."

The waiter retreated with the reassurance that his initial summation was not wholly incorrect, and that, despite his precise English, the Veddah was not quite as sophisticated as he liked to portray. Randul was pleased to see that nobody had appeared to notice his mistake. He munched on one of the biscuits and watched the flow of people through the lobby. There were very few locals. A number of guides had been standing in a group outside the entrance when he had arrived, waiting for their clients, but he did not recognise any of them and they did not know him.

As he lifted up the delicate porcelain cup containing the hot tea, Randul did not notice the suave young man who hurriedly entered the foyer, the fourth that morning. He looked around briefly until he saw what he was looking for and, with apparent relief, flopped onto a sofa a little distant from where Randul was seated.

The same waiter approached the new arrival and, after a brief exchange, left to collect his order. The young man studied his new mobile telephone but otherwise seemed to have no other purpose in the hotel other than to take some solitary refreshment.

Randul sipped his tea, still reflecting on the enthusiasm with which Stephen had embraced the opportunity to join him on a foraging expedition. He had been so insistent on learning more, repeating enquiries as to what all the ingredients were that Randul had supplied to Ranjid, what they were and where they came from. In some instances, even Randul could not categorise his discoveries with any great clarity. Some were new to him, the results of experimentation with foraged raw materials. His journal was meticulous in detailing his methods, but he had not thought to catalogue or name them other than allocating each new discovery a unique number. It worked for Randul, and anyway, names meant nothing to him.

The qualms over the evening were increasing with every sip of his tea. The inquisitive nature of his new friend was unsettling. He liked Stephen, they seemed to have a natural understanding. But by revealing his discoveries to a wider public, Randul ran the risk of exposing his forest, his home and his private sanctuary within the forest to invasion by an army of ignorant amateurs. Worse still, commercial hunter-gatherers would desecrate the land he loved so much.

Had he been foolish to admit that he was the source of Ranjid's culinary flourishes? He regretted his impatience in taking his latest discovery in that twist of paper. Maybe it was too early to try it out on Ranjid's diners. It was clear that Stephen's zeal for food was akin to Randul's curiosity for finding, collecting and processing ingredients.

It was this mutual quest for the unique that had united the two men. But they were from such different cultures. Randul, the young Veddah guide with an ancestral knowledge of foraging and a natural scientific gift that enabled him to manipulate plant material into inspiring ingredients. Stephen, a young English chef who has an apparent talent for creating great dishes that would delight diners.

And that was the problem, an apparent talent.

Apparent.

Randul's nagging doubts had suddenly coalesced during his perambulations around Kandy in the twilight hours of the morning. He suddenly realised that he had divulged to Stephen a great deal about himself without really knowing anything about Stephen. What he had been told by the self-proclaimed, prize-winning chef was just that. He was a prize-winning chef. Randul had taken it all at face value.

Immediately after he had completed his business with The Arab he walked to the centre of town, past the Clock Tower, to find one of the new internet cafes that were starting to appear in the Kandy. It was still early, and he knew that he would have to wait for it to open. He was the first customer to enter as the doors were unlocked. He ordered a tea and paid his fee to use a computer to do a search for Stephen Silchester on the internet.

He remained at the screen for half an hour and then left, satisfied that all that Stephen had told him was true. As he had delved deeper into the chef's background and read some of the reviews about his mastery of the intricate dishes that he had presented to the judges throughout the competition, Randul's earlier doubts lessened, and his enthusiasm was rejuvenated. This was an opportunity to try to meld his work with that of an undoubtedly talented young chef who was starting out on a promising career. Perhaps a short period of collaboration would be informative, maybe even enjoyable. On this basis, he would welcome the chance to get to know Stephen better. However, caution still sat on Randul's shoulder, and he decided that a final test should be set. Randul had slipped back to the guest house, knowing that it was a quiet time. His hosts only ever offering half board and so there was no lunchtime meal being prepared or served, hence the kitchen stood silent and empty.

He spoke briefly to Ranjid's wife who had agreed to Randul's rather unorthodox request, even though Ranjid had expressed some considerable reluctance. As a proud chef he did not relish another entering his domain and possibly surpassing his own skills. He was flattered that the English chef had eaten with them the previous evening, but he was a foreigner after all. Randul had attempted to convince Ranjid to grant the stranger admittance to his kitchen by pointing out that the Englishman had boasted how good a chef he was, but Randul wanted to see if this was true. Ranjid nodded his agreement to the wisdom of having proof as to any man's boastful claims. While he did not want to see the pleasant Englishman fail, to issue false boasts was not an attractive characteristic. If he failed the test then he would do it openly and be shamed. Ranjid eventually agreed, reluctantly stating that he might have to be out buying provisions for the evening meal.

"Good morning, Randul! How are you this fine morning?"

Stephen stood next to the sofa and Randul jumped, and quickly placed his cup and saucer noisily on the table. He stood, out of habit rather than respect, and greeted Stephen who was looking fresh and ready to experience whatever Randul had to offer for the day. He was dressed in a cotton shirt, open at the neck and untucked from his creased linen trousers. On his feet were a pair of scuffed leather sandals worn over grey woollen socks. A pair of glasses hung from a cord around his neck while his sunglasses were perched on the top of his head, partially obscured by his mop of blond hair. To say that Stephen Silchester was fat would be an exaggeration, but he was large framed, and it was only his height that masked his true weight. Randul noticed that even in the air-conditioned comfort of the hotel foyer, the taught skin of the Englishman's cheeks and forehead glistened with perspiration.

Stephen had slept very deeply despite, or perhaps because of, the elation he had experienced from the chance discovery of Randul and then the meal they had enjoyed together. This was the very essence of what Stephen had come to Sri Lanka to find and he could not allow the opportunity to slip from his grasp. Besides, he liked the young guide and would have welcomed the opportunity to work with him in some way and foster their friendship. However, that was not going to be easy with him in London running his new restaurant and Randul living his life in Sri Lanka. But if he could source some of the unique ingredients from him then he was sure that he could create a dining experience for the discerning clientele of Mayfair. Perhaps even achieve a Michelin Star or two?

Randul offered Stephen refreshment and Stephen accepted a tea as he sank into a chair next to his new friend. The same waiter efficiently appeared at Stephen's side anticipating that he would be making the order. He was taken aback yet again when Randul took the role of host and gave the order. He noted his requirements and bowed with a renewed respect for the local man who obviously was more important than he had initially assumed. He removed Randul's previous tray and disappeared.

"Well, what do you have in store for me today, Randul? I have to say, that meal last night was absolutely superb. Do you think Ranjid would come to England and work for me?"

He laughed at his own joke, the humour of which Randul had not appreciated, thinking that the suggestion was a serious one.

"Oh, no." Randul replied solemnly, "He has a wife and family here, as well as his business to run. I do not see Ranjid giving that up for England."

Stephen realised that his witticism had been taken too literally and started to explain, but then, when Randul looked at him quizzically, he decided to drop any attempt at levity.

The two men sat in silence for a short moment before Randul said,

"I wonder if you would do me a big service?"

"Sure, if I can." Stephen crossed his legs to reveal the thick grey socks beneath his sandals.

"I have asked Ranjid if you could borrow his kitchen for an hour or so," Randul watched to gauge Stephen's reaction before swiftly continuing. "So you can show me how you cook."

Stephen was slightly taken aback and hesitated. It was as if Randul was doubting his credentials, but then he realised that this was not so unreasonable. More importantly, it might give Stephen the opportunity to quiz Ranjid on some of his own techniques and recipes.

"Okay, I would be happy to do so, but I am not very prepared so don't expect anything too grand."

The waiter placed a fresh tray of tea on the table. He pointedly asked Randul if he would like him to serve and Randul nodded for him to proceed.

"I'll cook if I can use some of your ingredients. I would like to taste them uncooked and then decide how I might use them." The waiter listened to the conversation while serving the tea.

Randul shook his head, "I'm sorry but what I had I have given to Ranjid. He may have some bits and pieces left over as he normally uses them sparingly. Whether he will let you have them is another matter."

"Well, I'll have to charm him then, won't I?"

The two men continued to chat like old friends while they drank their tea. Randul was relieved that his request had not become an issue between them. When they were finished and ready to leave, Stephen called for the bill. The waiter looked to Randul for his instructions.

"No. I shall pay for these," Randul proudly announced as he dug in his bag to try to surreptitiously separate the appropriate notes from the large bundle of cash that Ziyad had handed over to him. He did not want to advertise how much he had in his possession, even in a prestigious hotel such as this. Stephen gratefully thanked his host, unaware that Randul was carrying around substantially more money in his bag than was currently in Stephen's bank account, including the prize money from the competition.

Randul paid the waiter who looked appreciatively at the notes in his hand. He wondered if he was duty bound to tell his unsophisticated guest that he had paid far too much. Sensing his consternation, Randul said,

"That's fine. Keep the change."

The waiter beamed with delight and thanked Randul effusively.

Meanwhile, the debonair young man across the foyer watched with interest and also began to prepare to depart, summoning the same waiter for his own bill. The two of them conversed for a moment and another generous tip was proffered by the young man to the waiter who could not believe his good fortune.

Stephen and Randul strolled past and, interrupting his conversation with the man, the waiter thanked them for their custom. The young man, still seated, watched their departure and then rose to follow them.

The walk back to the arched entrance to the guest house did not seem to Stephen to take as long as it had the previous evening. On the way he followed Randul into a tangle of narrow streets full of small shops selling vegetables, meat, herbs and colourful spices where he chose what he wanted for his menu.

The courtyard of the guest house was empty of people and in the daylight, it had a rather desultory air. Ranjid's wife was seated at one of the wooden tables that had been part of the large communal table. Now devoid of their white clothes, they looked scratched and tatty. She was studying some papers scattered across the surface with a cup of steaming coffee by her hand. She looked up as they entered and stated flatly that Ranjid had gone to the market, but the kitchen was theirs. She was sullen and it occurred to Randul that his request might have caused some disagreement between the couple.

He thanked her as Stephen tried once again to express his gratitude for last night's dinner. She looked at him without acknowledging any comprehension of his words, as Randul briefly translated before ushering Stephen through the door into the kitchen.

Stephen stood in the centre of the small room and started to professionally assess what was around him. He was not very impressed. The morning was going to be more of a challenge than he had initially thought. Almost as an afterthought Ranjid's wife poked her head round the door to ask if Randul knew where everything was. She told them how busy she was and hoped that she would not be needed. Stephen felt that the atmosphere in the house was decidedly frosty.

Randul nodded and, at Stephen's request, enquired whether she and Ranjid would be around later because Stephen hoped that they would join him to try his food. She mellowed slightly and, before returning to her paperwork, said she would if she managed to complete her morning's tasks.

After a more detailed inspection, Stephen satisfied himself that he would be able to master the basic equipment and quickly organised the provisions purchased from the market in preparation for creating a dish that he had made during the competition. He started automatically to get to work. Randul acted as his sous chef, running to and fro collecting ingredients as requested.

Stephen took on a wholly new persona in the kitchen, his attention focused entirely on the task at hand. He talked authoritatively to Randul who answered his questions, ensuring that each reply was factual but not too revealing. Randul found Ranjid's stash of herbs and spices that he had supplied on his arrival, all much diminished but certainly sufficient for the relatively small quantity of food that Stephen was going to prepare as a taster for the small panel of local judges.

As the two chatted, they found an ever-increasing communality of interests. Rarely was there a silence in the kitchen and Stephen was becoming increasingly respectful of Randul's depth of knowledge. Several of his preparations, Stephen discovered, required some minor adaptation to bring out the full effect on the taste or texture of a constituent part of his menu. Randul watched these minor changes and made a mental note to update his journal. Stephen carefully tasted each fresh element on its own and some he was still totally unable to classify but somehow, he intuitively knew where they would have most impact or would best draw out the flavour of another ingredient. It was as if they were able to speak to him, guide him and reveal to him their true purpose.

An invisible bond began to tie the two men as each worked their individual magic. Stephen held out wooden spoons that had been dipped in his pans for Randul to taste and make comment. As time slipped by, the smells that emanated from the simple kitchen reached the nose of Ranjid's wife and she inhaled appreciatively. While she had administrative tasks to perform, she had listened to the sound of the continual banter that passed between Randul and his friend. She did not understand what was being said but could tell from the tone of their conversation that they were content in each other's company. At times, Randul seemed to be almost lecturing Stephen, with occasional short and enquiring interruptions, and at other times Stephen was in command while apparently simultaneously seeking approval of a particular aspect of his work.

She was irritated that her own work was once more interrupted, a young man having silently slipped into the courtyard sometime after Randul and Stephen had arrived. He was not someone that she recognised but she knew the type and treated his arrival with immediate suspicion. This was not the usual prospective guest seeking a room for the night.

He was dressed in expensive western-style clothing with a gold chain hanging around his neck, a bracelet on his wrist and chunky gold rings encircling his fingers. The rolled-up sleeves of his silk shirt exposed a large-faced watch that she suspected cost more than her whole guest house was worth. He assumed a supercilious air but also seemed furtive and she was becoming increasingly doubtful as to his intentions. She met all sorts of people in her line of business and this one she instantly summed-up and had no hesitation in taking an aggressive approach to his invasion of her premises.

"We are closed!" She snapped.

He was not dissuaded by her less than gracious welcome and condescendingly looked around as if she was not there.

"Did you hear?" She stood up and pulled herself to her full, albeit modest height. Her stature belied the force of her authority that had now become overtly hostile.

"We are closed."

Thinuka looked at her with undisguised disdain,

"I don't seek lodging. Well, not here. I'm looking for a friend who I thought came in." He looked contemptuously at his surroundings as he continued to circle around the room.

"Although exactly why is beyond me." He approached the kitchen and stopped by the door when he heard voices beyond. He listened for only a second and then returned his attention to the proprietor of the guest house who now was standing directly in front of him.

Thinuka looked down at her and she wrinkled her nose at the smell of his sickly-sweet aftershave.

"I must have been mistaken."

Without another word he manoeuvred around her, strutted across the courtyard and left. Ranjid's wife watched his departure. After a while she wandered up to the first floor to look out from one of the rooms that faced onto the street. She was not surprised when she saw the same man lounging on the corner, smoking a cigarette while continually maintaining a watch over the entrance to the guest house.

She made a mental note to mention him to Randul.

*

Stephen had toiled in the stifling humidity for over an hour, perspiration running down his face and neck to be absorbed by the collar of his cotton shirt. He could feel the material sticking to his back and rivulets of sweat collecting around the waistband of his trousers. But he had come to the end of his labours. He spooned the aromatic food into small stainless-steel dishes and placed them on a tray. Randul collected three empty bowls and some cutlery.

He opened the door for Stephen who was more than ready to get out of the boiling kitchen for the relative cool of the courtyard. He took a cloth that was hooked into his belt and wiped the sweat from his face and neck before lifting the loaded tray and balancing it on one arm.

His hostess had returned from her upstairs vantage point and was seated at the table. The papers were pushed to one side, and she looked pensive. With the arrival of the tray of steaming dishes she dismissed her contemplative mood and looked appreciatively towards the two young men as they approached the table. She smiled as the wonderful smell of the food filled the expanse of the open courtyard. Had anyone remained in their rooms on the upper floors they would have been unable to resist the draw of the spiced aromas that wafted skywards.

"Has Ranjid returned?" Stephen asked through Randul.

"No," she replied, "he will be at the market until early afternoon." She knew that he had left the house in a mood. She had banished him from interfering in the kitchen while Stephen and Randul were using it. He would have preferred to watch and be involved, but in a fit of stupid pride he had stormed out of the house, and the same pride would not allow him to return.

Stephen looked crestfallen, he would have liked his host to sample his efforts and pass judgement on them. However, he consoled himself with the fact that Ranjid's wife was more than able to evaluate for herself whether he had done justice to her husband's chaotic workspace, sparse ingredients and Randul's mystical herbs and spices.

He placed an empty bowl in front of each of his two judges and the various dishes of food in the centre of the table. They all took small mouthfuls from each in silence. Stephen had sampled them throughout the various stages of preparation and execution. Now, as he sat at the table, the third bowl remaining empty, he felt the same nervous tension as he had when the critics were sampling his competition dishes. He wondered anxiously if he had misjudged their palates. Slowly, as if the flavours were a dawning sun within each of the diners, their faces turned towards him and shone with pleasure, swelling into delight and culminating in excited and voluble praise. Stephen could instantly see, and hear, that his efforts had been met with unreserved approval. He beamed with pride as the two talked over each other to express their awe and wonder at what they were eating.

When their enthusiasm had calmed, Stephen was able to sample the combined dish, which he savoured, allowing his taste buds to explore each aspect of the flavours. Once he had evaluated everything to his satisfaction, he allowed himself to swallow the combination to reveal any hidden surprises.

And surprises there were.

Stephen began to question whether Ranjid's wife's excited admiration for the food really was directed at him or at Randul. As he prepared the simple dishes, he thought that each additive was relatively innocuous when he had tasted them individually. He had scoured Ranjid's depleted cupboards for suitable ingredients and Randul had discovered that there was only a dusty residue of the yellow powder from the previous evening. Stephen had shaken and scraped every last grain from the twist of paper while Randul suggested that he did not taste it due to the limited amount available. Stephen thought nothing of the suggestion as he continued to regularly taste the contents of his steaming pots.

But now that each dish had been served, the combination of ingredients seemed to have undergone an obscure chemical reaction within the cooking process that resulted in his bowl of food providing a completely different experience to the one that he had expected. It was an explosion of every one of his most favourite flavours. A combination that would have appalled him had he been asked to create such a dish. It simply should not have succeeded - but it did. He was in awe of what he had produced and wondered if he was ever going to be able to replicate this alchemy in his kitchen in London.

The three of them consumed everything that Stephen had presented and Ranjid's wife waved her hands in ecstasy and chattered at such speed that Randul struggled to keep up with the translation of her praises. Stephen repeatedly attempted to give some of the credit to Randul and his magical ingredients, but she would have none of it. As they talked noisily, no one had noticed that Ranjid had returned using the rear entrance and was standing behind them. He was staring with incredulity, obviously thinking that his wife had been intoxicated by some liquor. To an extent she had, the intoxication was the effect of the food on her senses which even as he watched, was being absorbed by her body - and still her ecstatic gastronomic delight continued. The empty dishes showed the enthusiasm with which lunch had been consumed; any juices that had lingered in them had been mopped dry, leaving nothing more than a thin smear on the shiny surfaces. The table bore witness to the culinary orgy and Ranjid had arrived as all its participants basked in the afterglow.

He spoke curtly to his wife who, like a child caught in the act of doing something forbidden, looked shamelessly guilty. The elation of a few minutes ago dissolved and Stephen and Randul also sat quietly. Stephen presumed that she was explaining what had happened and he tried to get Randul to express his gratitude for the opportunity to cook in his kitchen. Randul waved him into silence and whispered that they should clear the dishes onto the tray. Ranjid ignored them as the married couple's voices rose.

Randul made for the kitchen, indicating that Stephen should follow. Once inside, they could hear the heated debate continue outside as Randul explained, "It is not right that we should be present at such a time. A man and his wife need privacy when he is chastising her."

Randul placed the tray by the sink and silently both men diligently washed up the last pots, pans and serving dishes, most of which had already been done by Randul while Stephen had put the finishing touches to his meal. The discussion in the courtyard was becoming ever more heated and once the various utensils had been returned to their rightful places, Stephen and Randul slipped out of the kitchen with the intention of leaving the guest house. Stephen felt he should attempt to express his gratitude, but Randul was insistent that they should just go.

As they started to cross the courtyard Ranjid's wife spied them. She held up her hand in front of Ranjid's reddened face. It was a commanding gesture and Ranjid ceased his haranguing, his jaw slack as his wife hurried over to stop them. She spoke urgently to Randul while Ranjid watched with a bemused expression on his face. He listened to the hushed conversation and then silently walked past them, out of the guest house entrance into the street beyond. Stephen saw him nonchalantly look to left and right while stretching, as if he had come from his hot kitchen for some fresh air. Presently, he returned and nodded his head to Randul and his wife, the former argument dismissed.

Randul was looking increasingly concerned.

"What is going on?" Stephen asked.

Randul turned to Stephen as if only just remembering that he was in the room.

"It appears that we are being followed. Perhaps you have a fan in Sri Lanka?" The levity of the question was misplaced and did not elicit a response. Their hosts had a brief exchange in whispered tones.

Randul thought that it was exceedingly unlikely that Stephen was the subject of any interest from the man loitering outside the guest house. The considerable sum of money and the larger Padparadscha that lay in his bag were far more likely targets.

A further hasty exchange took place between the three, Stephen being temporarily superfluous to their deliberations. Ranjid spoke in a muted voice and Randul listened intently until suddenly a look of relief cleared his furrowed brow. Kandy was not a large city, even though it was a tourist hot spot. Ranjid had seen the louche young man around Kandy and while he did not know who he was, he confirmed to Randul that he was a local playboy who spent most of his time carousing. Ranjid's wife also seemed ignorant as to the man's identity and only spoke of his rudeness to her. This riled Ranjid still further, his own argument with his wife set aside, his anger now focussed on the young man who had had the temerity to offend his wife in her own home.

Ranjid looked across at Stephen and asked Randul if he thought the Englishman was the one being followed. Randul could not admit that he thought that it was far more likely to be himself and so left the couple in the belief that Stephen was the target.

"I shall go and speak to him," Ranjid announced. "You can both go out of the back and by the time I have finished you will be long gone."

Randul collected up his precious bag and Stephen followed him out of the courtyard in the opposite direction to Ranjid, whose body language made it clear that he considered that the young man was not too old to be given a severe lecture as to the importance of good manners. Custom dictated that the young showed a degree of deference to the older man, and Ranjid knew it.

The two visitors departed unseen through the back street while Ranjid engaged Thinuka in a heated discourse on the benefits of young men having manners and respect towards women, and his woman in particular. Thinuka tried to bluff his presence as being coincidence but that only raised Ranjid's fury to explosive levels. Despite his many faults, Thinuka still retained the inherent respect that the young were required to hold for their elders and betters. He stood looking both chastened and anxious, glancing regularly over Ranjid's shoulder to see who else might emerge from the entrance. After some twenty minutes of being lectured and harangued, Ranjid did not quite clip him round the head, but eventually dismissed him from littering the street.

Thinuka walked away realising that his quarry must have flown and that he was going to have to start his quest all over again.

Chapter 12

Thinuka was livid after he had been released from the lengthy tongue lashing administered by Ranjid. He would have ignored the angry little man and his ranting were it not for his upbringing and inbuilt respect for a more senior male. He had been unable to escape until his accepted superior dismissed him and told him that he may go. Kicking out at a passing dog searching for scraps, he yelled at a group of children who were playing cricket in the street to get the hell out of his way.

With his head bent low, Thinuka hurried along the street towards the hotel where he had first seen Stephen and Randul drinking tea together. He could not work out who Stephen was or why Randul should have paid the bill. Was it possible that Stephen was a foreign gem dealer as Baba had suspected and that he was going to cut them out of any deal to buy the larger stone from the boy? Why were they in the kitchen of that stinking guest house and where were they now?

There were too many questions and not enough answers for Thinuka.

He estimated that he was only a year or two older than the Veddah, but he treated any tribesman with disdain. In his opinion, they were all savages, lacking any education or breeding that was inherent in those from his own social class. It had always baffled Thinuka why his father, a wealthy, self-made man, should perpetuate the image of an impoverished shopkeeper. Each morning Baba left his comfortable house in an affluent suburb of town dressed as a down at heel merchant working from a back street shop. He could so easily afford a clean modern shopfront on the main street. Why did he continue to wear that old, painful prosthetic foot when he had an expensive replacement that he used each evening as he retired to his study to drink his imported Scottish malt whisky? As a family, they never socialised or visited restaurants and consequently they had few friends. It was as if his father wanted to disappear from public view. It was an existence that Thinuka could not abide, and he did his best to escape from its repression.

The reasons for the subterfuge of the father were beyond the logic of the son – but reasons there were.

Thinuka was clear in his own mind that as soon as he took over, he would be moving the business into the 21st century. Branding and media exposure would be maximised to rapidly expand the operation such as to overwhelm his woefully inadequate competitors. He would not hide behind the present modest façade in the miserable backstreet. He imagined that his ambition vastly exceeded that of his father. For him, the unseen success of Baba's efforts would be exposed to the world, become a 'must-have' with the new social influencers and media celebrities who were spawned by the internet. He would be the new face of Sri Lankan design and flair within the jewellery sphere. His personal profile would echo his respected business acumen and exalted status within Sri Lankan society. But all that would have to wait.

At the present point in time his priority was more modest, albeit an important part of his future. He understood Baba's desire to discover where the boy had found that perfect Padparadscha sapphire and, perhaps more importantly, how many more he had in his possession. Were they still in his possession? In the bag he carried. Or were they hidden somewhere in the depths of the forest? Held in some revolting cave or hut where these people lived their heathen lives?

He was sure that he had recognised the uniform that Randul had been wearing and so he would start there. While the forest had many guides, he was certain that with a little financial persuasion, someone would point him in the direction of the one he sought. Then all he needed to do was wait and watch. He would eventually turn up. Thinuka would then stalk him until he went to his secret mine to retrieve more stones.

Simple.

What would be even simpler would be to steal what he had already. The boy was clearly involved in unauthorised mining so to whom would he complain? To whom *could* he complain? With whatever haul the boy had in his bag safely in Thinuka's possession, including the money he had clearly extorted from Baba, his father would issue the necessary certificates and the stones would legally become theirs – at little or no cost. This sounded a better plan to Thinuka.

But Thinuka was impatient. He did not want to waste time travelling all over the island trying to find a single guide. Besides, the north around Jaffna was a no-go area even though the fragile cease fire remained in place. If the savage came to Kandy from the Northern Province, then Thinuka could not risk entering that zone. Baba had already made discreet enquiries around town. It was clear that the boy was not a regular guide in the immediate Kandy area. The Veddah were not encouraged into the cities and seemed to have no desire to settle in them.

Thinuka's mind was reeling and, despite his earlier decision as to the best course of action, he found himself standing in front of the hotel where he had first found Randul and the Englishman. Why was he here? He knew that he had come here for a reason but in his confusion he was, well, confused. He looked vacantly at the entrance and the doorman in his traditional Sri Lankan uniform. Suddenly an idea flashed into Thinuka's brain and he rushed through the entrance and up to the front desk, pushing past a guest who was about to check-out. Breathlessly he asked the female receptionist about the Englishman.

Who was Thinuka?

He was a friend of the Englishman – sort of.

What did he look like?

Tall, heavy, untidy fair hair.

Was he a guest staying here?

He was here this morning. Left with a local man. A Veddah.

His name?

No, I don't know his name. I am a friend...well, an acquaintance.

What do you mean you can't help me?

But he must have walked out straight passed you.

Big.

Tall.

Mop of fair hair.

The young receptionist calmly tilted her head slightly to one side as a blustering Thinuka tried to expand on his vague description of his supposed friend. She was well trained and had her suspicions as to Thinuka's motivations. She had seen the smarmy Thinuka before, ingratiating himself with any solo male or vulnerable female tourists in the hotel bar on several occasions. It was more than her job was worth to give out information about a guest to anyone, let alone this fickle chancer. The fact that Mr Silchester had already checked out was none of his business and so she continued to feign ignorance as to exactly who Thinuka was attempting to describe.

On his part, Thinuka was becoming increasingly frustrated and agitated, raising his voice in his anger at her refusal to assist him. Eventually the deputy manager came across to calm the altercation that was beginning to gather a crowd of curious onlookers.

"Mr. Silchester is not here. He checked out a while ago." The receptionist's shoulders sagged as her efforts at discretion were instantly negated by the deputy manager. Thinuka shot her a vengeful glance and opened his mouth to glean what Mr Silchester was doing in Kandy and where he had left for, but the deputy manager immediately raised his hand to silence him.

"Please leave."

Thinuka stared at the man in disbelief. Did he not know who Thinuka was? He made no effort to move.

"Now. Or must I call the police?" The deputy manager looked over to the receptionist who picked up her telephone. Thinuka followed his line of sight, and he gave a malevolent scowl at the receptionist. She produced her sweetest smile and waggled the receiver at him. She raised her eyebrows fractionally as if challenging him to continue to argue. Defeated, Thinuka stumped off out of the hotel, thinking hard as he went.

What to do next?

He could not fail his father. Baba would be furious.

*

Some two hundred metres from where Thinuka was furiously trying to formulate his next course of action, Randul was trying to find an explanation for Stephen as to why a man was tailing them. It was helpful that Stephen had already, incorrectly, jumped to the conclusion that the motive related to him as a tourist, rather than Randul as the local. While this was convenient in some respects, it inadvertently seemed to place a responsibility on Randul to extricate Stephen from a situation that he found himself in, through no fault of his own. Randul should have ignored the agreement that he had reluctantly reached with Stephen to take him into the forest, and last night they should each have gone their own separate ways.

The simplest solution would be for Randul to return to the bus station and make a swift exit out of Kandy back to his home, but his bus did not leave for another three hours. Randul could not risk such a delay. While he did not know precisely who the person following him was, he felt sure that it had something to do with the Arab dealer. Through the diversion created by Ranjid, they had been able to slip away from the guest house and Randul wanted to use the time to best advantage. To remain in Kandy, particularly around the bus station would be courting fate.

Stephen stood with his bag at his feet as the two of them independently wondered what to do. He made a half-hearted suggested that perhaps he should get back to his original hotel as it might be safer there. Randul agreed but did not say so. With the unexpected appearance of the man who was following them, Stephen knew that the arrangements of the previous evening were in jeopardy, despite the fact that he was still desperate to join Randul foraging. Why he was being stalked, he had no idea? He watched as his companion, who now seemed to have adopted the role of his guardian, kept looking around anxiously to check if the man following them was anywhere to be seen.

Stephen bent down to lift his bag into the boot of the car, ready to leave Randul. Whether he would ever see him again he doubted, and he cursed the lost opportunity.

"Can I give you a lift anywhere?" Stephen asked in a dispirited voice.

Randul had to make an immediate decision as it was his safety that was on the line, not Stephen's. He had no wish to stay in Kandy for a moment longer than was necessary.

The bus was a non-starter. There was only one other mode of transport available to get him home.

"Do you still want to see where I forage?"

Stephen stared at his friend in delight.

"Of course I do."

"Ok, then. Why don't you come and spend a day or so with me and then go back to your original hotel?"

Stephen did not hesitate, having just resigned himself to the fact that he was going to have to cut short his friendship with Randul. Now he had the opportunity to learn all he could about Randul's methods of foraging and the forest in which he lived.

"Fantastic! That sounds great." Stephen's enthusiastic agreement accompanied his bag thudding into the boot. As he closed the lid he automatically asked, with instant regret,

"Are you sure?"

To his profound relief, Randul nodded in the affirmative.

"You would be doing me a favour. The bus is always a long, uncomfortable journey, and your car will be much more pleasant. I can then show you around." Randul removed his backpack from his shoulder and stowed it in the front footwell.

"Do you want to put that in the boot?" Stephen enquired, as Randul curled himself into the passenger seat, his feet either side of his bag.

"No, it's fine here," Randul replied, his eyes constantly scanning the street in all direction. "Come on! Let's get going!"

Stephen was overjoyed at the outcome and jumped into the car alongside his companion. He was more than happy to drive into the mystical forest, whatever direction that might be. He grinned as he imagined a distraught Celia welcoming the arrival of the TV crew and breaking the news that she had momentarily lost the star of the production.

Randul slid low in his seat while maintaining a watchful eye for anyone in the crowds who might look familiar. He kept down as far as he could without appearing too conspicuous. Stephen started the engine and pulled slowly out of the parking space, easing the small Toyota into the flow of traffic.

"Which way?" Stephen asked.

He had his window open and was constantly turning his head back and forth to monitor the chaotic vehicular activity all around him. Due to an inherent British sense of politeness to other road users, Stephen was defeated in every contest for possession of a space in the stream of traffic. His dithering and hesitancy were taken advantage of with alacrity by all the other drivers, accompanied by the angry frustration from those who found themselves in his stuttering wake. Randul cringed at the speed of progress and the look of incredulity on the other drivers faces as Stephen gave way or even signalled for others to move in front of him.

Still with his eyes roving across the faces of passers-by, Randul pointed Stephen down a wide boulevard. The car edged its way cautiously between the overladen scooters, battered vans and empty buses that were circumnavigating an area of road that purported to be a roundabout, but over which traffic travelled in all directions with no apparent sense of order. Stephen gently accelerated out of the chaos and followed the road along which Randul had directed him, away from downtown Kandy.

The wide thoroughfare was clogged with all manner of traffic while either side was bounded by a mixture of scruffy shops and offices; most being old, many with unfinished, open-fronted extensions to the upper floors. A small number of more modern styled offices housing banks or finance companies had been squeezed between the original traditional structures. Signs hung from anywhere that they could be safely secured, advertising a wide selection of merchandise and services. However, Stephen could only catch the briefest of glimpses of the facades as his concentration was exclusively reserved for the jumble of vehicles, animals and people that were fighting for positional advantage along the arterial escape.

*

Thinuka hurried down the road from the hotel towards where he had parked his car. He seemed to be going against the flow of people heading for the lake and the temple. He kept having to avoid collisions with innocent passers-by or roughly push others from his path. The traffic was heavier than usual, and he looked over at the noisy confusion around the junction in the centre of town. A white Toyota car was inching its way forward, the bulky driver appeared to be too big for the small interior of the vehicle. He looked flustered and out of place amongst the seasoned campaigners in this busy part of town. Gradually the vehicle negotiated its way through the confluence of various streets and, after a final fusillade of horns and raucous gesticulations, managed to extricate itself from the melee and escape down a less congested road out of town.

Thinuka looked at the driver one last time and was galvanised into action. He raced across to his car and jumped in. The powerful engine of the Mercedes roared into life and the wheels spun on the smooth macadam as the powerful vehicle shot out into the traffic. He had no qualms about forcing his way through the resulting carnage that had been wrought by the Toyota. Far ahead, he saw the white car tentatively pull out past a stationary bus.

The Mercedes was quickly catching up with the Toyota and he needed to slow down and pace himself so as not to crowd the driver or raise any suspicions that he was following him. Thinuka was sure that the driver was the English gem dealer that he had seen in the hotel having a coffee with the boy. He could not see if there was a passenger in the car, but he was pretty sure that the departure of the Englishman was too much of a coincidence.

As he paced himself a couple of cars back from his quarry, Thinuka could not believe his good fortune. As they emerged gradually from the suburbs of Kandy, he was overjoyed to see a head rise above the headrest as the tall passenger sat more upright. The savage had obviously been hiding through the traffic and now felt it was safe to emerge. A grin spread across Thinuka's face, and he settled down in the soft leather seat, turned up the air-conditioning and flicked on the radio. It was hardly a challenge to follow the Toyota, but it was important to maintain a good distance between them so as not to be detected.

The traffic was thinning out quickly and Thinuka had to pull further and further back until he could only just keep the Toyota in sight. Occasionally he tucked himself behind a bus to catch up and check that they had not turned off. However, the buses either unexpectedly stopped or roared pass the white car to suddenly exposed the Mercedes. Each time he would veer to the edge of the road and wait a few seconds for a few vehicles to pass him and fill the gap. Such erratic manoeuvres did not cause any disruption to the sparse traffic and certainly would not be considered unusual on these outlying roads.

Stephen relaxed slightly as the traffic diminished and Randul straightened up in his seat, relieved to have survived the terrifying ordeal of Stephen's indecisive urban driving. The air that flowed through the open windows was much fresher and they both began to breath more deeply. Randul still had some reservations about taking Stephen to his home but the need to escape from the city was more important. He started to explain that his home was modest compared with what Stephen might be expecting. He felt a twinge of embarrassment, fearing that Stephen would think him a peasant rather than an educated man. He emphasised repeatedly that Stephen should not expect too much.

"Please stop being so apologetic. I'm sure that I shall love your home. I hardly grew up in a palace."

Stephen was pleased to be out of Kandy and a sense of contentment, mixed with expectation, filled his heart. He did not care how basic his friend's house was. All he was really interested in was collecting original ideas for his opening menu at The Sauceror's Apprentice. But deep-down Stephen experienced a desire to know this contradictory man better. An aboriginal who was treated by his peers as a second, or possibly third- class citizen, a throwback to more uncivilised times. The fact that he had an education and a talent that many could only aspire to, seemed to be lost on those who encountered him. Stephen looked across at the strikingly handsome young tribesman and he smiled awkwardly as Randul caught his gaze.

Randul, whether out of embarrassment at Stephen's sideways glances or the relief of escaping from Kandy, talked animatedly about his time at Colombo university and how he had lost his father just after he graduated. Stephen was amazed to hear that the old man had made a living from his foraging sufficient to support his family and educate his son. Randul was not sufficiently comfortable with his companion to make any mention of the income earned from the odd sapphire, emerald or ruby extracted from the river. Randul asked Stephen about his life in London, the cooking competition and was intrigued by Stephen's plans for the restaurant. They slipped into a game of devising dishes and menus and Stephen came to realise that Randul had a natural affinity with flavours and how to use them to best advantage. It seemed that, were he to be so inclined and the circumstances different, Randul could have become just as accomplished a chef as Stephen intended to be.

Throughout the conversation, Randul kept a wary eye on the wing mirror and noted that the blue Mercedes was still behind them.

*

Thinuka had become drowsy and was daydreaming about his future and the possibility that the savage might have something truly exceptional that was going to transform his life – Thinuka's life, not that of the heathen. By the time he was winding his way up into the hills, he had opened a branch of his jewellery business in New York. His image of New York was one gleaned from the movies that he had watched, but for a global dealer in high-end gems, it would be foolish not to have a New York outlet. And Singapore, or perhaps Dubai. And then there was London. He felt that he knew London better and wanted to have a flat in Eaton Square, which he had read was the most expensive part of the city to live in. He was fascinated by the fact that the whole area was owned by a Duke.

How did one become a Duke? Maybe…. but no, that was unlikely even in the most fanciful of Thinuka's daydreams.

The fantasizing ended abruptly as he suddenly realised that the Toyota had stopped and was parked by a small tea house on the side of the road. It was too late for him to take any immediate action as he was already alongside. The heavy-set, fair-haired Englishman was seated outside at a small metal table mopping a handkerchief across his forehead. The savage was exiting the shack like a slave, serving his master, a cup in each hand.

Thinuka swept passed the spot before he was able to absorb any more information and continued fretfully driving down the road, constantly watching in his rear-view mirror, unsure as to whether either man had noticed the dark blue Mercedes. After a short mile there was a small collection of shacks with an incongruous single-pump petrol station, a fruit stall and little else. Thinuka swung the car into the forecourt and parked as unobtrusively as he could on the inside of a decrepit flatbed truck. He repositioned the mirror to give him a clear line of sight back along the road and settled down to wait.

*

The decision to take a break was at Randul's suggestion and Stephen welcomed the opportunity to unwind himself from behind the steering wheel. He stretched his back while Randul disappeared inside the tea house to get them both some refreshment. It was little more than a timber frame clad in an assortment of salvaged timber and iron sheets built on the edge of the highway. Tall trees overhung the structure providing a dappled shade to the rutted and baked mud that served as a veranda. If Stephen were alone, he would never have chosen this place for a relaxed break. However, he had come to trust Randul's judgement and was looking forward to some black tea to refresh his parched mouth. Whether he relished the prospect of visiting the toilet signposted on a battered piece of cardboard nailed to the side of the shack was a matter for conjecture, but he would deal with that possibility later.

As they appeared to be the only customers, Stephen chose one of the two tables positioned on the uneven kerb. A thin layer of dust attached itself to the surface and, as he wiped it with the side of his hand, he discovered that the dust was held in place by an invisible sub-coating of unidentifiable stickiness. A grey wave of grime formed on the edge of his hand that turned into a tacky smear when he attempted to clean it away with his handkerchief. Stephen considered risking the men's room to wash but at that moment Randul emerged carrying two steaming cups together with a couple of bottles of water lodged firmly under his arm.

He looked up briefly to locate where Stephen was sitting and saw the immaculate blue Mercedes rumble by in a cloud of dust. The driver appeared to be startled, as if caught unawares as he passed. He was looking at Randul but made no effort to slow down or stop. Randul calmly set down the cups and the bottles of water as Stephen, unaware of any concerns that his friend may have, started chattering once again.

He had become increasingly garrulous as the journey had worn on, but at this point in time Randul just needed some peace and quiet to think. He silently sipped his tea and shut out the babbling Englishman from his mind.

*

Thinuka sat silently cursing his loss of concentration to another of his daydreams. It would be fortunate if neither the savage nor the foreign gem dealer had noticed him passing the tea shop. He hoped that when they had finished their break, they would continue their journey along this road. He had not seen any other tracks or lanes that turned off it so he should be able to spot them.

After what seemed an age, the white Toyota did reappear and Thinuka slid down in his seat to make sure that he was not seen. Dust swirled around the truck that partially hid the Mercedes as the white car passed. Thinuka paused for some seconds to let his quarry get a reasonable head start before he pressed the ignition button and cautiously pulled out from his concealed parking space. The car ahead was travelling at a much faster pace than previously and Thinuka was surprised at the lead it had drawn out between them. However, he always welcomed the opportunity to open up the Mercedes, albeit having to carefully watch for any sharp potholes that unexpectedly pitted the country roads. The car was not made for rural byways, much preferring the urban environment where both car and driver could be admired by the envious residents of Kandy, Galle, Colombo or Negombo.

This time, he kept a wider margin between the two cars as he followed. The speed of the Toyota threw up a cloud of dust that partially obscured the view behind the driver of the leading car. Gradually the vegetation closed in on either side of the road, becoming denser with shafts of bright sunlight flickered through the canopy and across Thinuka's face. He screwed up his eyes as he took a sharp bend and the sinking sun suddenly shone straight through the windscreen onto him. He was momentarily blinded, and the road disappeared. He instinctively slowed his speed for fear of slipping over the edge of the tarmac into the treacherously deep rut that had been created by other vehicles taking avoiding action from on-coming traffic.

Thinuka stabbed at the windscreen washer and a spray of soapy water showered the glass to be smeared into a thin film of grease and dust that completely obscured his forward vision. He hit the brakes hard and, with more water and the frantic windscreen wipers slapping across the screen, he cleared the gritty mess, only to discover that the road ahead was empty. It was long and straight, and the Toyota was nowhere to be seen. He cruised along for a mile or two and then turned around and retraced his steps looking for turnings or tracks that he might have missed.

He knew that the speed of the Toyota could not have outstripped his vehicle by much, even allowing for the fact that he had had to slow down when blinded by the sun and filthy windscreen. He turned around once again, and for a third time the Mercedes crawled down the road while its driver studied every possible point at which the Toyota could have disappeared into the forest.

*

Randul stopped the car with a jerk and Stephen sat holding onto the passenger door handle. The sudden manoeuvre had taken him completely by surprise to the extent that he had cracked his head on the pillar of the door as Randul had yanked the steering wheel over to slip the car between two trees and down a leaf strewn path that Stephen would never have seen. The car had careered along the track as Randul expertly slid it around a couple of corners and then came to a sudden halt.

Stephen quickly regained his voice and screamed in shock at Randul.

"What the fuck are you doing?"

He had had reservations when Randul had suggested that he took over the driving for a spell.

"Shut up, my friend. Be very quiet."

Stephen had not heard Randul speak with such authority before, having previously taken him to be a rather timid sort of a character. The effect was startling in that it silenced Stephen immediately. Randul turned off the engine and twisted round to look behind him. As the engine of the car cooled it made its usual soft plinking sounds while in the trees all around the briefly interrupted birdsong resumed. There was nothing to be seen of their unexpected arrival save for enveloping vegetation and the swiftly settling dust and leaves.

Stephen could wait for an explanation no longer, but kept his voice at a whisper,

"What the hell are you doing? Why have we careered into the trees?"

"We are being followed and I wanted to lose whoever it was."

"What?" Stephen was stunned, "Who is following us? Why?" He was shaken by both the unexpected move from road to undergrowth, as well as the explanation given by Randul. For the first time, he became very aware of his vulnerability as a lone tourist in a car with a stranger in the middle of an unknown forest. Nobody knew where he was and if anything happened to him, then no one would find him. Stephen surreptitiously moved his hand onto the door handle with a view to making a quick escape should it be necessary. Whether he could outrun Randul back to the road he was unsure, but he would make a damn good attempt.

Randul relaxed momentarily feeling that he might have temporarily shaken off their tail but knew that they only had a limited amount of time before the Mercedes would inevitably find some evidence in the dirt of his detour between the trees. He twisted back to face the still shocked Stephen. He held his attention with a stern face and direct eye contact.

At the tea stop Randul knew that he would have to tell Stephen the truth.

"I think whoever is following us is after me. Or more particularly, something I am carrying."

"What do they want?" Stephen asked, perplexed, unconvinced and suspicious.

"It is better that you don't know, but I want you to listen, and do exactly as I ask."

Stephen listened slightly incredulously to what Randul was instructing him to do but concluded that whatever trouble the young man was in was of no concern to him. If it meant that he would be free of both Randul and the person following them then he was more than content to follow the instructions given to him.

*

Thinuka stopped his car and got out to study the road surface more closely. There were faint signs of black tyre marks from a vehicle suddenly swerving to the right. Such an abrupt change of direction was not unusual on Sri Lankan roads but even though relatively indistinct, this was obviously fresh. He followed the direction of travel and saw that the vehicle appeared to have left the road and sped between two trees. It was a narrow gap and there was no way that Thinuka was going to get his car through to follow. Even if he wanted to, the unforgiving edge to the road surface would catch his sump and do considerable damage to his beloved Mercedes. The only alternative was to continue on foot.

It was clear to Thinuka that the boy was aware that he was being followed and that made Thinuka naturally cautious, if not nervous. The reputation of the Veddah people as excellent hunters was no secret, a talent they were proud to demonstrate should anyone want to bear witness. Thinuka had no wish to find that he was the quarry for this particular native. He returned to his car and opened the glove compartment. He cautiously withdrew Baba's handgun that he had taken earlier from the safe in the shop. If Ziyad had been aware that his son knew the combination of the safe, then probably he would never have kept the gun in it. The fact that the door had been left ajar made its removal all the easier and was to be regretted for as long as Ziyad lived.

Thinuka liked the feeling of omnipotence that the weapon gave him and, as he was on a mission for Baba, he felt justified in taking it with him. He caressed the blue metal barrel and checked to make sure that it was loaded. His father would not notice its absence and, anyway, it would be returned by the end of the day.

Previously, Thinuka had only ever played with the gun in the confines of the shop. Unbeknownst to him, this was its first outing since Ziyad had had occasion to use it some years back. He slipped the gun into his waistband at the small of his back. He had seen this done in the movies and while it was uncomfortable and dug into his skin, it was out of sight. His silk shirt hung loosely untucked to disguise any bulge caused by the weapon.

He locked his car and started into the forest following where the Toyota had disappeared. As he proceeded along the path, the tracks became clearer in the forest litter, the leaves having been scattered by the speeding vehicle as it sought to grip onto the loose, dry surface.

After four or five hundred yards, Thinuka froze and sank onto his haunches when he saw the stationary white car ahead. There was no sign of anybody in it. Slowly, he approached the vehicle and felt the bonnet which was still warm. He looked around and could see nothing out of the ordinary. There were no obvious tracks made by anyone moving further into the forest. He opened the driver's door and checked the interior, but it was empty. In the boot was a single bag that he assumed belonged to the gem dealer. Despite a sense of vulnerability with his back to the forest, he unbuckled the top and swiftly rummaged through the contents. From a cursory inspection there was nothing he could see of interest apart from clothes and a couple of books. He slammed down the boot lid, his senses alert for any signs or sounds of movement, but nothing stirred save for the cries of birds that had flown in alarm at the sudden thump.

Thinuka leant against the car and tried to decide between lying in wait, entering further into the forest or returning to his car.

*

Randul remained motionless behind the broad buttress of a tree some fifty yards from the car. He could hear the door being opened and shortly after the boot lid slamming shut. He waited and listened as intently as he suspected the other man was doing. After a minute of inaction in the vicinity of the car, Randul crouched down and picked up a dry stick. He bent it until it cracked loudly and then he moved, swiftly and easily through the trees and over the uneven forest floor.

Thinuka had involuntarily jumped at the sound of the broken twig and tightened his grip on the butt of the pistol. His quarry was in sight and running. No longer was there any attempt at deception. The decision was made for Thinuka. The savage had carelessly revealed himself and in the bag on his back was something Thinuka wanted. It was a simple task of catching him and relieving him of it.

Randul was undoubtedly the fitter man, and he knew the forest well so he could travel at speed, while Thinuka stumbled and gasped for air. However, at no point did Randul allow the gap between the two men increase, he merely remained just in sight while ensuring that the route was suitably convoluted, drawing them both further into the depths of the forest.

Thinuka continued doggedly in the chase, driven on by the thought of dispossessing the local boy of the exquisite Padparadscha that was safely stowed in the bag strapped to the back of his quarry. His eyes never left that bag despite the sapping of his energy and his increasingly weakening legs. Deeper and deeper into the forest the two men sank, one perfectly relaxed as to his whereabouts, the other without a clue.

Stephen saw the two men disappear into the undergrowth and, complying with Randul's instructions, he allowed them a few minutes before he came out from his hiding place and took the car keys from his pocket. Carefully he reversed the car out of the forest and onto the main road. Pointing the car back in the direction that they had come, he drove off towards the tea shop.

Stephen had been seated at the same small metal table for long enough to allow the darkness to descend and the owner of the tea shop to have locked up and gone home. Headlights flooded the road every so often and Stephen tensed as he anticipated the Mercedes returning. Randul had been insistent that Stephen remained at the tea shop until at least nine o'clock that evening. After that, if Randul had not turned up then he should drive back to Kandy, alert the police and tell them what had happened.

Stephen looked at his watch and saw that it was 20:45. He was becoming increasingly anxious, fearing for the safety of his friend. He chided himself for having had any suspicions as to the motive for Randul inviting him to his home or taking over the driving. Earlier thoughts of deserting his friend were now banished. The events of the afternoon had served to strengthen the tie that had grown between them. When he saw the man arrive at the car and start searching it, Stephen experienced a quiver of excitement. The adventure took him outside his usual mundane existence, well beyond his comfort zone. Besides, there was no real danger. Surely this was a simple misunderstanding? A case of mistaken identity that would prove to be an escapade that he would recount to friends back in London.

Even so, curiosity gnawed at him as to the reason why Randul thought that he was being followed.

Another car appeared in the distance and as its lights illuminated the road, he saw in silhouette the rangy figure of Randul jogging towards him. His heart missed a beat, and he hurried to meet him. Whether in relief or for some other unknown reason, both men opened their arms and embraced, Randul breathless from his run and Stephen out of sheer delight at his return. Stephen had so many questions, but he was stopped from pursuing his enquiries by Randul ushering him towards the car.

"We must get going." Randul slung his bag onto the back seat and jumped into the driving seat.

"I'll drive as I know the road."

Stephen offered no objection and hurried round to the passenger side and squeezed himself back into his seat, securely fastening the seatbelt in case Randul was intent on repeating any more sudden off-road excursions. Once the car was back on the road and retracing its tracks towards Kandy, Stephen was permitted to ask some of his many unanswered questions.

Randul told him that the man who was following them was going to spend an uncomfortable night in the forest before finally find his way out. If he was sensible, he would walk either due North or due South as he would eventually come to a road or some form of civilisation. He could then retrieve his car, which Randul had ensured had developed a couple of flat tyres since he last saw it.

As to the reason why the man was following them, Randul was much more circumspect in his response and left Stephen none the wiser. Stephen tried again to coax an explanation from Randul, but he remained tight lipped on the matter, driving swiftly and surely along a narrow road that ran deep into the forest. There was no other traffic, and it was evident that Randul must have been very conversant with each undulation, twist and turn. He guided the car effortlessly at speeds that made Stephen subside back into his seat in a horrified silence.

After a couple of hours of rollercoaster driving more suited to a rally driver than a native guide, they arrived outside a secluded bungalow with a veranda and a picket fence boundary. Randul took the car to the back of the building so that it was not visible from the final dirt track that they had travelled along to the house. Both men stretched as they extricated themselves from the cramped interior of the car. Stephen looked across to the simple, single storey building.

"Is this your home?" Stephen enquired. Randul nodded and leant into the car to retrieve his bag from the back seat.

"It was my father's."

Randul looked at Stephen to gauge his reaction to his humble abode.

"It looks simple, but homely." Stephen was not sure what else to say.

"It suits me."

Randul led the way up the steps to the veranda, past a Windsor backed chair and a rusty topped table into the house. Stephen noted that the door was not locked and there appeared to be no electricity. Randul lit a glass domed paraffin light just inside the front door. It smoked initially until the wick was trimmed to provide a pale light that dimly revealed the interior of the house.

The single room was functionally divided into various areas, kitchen, dining, sitting, sleeping, all perfectly clean and tidy. To the rear was a door that led out to the back yard where the engine of the car cooled after its harsh journey. There was no sign of an internal bathroom and so Stephen assumed that such facilities were to be found outside somewhere.

Stephen realised that neither of them had eaten since lunch and it was now late. Randul made no signs of wanting or offering any food to his guest and so Stephen decided to surrender to a deeper sensation, that of an overwhelming tiredness. He took his bag to the sofa along one wall, flopped onto the sunken frame and wished a distracted Randul a good night.

Chapter 13

Aloka had arrived at the empty shop especially early to try to ingratiate himself with Ziyad who had become increasingly tetchy and unreasonable. It had started a couple of days ago and escalated from that point until the previous evening when Ziyad had impetuously struck the unfortunate Aloka. His anger erupted after Aloka dropped a tray of rings, scattering the overpriced trinkets across the floor. That the accident had occurred due to Ziyad having turned unexpectedly and bumped into his browbeaten assistant in the confined space behind the counter was irrelevant. He soaked up the vitriol that poured out from Ziyad's mouth before crawling around on the dusty floor until he had retrieved all the items and placed them back on the tray.

Now he waited, all his chores for the morning completed.

When Ziyad eventually arrived, it was later than Aloka had ever known. He ignored his assistant and went straight through to the back room where he threw himself into a worn armchair in one corner and placed his head in his hands. Aloka hesitantly approached the door and tapped on the chipped paintwork of the frame. Ziyad did not move when Aloka spoke,

"Can I get you your coffee, Master?"

There was a long pause and Aloka wondered if Ziyad had heard him. He had purposely used the word 'Master" as he knew that Ziyad appreciated the subservience shown to him by the lowly Aloka.

"Master? Are you alright?"

Ziyad still made no response apart from looking vacantly across the room with tired, slightly blood-shot eyes. He gave a perfunctory nod of his head. Aloka grasped this wan acceptance with alacrity and set about making his employer the best cup of coffee that he had ever tasted. He was keen to please Ziyad, not least because, somewhat surprisingly perhaps, he held him in respect and felt strangely sorry for him. That did not mean that he liked the man, but he did admire the fact that he had arrived in Sri Lanka as a refugee, with nothing and had worked hard to become a successful businessman within the community. The fact that Ziyad shunned most social interaction had always puzzled Aloka, but he concluded that Ziyad was just a very private man who lived his own life and avoided involvement in anyone else's.

Over the last few mornings, he had seen a fundamental change in his master. He had lost his self-confidence and was obviously troubled by something but would not think of sharing his worries with his lowly employee. Ziyad was clearly distracted and Aloka was intelligent enough to guess it might have something to do with his son.

Thinuka was a brash young man. His father knew that he played the gigolo and was regarded as a bit of a louche character, too fond of the trappings of an affluent upbringing. Ziyad privately admonished himself for having spoilt the boy to whom he had provided such a privileged existence, an upbringing that had been missing for Ziyad in his formative years. His was a life that had its foundations in poverty and deprivation. His parents scraped a living from the land until his father was murdered by ill-disciplined, renegade soldiers – from which side of the many warring factions, Ziyad would never know. His mother was abducted for several days by the soldiers. When she returned, she was a broken woman, crazed and completely incapable of fending for herself, let alone her children. In his early teens he was made to enrol into an unidentifiable militia group that randomly roamed the countryside raping and extorting wherever they went. He was roughly treated and poorly trained by the men who provided him with scant food and a place to sleep. What the militia did give to the young Ziyad was a sense of belonging, something that he craved as a dispossessed young teenage orphan.

Ziyad was popular with the men and caught the eye of the leader of their band of brutes. He took a liking to the short, stocky youth who had proved himself in several disorganised skirmishes with the enemy. He was bright and learnt quickly, showing a particular talent with figures. He was removed from front line combat duties and started working with a smart, middle-aged Lebanese fighter whose family had connections with banks and financial institutions in the Middle East. Ziyad was a runner, taking messages and packages and collecting replies from the various modern office buildings that had avoided the years of bombing and conflict.

Gradually Ziyad came to recognise, and be recognised by, the financial players that his mentor had introduced to him. He was liked and trusted by all.

Over the years he became more deeply involved with the intricacies of the financing of the militia, and his role expanded along with his influence. Substantial sums of money came from a web of sources that stretched into countries and continents far removed from the conflict. Each realm saw advantages to be had from supporting one faction or the other, or even both. These countries and global corporations spent their considerable budgets and foreign reserves like punters placing wagers with bookies. Each betting on which side might emerge victorious, the spoils of war being their winnings for aiding and abetting the mayhem inflicted on the general population.

Ziyad did not see this as a career with a long-term future. He began to look for any weaknesses - and there were plenty - in the financial structures that supported the militia. Then it was just a question of which to exploit to best advantage. He surreptitiously siphoned off sufficient money for his needs but not so much that he would be a marked man for the rest of his life. A naïve expectation for an inherently avaricious man. He subconsciously knew that if he followed through with his plans, he was forever going to be on the run. At least he would be a comfortable fugitive and if he could cover his tracks successfully then he might live to enjoy the fruits of his fraudulent endeavours.

What was 'sufficient' was a matter of speculation. He started to implement his scheme with subtlety and care. Stealthily using his detailed knowledge of the leaky systems and exploiting his collection of corruptible contacts, contacts that he had nurtured separately from his role as military banker, he created a web of interlinked corporations and trusts in far flung locations. When all the detailed preparation had been completed, he pressed the button and watched millions of dollars gradually trickle out of one rogue account into another, and then another, and another still, the constant stream being under his invisible control.

Constantly fearing discovery and execution in the foulest manner possible, he planned his own escape.

But that was when things went awry.

Whether someone unbeknownst to him had been covertly watching him or whether one of his corruptible contacts had been corrupted (you just could not trust anyone in those days), he did not know. Perhaps someone had their own links to the militia's web of informants, but for whatever reason, he was unexpectantly summoned to the militia's commanders temporary headquarters - by necessity, the headquarters were constantly being relocated. Ziyad had been a 'chosen one' by the militia leader, he was his protégé, and therefore under his protection. So, it was an unpleasant shock to be told that there had been a putsch and his mentor was distributed across the street in some Syrian village, together with the remains of his car.

It was even more rare that there would be face to face contact between the commander and the backroom financiers. The separation of the roles was felt to be imperative to keep all the political backers from foreign countries removed from the killing and raping that was undertaken in the name of freedom.

All the plans that Ziyad had cautiously put in place had to be suddenly brought into play. He spent the twenty-four hours before the meeting in his small office in a suburb of Sana'a. He would not be able to escape from the country prior to the meeting but he had arranged for his wife and two small children to be spirited out of the country as soon as he had been called to the meeting. Perhaps this precipitous action would seal his fate, but it was set in the plan and there was no time to make any alterations to his arrangements.

The price that Ziyad had to pay was high.

When he was sure that his family were safe, or as safe as possible, he made a final telephone call. This was the most dangerous, but the most necessary if he was to stand any chance of survival. Once he had completed the brief conversation, he knew that there was no turning back. The die was cast for him and for those who wanted to unseat him.

Immediately after morning prayers, Ziyad was collected and driven into the desert to an area that was unknown to him. The HQ was hidden in the burnt out remains of an insignificant village with crumbling walls, vacant windows and the dismembered bits of machinery of war littering the streets. Heavily armed men and young boys stood or sat around in groups smoking or talking. None of them took any notice of the car that sped down the streets strewn with rubble, the vehicle slewing between the detritus, the driver well versed in the art of avoiding such everyday obstructions.

Ziyad became increasingly nervous as they approached the end of their journey. He frequently took out a handkerchief from the breast pocket of his only business suit to dab at the sweat that beaded his brow. The driver kept an eye on him through the rear-view mirror. Not that there was any chance of escape. Ziyad knew that the door handles on the inside would have been disconnected. The only way out of the car would be when the driver opened the door for him at their destination.

He was met at the entrance of a house in the centre of the village that seemed to have miraculously evaded the conflict. A gaggle of four scruffily uniformed guards swarmed around his door. Whilst his security was normally assured on account of his role, Ziyad could not help but feel that this was more than just a shield for his protection.

He was being delivered to this meeting like a kid goat to the feast.

Ziyad checked the time on his watch. Not long.

The driver hurried round the car and opened the door for Ziyad to emerge. He was made to stand in a star shape by the guards, legs and arms held apart, his empty briefcase by his feet. They frisked him, removing his bulky mobile telephone. He remonstrated but his protestations fell on deaf ears. His shoulders slumped and the false bravado that he had tried to show dissipated. With a heavy heart he realised that the chances of him ever seeing his family again were diminishing by the second.

One of the guards tried to remove his watch but this was a step too far for Ziyad who snapped that the man was out of order. Ziyad tried to shake his wrist free, but the guard maintained a tight grip until the more senior of the guards told him to back down.

Time was running out.

In the middle of the house was the usual courtyard with the calming sound of water trickling from a fountain. The serenity of this oasis of civilisation defied the scenes of devastation that engulfed the remainder of the village. A series of fine stone columns supported the upper floors and created a colonnade around three sides of the courtyard. In front of Ziyad was a group of four men huddled over a table studying maps that were strewn across its surface. One of them, a thin, willowy figure, looked up at the new arrival and broke away from the others who ceased talking and stepped back into the shadowy depths of the colonnade.

"Welcome, my friend. How was your journey?"

Ziyad recognised the new leader and trusted him as much he would a cobra ready to strike. Colonel Qasim was a hard, seasoned rebel who had watched the meteoric rise of the young Ziyad from boy-warrior to rebel banker. Like Ziyad, Qasim was also an acolyte of his predecessor, who he assassinated without compunction for displaying weak and over sentimental ideals. Ziyad knew that he was part of the old guard and so the self-promoted Colonel was automatically suspicious of his loyalty. The problem for the Colonel was that Ziyad had proved to be so successful at sourcing, extracting and then managing the funds that supported his military adventures, he had had to rely totally on his knowledge and expertise. The complexity of the financial structures that Ziyad had created were partly for reasons of obscurity, but mainly for his own preservation.

Ziyad involuntarily glanced at his watch.

Soon.

Qasim walked towards Ziyad, smiling as he took another Black Sobranie from a gold cigarette case that he kept in his tunic pocket. He lit it from the one that was held between his lips, inhaled deeply and then blew out a cloud of smoke upwards towards the blue sky. He moved smoothly, like a dancer, his limbs lithe and strongly muscled with not an ounce of fat visible. His face had a hard, weatherworn angularity, his nose hooked and flared at the nostrils.

He eyed Ziyad as he approached and greeted him with the customary kiss on each cheek. Ziyad could smell the stale tobacco on his breath and knew that there was little warmth in the welcome. They stood by the fountain, the water playing into the wide pool sent expanding ripples across its surface.

The men in the colonnade watched the charade, unsure whether to pity or despise the banker. Qasim looked over Ziyad's shoulder at one of the guards who confirmed silently that Ziyad had been searched and was clean.

"Forgive my impertinence for dragging you out here to see me at such an early hour." He took another pull on his cigarette and brushed the slim middle finger of his other hand to smooth his eyebrow. "Come. Have some coffee as we talk."

Ziyad had a mouth that was so dry he had no need of coffee.

"A glass of juice, or even water would be good."

Qasim looked to one of the guards and asked, "Have you checked his telephone?"

The guard held out his hand to reveal the only item that had been taken from Ziyad.

Qasim recoiled in horror and shouted, "Don't bring it in here, you fool. Take it away. Now!"

Ziyad looked at his watch.

It was time.

Almost simultaneously, two things happened. Ziyad flung himself into the water of the pool and flattened himself against the bottom.

Qasim jumped in surprise and confusion, but then in comprehension. He spun round to shout a warning, but it was too late.

There was an enormous rush of hot air and an explosion that dissolved everything around the courtyard. Ziyad felt the searing heat from beneath the shallow water and then a scorching sensation on the left side of his face. His ears rang and when he raised his head, he could see through a blurred haze of red a pair of legs twitching on the floor in front of him. There was no torso attached to the legs, but a sodden Black Sobranie was floating in the water just in front of him.

Unsteadily, he crawled to his knees and shook his head but the shrill screech in his ears did not diminish. There was just swirling dust and debris all around him – and silence apart from the high-pitched wail that rang in his ears. He stood half blinded, pain stabbing down one side of his face, and turned towards the door but there was no door, no wall, just an opening onto the street. The car in which he had arrived was on its roof on the other side of the road. Limp bodies lay broken and those less wounded were slowly picking themselves off the floor and stumbling around in shock and pain.

Ziyad knew that he had to take advantage of this short period of chaos before anyone took command. He ran through the opening and yelled for help. Half a dozen men were running towards the debris that had been the HQ and Ziyad ran in the opposite direction, shouting misleading orders to anyone who would, or could listen.

He kept running, aware that his face was burning, and he had blood running down the front of his shirt. His jacket appeared to be missing, blown from his body when the rocket had hit its target. He cleared the edges of the village and headed along the side of the road, looking over his shoulder every so often to see if he was being pursued. There was a pall of dust hanging over the centre of the village, but Ziyad kept sprinting. His chest heaved as he sought to draw sufficient oxygen into his lungs to continue at the pace that he had set himself. He knew that at some point there would be an exodus for fear of a second strike.

When he was half a mile away, he slowed and looked back. His sight was badly impaired, but he could just make out the tell-tale eddies of dust thrown up by speeding vehicles. He turned from the road and started to move cross country having spied a stand of palms off to his right. He pushed himself harder, his lungs screaming for air but his legs refusing to let up. His feet slipped in the soft sand that collected in his shoes and he stumbled, falling onto his knees. Thick, congealing blood dripped onto the sand in front of him. He briefly lifted his shaking hand and felt with sandy fingers the place where his left eye should have been. A soft and sticky socket was all that remained. Terror lifted him back onto his feet and forced him to run again.

One step.

Two steps.

Three.

He could neither see where his speeding foot was landing, nor did he hear the click of the landmine and the subsequent detonation. He felt the whoosh of hot air and the bizarre sensation of being lifted into space. He pirouetted and was spun like a rag doll, arms and legs flailing uncontrollably, dancing through the dust, shrapnel, shards of bone and globules of flesh. The trajectory of his body seemed to be played out in slow motion. He was watching himself as if he were a passing bystander who, having witnessed the incident, slithered back into the broken shell that was his body.

Ziyad hit the soft sand, slumping onto the ground in an untidy heap. Blood leaked from his shattered body into the thirsty desert and was silently consumed.

Everything went blank.

Aloka knew none of this and stood at the door to the rear room of the shop and observed his dishevelled employer. There he sat, drawn, with three days stubble on his face, a permanently hunted look in his one good eye. A man who wanted for nothing, but a man who appeared to have the weight of the world on his shoulders. No matter how often he asked, there was nothing that Ziyad would permit Aloka to do for him.

Ziyad felt strangely touched by Aloka's concern for his well-being but could not bring himself to talk to him about his night-terrors. He had always had the nagging dread of discovery, constantly living in fear for his life.

And now, he had a second dread.

Thinuka, his only son.

Why, oh why, had he sent him after the Veddah? What had happened to him? Where was he? While he was often out for a night it was not possible that he would go missing for three nights in a row. His car had disappeared and, even more alarming, it appeared that he had removed the pistol from where Ziyad kept it in his safe. It was stupid of him not to have changed the combination on the safe the first time he discovered that Thinuka knew the code. The occasional removal by his son of a couple of thousand rupees did not concern him terribly, but the taking of the gun was something else entirely.

Initially Ziyad had asked Ameesha, Thinuka's sister, to ring around his friends, but she reported that nobody had seen or heard from him for the three days. How was Ziyad going to ask the police to search for him if he was carrying a gun? He had constantly impressed on all his family the importance of maintaining a low profile and while the children did not know why, his wife did. Most of the time they complied with his demand – but not Thinuka. Why did he have to be such an extrovert? Why did he have to show off to his friends? Why had Ziyad succumbed to all his demands and indulged him?

Ziyad had no desire to involve the authorities, but it seemed inevitable if he was to find his son. The coffee that Aloka had so carefully prepared for him sat cold and untouched as Ziyad tussled with his predicament. Reluctantly, he picked up the old fashioned black, Bakelite telephone on his desk and dialled the number.

Chapter 14

Stephen had never experienced such an idyllic three days. He and Randul had hiked over miles of the forest and his guide had introduced him to the bountiful harvest of ingredients that lived in the forest and its surrounds. Each evening Stephen had cooked for them on the ancient stove that formed the focal point of the living room to the bungalow.   What Stephen had not expected was the content of a timber clad shed that was located towards the back of the plot on which the bungalow stood. On the second morning Randul took Stephen into the building, and he was amazed to see that it was set up as a laboratory with all the accoutrements that one might expect - gauzed tripods, glass tubing and dishes, Bunsen burners fuelled by portable gas bottles and a range of shelves that held a vast array of glass bottles filled with powders and fluids of differing colours. In any other situation Stephen would have assumed that this was a lab producing illicit drugs but Randul assured him that there were no illegal substances that would interest the enforcement agencies.

Randul explained that it was a mere extension to his academic degree. Research that he had continued to pursue from his home. Some of the items that he foraged from the forest, he had explained, were better if combined, refined or distilled. Stephen was given practical demonstrations and the flavours of the various concoctions that Randul produced were beyond anything that he had experienced in his life.

In deference to the extraordinary knowledge that Randul had displayed, Stephen pushed his inventive skills to the limit, creating dishes that paid homage to the foraged ingredients and the compounds that Randul had designed. They worked expertly together, and Stephen was only sorry that there was no opportunity to present to the general public the incredible plates of food that were appearing from their combined efforts. Randul was delighted with the flavours encapsulated within the dishes that Stephen was inspired to produce.

As he worked, Stephen made copious notes of the names of the ingredients - when they had names - the quantities added and a brief comment as to their best use.

Where there were no names, numbers were applied by Randul for reference purposes. Up to that point, he was the only person who had known of their remarkable properties. It continued to worry Stephen that it was possible that Randul had inadvertently, or through intent, created some illegal opiates, but as he was not a chemist, he had no way of knowing. Randul had laughed at the suggestion and convinced Stephen that they were all natural and harmless – unless they could be considered addictive because of the sheer joy they provided to the user. Stephen was comforted by the fact that he and Randul had eaten the dishes regularly over the few days that they had been together with no ill effects. The only addictive trait was the desire to try a new combination or refine a previously tested creation.

In his pleasure and the excitement of having stumbled across ingredients that he believed would provide a truly unique dining experience, it never occurred to Stephen that the desire of anyone who had eaten his food to repeat the experience might become so desperate as to be defined as a form of addiction.

At night, Stephen lay on the lumpy sofa and, by the dull light of an oil lamp, methodically edited the hasty notes he had made during the day. It troubled him that he had found the holy grail of the culinary art without a clear plan of how to turn it to his advantage. How was he to harvest and transport the freshly foraged herbs and spices from the depths of the Sinharaja to The Sauceror's Apprentice in the heart of Mayfair. The products from the laboratory were relatively simple to move as they were in powder or liquid form. The added advantage for Stephen with these latter items was the fact that Randul had limited facilities, hence he would only be able to supply Stephen. He doubted if Randul had any desire to scale up production, his primary interest being the discovery and creation of his unique constituents. Stephen had gained the trust of Randul, but Randul still remained highly protective of his discoveries and, to date, had not wanted to see them exploited for commercial gain. Inevitably, to expose the world to his extraordinary products would attract less scrupulous enterprises that would seek to copy or devalue the currency of the commodity.

The potency of each of Randul's ingredients was such that Stephen had to use only a very small amount in each dish, which would also prove to be an advantage.

A little went a long way so the volume of the materials to be transported would be relatively modest to satisfy the demands of his restaurant turnover.

Over and above the euphoria of discovering a whole new vocabulary of dishes and cooking techniques, Stephen was elated that over the past few days he and Randul had forged such a strong friendship in the most unlikely of circumstances. He was flattered that Randul had been sufficiently captivated by Stephen's knowledge and passion for the food he cooked that he had brought him to his home. While a basic knowledge of foraged ingredients was required by all chefs of note, the immersion into Randul's world of foraging was far deeper. It verged on a religious experience.

What was a surprise to Stephen was discovering Randul's expertise in the scientific approach to his work. The basic natural ingredients that he found were transformed in the home laboratory to create additives that were unknown and unavailable anywhere else. Stephen was sure, no, he was convinced that the combination would make him invincible in the competitive London restaurant market. Any doubts that Stephen had had about his future enterprise had been completely dispelled. He was confident that he would crush the food critics and that his future was assured.

He was also aware that he had extended his solitary escape from the clutches of Celia into the period when he was due to be filmed on location for the cookery programme. Celia would be apoplectic at having lost her charge in the depths of rural Sri Lanka. The television producers and directors, as well as the crew would have been kicking their heels for two days. Stephen had not contacted her since he spoke to her from the hotel in Kandy and he did feel slightly guilty. However, it was not entirely his fault as a mobile phone did not work at the bungalow and he had been too immersed in the revelations that materialised on each foray into the forest or experimental session in the home laboratory. He hoped that the results of this personal voyage of exploration would be sufficient to quell their understandable irritation and impatience to get the filming completed.

On the third evening of his stay Stephen knew that he had to address the issue of supply with Randul. They had dined on a variation of a polenta dish using the smallest pinch of something Randul called 'Midnight Dust' – he told Stephen that he had completed his discovery at midnight, hence the name. The result was like nothing

Stephen had ever managed to produce before from a simple base such as polenta. After dinner Stephen was scribbling some comments in his battered notebook when Randul announced that he was going for a walk. Stephen was too immersed in his notes to offer more than a grunt of acknowledgement.

Randul left the house and disappeared into the night. There was nothing unusual about this, and Stephen waited for his return, determined to raise the issue of securing a regular supply of ingredients for his restaurant.

He dozed in the soft old armchair and recalled the chase in the forest with the man in the Mercedes. Stephen had raised it with Randul on a couple of occasions just after they had arrived at the bungalow, but Randul had dismissed it as just one of those things. Stephen had no idea whether such events were a regular occurrence on the island. Each time, Randul dismissed it and told Stephen that the silly fellow had probably spent a very uncomfortable night in the forest before returning to Kandy with his tail between his legs.

However, it was a disquieting episode that had put a blemish on the trip as far as Stephen was concerned. He had, up until that point, felt very safe amongst the friendly locals and did not like the possibility that there was an ugly underbelly to these happy and seemingly contented people.

Some hours later, Randul entered the bungalow quietly, thinking that Stephen had dropped off to sleep. He had walked the mile back to the tourist reception building, as he had done each evening since deserting the man in the jungle. He chatted with the other guides who congregated in the building most evenings after their duties were completed for the day. While not asking directly, he listened to the local gossip but had heard no tales of anyone being found or reported lost.

Tonight, however, one guide did mention the fact that a new Mercedes car had been abandoned on the main road near Kolonne. To find an abandoned old jalopy was not newsworthy, but an expensive luxury car was worth reporting, even if it had two flat tyres. The others speculated as to whether the owner had gone hiking in the hills or perhaps, he was visiting a mistress. Either way, after a short debate the conversation moved on to other more parochial matters. Randul had heard enough and bade everyone goodnight before hastily leaving for home.

Stephen was breathing slowly and regularly so Randul went across to the kitchen and quietly pulled up the loose floorboard where he hid his hoard of gems. In the void were four or five soft leather pouches, each one containing a different colour or grade of stones. The one on the top held the remaining two large Padparadscha stones and to these Randul added the single specimen that he had returned with from Kandy. He had been foolish to allow his haul to reach such a size. After his meeting with The Arab and the events that followed, he knew that he was going to have to find other dealers if he was to reduce the quantity he had amassed over the last few months – or was it years? Randul could not remember when he had last sold some stones.

More recently the little rock pools had produced an array of beautiful stones, culminating in his latest extraordinary find. The Padparadscha were completely unexpected and put his other finds into the shade. He wondered if someone had started illegal mining further upstream. If so, they had located a rich seam but their inexperience in the traditional methods of finding gems in the silt of the fast-flowing streams and rivers was only too evident. The result was that flushes of gems were periodically dislodged and washed onto the rocks at Randul's swimming spot, finding a resting place in the smoothed-out holes where they remained until found by Randul.

He had kept each tiny find and day after day, month upon month, placed the valuable stones into his small pouches. A couple were so full that the draw strings around the top were straining to keep the contents in. Occasionally small gems would slip out to lay on the earth subfloor. Randul would carefully pick them out, blow off the dusty soil and put them back into the relevant bag.

He quietly slipped the pouches into his backpack and then folded a clean teacloth over the top before replacing the floorboard. When he stood up, he turned to find that Stephen was seated fully alert and watching his every move. Both men looked at each other but said nothing, wondering if their supposed mutual trust was about to be tested.

"What on earth are you doing?" Stephen asked.

An expression of both guilt and resignation spread across Randul's face. He could either take this man into his confidence or adopt a belligerent approach. It was none of Stephen's business what he did in his own home. He was Randul's guest and could get out now.

But what would that achieve?

Randul had been thinking hard on his walk back from the reception building. With the events of the past few days, Randul had had to reappraise his earlier plans for quietly liquidating his cache. The arrival of Stephen into his life and the natural rapport that had built up between the two of them over the past few days meant that Randul felt an affinity sufficiently strong to confide in his friend. The consequences could be no worse than the current position in which he found himself. In fact, it might be a relief to share his predicament. Besides, he had concocted a story on his walk back to the bungalow that was believable enough without revealing all the details.

He was going to have to see if his plan was practical at some point and now was as good a time as any.

"I think we need to have a chat." Randul carefully placed his bag to one side and, taking a hard chair from next to the table, he placed it in front of Stephen and sat down.

Stephen was immediately wary. His mind raced back to the other night on the road, to the man who had tailed them and his disappearance into the forest after Randul.

"Is it about that chap who followed us?" he enquired. "Who was he after? Me or you?"

Randul looked uncomfortable, "I'm sorry, but I think it was me. You see, I have something that he, or whoever asked him to follow me, wants." Randul pulled his backpack towards him and placed it on the floor at Stephen's feet. He cleared the low table of a half full glass of water, along with a bird book that Stephen had been idly flicking through. He took out the teacloth, spread it on the table and then delicately set three of the pouches in a row facing Stephen. A fourth, containing the Padparadscha, he placed slightly to one side. Grains of soil settled under each pouch, and Stephen watched in fascination. Randul methodically untied the top of each of the three pouches and then lay them open for inspection.

"Take a look," he said, leaning back in his chair.

Involuntarily, Randul looked towards the door as if he expected someone to burst in as Stephen bent forward to reveal their secret. He gently took one of the bags in his hand. It was heavier than he had expected. Gently he tipped it forwards and emptied the contents onto the dish cloth. He whistled as the sparkling stones rolled and settled in the fold of the material.

"They are beautiful. I don't know what they are, but I assume they're valuable?" He could not take his eyes off the gems and went on to inspect another two bags, his eyes sparkling almost as brightly as the stones that rolled onto the cloth.

Stephen reached for the fourth bag that had its draw strings tightly wound around its neck. Randul stayed his hand.

"What you have seen are beautiful and valuable, but the bag you have in your hand contains something slightly more so." He then released Stephen and watched as he slowly undid the strings and tipped the bag to release the three orange-pink coloured stones that tumbled out of the opening.

They were pretty.

Very pretty.

The colour was subtle yet shone with a lustre and a clarity that allowed the light to be refracted through even the uncut surfaces. But what struck Stephen most was the size. These were rocks, not stones, pebbles or grit.

"Wow." Stephen looked at the other bags, and then back to the last one he had opened. He nodded towards the three stones, "Why are these more valuable?"

"Have you ever heard of Padparadscha sapphires?"

"No." Stephen picked up the biggest stone and weighed it in his hand. It was the size of a small tomato or plum, but much heavier,

"Well, they're considered to be the most rare and valuable of all sapphires. They only come from a few locations in the world and in Sri Lanka we have some of the best."

"But if they are so rare," Stephen picked another one up and rolled it between his fingers, "how come you've got three of them?"

"I used to have four, and that is the problem." Randul regretted his swift, ill-considered reply, but Stephen was mesmerised with what was on the table.

"But these are really big?" Stephen had picked up the largest again. He held it up to the light in an expert manner but without really knowing what he was doing, apart from admiring its beauty and its size.

"I was very fortunate." Randul paused but then decided that he had gone so far and might as well complete the story.

"I have a place, a private spot, on the river that my father used to take me to when I was a child. It's where I disappear every morning while you are snoring." Stephen was about to defend himself, but Randul continued swiftly, "There are rocks that you can lie on or sit and meditate as the sun rises. Most days I explore the many holes that have been eroded by the river. Over the monsoon the river is violent and rips into the banks further upstream, depositing silt and stones into these holes. Recently, there's been some exceptional flushes of stones, and I've been lucky enough to be in the right place at the right time."

Randul started to collect up the stones and replace them in the bags. Stephen collapsed back into his chair and stretched up, placing his hands behind the back of his head. He looked up at the ceiling before asking the obvious question.

"What are they worth?"

Randul remained cautious in his answer, "These coloured ones," he lifted one of the other three bags, "they have a value if of good quality, mainly down to the clarity and colour. The market wants the mid hue of the blue and yellow. Most chance finds will merely be shards that are ground down for industrial use."

"How many of yours are of industrial quality?"

Randul could not suppress the smile that exposed his even, white teeth.

"Not many. I've discarded those already. The authorities turn a blind eye to the very low level of mining that some forest residents discreetly undertake. But if there was a sudden flood of quality sapphires, let alone these, onto the market then questions would be asked." Randul replaced the last of the bags into his backpack and once again covered it with the tea-towel.

Stephen did not look at Randul and spoke to the ceiling,

"Presumably your collection would raise questions?"

"Almost certainly. I've already sold one small Padparadscha to a dealer in Kandy. That's why I was there when we met. I had just come from his shop. He knows that I have another, larger, better stone because I told him I'd sell it to him if he would certify others for me. I suspect that his greed and impatience got the better of him and he sent that man to acquire or steal the other stone."

Stephen thought for a moment longer.

"Does he know the true extent of your haul?"

"No, certainly not. That would be very foolish of me." Randul revealed his dilemma to Stephen.

"The trouble is, I can no longer trust that dealer even though he's expecting me to return. I need to find a different one, but above all, I need to avoid that dealer."

He allowed the information to sink in and Stephen took little time to come up with a solution, but first he had a more pressing question.

"What did happen to the man you led into the jungle?"

Randul chose his words carefully when recounting how he had laid a trail and the man had followed. He had ensured that he became totally disorientated in the forest and then Randul had slipped away to return to the tea shop where he met up with Stephen.

"I believed that I had left him stumbling around in the thick undergrowth. He was perfectly healthy, a bit dirty perhaps and very angry."

"You promise me that you did him no harm?" Stephen lowered his line of sight to stare hard at Randul who felt like a small child being spoken to by his father.

"Only to his pride. That's the full extent of the harm that I inflicted on him."

Stephen watched Randul who averted his eyes. It was impossible to determine whether he was telling the truth. Stephen stared at the backpack on the floor and Randul wondered if his friend had believed him.

Randul added, "I learnt this evening that his car is still on the side of the road." He saw Stephen's brow furrow. "It's not been moved. Of course, it did have two flat tyres."

Several questions now fought for priority in Stephen's brain.

"Has he been seen?"

"Not around the forest."

"Did you recognise him?"

"No."

"But you think that he must have something to do with this dealer you visited?"

"Probably."

"So, the dealer is going to suspect that you were behind getting his chap lost in the forest?"

"I suppose so." Randul was feeling more and more like an unruly schoolboy being interrogated by his headmaster after some misdemeanour had been discovered.

"You'll be under suspicion and the man who followed us will be looking for you, and possibly me?"

Randul remained silent as he nodded his head in affirmation. Stephen continued his line of questioning, trying to obtain clarity. He hoped that a simple solution might emerge at the end.

"Are you known to the dealer?"

"I don't think so. I have never used him before. That's why I went to Kandy rather than Ratnapura"

There was a pause as Stephen considered further the predicament that faced Randul and, by implication, himself.

"It seems to me that you need to remove any trace of suspicion from you. But that means having to go back to the dealer as if nothing has happened. You said that you had arranged to return. When?"

Randul was looking pale and exceedingly uncomfortable. It was clear that he had no intention of returning to see the dealer. As far as Stephen was concerned, he could not be sure that the man had not escaped from the forest and told the Arab what had happened. If he was a hired professional, would he want to admit to his employer that he had failed in a simple task of tailing Randul? He could not be sure that there was any intention to steal the second stone from Randul, but it was possible.

What was a much more unpalatable thought was; what if the man had not come out of the jungle, despite Randul's rather unconvincing assurances that he had not harmed him?

Randul answered Stephen's earlier question,

"I only loosely agreed to return but I did not specify exactly when, just that I would return."

"Well, I think the time has come to take the risk. You need to find out if the dealer knows what has happened." Stephen seemed to have taken control of the situation and Randul accepted, with extreme reticence, that he should return to try to dispel any suspicions that the dealer may have. However, he would still have to find another way to trade his stones. He did not trust the Arab, but at least by returning he would demonstrate that he knew nothing of being followed and was not involved in getting anyone lost in the forest.

With the four pouches stowed safely in his bag, Randul was thinking that his finds had become more of a hindrance than an asset. In his mind, Stephen was his solution, even if he exacted a price for his cooperation. At least he did not think that his friend would cheat him as much as the dealer would or be a threat to his life.

The two continued talking late into the night, exploring alternatives, until Randul was forced to retire to bed with his own sense of foreboding.

Chapter 15

The arguments had been constant over the last two evenings and Ziyad had become more and more reclusive in his study, seeking the comfort of copious quantities of malt whisky in preference to the recriminations of his family. His wife was threatening to call the police even though Ziyad assured her that he had already spoken to them. They had taken all the details but because of his son's age, and reputation, Thinuka was not felt to be a priority in their schedule of work. Ameesha, his quiet and scholarly daughter cried and, uncharacteristically, criticised him for the fact that Thinuka got everything and gave nothing in return. Each accusation hit home and deeply wounded Ziyad. Not because of the vitriol with which each charge was delivered, not because he lived in constant fear of exposure, but primarily because he knew in his heart that every denunciation was fair and just.

Like a wounded fox, he retired to his den and sought the solace that was to be found in the bottom of a glass. Sleep was taken on the couch opposite his desk for fear of waking his wife with his drunken arrival in the marital bed. He continued to run his investments with a fervour that partially dispelled familial rejection, focusing his concentration elsewhere. He undertook a full inventory of his assets, both those held through his network of corporations and trusts in Grand Cayman, Dubai, Delaware and Singapore as well as those held elsewhere.

The stock in the shop was much diminished, as were his cash reserves. These had been depleted due to his purchase of the Padparadscha sapphire. He knew that it would be a most lucrative trade in the longer term. He had paid a heavy price for the Padparadscha sapphire that by day lay in his office safe. In the lonely evenings he would sit and admire it, the soft colouring and sheer size eased the tensions and soothed his nerves that had been in a constant state of fear since the disappearance of Thinuka.

Regardless of Honey and Ameesha's iciness, he had to contend with his own self-loathing for having sent Thinuka out on a fool's errand. Now he had disappeared, Ziyad feared for his son's safety. What had also disappeared was that damn native, the subject of the errand. He had said to Ziyad that he would return with the second Padparadscha, but he had not and that made Ziyad more than a little suspicious.

He had not mentioned to the police the task that he had set his son. What was the point? He had no certainty that the two events were linked. Perhaps it was merely a coincidence? But Ziyad did not believe in coincidences. Perhaps his son was holed up with some pretty little tourist in a hotel somewhere, sating his sexual appetite that seemed to drive his every decision. He had become a slave to the carnal delights that these young western girls offered with such ease when they escaped the limitations of their families or educational institutions. No doubt he would return looking pale and exhausted as his latest conquest moved on.

Ziyad heard movement in the house as the staff awoke to start to prepare breakfast and undertake the chores of the day. He had no wish to see any of them that morning and so, unshaven and having had no shower, he silently left the house. He did not bother to change out of his comfortable prosthetic foot or the clothes that he was wearing from the previous evening. He no longer cared who might see the Arab without his limp and attired in smart, albeit crumpled, clothes.

It was dark when he left. His taxi was not due for an hour and so he decided to cancel it and walk to the shop. The morning was fresh, and the clear air would do him some good, blowing away the fog that enveloped his brain as a result of the alcohol consumed last night. He walked as if in a daze through the affluent area in which he lived, with its detached villas encircled with high security fencing. He felt comfortable in these surroundings.

As he progressed along the route the houses diminished in stature, until they were nothing more than rows of simple timber and corrugated iron structures with open areas around them into which anyone could wander. Dogs sniffed at the dying fires looking for scraps from the previous evening's meal. A small number of residents who worked in the centre of town were beginning to rise and collect whatever they were going to sell in the market that day.

No doubt Aloka lived in a similar area, maybe even this area. Ziyad had no idea, nor had he really cared up until the moment Thinuka had disappeared. He should know more about his employee. Ziyad began to think that perhaps he would give up the gem dealing business, let Aloka take it on. Thinuka was too impetuous, too willing to let his heart rule his head. Aloka, on the other hand, was perfectly capable and very level-headed. More particularly, he was loyal and hard working. What was more, Ziyad knew that he was unlikely to cheat him. At least, he would not do so initially. Everyone eventually succumbed to self-interest and if Ziyad stepped out of the picture it was inevitable that, over time, Aloka would become more and more ambitious and seek to maximise his own returns for his efforts. It made increasing sense to Ziyad to entrust the future of the business to him, although he accepted that Thinuka might have different views.

Ziyad had personal reasons for seeing Aloka progress.

After walking for an hour or so, Ziyad arrived at the shop feeling slightly refreshed, his mind much clearer. As always, before inserting the key into the lock, he took a quick look around to check that the coast was clear. He did not expect to see anyone at this hour and so was taken aback when he thought he detected some movement in the shadow thrown by a dim streetlight further down the road.

It was a long time since he had had to consider how to react if his fear of finding someone there materialised. Momentarily he was unsure what he should do. He casually looked again, but the movement had ceased. He was becoming paranoid. It was probably a feral cat or a mangy dog. Quickly, he slipped the key into the lock and turned the handle to open the door. Before he had managed to extract the key, a body had silently appeared from nowhere to stand over him. He gave a sharp in-take of breath, stunned that the person had covered the ground with such rapidity and stealth.

He turned with trepidation and was relieved to see that it was the young Veddah. Anger flared momentarily to accompany his relief.

"Damn it, boy, what the hell are you doing?"

The boy was larger, more imposing that he had remembered and had wedged himself tightly by Ziyad so that he could move neither in nor out from the doorway. The relief ebbed from his body, and he attempted a wan smile of welcome. Randul said nothing save to nod that Ziyad should enter and let him in at the same time. He stepped back slightly to allow Ziyad to pass across the threshold before immediately following so as to deny the shopkeeper any opportunity to close the door on him.

Ziyad attempted to recover some of his authority, but the balance of power had shifted to the Veddah's advantage. Ziyad's heart was pounding and he was flustered, he still tried to greet Randul in as natural a voice as he could muster.

"You are very early, again. Where have you been? I was expecting you a day or so ago."

Randul looked around the shop to ensure that they were alone.

"I needed to collect some things, before I came back to see you."

Ziyad moved to his accustomed position behind the counter, placing some distance between himself and the other man. He doubted that there was any violent intent, but he was not going to take any chances. He needed to ascertain if the Veddah had anything to do with Thinuka's disappearance without raising any suspicion.

"I assume you are here on business?" Ziyad automatically felt below the counter for the velvet cloth that he spread on the top, smoothing it over the glass with his long slender fingers, trying to avoid any sign of fear or nervousness.

He had no need to worry, surely?

Randul took his daypack from his shoulder and pulled out a single pouch that appeared to have little in it. Ziyad acquisitively eyed the bag, trying to predict the size of what might be revealed, praying that it was another Padparadscha. The anticipation was almost unbearable as Randul fumbled with the drawstrings. Finally, he opened the top and rolled two blue sapphires onto the cloth covering the counter. Ziyad was crestfallen, and he looked up into the eyes of the prospector who returned his stare without flinching.

"Forgive me," Ziyad stammered, "but I thought that you were bringing me a Padparadscha? These look good stones but nothing spectacular." Any attempt at taking commercial advantage evaporated with the disappointment in what he saw.

Randul had prepared his innocently naive response to the anticipated dismay,

"I sold that directly to a German tourist. I based my price on what you paid me for the first one."

Ziyad was visibly shaken at the lost opportunity.

"What!" Ziyad had to sit down with the shock of the news. "I hope he gave you something better than that. It was much larger. You are a fool not to have come back to me."

"Oh, I was happy with the price," Randul lied smoothly. Ziyad was even more dismayed. He had weighed the stone and knew that it was a serious gem that would have commanded a premium when cut and polished. The savage was an idiot, which Ziyad knew him not to be. He was too bright to make such a stupid transaction and Ziyad did not believe him but felt that he could do little more than to play along.

"Congratulations." There was no sense of approval in Ziyad's voice. "I hope you are satisfied, but I suspect that we could have done a much better deal, especially with my contacts." Trying to return to his usual business-like approach that he adopted to any illegitimate miner seeking to sell him stones, he inspected the offering before him.

"Well, these are reasonable stones, but I have a lot of these at present and they're not selling very well at this time of year." Ziyad shrugged his shoulders in a dismissive manner and pushed the cloth back towards Randul, "I'll take them off your hands, but the price will not be anything like as generous as last time."

Randul watched the sly old Arab deliberate and then make his derisory offer for Randul's consideration.

"Of course, if you have any more Padparadscha sapphires then I might be able to improve on that price, but I must know where they come from and how you got them." Ziyad and Randul were now eyeing up each other like a mongoose and a cobra, neither wanting to make the first strike.

"Do I detect from your silence that you might have some more?" Ziyad waited and then turned to go into the back office, "I appreciate that you are not keen to give me any detailed information, but you do know that I can be trusted, otherwise why are you here? Let us have some coffee and discuss this business a little further? I have the time. What is your name, by the way?"

Randul accepted the Arab's dubious hospitality with some hesitancy, wishing to complete his business with him and get out as soon as possible. But equally important was to try to find out if Ziyad had sent the man who had followed Randul and Stephen. Was he aware of the possible disappearance of that man? So far there was no indication of any such involvement.

Ziyad returned with two small cups of his powerful black coffee and placed them onto the counter. He held out his hand towards the cup nearest Randul.

"Please."

Randul lifted it to his lips, but the thick, steaming, liquid was too hot to drink. Ziyad seemed impervious to the heat and sipped thoughtfully. He watched the young man and after a while seemed to reach a conclusion. Playing the patient game was proving fruitless.

He placed the cup down decisively and noisily, cleared the back of his throat and swallowed the result.

"You know, after we last met, I was naturally curious where you had found the beautiful Padparadscha that I bought from you. I have a confession to make," he paused and took another sip, looking over the lip of the cup at Randul.

"I asked someone to keep an eye on you."

Randul started and looked shocked. Ziyad was uncertain if this was a reaction to the boldness of the admission, or the fact that he had made the admission at all.

"You did what?" Randul exclaimed.

"I apologise. It was silly of me. Did you not notice? Did you not see him? He wasn't a professional." Ziyad kept taking small sips of his coffee, hoping that his relaxed appearance would encourage the Veddah into making some admission of his own, or a mistake.

Randul slowly shook his head from side to side.

"I can't believe it. Why would you do that?"

Ziyad studied the boy who was either an honest innocent or a good actor. He could not quite decide which. He had underestimated him once and did not wish to repeat the error.

"As I said, I was intrigued and, to be honest, I was concerned for your well-being. You know, with such a valuable load in your bag." Ziyad nodded towards the backpack at Randul's feet.

"You people are not very worldly and there are unscrupulous people out there." This was the first lie with which Ziyad embellished his confession.

"Naturally, I was keen to ensure that it was me, rather than some strange German, who secured the other Pad." He took another few sips and looking into the sediment at the bottom of his cup, before adding "You do have more I assume?"

Randul took up his cup and also drank some of the foul liquid that Ziyad called coffee. He ignored Ziyad's question.

"What were you hoping to gain from having someone follow me?"

"Your safety? Oh, I don't know. Look, young man, let's stop sparring with each other. I thought you might lead him, and therefore me, to where you found them." Ziyad was almost matter of fact about his revelation.

"So you could cut me out, no doubt," Randul snapped. Ziyad raised his eyebrows and turned down his mouth as if such a suggestion was a personal affront.

"It was merely a part of standard business practice."

"And you say I can trust you?" Randul thumped his cup down on the counter and snatched up the two blue sapphires.

"Who was this man you set on me?" Randul asked as he thrust the stones back into his bag. Ziyad winced at the question.

"How did you know it was a man, my friend?"

"You're an Arab. You wouldn't use a woman," Randul replied.

Ziyad looked deeply into Randul's eyes with his own single, cold, accusatory eye before quietly responding, "He was my son."

Ziyad was unable to conceal an emotional chink in his armour that escaped out of a genuine concern for a loved one.

"He was your son?" Randul was incredulous - and scared. Suddenly Ziyad was certain that there was some link between the savage and his son's disappearance. Although only very feint, there was an infinitesimal reaction from the Veddah, a tensing of his body, a flicker in his eyes.

"You wouldn't know anything about his disappearance, would you?" Ziyad suddenly pointed a dirty fingernail at Randul, rising slightly from his stool. "He hasn't been home for over four days. Where is he? I'm worried, his mother is worried." Ziyad paused for maximum effect, "What have you done?"

Ziyad was on the offensive and Randul felt the pressure of a father's justified wrath. Now he wanted just to get out of this accursed shop. The Arab moved from behind his counter towards Randul. The approach was deliberate and purposefully intimidatory. Randul was fearful that Ziyad intended to trap him in the shop and he was just about to protest his innocence when the door behind him rattled and opened. Ziyad stopped instantly in his tracks and Arabic exploded from Ziyad's mouth.

"Tozz feek! Tozz feek!"

Randul spun round to see what had caused the furiously foul-mouthed outburst from the man who a moment before had virtually accused him of abducting his son.

Standing in the doorway was the large frame of Stephen, looking the picture of innocence.

"Good morning, old chap." His voice had adopted a theatrically English mannerism, "I saw that you were open and wondered if I could have a jolly old look around?" He glanced expectantly from Ziyad to Randul and back again, "Oh, I say. Have I interrupted you?"

Randul took his cue and immediately gathered up his belongings.

"No. I am just leaving." He brushed hastily past Stephen not looking at him on the way out of the door.

"Wait!" Ziyad went to catch his sleeve, to detain him, but failed as Stephen bumbled between them. His eyes followed Randul as he made his swift escape and his demeanour hardened. His expression became murderous and he pushed hard against the interfering Englishman.

"Steady, old man."

"Fuck off! We're closed." He angrily ushered a blusteringly apologetic Stephen back through the door, pushing him roughly into the street.

"I say, old chap, there's no need to be rude." Stephen stopped in front of Ziyad to delay him as he rushed from the shop into the street. Desperately he searched for Randul but he had disappeared from view. Ziyad stood in front of Stephen and glared at him.

"Go! Go!" Ziyad stabbed his fists onto his waist and stood with his legs apart to bar any attempt by Stephen to re-enter.

Randul had gone. There was no sign of him in either direction. Ziyad maintained a vicious snarl to his voice,

"Now!"

Stephen looked perplexed and after moment of indecision, he waved a cheery goodbye and set off up the street.

Ziyad stumped back into the shop and slammed and locked the door behind him.

Barely had he retaken his seat and grasped his now cold cup more tightly than necessary, but there was renewed tapping on the glass. There appeared to be two men at the door, and they persisted with their knocking impervious to the fact that Ziyad was ignoring them. Finally, Ziyad smashed his cup down on the counter and flew to the door, his fury boiling over at yet more interruptions.

As he came close to the entrance, he saw that both men were in uniform – police uniforms.

He fumbled for his keys, unlocked the door and flung it open.

"Yes?"

The policemen showed him their identity cards and asked if he could give them a moment of his time - inside.

Ziyad backed through the door, his face paled, his mouth opened slackly, his hands shook involuntarily. At no point did he turn away from the advancing uniforms. They suggested that he should sit down before the taller officer spoke,

"It's about your son." Ziyad slumped onto his stool.

*

"He knows! He definitely knows!" Randul was in a terrible state by the time Stephen had caught up with him at the bus station. "I must get away from here. Go home. Forget I ever came here."

Stephen tried to calm him, but Randul was too wired to listen to any logical argument.

"Here! Take the things." He hurled his backpack towards Stephen. It skidded across the ground and came to a halt at his feet. A couple of passers-by watched the altercation, bemused as to why the young Sri Lankan was throwing his bag at the European.

"Don't be ridiculous. Just calm down." Stephen picked up the bag and handed it back to his friend. "I've got my car and we can go to my hotel outside Negombo. You'll be safe there. I should've been back a couple of days ago anyway. They'll be thinking that I've gone missing as well." The quip did not sit well with Randul who looked at him unhappily for taking such a cheap shot.

"I don't want to go back to your hotel." Randul sounded like a petulant child. "I need to go home, without being followed."

"OK." Stephen tried to adopt a conciliatory tone but was slightly irritated by the attitude Randul had adopted. His predicament was not of Stephen's making. "I'll take you back to your place and you can pack a few things. You need to put some space between you and this guy's father."

Reluctantly Randul accepted the suggestion and walked sullenly back to Stephen's car. He constantly checked the streets and pedestrians to make sure that there was no sign of the dealer or anyone else of suspicion. No-one appeared to be following or taking any interest in either of them.

They drove out of town as Ziyad sat apprehensively in front of the two policemen.

The body of a young man had been found at the base of a cliff in the Sinharaja Forest Reserve, close to Mala Ella Falls. It appeared that had been there for a few days and was being brought back to Kandy. The body had been provisionally identified as his missing son, but he was required to provide a positive identity when it was delivered to the hospital.

The two policemen expressed their regrets and condolences. Ziyad was in a trance. He could not believe what they were telling him. He tried to pull it all together but was incapable of grasping the implications of what they said had been found. How was he to break the news to his wife? To his daughter?

His life had imploded.

"How did it happen?" he asked blankly, his eye staring unseeing into the distance.

"We do not know for certain, but it seems that it was an accident. A fall from a cliff edge. It is a notoriously dangerous area to walk unguided."

"No sign of foul play?"

"None."

Ziyad nodded his head in disbelief. He recalled the clothes that the young prospector had worn the first time that they had met. Now he recognised them as those of a tour guide from the Sinharaja Forest Reserve.

Should he tell the police of his suspicions? Where was the gun? He could hardly ask.

It would probably be best if he handled the matter himself.

Chapter 16

When Stephen and Randul arrived back at The Kithul Hotel, outside Negombo, Celia greeted them with a mixture of relief and rage. She had spent days trying to contact him and was on the verge of informing the police that he had gone missing. It was the producers of the TV show who had persuaded her otherwise, fearful that any bad publicity would result in the BBC withdrawing from the deal to televise both the series and the cookery programme that was to follow. A lot of money had been invested already and the production company could not afford to write this off. It would break them, just as they had found a success on their hands.

The small crew, comprising of a cameraman, sound technician and second unit director were perfectly happy lolling around the pool overlooking the sea and enjoying the all-expenses paid trip. They were not overly concerned if Stephen reappeared or not. However, his eventual arrival meant that all thought of relaxation was banished, and they mustered themselves to their task.

Celia viewed Randul's arrival with suspicion but did not make any comment. Stephen had not seemed to be gay to her but then it was becoming increasingly difficult to identify who was and who was not. A room was found for him, a basic, windowless ground floor store, that was sometimes used by the Assistant Manager of the hotel when he had to stay over. The quality of the accommodation was of no concern to Randul, he was relieved just to be away from the Kandy area for a few days.

Randul watched with fascination as the various shots planned by the second unit were executed. He tried to correct the liberties that were taken by the TV company in portraying for the audience back in the UK their version of traditional Sri

Lankan life. Tongue in cheek, Stephen had introduced Randul as his "Consultant Herbologist" and, to the amusement of both, nobody gave the matter a second thought – except for Celia who had smirked.

The sound man, wearing tight white shorts that were very tight and very short, was quite covetous that Stephen had managed to pick up such a good-looking young man. Despite his best efforts, he had had a singular lack of success on that front. He was obsequiously willing to explain to Randul the intricacies of his job and tried to ingratiate himself as much as possible. Randul was not as naïve as the soundman obviously thought and he retained a polite, but detached demeanour. This frustrated the soundman even more, thinking that Randul was teasing him. However, he was unable to pursue his infatuation further due to the pressure that the unit was under to make up the lost time as a result of Stephen's unexplained absence.

Randul became the 'go-to' man for the crew, offering advice and a taste of ethnicity. Stephen encouraged his participation, seeing it as a welcome distraction from his worries about the dealer in Kandy. Very reluctantly, the tribesman appeared in the background to several of the shots, ever mindful that he was here to lie low rather than expose himself to attention. The crew were insistent and he managed to keep himself as much in the shadows as he could.

Celia was also not immune to Randul's charms, encouraged by his rejection of the advances of the sound man. She became his self-appointed chaperone at all the locations, most being in or close to the hotel garden or shoreline (even though they were purported to be from every corner of the island). Randul was no more susceptible to Celia's attentions than he was to those of the sound man. He resisted the temptation to politely rebuff her, aware that this was important to Stephen, and he did not want to do anything that might adversely affect the success of the shoot.

The Kithul Hotel was one of Sri Lanka's most expensive and catered for only the upper echelons of the tourist market. It had its own private beach, gardens, a wellness centre, a couple of pools, spa-baths, a yacht for charter that was moored offshore and luxury cars with uniformed drivers to ferry guests to wherever they wanted to go. It was all a far cry from the tourists that Randul was used to, and he observed with distaste the excessive consumerism and the waste of natural resources that seemed to be deemed essential in order to satisfying the peccadillos of their overtly wealthy guests. Initially Randul was intrigued to wander through the hotel and watch the antics of the rich, but quickly became bored with the superficiality of it all.

While Stephen was busy, Randul roamed along the shoreline or into the surrounding country to forage for items that could be used by Stephen. On the final night of the trip, it had been arranged for Stephen to take over the hotel kitchen and prepare a taster menu for all the other guests, along with a few notable local dignitaries. The event was proving to be the talk of the hotel and would enhance Stephen's profile to some influential potential customers who might be useful in promoting his restaurant.

Randul took his role of "Consultant Herbologist" seriously and made sure that he discussed the menu with Stephen the day before so that he could ensure that he had all that he felt was needed for the various dishes.

When Stephen had driven back to the bungalow with Randul following the truncated meeting with the Arab dealer, they had packed up all his stock of ingredients. Many were in dried or powdered form and so could be easily transported. Those items that were fresh he packed in plastic bags, and they had vacuum packed them immediately they had arrived at the hotel. As might be expected in a hotel of such renown, the kitchen had every modern piece of culinary equipment that could be imagined. Randul was absorbed by the variety of tools at the chefs' behest and quickly took advantage of as many as he could. The kitchen was as technically challenging as any laboratory that he had worked in during his time at the university.

The following day was very hectic as Stephen went about his business prepping for the Gala Dinner for the guests. Randul was determined to ensure that he had fully played his part and that there were no last-minute panics. He had stocked the kitchen with a wide selection of his foraged items already, leaving explicit instructions that they were solely for the use of Stephen. The hotel management and head chef had ensured that Stephen had more sous-chefs than he could keep gainfully employed and so Randul had retreated to the pool. He lay on a lounger, a tray of tea at his side and closed his eyes.

A pool attendant in a white shirt and black Bermuda shorts sidled up and asked, "Is there anything I can get you, sir?"

He waited for a response as Randul opened his eyes and squinted into the sun that was behind the waiter's head. Pulling himself up into a seated position, Randul saw that tucked under his arm was a crumpled newspaper that the waiter had cleared away from a vacated lounger. He asked if he could read it and the waiter looked at the paper as if he did not know how it had slipped itself under his arm.

"This thing? But it's creased, sir. Let me get a fresh one for you."

Randul chuckled and assured him that it was fine as it was, and the waiter handed it to him, wondering why any guest would want a despoiled newspaper when a crisp, fresh one was available.

Shaking the pages open his eyes flitted from article to article until he focussed on a small paragraph beneath a grainy photograph on page four.

> The body of a man has been found at the bottom of a cliff close to the Mala Ella Falls. There are no suspicious circumstances, and it is being treated by the police as a tragic accident. The man was named as Thinuka Al-Quadi, aged 24, the son of a local businessman. What he was doing hiking alone in the forest is unknown. The Head Ranger for the Forestry Department warned that the Sinharaja Forest, like any other wild area, had its dangers and that it is extremely unwise for anyone to wander off into the area without a trained guide.

The photograph was of a grieving father leaving the hospital mortuary. Clearly, he did not want to be caught on camera as the picture showed him with his hand ineffectually trying to cover his face. Despite his best efforts, it was impossible to hide the distinctive facial characteristics that made Ziyad so instantly recognisable.

Obviously, the photographer had caught Ziyad unawares and, from the look on his face, he was not pleased.

Randul felt sick and, taking the paper with him, retired to his room leaving his tea unfinished.

*

When Stephen eventually caught up with Randul, he was unusually animated as he described the filming and his day generally. Randul remained strangely quiet throughout. They were both seated at a table overlooking the pool. The terrace was buzzing with guests all discussing their own days activities over iced drinks. Now and again, one would look furtively in their direction, aware that they had a minor celebrity in their midst, but not wanting to display any obvious interest. Noting the lack of enthusiasm from Randul as he recounted his exploits, Stephen sank back in his chair to drink his gin and tonic. There was something troubling his friend and he surmised that it could be because his trip was coming to an end and that they would be parting. Stephen had to admit that he too was not looking forward to their separation.

After an extended period of silence, he asked as gently as he could, "What's up. You are very quiet this evening. Something wrong?"

Randul merely looked across at Stephen before he took a scrap of paper torn from the newspaper. He handed it across to Stephen without any comment or explanation. Stephen took the cutting and read it. When he had finished he glanced back open-mouthed at Randul.

"And?"

"And what?" Randul responded, picking up his glass of beer.

"Was it an accident?" Stephen asked cautiously.

"I have already told you that it was, haven't I?" Randul was irritable because he feared that the father would not accept the conclusion of the police that there had been no suspicious circumstances. No father whose son died unexpectantly would ever accept that it was an accident. There would always have to be someone responsible for an accident. The friend? The girl? The lorry, bus or tuk-tuk driver?

A Veddah? Randul?

Anyone? Anyone who was close to the victim or near to the incident. He would never believe that his boy had stumbled and fallen to his death through his own misadventure.

"Did you see it happen?" Stephen's eyes had not left Randul's taut face. He appeared to struggle to find the right words in reply.

"I heard him fall." Randul could not look at Stephen and his hands fidgeted in his lap. "I heard a cry behind me but thought he had just fallen over."

"Did you not go back to find out?"

"Yes. I went back up the path that I had led him onto. It skirted the cliff but was not particularly near the edge," Randul's reply was seeking mitigation where it could. "I couldn't see him and was careful not to get too close in case he was feigning an injury and attacked me. I hunted around and finally gave up. I knew that I should have continued to see if he was injured but it was dark, and I was keen to get away." Randul took a sip of his beer to moisten his dry mouth before continuing, "I decided to go along the ridge, scramble down to the river and then I could double back on myself. I guessed that he would stay following the upper path, continue further into the forest and then get even more lost. I retraced my steps along the river until…" Randul raised his glass to swallow a mouthful of his drink before realising that it was empty. Randul stopped and stared into the bottom of his glass.

He took his battered tin from his pocket and started to prepare a betel leaf to calm his nerves.

"Until what?"

"Until I came across his body. It was lying at the base of a steep escarpment."

"What the fuck!" Stephen interrupted. A couple of guests looked across at Stephen and he lowered his voice to a whisper, "Why didn't you mention this earlier? Was he dead?".

"Yes."

"You're sure? How did you know?" Stephen was alarmed.

"I'm a professional guide. We're trained in first aid. I know when someone is dead. Anyway, you only had to look. His neck was obviously broken." He placed his tin gently onto the table and popped the green folded leaf into his mouth.

Stephen thought for a moment.

"So, it was definitely an accident? You're in the clear?" He sounded uncertain, hoping that the matter was closed.

"In your eyes and in mine, perhaps. But I doubt that his father will see it as that clear cut." The waiter reappeared and Randul ordered his third beer. He was not accustomed to drinking any quantity of alcohol and it was already going to his head.

"Do you want to tell the police what happened?" Stephen waited for a response with selfish trepidation. Randul was slow to respond, and Stephen added, for clarity, "Just don't mention my name, that's all. It wouldn't be good for the show."

Randul realised he was seeing a different Stephen Silchester for the first time. A man more concerned about his career than a friend's predicament. Randul felt a tinge of disappointment that he might have misjudged Stephen.

"I have already thought about that, but it's not that easy."

Stephen was confused, "What's so difficult?"

"You wouldn't understand."

Stephen persevered, "Try me."

"The police are not going to accept my word against an apparently successful and respected businessman like Ziyad Al-Quadi."

Stephen needed an explanation, "Who is Ziyad Al-Quadi? Not that scruffy little dealer that I met the other day in that back-street shop. He hardly looked to be a pillar of the establishment."

Randul pursed his lips at the innocent gullibility of the Englishman. "That scruffy little dealer is, by all accounts, a very wealthy dealer. I suspect that he lives a life that is completely at odds with the image he portrays for his customers, most of whom are simple tourists looking for a bargain. Al-Quadi provides them with what they seek and makes a very good living from it."

"Is he a local?" Stephen asked, motioning to the waiter that he would like another gin.

"No, not to look at him. And with a name like Al-Quadi? It sounds more Middle Eastern than Sri Lankan."

"Well, there you are. Surely the police would take the word of a local over that of a foreigner?" The waiter removed Stephen's glass and replaced the wet coaster with a dry one. Randul waited until he had left.

"I suspect his relationship with the police is supported financially, if you understand me. Secondly, I am a Veddah. In the social hierarchy I lie just above a Rodiya."

Stephen was none the wiser.

"What is a Rodiya?" he asked.

Randul took a deep breath,

"Filth. That is what the word means, and I am, in the eyes of many, no better than filth. A lower caste, an outsider."

Stephen was stunned, "Surely that doesn't apply now? We're in the 21st century."

"You would be surprised. I was fortunate to have had a father who fought for my education and who supported me throughout my time at both school and university. But it was not easy for me, or for him. I had few friends and always welcomed the holidays as a respite, a time when I could retreat back into the forest."

Stephen sat in silence, his perception of his comfortable, orderly middle-class world turned upside down by the feudalism and bigotry that was being experienced by someone of his own generation, an educated and erudite man. A man perfectly capable of taking a leadership role in any administration worldwide, and brighter than many that do.

"So, if you go to the police, you are telling me that they will ignore you? Just because you are a Veddah?"

"What do you think."

*

Two thousand, four hundred and eighty-four miles to the west sits a solitary woman wearing a black embroidered abaya. She is tediously scrolling through foreign web sites. The room is silent save for the continual hum of fans that take the warm air from a bulky computer's hard-drive and pumps it into the stifling heat of the room. She has several 'favourites' and now and again one would pop up with a snippet of information that is noted and carefully stored away for future use. She would not have bothered with a random death in Sri Lanka were it not for the photograph. It is grainy and not of the best quality. Despite its imperfections, the latest face recognition software that had recently been stolen from the US and installed on her machine had picked him out. She stares at the unknown man and transfers the image to another application. After a succession of taps on her keyboard the jumble of pixels slowly finds form, the photographic defects are corrected and a perfectly rendered image of the father of the deceased appears on her screen.

All information of 'persons of interest' had to be sent to a pre-set site and, being a loyal servant of her God and Leader, the woman assigns the face and accompanying short article a reference number and forwards it to…she knows not where.

It was immaterial, her task is done.

Chapter 17

The news of the English TV chef cooking at 'the beautiful and luxurious Kithul Hotel at a beachside location on the outskirts of Negombo' had spread far and wide, predominantly through the efforts of the TV company that was heavily promoting the event. The hotel was fully booked, as were several other lesser establishments in the immediate vicinity. There was a high level of expectation placed upon Stephen's shoulders and the pressure was beginning to get to him. The atmosphere in the kitchen was tense for most of the day and increased as the time for the guests to sit down for dinner advanced.

Randul remained on hand should he be required but was peripheral to the feverish activity in the stainless-steel kitchen. Four under-chefs had been supplied by the hotel as well as attendant assistants to wash and tidy and clear space. Randul was impressed by the work rate of his friend who, once he had settled to his brief, prepared his dishes with an exactitude more becoming of a surgeon than a chef. Each element gradually built into the story that he was seeking to tell of his time in Sri Lanka. The literal story was much abridged but the TV producer, who had flown in first class specifically for the dinner loved the concept. The following morning, he would fly out again for Heathrow taking Stephen with him.

Any reference to Randul's contribution to the culinary artistry of their protégé was omitted, the local foraging for indigenous ingredients being portrayed as purely an initiative of Stephen. The producer was euphoric as to the impact this would have on the environmental credentials of the programme and, consequently, on his production company. Sustainability, ESG and global responsibility were all good greenwash phrases to sell programmes around the world. Stephen would be marketed as the vanguard to a new generation of chefs who would use natural products and constituents to create food that would delight both the palate and the conscience of their diners.

When the time came for the dinner to commence, the Kithul was packed with excited guests. Residents lucky enough to be staying mingled with local dignitaries, along with some celebrities who either had been staying in the area or had been flown in at the expense of the TV company. The latter were the new phenomenon known as the 'Influencer'. These vapid youths would wander through the crowd with mobile phones held aloft to capture what had become known as 'selfies'. This was the gift that the new millennium had given to the world of the internet. Whether the concept would flourish, no one knew, but for the moment it and sprouting social media platforms were the new promotional tools that publicists were grappling to control and exploit.

As Randul hovered on the outskirts of the congregation he caught glimpses of the 'nipped and tucked', the botoxed, the tattooed, the expensively and minimally dressed, the extroverts and the unnecessarily obese. To a man, woman and, to Randul's confusion, the gender-neutral all competing for exposure. Each ensuring that their exaggeratedly preened faces were providentially caught in shot with the other more traditionally established stars. Every picture would be accompanied by an inanely brief post saying nothing of value, just another flash of self-promotion in pursuit of more 'followers'.

Randul thought, 'What a waste'. They would never have any appreciation of the artistry in Stephen's efforts. His creations were entirely for their delectation and gratification but the subtleties of flavours as well as the balance of textures that he was at such pains to fashion would be lost on these morons. The TV company was expending so much money in promoting Stephen in the anticipation of the opening of The Sauceror's Apprentice, and these flaky individuals were to be his ambassadors.

For Stephen, it was all becoming very real. Earlier in the day he had spoken to the producer who had reported that the fitting out of the restaurant was well in hand and that completion would be achieved in time for the opening. Normally he would have had time to revel in the anticipation of the opening night, but this would have to be deferred until the morning. In the meantime, there was a hoard of hungry guests in the dining room who were eagerly awaiting his first dish. He finished plating up his prima course of seven.

To the waiting queue of uniformed waiters he called, "SERVICE!"

Randul slipped away from the hurly-burly of the kitchen and the noisy babble of the expectant diners. Quietly he took himself off across the terrace and beyond the lawn to walk in solitude on the moonlit beach. Tomorrow Stephen would be leaving, and he might not see him again, which saddened him. He had enjoyed his company at the bungalow and felt a sense of purpose to his life through his contribution to Stephen's gift as a chef.

Previously, the foraging had been a hobby more than anything else, a bit like the gemming down in the rock pools of the river. An innocent pastime that he had pursued with enthusiasm, but without any real ambition or expectation. However, when Stephen combined Randul's extraordinary ingredients with his own talents then they were an incontestable duet.

Randul grimaced to himself as he realised that neither of the two riches that he held within his control could be fully realised. He was the catalyst that could launch Stephen as a renowned, world class chef. Without his foraged ingredients, and more particularly his alchemy, the food that Stephen put onto his clients' plates would undoubtedly be delicious, but unexceptional. Randul was the spark that set the dishes on fire. He and Stephen had a symbiotic relationship – the one dependent upon the other for survival. So how was he to capitalise on his contribution to the partnership?

As he walked along the beach the cool water ran up the sand, flowed around his feet and then slipped back out to the sea.

Then there was the issue of the stones. Randul had in his possession enough to set himself up anywhere in the world, if only he could maximise their real worth. He would like to expand his horizons beyond the forest, beyond the island. With the arrival of Stephen, his interest in widening his horizons was becoming a strong impulse. He was committed to his homeland, of course, but not to the exclusion of everything else that the wider world might have to offer. Ever since he had decided to sell his Padparadscha and blue sapphires, he had become ensnared within a web of deceit and mistrust that emanated from the dealer who now he knew as Ziyad Al-Quadi. The Arab sat in the centre of that web, a voracious spider watching and scheming as Randul fought to extricate himself from the sticky fibres that had been spun around him.

The newspaper reported that the death of the Al-Quadi boy was a tragic accident, but Randul was certain that the father would not accept that conclusion. In fact, Randul was certain that he suspected Randul of being complicit, and to an extent he was right. If Randul had not made a conscious decision to lead Thinuka into the forest, then he would not have stumbled or fallen over the edge of the cliff. He would be alive now.

The brief stay at Stephen's hotel had merely been a stay of the inevitable, but Randul knew that he would have to return home at some point. The people from the TV company were hardly going to pay for his room beyond their departure the next morning. The fact that the three huge stones Randul had in his chamois pouch, if carefully cut and polished, would be sufficient to purchase the hotel a few times over did not help his thought processes. They were unrealised assets and to liquidate them was not going to be easy in the confined markets of Sri Lanka.

Randul continued to walk along the sandy beach as the water was ruffled by a breath of warm night air, the peaks of the ripples reflecting iridescent flashes of moonlight that flickered and bobbed across the mirrored surface. The sea and the sky were as black as ink, the canopy above his head punctuated by bright pinpricks of patterned light that performed a slow, circular dance across infinity. The peace and tranquillity of his surroundings calmed him. He sat for a while, cross legged on the sand inhaling and exhaling deeply, holding his breath for a few second between each.

Amid his inner serenity and the betel leaf, he found inspiration.

*

The only emotions experienced by Ziyad at that moment were frustration, anger and despair. The Mercedes had been recovered from where it had been abandoned and both the police and he had searched it thoroughly for any clue or hint as to what had really happened to his son. The car yielded no information that assisted either of them.

Two questions continued to elude him. Firstly, what had really happened that night in the forest, and secondly, where was the gun?

He had buried Thinuka swiftly after the authorities had released his body, the remaining members of his small family silently weeping while simultaneously laying the culpability for the death of his only son firmly at his door. It was impossible for Ziyad to admit to anyone that he accepted any responsibility, even though he rued having ever asked his son to tail the savage from the forest. And now, to compound his woes, the newspapers had picked up on the story and were starting to dig around into Thinuka's life and his many peccadillos. Some locals who purported to know him were divulging secrets and facts that Ziyad found hard to believe, let alone acknowledge.

He spent more and more time at the shop or in his study as neither his wife nor his beloved Ameesha would speak to him. He could live without the appreciation or respect of his wife. But Ameesha, his beautiful daughter whom, save for his dead son, he loved above anything, appeared to have sided with her mother. She had become oblivious to both Thinuka's weaknesses and his excesses. Despite Ziyad's best efforts, including giving her the Mercedes (having had new tyres fitted), still she ignored her father or treated him with undisguised disdain. He had tried to speak, no, plead with her but all was to no avail. He had been forced to repeat the abridged version of why they had had to leave their homeland, why Thinuka's constant desire for the bright lights was unwise and why his socialising caused her father such anxiety. But she would not listen, and so he became angry and shouted at her, reducing her to more tears.

Too many tears had been shed already in his house. Too much had been said, or not said.

His study remained his refuge, his shop his temple and he threw himself single-mindedly into his work and the running of his investments. He spoke almost every evening to his advisors in the Cayman Islands, in London, in Dubai, in Frankfurt, in Singapore. He watched as financial markets fluctuated against the illiquid property markets, cryptocurrencies defied traditional pundits and behaved with a ferocious volatility that favoured the alert and fleet of foot. Most of his real estate was in the UK and more specifically in London and he was constantly harrying his agents, his solicitors and his managers to swiftly expedite what was not possible to swiftly expedite.

When it was explained yet again in patronising tones by his agents and contractors that they were moving as fast as they could, he lost his temper and screamed across the internet that he would not accept their incompetence a moment longer. This time, he was standing arched over his computer, glaring at the screen and the four faces that stared back.

"Ya Ibn el Sharmouta! You imbeciles! I'm coming to London!" he screamed with finality.

Ziyad punched the 'Leave' icon on his screen and fell back into his chair in exhaustion. Across the room the television that he had constantly on, was winding up a depressing report on one or other of the continuing conflicts that engulfed the trouble spots of the world, before moving on to news nearer to home.

A local reporter was being filmed standing on the terrace of one of the up-market tourist hotels on the coast, jabbering on about a dinner that some celebrity chef from Britain was giving. There was a crowd of exotically dressed guests seated in the background and Ziyad allowed the nonsense to wash over him as he poured another whisky from the cut glass decanter that now permanently stood on his desk.

The pale, peaty spirit slipped down his throat easily and went some way to calming his mood.

"I have with me the English celebrity chef, Stephen Silchester, who has chosen a fusion of Sri Lankan and European food as his signature style. Good evening, Stephen."

"Good evening."

Ziyad suddenly looked up at the sound of the second voice responding to the interviewer. On the screen was a large-framed young man with a three-day growth of stubble on his face. He was fresh faced, and his eyes glinted in the lights. Ziyad had seen before the effect of adrenalin in the eyes of men. The dilated pupils, the speeding heart rate, the increase in blood pressure as it courses through the veins to the muscles in readiness for flight or fight. Ziyad had experienced such feelings as a reaction to abject fear, but to the young man on the screen it was derived from euphoria.

The face was familiar, and it did not take Ziyad long to place it in his shop, early one morning, when it had interrupted his inquisition of the young Veddah. The voice was easily identifiable, even though it was not as patrician as it had been when he had unexpectantly and, apparently arbitrarily bumbled into his shop. He sat forward to listen resting his elbows on the desk and supporting his chin in his hands.

"This trip has been revelatory as to the incredibly wide diversity of spices and herbs that Sri Lanka has to offer," boyish enthusiasm fizzed from Stephen as he addressed each question put to him by the interviewer.

"I understand that you have been away for a few days in the forests foraging for ingredients. How did you know what to collect? Do you use foraging in England?" The camera panned back and caught a second face, not quite in focus, in the background and Ziyad slowly sat up straight in his chair, his eyes glued to the person to the right of the chef.

"Foraging is a crucial element to the future of our profession," Stephen replied. "Such ingredients being completely natural and plentiful. However, what I've discovered, thanks to the invaluable assistance of my Consultant Herbologist and good friend Randul, here." Stephen turned slightly to try to draw Randul into the interview, but he had purposefully moved out of camera shot. Waving a hand vaguely in the direction of where Randul had been standing, and unable to find him, Stephen continued to speak.

"What I've learnt is that there is so much more that's available here on your beautiful island than at home. Using simple techniques your abundant larder can be adapted or refined to instil into these natural ingredients properties that will delight everyone who enjoys delicious cuisine." Stephen beamed into the camera with self-confidence.

The interviewer was about to ask another question when the anchor-man interrupted her to say that they had run out of time. When the camera cut back to the studio, the presenter made some fatuous comment about wishing that he was there, rather than reading the news, but Ziyad was not listening.

He pensively sipped more of his drink. So, the unexpected arrival of Mr. Silchester at his shop was not quite as arbitrary as might at first have appeared, and now Ziyad could put at least one name to the Veddah. Randul. It would be easy to find out where he lived through his contacts in the police. Before his trip to London, he intended to pay a visit to young Randul for a long chat.

He drained his glass and got up to stretch his weary muscles from having been seated at his desk for too long. His countenance was much improved, and he replaced the glass stopper into the neck of the decanter before he went up to the spare bedroom to sleep soundly.

*

The camera crew packed up their gear and chatted in the bar over some complimentary beers. Stephen, meanwhile, was having his hand enthusiastically shaken and being clapped on the back by various guests, all of whom extolled his culinary mastery, promising to visit The Sauceror's Apprentice as soon as they returned from their holidays. The producer stood by proprietarily, already planning how the company would profit further from their newest asset, as Stephen soaked up the accolades from his fans. He was impressed by the young chef's unruffled eloquence when being interviewed, seemingly unfazed by all the attention that this gala dinner had generated. It had been expensive, but the producer had twisted a few arms and greased a few palms to persuade TV Derana, the local station, to do a piece on its main news. Hopefully this would be picked up by BBC News Sri Lanka and then syndicated wider afield, possibly even getting a small slot on the BBC UK News.

All in all, the producer was very pleased with himself and eager to return to London to put the wheels in motion for more commercialisation of Stephen Silchester. The contract between them was suitably tight and basically anything Stephen created or spun off from his fame as a result of the competition was financially tipped in favour of the production company. Intellectual property rights had similarly been scooped up. That was business and the eagerness of the applicants to secure a place in the competition had blinded them to the usual principle of seeking legal advice, let alone actually reading the document, before signing any contract. Thankfully the pursuit of fame overwhelmed common sense, and his production company prospered.

The next day his team would return to London triumphant. However, he needed to make sure that his newest discovery was fit and ready for the grand opening of The Sauceror's Apprentice before the publicity dwindled. The only slight fly in the ointment was the local native who Stephen had picked up and now treated as his 'Consultant Herbologist". It seemed that Stephen's newfound confidence and his incredible dexterity in the use of the foraged additives that were sourced by the Sri Lankan had become fundamental to his creativity. Stephen had acknowledged this fact when he spoke to the producer earlier in the evening but to what degree Randul was going to prove a problem as a possible 'hanger-on' was unclear.

He had taken the opportunity to gently quiz Randul when he was loitering around the edges of the kitchen as Stephen laboured to craft his dishes. The Sri Lankan assured him that he could continue to provide a reliable supply of good quantity ingredients if Stephen wanted him to do so. It would help if he had similar packaging and storage equipment that was to be found in the hotel kitchens and it had taken the producer but a second to confirm that this could be arranged, as would the necessary freight contracts with Sri Lanka Airlines. Randul seemed to be satisfied with the arrangements, together with the modest retainer that the producer had promised for his trouble. The question of whether Randul could accompany them to London did not arise, much to the producer's relief.

He did wonder whether there was more than just a simple culinary relationship between the two men and weighed up the pros and cons of such a relationship in commercial terms. On balance, he decided that it was a distraction from the main purpose of the current programming. Perhaps later it would be an interesting feature, particularly if ratings fell too quickly and they needed to garner the support of the gay community with an injection of topicality.

Randul was feeling like a pawn in this commercial roundabout that had consumed Stephen's attention. His friend had been generous in his praise of Randul's contribution to the phenomenal success of the evening. The producer, on the other hand, was somewhat dismissive of Randul, once he had secured his agreement to providing a continued supply of the special ingredients that Stephen relied upon.

The bright lights of celebrity and media attention held no attractions for Randul who had watched with both amusement and disgust at the antics of those who sought to maintain a hold on the spotlight of fame. He still held a desire to one day travel to London, but the excessive exhibitionism of those who surrounded Stephen or wanted to be part of his entourage discouraged him from making such a suggestion. Instead, he quietly slipped away from the celebrations that were becoming louder and more boisterous as the night wore on. In his room he collected all his belongings together for the journey back to his modest bungalow in the Sinharaja Forest Reserve.

Once packed, he returned to the deserted kitchen that had been cleaned and left ready for another cycle of meals to be prepared the following morning. The remnants of his boxes of ingredients had been stacked tidily and left for collection. Randul took two of the cardboard boxes and carefully slid a knife down the gap between the sealed flaps that formed the lids. He removed and then repacked the contents with a couple of additions in the middle of each. Randul sealed the tops with brown sticky tape that he had found on a shelf above the boxes.

He hunted for a pen and found a black permanent marker in a pot on the same shelf. He took off the top and smelt the hydrocarbons from the thick felt tip. On the front of each of the boxes, he wrote in large, clear, block lettering:

FOR STEPHEN SILCHESTER EYES ONLY

STRICTLY PRIVATE AND CONFIDENTIAL

DRIED AND PROCESSED HERBS AND SPICES.

Restacking the boxes where they had previously been left for collection, he went back to his room to settle down for the night. He would be up early and long gone before Stephen and his entourage were roused from their celebrations.

Chapter 18

For once, Ziyad had slept well. He awoke refreshed and revitalised as he shaved, showered, and dressed. He was looking forward to his trip to London and his absence would allow a period of peace between him and his disapproving family. The enjoyment would be heightened even further if he took his mistress, Eleni, with him. It would be a pleasant surprise for her as he had ignored her over the last week or so due to all that had occurred.

Since the death of Thinuka he had eschewed the ill-fitting prosthetic foot and the shabby clothing. While he avoided being ostentatiously overdressed, he did improve his overall appearance. He had also broached the possibility of Aloka having a more elevated role at the shop so he could withdraw into the limelight and concentrate on other interests. This had been accepted with alacrity by his assistant who had suddenly taken to arriving before Ziyad and staying after he had left for home in the evening. The shop was tidier, the customers greeted with charm and courtesy, and, to Ziyad's great surprise, takings had risen.

It had been agreed that there would be a three-month trial period but already, from what he had seen, Ziyad was relatively relaxed and was seriously considering putting Aloka solely in charge while Ziyad travelled to London. Upon his return, he would then be able to see how Aloka had coped before making any final decision as to whether to make the promotion permanent.

Ziyad took for granted that such an arrangement would infuriate Ameesha who had assumed that, with Thinuka no longer the heir apparent, his mantle would fall to her. But Ziyad kept some traditional views about business and commerce not being a suitable setting for a young woman. They should be satisfied with a supporting role for their husbands or fathers, and in the latter case this did not include running even a minor part of Ziyad's business empire. She was twenty-one and, although he had reluctantly agreed to her continued education (although to what purpose he was never entirely sure), the time had come for her to be married and off his hands.

As he had expected, when he arrived at the shop the lights were on and the area in front of the window had been swept clean and washed down. The glass gleamed and the shelves were ready to receive the display cases from the vault. Aloka had not been given the keys to the safe yet, but Ziyad accepted that he was going to have to award this final badge of office when he left for England. This would necessitate Ziyad clearing any surplus cash that had built up over the period of Aloka's probation together with the Padparadscha and a few other precious items that Ziyad had stockpiled for a rainy day. These had not and would not appear in the formal accounts of the business.

Ziyad proprietarily strode into his emporium and immediately smelt the strong aroma of freshy brewed coffee. Aloka greeted him and was handed the keys to the safe as Ziyad took the proffered cup of coffee and settled onto his stool behind the counter. He watched as Aloka busied himself collecting trays of jewellery and placing them meticulously into the window. After each shelf was complete, he would scurry out of the door and check that his handiwork met with his own meticulous standards, standards that he had learnt from his employer.

Finally, he was satisfied with all his preparatory tasks and stalked back and forth across the shopfloor, making minor adjustments to items on the counter in order to assuage the impatience of awaiting the arrival of his first customer.

The person who walked through the door was unexpected to both men. Aloka looked across at his employer who wearily stared at the new arrival in anticipation of yet another argument.

Ameesha was clothed in a modest full length Batik dress that had a large flower motif on the front. Her height was enhanced by the cut of the dress and her shoulders were just visible beneath a thick blanket of tumbling ringlets of dark hair that shone with expensively subtle highlights of auburn. Beneath the hem of the flowing dress her feet were clad in simple open toed sandals, perfectly manicured, the toenails painted a deep red to match her perfect fingernails. She was unadorned by any jewellery save for a thin gold chain around her neck with her name written in Sinhalese that settled on her chest.

The piece was her eighteenth birthday present from her father and every time Ziyad saw her wear it his heart swelled with pride. She would make any man very happy to have her as his bride. She was too good for a guileless youth. He knew that she needed a more mature, worldly man who could control her wilfulness but also provide her with the lifestyle that he would expect for his daughter. A man did not display such attributes in youth but gradually accumulated them with age. There were advantages for Ziyad too. An older man would have more in common with his father-in-law and they would be able to commune on matters of business and politics, their two dynasties growing in power and influence.

"What are you doing here at this hour?" Ziyad enquired warily.

Ameesha smiled innocently at Ziyad with wide eyes and her father felt the warmth of his paternal affection spread across the shop.

"Baba, you left so early, and I wanted to see you before you went." She came over to Ziyad and kissed him fondly on both cheeks. He took her face between his hands and kissed her forehead softly. Ziyad knew his daughter too well to fall for the sudden shows of overt filial tenderness that were now being poured upon him. Only the other evening she had yelled at her father for continuing to put her and her mother under virtual house arrest. She had complained that she had no real friends and that they never wanted to visit her because of the monastic conditions they lived in. Once again, the fact that Thinuka had had the freedom to do as he wished was thrown back at him. Ziyad tried to explain that it was different for a boy, that there were not the same threats to a man as there were to a young girl. All such reasoning fell on deaf ears.

"No threats? No threats!" Ameesha had bawled at him. "And now look. Thinuka, my beautiful brother, your only son, is dead." She had then stormed out of the room and taken refuge behind her locked bedroom door, accompanied by thumping rock music that shook the fabric of the house. She knew that he hated the sound, let alone the lyrics, of Iron Maiden, AC/DC, Faith No More or whichever band she currently favoured. Ziyad looked across at his wife who was seated, quietly reading. She paused and raised her eyes from her magazine.

"What did you expect?" she asked before returning to the latest fashion report.

Ziyad knew that women could be contrary, but he was chary of this morning's apparent transformation in his daughter's demeanour. She was wily and he was not going to be stalked and caught out by his little vixen.

"Baba? Can we talk. Privately." Ameesha flicked her eyes in Aloka's direction. He had been observing her and was wondering if the exchange and her doting tone might herald a reconciliation between father and daughter. That would undoubtedly please Ziyad but not Aloka. Such a harmonious ceasefire could only result in Aloka's elevation in the business being rescinded.

He understood the girl's despair at always being treated second best to Thinuka. The last time he had had words with her brother was just before he had arrived at the shop on the day he disappeared.

Sharp words.

Hurtful words.

Words of rejection.

Aloka had misread his own craving and was wounded by the heartless treatment received from the man whom he thought had affection for him. For whom Aloka had developed a deep affection. But this was all a game to Thinuka. He enjoyed toying with other peoples' emotions.

Aloka dismissed the recurring pain of the memory from his mind as Ziyad announced that he and Ameesha were going round the corner for a coffee. Ameesha beamed with pleasure and slipped her arm through his.

"Aloka, you are in charge. I will be as quick as I can."

"Baba, Aloka has been your assistant for many years." Ameesha put her head on her father's shoulder playfully, "You know what to do, don't you, Aloka?"

Ameesha gave Aloka a strange look, the smile remaining on her lips but the hardness not leaving her eyes. He assured them both that he would cope and, hurrying across the shop to open the door for them, hoped that they would have an enjoyable coffee.

What else could he say?

When he thought back, after they had departed, he became concerned. The arrangements for him to take over the management of the shop while Ziyad travelled to London were proceeding well and Aloka was looking forward to taking up his new responsibilities. This compliant, and doting behaviour from Ameesha was contrary to what he had understood to be the atmosphere in the Al-Quadi household. Of course, Ziyad never disclosed the details of his family life to Aloka, but in his grief and frustration he had let slip at times that all was not well. Aloka knew from Thinuka that Ameesha was a pent-up rebel who hated the restrictions that her father had placed on her life. He knew that sometimes she secretly rebelled and crept out to join Thinuka on some of his more innocent escapades. In fact, she had joined them both on one occasion when Thinuka had somehow obtained an invitation to the opening night of a new restaurant. They had had dinner together and then Thinuka had run her home, amidst vociferous protestation from Ameesha, before returning to join Aloka for the rest of the evening.

Aloka needed to be on his guard and make sure that Ameesha did not impede or derail his ambitions.

*

"I wanted to apologise for my behaviour last night," Ameesha said. She looked down at her hands that were folded demurely on her lap. She was sitting across the low table from her father, the early morning sunshine shone through a tall stained-glass window to one side of the coffee shop. It softened her features, and she radiated a youthful beauty that some of the other customers in the café could not ignore. This provoked a mixture of pride and possessiveness in equal measure from her father.

Their coffee was cooling in the bone china cups that had been carefully centred on paper doilies. Ziyad was perched on the edge of a sofa, alert but receptive to whatever his daughter wished to talk about. An outright apology was a surprise, but Ziyad accepted it and was conciliatory in his admission that he too had over-reacted at an emotional time.

There was a hush and Ziyad wondered if that was all she wished to say. He had to admit to himself that he was pleasantly surprised with the conversation so far.

Ameesha took up her cup and saucer and tentatively tried the coffee. She licked her lips, that had a tad too much lipstick on them for Ziyad's taste, but he would let that ride for today. She was obviously contemplating her next sentence with care. Finally, she spoke.

"Did I hear that you are going to London?"

Ziyad had made no mention to his family of the impending trip and so presumed that Ameesha had been eavesdropping on his telephone conversations in his study. She could only do that by being close, if not at, the door.

"I may be," his answer was cautiously non-committal. "I have just bought a building there and at some point I need to go and see it." He picked up his own coffee, swallowed a mouthful of the insipid liquid and wrinkled his nose in distaste. The proprietor, who knew his taste, was not present when he ordered and an unknowing assistant had served him.

"How can they serve this stuff and call it coffee?"

"Baba," Ameesha scolded him with a grin, "if they served what you call coffee, they would kill most of their customers."

They both hesitated and then laughed together and Ziyad relaxed momentarily, enjoying his daughter's company for the first time in many weeks. They should do this more often.

"Baba, I know that Thinuka was your favourite." Ziyad went to protest but Ameesha silenced him by raising her perfectly manicured hand. "Hear me, please, Baba." He returned to the edge of the sofa to listen carefully to what his daughter had to say.

"I know that he was your favourite and I do not blame you for that. He was your son; he was your eldest child. But Baba, he has gone. It was a tragic accident, but he is not here anymore, and you have shut Mama and me out of your life."

Ziyad opened his mouth to protest but again was stopped from making any comment.

"Please, Baba, do not exclude me of all people. I want to be here for you. I know that I can't replace Thinuka, but I can support you. I can help you. I love you, Baba. You can trust me, and I want to become more involved in what you do." She looked directly into his eyes, and she allowed tears to fill the edges of her eyelids, "I love you, Baba, and I want you to love me."

Ziyad swallowed hard as he felt a lump form in the back of his throat. He started to speak, but the words were choked off. Instead, he leant forward and stretched his hands across the table. Ameesha took them in hers and squeezed them gently without releasing.

For a moment they sat, hands entwined looking at each other until Ziyad regained control of his emotions.

"I do love you, Ameesha. I love you very much. But you know nothing about what I do. You are a woman, a very beautiful woman who will make any man very happy to call you his wife."

"Stop!" Ameesha flushed with anger, "This is the 21st century, Baba, and you cannot dictate what I do with my life. I am too young to marry, and when I do so, it will be to the man of my choice. Not yours…or Mama's."

Ziyad suppressed any hint of paternalistic authority in his own voice and tried to remain calm, while internally he seethed with frustration.

"Ameesha, commerce is not for women. It is a dirty world, it is a world of distrust, dishonesty and …"

"And why is that Baba? Because it is a world dominated by men." Ameesha slapped her hand onto the table making the cups rattle in their saucers. Ziyad rocked back on the sofa in shock at her vehemence. Those in the immediate vicinity fell into an embarrassed silence before returning to their own conversations, each keeping half an ear on the more interesting discussion than their own.

"Please, Ameesha, do not make a scene." Ziyad looked around and smiled apologetically to those who still openly observed the arguing father and daughter.

"Then take me seriously, Baba." Ameesha almost hissed the words and Ziyad was back on the edge of his sofa, straining forward so that she could hear his gentle but insistent voice.

"Why do you want to work? What is so bad about marriage? What about us, your parents? Don't you want to give us grandchildren?"

"I will give you grandchildren all in good time, but not now. I am only twenty-one and you have provided me with a good education. Let me use it."

"Ah," Ziyad said mournfully while shaking his head slowly from side to side, "perhaps that was an error?"

"Not an error," Ameesha's voice had risen again and Ziyad placed his hands out flat above the surface of the table, bouncing them up and down to ask her to calm down. She lowered her voice in obedience, but not in surrender. "I am just as able as Thinuka to work with you, better in some ways. At least I can be relied upon and don't disappear on wild excursions."

Ziyad nodded an acceptance that his son had not proved the most reliable of people and displayed a certain hedonistic tendency that had displeased Ziyad on several occasions.

"So, what do you want," he asked. "To shadow me, or is this just a ruse to get me to take you to London?"

Ameesha looked knowingly at her father,

"That would be a bit of a crowd, wouldn't it?"

"What do you mean? Your mother isn't coming."

"I wasn't referring to Mama." Ameesha let the words fall onto the table and Ziyad's mouth dropped open.

"What do you mean by that?" Ziyad's voice was icy, his lips tight across his mouth, but his good eye was wide open in trepidation. "Be very careful how you answer."

"I know about Eleni."

There, it was out.

Ameesha had not intended to go this far but the disclosure was inevitable at some point, and that point had arrived. The colour drained from Ziyad's face and his eye blazed. Ameesha had no alternative but to add the coup de grace, "And Mama knows. Has known for years. Why do you think that she's so cool towards you? She doesn't want to share a bed with…"

"Enough!" This time the whole coffee shop fell into silence as Ziyad exploded with rage. He stood up and threw down some notes onto the table to pay for the coffee. "You have spoken out of turn and without respect. Is this what education in the 21st century has done to the young women of this country. Is this the price of Western influences? I did not fight for this. I do not deserve this."

Ziyad spun round and stormed out of the coffee shop as an excited buzz of conversation swirled around the other tables. Ameesha sat coolly and took up the coffee pot to refill her cup but, unable to prevent her fingers from trembling she spilt the tepid liquid onto the table. A waitress hurried over and asked if she would like a fresh pot and Ameesha gratefully accepted. She saw that in his fury her father had inadvertently thrown down notes of far too large a denomination. She quietly collected them up and placed them in the pocket of her dress.

She would tip the waitress well, but not that well.

*

Ziyad walked at a fast pace back to the shop and, as soon as the door smashed open against the window cabinet, Aloka knew that the reconciliation had not gone well. He fretted as Ziyad turned his ire towards the inside of the safe, rummaging around in the drawers and boxes. Did this black mood mean that his own future at the shop was in jeopardy? Aloka knew better than to try to ask any questions of his employer when he was in such a state.

Ziyad was noisily banging around in the backroom. Aloka took a quick look and could see that the safe was open and the contents was being rummaged through. The side table was untidily littered with trays, small envelopes that held individual gems and private papers, some slipping from the surface and scattering onto the floor.

Aloka need have no qualms about his future. Ziyad had made up his mind that his assistant, correction, new manager was to take up his role forthwith. He was almost blind with fury at the affrontery of his daughter.

No daughter should speak to their father in such a manner on such a sensitive subject.

He threw the last few wads of low denomination notes, tied in bundles, into a battered leather briefcase and afterwards he started to empty trays of gems in, the loose stones tumbling to the bottom of the bag. His anger was overwhelming him. Aloka knew better than to timidly enquired if there was anything he could do, because Ziyad would only yell at him to get out and slam the door in his face. Quietly, Aloka pulled the door closed and left his employer to cool off in his own time.

It was in the solitude of the room that Ziyad felt his anger slowly subside. It was replaced by a renewed sense of loss that flooded through him. The grief resurfaced and Aloka heard a gentle sob that built in intensity until there was no disguising the abject distress that had consumed his employer. In deference to his master's feelings, Aloka turned the sign on the door to closed, quietly slipped out into the street and locked the door behind him.

He covered the distance back to the coffee shop in not much longer than Ziyad had on his return. Through the plate glass window he saw Ameesha still sitting calmly drinking her coffee as if nothing had happened. He went into the café and sat down where Ziyad had previously been seated. Ameesha made no attempt to acknowledge his presence and the pair sat in silence. Aloka was patient, knowing that eventually Ameesha would speak, but it had to be in her own time. Although she was outwardly serene, inside her mind was in turmoil. She had not intended to blurt out the fact that she and her mother knew about his mistress, Eleni. She had not wanted to end the conversation with a scene, or with her father storming out of the coffee shop. That was the last thing she had wanted but she just could not help herself. She was hurt at his exclusion of her. Did he not recognise her grief? He had just cut himself off, retreated into that study of his, buried himself in his work, spoke to no one save for his advisors while drowning himself in a sea of malt whisky.

The whole plan had proved a disaster and as far as she could see, she had blown her chances of convincing her father that she was the natural successor as his business protégé.

Initially Ameesha did not acknowledge the presence of Aloka. He sat quietly and watched. There remained a dispassionate expression on her face, her mouth set in a hard line, her eyes dry and clear. No tears in evidence. Eventually she spoke.

"What are you doing here?" Ameesha did not make eye contact with Aloka as she spoke, "Shouldn't you be in the shop?"

"Your father is there, and it is better that I keep out of the way." Aloka was apprehensive at what had passed between father and daughter, "You know what it's like." Ameesha nodded, only too aware of the wisdom in not being around when Ziyad was in one of his tempers. And when he had left her, he was in a mighty temper.

"What did you say to provoke him?" Aloka asked.

"Don't worry, your little secret is still safe with me."

Aloka let out an instinctive sigh of relief and then checked himself to regain his composure, but it was too late. Ameesha noted the reaction with satisfaction.

"Okay," Aloka said in a matter-of-fact manner, "So what drove him into such a rage?" Aloka felt a huge weight lifted from his shoulders.

"I told him that we, Mama and I, knew about his trip to London with Eleni." Ameesha had not moved since Aloka had joined her, but she stretched and sat upright in her chair as if awaking from a deep sleep or having reached a momentous decision. Aloka's anxiety returned as he knew that he had disclosed the proposed trip to London. The identity of Eleni as Ziyad's mistress was old news, but again he was the culprit.

"What's he doing now?" Ameesha asked.

"Clearing the safe, or that's what it looked like. What shall we do?"

Ameesha thought for a moment, "Nothing. Let's let him cool down and then you and I will return to the shop."

"Is that a good idea. I mean, for you and me to be seen together?"

"Perhaps I can use your return to my advantage. Bringing back the absentee employee, that sort of thing." She smiled sweetly at Aloka and he noticed that there was such a resemblance to Thinuka that he felt his heart miss a beat while his soul was crushed at the prospect of never seeing him again.

"I'm not sure that I want to be a pawn in your game."

"If you want me to remain silent as to your, what shall we call it, friendship with my brother then you will do as I say." She fixed him with her cold hard eyes, "I would not want to be in your shoes if my father, or for that matter, the police found out about you and Thinuka. Don't forget that what you two did is still illegal in Sri Lanka."

Aloka shuddered at the prospect of being incarcerated and persecuted merely for his love of her brother, even though Thinuka considered it a dalliance. Thinuka was dead and he was the sole remaining guilty party of the relationship.

It was a sullen Aloka who accompanied Ameesha back to the shop. She marched ahead of him, and he followed dutifully two paces behind. She had a long stride and he had to skip now and again to keep up with her.

The closed sign was still in the window and the front door remained locked. Aloka put his hands up to the glass and placed his face against them to shade the glare. Inside there was a figure moving around the back room. Aloka took his keys from his pocket and unlocked the door. Ameesha indicated that he should precede her. He was not sure if that was because she was fearful of her father's reaction to her reappearance, or if it was part of the charade of returning the errant assistant to his place of work.

They had covered half of the depth of the front shop when Ziyad appeared in the doorway to the back room. He looked from Aloka to Ameesha and then back to Aloka before he shouted at Ameesha,

"Out! Out now!"

"But Baba…"

"Don't Baba me. You have disrespected your father. In my book, that is unacceptable…unforgiveable. Get out of my sight!" Ziyad pointed his finger towards the entrance and glared murderously at his daughter. Ameesha tried one more plea but was met with the same ultimatum that she must leave. Suppressing a sniffle and a slight sob, she turned and sloped out of the shop, looking back just once to see if her tears of remorse were warming her father's frozen heart. They had no impact as Ziyad told Aloka to lock the door behind her and come into the back room.

Ziyad took a few deep breaths before addressing his employee.

"Aloka, you've been loyal to me for many years and, as you know, I'm due to fly to London on business in a few days." Ziyad had regained some of his equanimity and even showed a degree of warmth towards his young assistant by placing a paternalistic hand on his shoulder and giving him a pat. "You've done well since I gave you greater responsibility and I think you have earned the next stage of the proposed transfer of the management of my shop to you."

Aloka stood more erect, and a look of self-importance spread across his face. He started to make appreciative noises until Ziyad continued with his instructions.

"I have cleared the safe of my personal effects, and I have left you with sufficient cash for you to buy and sell as you see fit." He turned and took a box out of his briefcase and handed it to Aloka who looked in amazement at the package. "You need to be able to contact me and so you are to have this mobile telephone for that purpose."

"Thank you, Mr Al-Quadi." He hastily opened the box and took out the black screened telephone and turned it on.

"I have pre-set my number into the contacts so it is easy for you to use it at any time should you need to do so." Ziyad made sure that Aloka had understood what he had said and then continued by handing him the keys to the safe. "You know what these are. You must guard them with your life. You now have responsibility for everything in this shop. I have an inventory of what is here, and I expect you to increase that inventory and provide a profit by the time I return."

Aloka placed his hands together and bowed formally to Ziyad, uttering words of assurance and appreciation at the same time. Ziyad nodded an acknowledgement of his new manager's gratitude and bent down to pull the sides of the briefcase together. It was not easy but eventually he slid the catch into place for it to click shut. As he lifted it Aloka noted that it was obviously heavy.

Ziyad passed him in the doorway and Aloka went to open the front door for him.

"Where are you going?"

Aloka looked surprised, "To open the door for you."

Ziyad turned and stood looking into the room they had just vacated, and more particularly at the safe with its door wide open. Aloka immediately realised his error and rushed back to close and lock the steel door.

"I hope I have not made my second error of the day?" Ziyad stared at Aloka and Aloka assured him that it would never happen again.

"I hope not." He turned back towards the door and waited, adding, "Now you can open the door for me."

After his employer had left, Aloka walked around the shop relishing the freedom that he was experiencing as the master of his new domain. His sense of proprietorship was swiftly deflated when Ameesha reappeared a few minutes after her father had left. She had been watching for Ziyad's departure.

She sashayed into the shop and stood opposite Aloka with her hands held out in front of her, her body leaning slightly towards him.

"Keys, please."

Chapter 19

It was hot as Ziyad strode his way up Kandy's main street towards the hotel where, so he had been informed by one of the drivers on his payroll, that Thinuka had been seen, and the Englishman had briefly stayed. He doubted that there was anything new to be learnt from going there but something nagged at him suggesting that a quick visit would do no harm. He had already discovered from the media reports the name of the Kithul Hotel, near Nagombo, where the Englishman and his 'Consultant Herbologist' had held their gala dinner. Stephen Silchester's departure the following morning had been another media scrum, but the man they called Randul had not been in evidence. Ziyad had repeatedly watched the many TV reports, but in none of them could he see the young Veddah.

As he puffed his way along the street and entered the central square, he regretted having brought the weighty briefcase with him. Thinuka's Mercedes, now belonging to Ameesha, was still parked in the same slot as it had been when he and his daughter passed on their way to the coffee shop.

Was that only an hour or so ago?

He was still fuming at his daughter's disgraceful behaviour although the initial shock at the disclosure that all his family, presumably including Thinuka, knew about Eleni had dissipated. When he thought about it rationally, it was clear that the relationship between him and Honey had cooled over the past few years, the same years that he had spent wooing and bedding the delicious Eleni. After the birth of Ameesha, Honey had shown no great desire to satisfy his physical needs and his pride would not permit him to beg for her sexual favours. As her husband, he knew that he had the right to force himself upon her but some respect for her remained in his heart and he could not bring himself to use violence in order to exercise his connubial rights. Besides, it was not difficult to find a substitute for such simple pleasures and

Eleni had fulfilled the role perfectly. He ensured that his wife was well cared for, but he was aware that she would not miss him very much in her bed.

The heat and exertion from carrying the heavy briefcase sapped his strength and he arrived at the entrance to the hotel red faced with his clothes sticking to his back with sweat. He was unused to taking any form of exercise, let alone in the hot morning sun. The doorman opened the door for him, and Ziyad stumbled into the cool of the foyer. He put down the bag and straightened his attire as best he could.

No longer the scruffy down at heel shopkeeper, he blended with the surrounding clientele who gave him but a passing look, some sympathising with his suffering at the heat of the day.

Ziyad approached the reception desk and after a brief, fruitless exchange with the receptionist was about to depart when he vaguely recognised the assistant manager. He was talking to an elderly gentleman at a table across the expansive foyer. The conversation terminated with the assistant manager shaking the hand of the other man and laughing as he departed. He strode towards Ziyad and gave a brief nod of recognition without being able to put a name to the man with the eye-patch. Ziyad stepped forward and greeted him like an old friend, but also struggling to find a name.

"Good morning, how are you?" Ziyad cheerily enquired.

The assistant manager smiled a welcome and, as he had been trained, bowed with his palms together in front of his chest and replied,

"Ayubowan."

He had seen this unfortunate man in town on several occasions as his face was instantly recognisable. But there was something different, not right, about him that made his usual gift for putting names to faces, even faces as recognisable as the one before him, fail him.

Ziyad quickly returned the formality and then tried to give credence to his presence,

"I am trying to find a young friend of mine who I think was in your hotel a few days ago."

The assistant manager immediately adopted an expression of apology before he stated the company policy on confidentiality. Just as he was about to speak the image from the newspaper report on the tragic death of the young man flashed across his mind and he recognised where he had seen the man. He immediately adapted his look to one of sympathy.

"You are the father of the young man who died recently. I am so sorry for your loss. On behalf of the hotel and its staff may I extend to you our sincere condolences?"

"Thank you. You are very kind," Ziyad mumbled.

Ziyad was taken aback by the fact that he had been so easily recognised and looked around the foyer to see if others had also worked out who he was. There was no attention being paid to either of them. His briefcase weighed heavily in his clenched fist and Ziyad felt a strong desire to complete his business here as swiftly as possible.

The assistant manager continued in an attempt to be of some help to the unfortunate man.

"My staff reported to me that your son was here the day of the accident. In fact, I had occasion to speak to him." The assistant manager saw no reason to elaborate to a grieving father on his argument with Thinuka.

"You spoke to him?"

"Yes, he was asking similar questions to your own and I was unable to assist him, as I am unable to assist you. I am sure you understand."

The assistant manager was feeling increasingly uncomfortable. He looked around in the hope of finding something that required his urgent attention.

"He left shortly after we spoke. He seemed to be in some haste."

"Do you know where he was in such a hurry to go?" Ziyad enquired.

"I am afraid not. Again, my condolences on your loss."

*

Ziyad walked across the square and wondered why Thinuka was in such a hurry. Had he seen the Veddah and was he following him? The blue Mercedes was still parked in its same spot. The bag seemed to weigh a ton and he tugged at the door handle that did not yield. He impatiently lowered the bag onto the dusty street, which provided some relief to his aching shoulders. He pulled out the spare key fob that he carried with him ever since Thinuka's disappearance and manually unlock the front passenger door before slinging his briefcase into the footwell. He opened it and retrieved a dog-eared notebook from inside, walked around the car, climbed into the driving seat and slammed the car door shut.

Ziyad sat and gathered his thoughts while looking out of the windscreen in the direction of his shop. He wondered what was happening inside, in the certainty that Ameesha would have returned to try to bully poor Aloka. He hoped that the boy would stand up to his daughter but suspected that she was too wilful for him to resist her demands.

However, what was in the forefront of Ziyad's mind was the whereabouts of Randul. While initially his priority had been the source of the Padparadscha sapphires, now it was to discover what involvement he – and the Englishman – had in the death of Thinuka. He knew that his son had left his shop that fateful morning on a mission for him. From the comments made by the assistant manager at the hotel, Thinuka had been there and had left after the departure of both the Veddah and Silchester. Did he know that the Englishman and this Randul scum were working together? This had become a burning issue for Ziyad, beyond ownership of the Padparadscha.

The Silchester man was undoubtedly the bumbling tourist who had interrupted at a crucial point the meeting he was having with Randul. The Veddah, in turn, had disappeared as soon as the diversion gave him the opportunity. That was no coincidence. Ziyad realised that he had sent a boy on a man's errand. He had badly underestimated the skulduggery that his nemesis was capable of and regretted it every time he thought of his dead son.

Now it was time for him to finish what he had set in motion.

There were three objectives. Firstly, he wanted to know what the real cause of his son's death was. Secondly, Ziyad wanted revenge, and thirdly he aspired to being the owner of a beautiful, unique Padparadscha. He suspected that this Randul man was the link between all three. He had run, which implied guilt. He was frightened, and he did not know how to dispose of his most precious stone, or stones, without raising questions with the authorities. Ziyad was working on a solution that would satisfy him, but not them both. This time everything was to be on his terms.

Ziyad flipped through the pages of his notebook as the engine idled quietly. He found the hastily scribbled note that he had taken on hearing the report on the local TV news about the hotel where Stephen and Randul had prepared the gala dinner. He snapped it shut and threw it onto the passenger seat.

As he pulled out of the parking space, Ameesha entered the square and saw her Mercedes slide into the traffic and disappear down the Colombo Road. She knew that it had not been stolen, the profile of the driver was unmistakeable. She stamped her foot in frustration and flailed her arms as she shouted down the street – but all to no avail.

Even if Ziyad had heard her, he would not have stopped.

*

The young receptionist behind the desk at The Kithul Hotel smiled sweetly at Ziyad and asked if she could be of any assistance. Ziyad had prepared his cover story as he had driven to the hotel.

"Well, yes I hope you can." He placed the briefcase between his feet for safe keeping. "I represent a newspaper that wishes to do a feature on the young Sri Lankan Herbologist who was here at the dinner the other evening. I saw him on the local television news report. You probably met him. The one who worked with the English chef, ...er, ...Stephen Silchester." The girl cautiously regarded the reporter with the eye-patch and crinkled facial skin. He did not look like a reporter.

"I think his name was Randul?" Ziyad used what he hoped was his most obsequious expression. "Unfortunately, he left before we could contact him, and I wondered if you knew where I could get in touch with him. Do you have his address or telephone number?"

The girl clearly remembered Randul but said that she did not know where he lived. If it would help, she could ring the manager to see if he knew? Ziyad thanked her profusely and followed up by assuring her that the hotel would be favourably mentioned for supporting an indigenous local who was trying to succeed in life. The girl turned round and picked up the telephone on the desk behind her. She spoke briefly and then returned her attention to Ziyad.

"If you would care to take a seat in the foyer, Mr Amal will be right out. Can I get you a coffee?"

Ziyad smiled and accepted her offer. She returned to the telephone and requested a tray of coffee. A waiter at a serving station to one side of the foyer replaced his handset and looked across to the receptionist. He gave her a knowing wink. She blushed and lowered her face to studiously attend to the papers on her desk.

It was only a short wait until a tall, distinguished, moustachioed man in a dark suit, white shirt with a red tie and shiny shoes strode up to where Ziyad was seated.

"I am Mr Amal, the manager. I understand that you are seeking Mr Ranatunga?"

Ziyad looked confused at the surname, "No, I am seeking the young man called Randul who was here with the English chef...Mr Silchester?"

The manager nodded, "Yes, Mr Randul Ranatunga. That is his name."

Ziyad laughed at his error, "I'm sorry, I thought you were referring to The Lions cricket captain."

"Yes, an easy mistake." Mr Amal laughed along with Ziyad, "He does bear the same name, but I do not think that he is related, or as talented in that particular direction."

Ziyad was developing a crick in his neck constantly looking up at the manager and rose from his seat, his briefcase remaining at his feet.

"My receptionist said that you represented a newspaper?" Mr Amal was always open to free publicity but was simultaneously chary, wanting to ensure that it was the right kind of publicity.

"What is the publication you represent?" He had already surveyed the Arabic looking man seated in his foyer before he came and introduced himself to Ziyad. He did not think he looked like a journalist either, but they came in all shapes and sizes nowadays. The eye-patch made him look more like a pirate, but his clothes were well cut and obviously not cheap.

"The Khaleej Times," Ziyad replied without hesitation. Amal looked enquiringly at Ziyad, not immediately recognising the name of the paper.

"It's a Dubai publication," Ziyad explained smoothly, "and has a global, as well as a UAE, readership. We cover financial affairs, and it is directed particularly at the HNW readership."

"HNW?" Amal was struggling with the foreign acronym.

"Sorry, High Net Worth…HNW. We have a large readership of very wealthy people who have global business and leisure interests. Obviously, the introduction to the world of this chef here at The Kithul will be an important element of my piece."

Mr Amal was hooked on the potential of a global exposure for his hotel and so felt that the risk was worth taking. He started on his usual promotional pitch and Ziyad, consistent with his adopted persona, took his notebook from his bag. Mr Amal clicked his fingers for a waiter to attend to their needs and the overdue tray of coffee appeared instantly.

It took Ziyad forty minutes to elicit the small piece of information that he had really come for, Mr Amal describing in excruciating detail all the benefits of the hotel and its strong support for local talent. Throughout, Ziyad had to listen politely before Amal paused and Ziyad took advantage of the lull in his dialogue to thank him for the very useful background information. As he rose to leave, he promised an anxious Mr Amal that he would let him see his article just as soon as he had sent it to his editor.

He would be waiting a long time, Ziyad thought, as he pushed his way through the rotating doors onto the street outside.

He read the scrawled address and, although he knew roughly where he was going, he put the details into the Mercedes' Satnav. The destination flag appeared to be in the middle of the Sinharaja Forest and another piece of the jigsaw slotted into place.

Chapter 20

"Mr. Ranatunga? You are not an easy man to find."

Randul looked thunderstruck at Ziyad standing impassively in front of him on his veranda. The Arab had parked his car out of sight a little further back along the track that led to the bungalow. He wanted his visit to have an element of surprise and he seemed to have succeeded spectacularly.

Randul was rattled and at an immediate disadvantage. He stepped back and tightly held the door, ready to slam it shut. Was this man here to seek revenge for the death of his son? Did he know that Randul had led him into the forest where he fell to his death? What else did he know? Randul was uncertain what to do except to stall for time.

Ziyad calmly and politely, overly politely, to the point of intimidation, continued on a completely unexpected course.

"I would like to make you a proposition. A partnership, if you like." Ziyad watched for any reaction, but Randul was still trying to get a grip on what was happening. He looked over Ziyad's shoulder to check if there was anyone with him and was relieved to see that he was alone.

"My name is Ziyad Al-Quadi, and I now know you to be Mr Randul Ranatunga. Are you any relation to the cricketer?" Ziyad was relaxed and sounded genuinely interested in Randul's answer.

Randul shook his head to confirm that there was no relationship and Ziyad pressed on.

"Ah well, no matter. Now, first, let us discuss your gems." Randul tensed in the entrance, giving no response and still ready to slam the door shut. Ziyad took a step forward and Randul re-tightened his grip on the door until his knuckles where white.

"Is there any possibility that I could have a cup of coffee or a glass of water?"

Randul gathered his wits about him and, blocking the entrance with his body, indicated that Ziyad should take a seat at the table on the veranda,

"Sit there and I'll get one."

Ziyad made no effort to move. He had already taken a scout around the building and had no intention of letting Randul slip out of the back of the property. His cold eye held Randul and, lowering the pitch of his voice he added,

"Then, perhaps we should discuss my son's disappearance, and his death."

Randul flinched and felt a frisson of fear as he involuntarily moved away from the advancing figure. Ziyad placed his false foot between the door and frame and then gently pushed a compliant Randul into the bungalow. Both men moved in unison like ballroom dancers, until Randul broke away. With shaking hands, he filled a glass of water for his unwelcome visitor. Ziyad looked around the open plan space with feigned interest.

"Charming. It is extraordinary how a simple hovel can be made homely."

Ziyad continued to appraise the room. He wanted to ascertain whether there was any obvious site for a safe or other form of secure storage. He had already surmised from earlier encounters with the tribesman that he was not stupid, so it stood to reason that he would keep such valuable gemstones somewhere safe and away from prying eyes.

Ziyad became surreally business-like, without any sense of the earlier menace or reference to his son. He spent the next few minutes explaining to Randul that, as a certified dealer, he was able to work with Randul in authenticating his exciting finds from his illegal gemming activities. He, Ziyad, would be able then to sell them on the open market as being fully certified. He explained that by using his contacts outside of the confines of Sri Lanka they (Ziyad was at pains to use an inclusive pronoun) could obtain a much higher price for each one. The proceeds they could then split.

Starting with a 75:25 share in Ziyad's favour was ambitious, he knew, but he had to start the negotiations somewhere. The wily dealer was not at all surprised to find that Randul was more than able to hold his own in any negotiation. In fact, Randul proved to be adept, if not a natural, and Ziyad continued to develop a disarming respect for the young Veddah. He was no country hick, and it might transpire that a longer-term working relationship between the two of them could prove to be good for both parties. Thinuka had obviously underestimated his quarry, a mistake that Ziyad was not going to repeat.

Randul felt no reciprocation of respect for Ziyad. He treated him with the utmost distrust. He listened and seemingly went along with the proposals merely to give himself time to find an alternative strategy. No ideas were forthcoming, and he resorted to just trying to get Ziyad to depart with an impression that Randul would be cooperative.

That was not going to happen.

Randul handed Ziyad his water and walked out to the veranda to sit at the small table. He needed fresh air and wanted to get the Arab out of his house.

Ziyad followed.

To the casual observer, the two men on the veranda were friends having a chat and a drink together. But for the whole time that Ziyad was talking Randul's mind was racing trying to find some way of extricating himself from what he was sure was a dangerous situation. Ziyad was persuasive in an authoritarian manner. At this point of the visit, he had only one real objective and that was to take control of the gems that Randul already had in his possession, and then any that he might find in the future. What had been an amusing pastime for Randul during moments of relaxation was evolving into an unpleasant commitment to this rapacious Arab. Randul was only too aware that once he was in the clutches of this man, he would be beholden to him forever and the demands made of him would become ever more extreme.

Throughout the conversation, Ziyad kept obliquely referring to the penalties for illegal gemming and the effects that it had on those who were found guilty. The blackmail was hardly subtle, but effective, nonetheless. Randul had no desire to get the wrong side of the law. Life had been so simple, not to say charmed, before he had found the Padparadscha sapphires. Now they hung like small, glistening millstones around his neck.

Too impossibly beautiful, too impossibly valuable, and yet, too impossibly destructive.

While Randul did not consider himself to be a greedy person, the lure of the potential riches that his gems could provide was increasingly difficult to resist. All dreams of travelling and foraging in different lands, to seeing places that he had only read about in books or seen in photographs at college would be within his grasp. To make those dreams a reality did not include being dependent upon the man who sat before him. But the chances of a lowly Veddah guide in the Sinharaja Forest being able to legitimately sell his extraordinary find was merely going to force him into the clutches of another dealer, another dishonest man, another crook who only had his own interests at heart.

Alternatively, to declare the stones to the authorities would certainly end in some form of detention and a criminal record. Perhaps he would be better off to ignore them and leave them in the cavity under his kitchen floor for someone else to find.

But it was impossible to ignore them.

Randul weighed up his swiftly formulated alternatives, hardly listening to Ziyad who continued to argue his case.

"The issue is, my friend, whether I can be confident your gems come from a location that is unregistered or if they come from someone else's holding. If that is the case, then the task is far more difficult." Ziyad had not touched his water. He was finding it difficult to maintain the attention of Randul, who seemed to be far away from the topic under discussion.

"It would be helpful if you could show me on a map where you pan for the stones?" The question hung in the air, Randul apparently still not listening.

"Boy?" Ziyad snapped and then reverted to a softer tone. "Randul, are you with me?"

Ziyad was becoming increasingly impatient and irritable. What was it with the younger generation? They lacked the basic manners that were forcefully instilled into him from an early age by his father. It was the same with Thinuka, and now Ameesha.

Randul returned his attention to Ziyad without banishing his incomplete plans.

"Yes. Yes, I heard you." For Randul, it was a watershed moment, but he needed a respite to be sure that his decision was the right one.

It was. Surely?

Would the spell of the Padparadscha retain its magic?

"Forget the map," Randul said with undisguised resignation. "I can do better than that," Randul suddenly stood up. "Why don't I show you where I find them?"

While Randul had no intention on revealing the location of his finds, the prospect of leading Ziyad, as he had led Thinuka, into the forest had a certain symmetry to it. But would the father let his desperation to discover the source of the gems overcome his natural distrust of the Veddah who was a native to the forests, while Ziyad was not?

Ziyad sat back in his chair to consider the proposal. He was not to be made a fool of and his suspicions remained that Randul had had something to do with Thinuka's disappearance in the forest, if not his death. However, the lure of the source of the raw Padparadscha gems was stronger than his sense of self preservation. He looked Randul up and down, re-assessing him for his strength and ability to overpower Ziyad. He was younger and of a slimmer build than Ziyad, but Randul had not had the combat experience that had dominated the formative years of Ziyad's manhood. The balance between untold riches and personal injury was weighed up and then dismissed. It was a risk, but it was also a risk for the younger man. He did not know whether Ziyad was still out for revenge over the death of his son. In fact, if it transpired that his suspicions were true, then Randul had every reason to fear for his life.

Of course, he might have reason to fear for his life anyway…but Ziyad would review that option later.

*

The trek into the forest was far more arduous than Ziyad had expected. They had walked hard for two hours, and he was not dressed for the terrain. His leg ached and the insects buzzed around his face, biting whenever and wherever the opportunity arose. He was hot and thirsty, but worst of all, he was lost. Randul had led at a punishing pace and Ziyad was beginning to wonder if the balance of risk was gradually tipping in favour of the Veddah.

Was this how it had been for Thinuka?

The only difference was that Ziyad was prepared. Thinuka had let his enthusiasm get the better of his caution. He had assumed that the man in front of him was incapable of subterfuge. Ziyad had no such preconceptions. On their way out they had passed the Mercedes and Ziyad had made sure it was locked and his bag was out of sight through the darkened glass of the windows. It was unlikely that anyone would pass the remote little building and if they did, he doubted that they would bother to break into the car. He knew he was being overly cautious, but that was what had kept him alive this long.

Under the pretence of his diligent security measures, Ziyad had taken the opportunity to remove from the glove box the can of mace spray that he insisted Ameesha carried with her wherever she went. Not that any callow youth would ever try to take advantage of his daughter, she was far to feisty for most of them.

His jacket was dirty and damp from the humidity and his sweat had soaked through his shirt that now clung to his body. A ragged hole was visible in his trousers and Ziyad was becoming increasingly exasperated.

"How much further, boy?" He puffed, short of breath and patience.

Randul stopped, breathing calmly, his fitness showing over that of Ziyad. He had purposely kept a good distance between himself and the Arab during the walk. The fast pace had been maintained to assess the fitness of the older man. He could see the effect on Ziyad as he stumbled once again on the rough terrain.

"It's not much further, then we can take a break." Randul added a decisive lure, "You will then know where I find my gems."

Randul pushed on up a steep incline and Ziyad, swearing in his native tongue, grabbed a fern to stabilise himself for the climb. His leg was killing him, and he had to resort to going onto his hands and knees to make it to the top. He was regretting his rash decision to accept Randul's invitation to see where the stones came from. Scrambling up the last few feet, he collapsed at the summit of the slope, his breathing wheezing and laboured, his head bent forward from his exertions and his focus on the plate of hard rock on which he knelt.

When he looked up, Randul had disappeared.

The forest was empty and the only sound he could hear was the air rasping in and out of his lungs. He called out and there was no response save for the natural sounds of the forest. He pulled himself upright to get a better look at his surroundings, but he could see no evidence that indicated that Randul had merely continued on ahead.

Ziyad rummaged in his pocket for his mobile 'phone.

No signal.

He looked back down the slope intending to retrace his steps. As he had followed the path trodden by Randul, he had had the foresight to snap stems or scuff the earth in anticipation of just such an eventuality. Now, by his actions, Ziyad was satisfied that Randul had as good as confessed to being implicated, if not being the primary cause, of Thinuka's death.

He could feel the anger rise in his heaving chest and a growl rose in his throat to a shriek of fury directed towards Randul. His fists were clenched by his side, the muscles in his neck tightly bunched and he shook with rage. He took a huge breath and yelled in frustration at the trees and vegetation that surrounded him, that enveloped him. Once his long, hoarse cry dissipated into the heart of the forest, he turned and slowly slid down the incline to follow his markers back to the car. With each painful step he plotted his revenge against Randul, a revenge that would rely upon skills that he had acquired in an earlier life but had had no reason to use for many years. Such skills are never forgotten.

Ziyad rescinded all prior assurances.

No partnership.

No forbearance.

No mercy.

Meanwhile, Randul sat silently behind the broad trunk of a tree some fifty yards from the bellowing Ziyad. The carpet of rain sodden leaves had deadened his footsteps as he had made his break. He saw Ziyad stumble and then mount the crest of the hillock on all fours. Randul knew this mound, it being the start of the climb to the top of the cliff from which Thinuka had fallen.

Randul watched as Ziyad slowly and cautiously slithered his way back down the slope and out of sight. The path back to Randul's house would not have been difficult to follow if Ziyad's rather obvious markers had remained undisturbed. The fact that Randul had supplemented some of these with his own meant that Randul knew he could outpace the older man, thereby giving him enough time to vacate the bungalow before Ziyad eventually found his way back.

It was clear that the Arab was not a man to be trifled with and for that reason alone Randul knew that he would have to disappear for a while. The North seemed the best solution, despite the fact that it was a rebel stronghold and therefore fraught with danger. It had never been his intention to run but he saw no alternative. He needed time to think and once the dust had settled, he might then be able to quietly return.

There was a noise of movement in the distance and Randul continued to skirt in a wide loop around the path that Ziyad was attempting to follow. Randul's confidence that his alternative clues on the route would confuse Ziyad into taking some wrong turnings was proven. Once in unfamiliar surroundings, hopefully the Arab would be criss-crossing the forest for some hours.

Randul sure-footedly followed his own separate route and saw the familiar outcrop of rock that he knew as the 'Monkey's Head', so named because of its distinctive shape. He went to the far side of the skull where there was a small hole forming a mouth to the skull into which his hand would just fit. Once in, the hollow opened out to form a slightly larger chamber. He pushed his arm in as far as it would go. His fingers searched around in the soft, damp floor and touched the far wall. He recoiled when something ran across the back of his hand but continued to feel around until he found what he was searching for and grasped it. Gradually extracting his arm, his clenched fist jammed on the tunnel of rock. As swiftly as he could, he manipulated the awkward shape until it was lengthways in the shaft. The entrance was still too narrow for him to extract his hand while holding the package, so he lay it on its side and using his thumb and forefinger eased the bundle out.

He hesitated and questioned if this part of his plan was wise, before reluctantly stowing the retrieved parcel into his backpack. Randul turned and took up a loping trot through the undergrowth, watching the forest floor to ensure that each footstep landed silently on the leaf litter, avoiding any sticks that might alert Ziyad as to his position. As he ran, Randul planned the packing of his possessions from the bungalow. He was as certain as he could be that the man who offered to form a partnership with him had no intention of allowing that partnership to last beyond the point at which he discovered the location of the rock pools.

It took Randul no more than forty minutes to reach his home. He approached with caution just in case, by some miracle, Ziyad had managed to get there first. It was exceedingly unlikely as the Arab had been limping and moving slowly when

Randul had left him. Even without the misdirection, Randul estimated that he was going to take a couple of hours to retrace his steps.

But Randul should have known that it was unwise to underestimate his adversary.

The first task upon his arrival back at the bungalow was to go to his laboratory and collect as many of his journals as he could reasonably carry. The remainder of the journals and the last vestiges of his various ingredients would have to remain for his return. He knew that if he had at least a few of his journals, then he could replicate his experiments wherever he eventually found himself.

Slipping into the bungalow through the back door, Randul crouched in the shadows, listening. When he was satisfied that the building was empty, he unpacked the contents of his daypack onto the table and swapped it for a larger, more robust rucksack. Packing his immediate needs took no time at all and with the journals safely stowed, he turned his attention to the void beneath the kitchen floor. Carefully he started to withdraw the various pouches and place them on the boards beside him for packing into the rucksack.

*

Ziyad slid down yet another incline and attempted to maintain a steady pace even though his stump below his calf was blistered and bleeding. Anger and adrenaline drove him on. Neither blisters nor pain were going to distract him from his target. Twice he had been diverted by the boy's attempts to deceive him and he had wasted time as he retraced his steps. His adversary had miscalculated Ziyad's tenacity, a tenacity that was honed by forced marches through harsh terrain as a young militiaman. Yes, he was out of practice and yes, he was out of shape. But his single-minded determination to teach Randul a lesson he would never forget was all the motivation he needed to set aside the discomforts that were assailing him. In fact, he was gratified that after so many dormant years he had retained many of the techniques drilled into him during his youth. He covered the ground relatively well, gritting his teeth against the pain, moving on, whatever the cost.

At last, he recognised a path as one running close to the bungalow. Ziyad followed it until he was sure that he was near the house before deviating off. He was unarmed and had no wish to make any signal of his advance on the front of the building. He regretted that Thinuka had taken his pistol from the safe, he could do with it now.

What continued to worry him was the fact that still he did not know where the gun was. Had the police found it near Thinuka's body? They made no mention of it when they came to inform him of his son's death, or even when they handed over the body for a swift burial. No suspicious circumstances, a tragic accident, no reason to create reams of paperwork. An open and shut incident.

Open and shut indeed.

The silhouette of the Mercedes was just visible through the gloom of early evening. Ziyad was reliant on the fact that Randul had misjudged the strength and resilience of an old soldier. He might have outsmarted a naïve Thinuka, but Ziyad was an enemy of a very different kind.

A much crueller, more dangerous enemy.

Ziyad guessed that Randul was preparing to escape, flee to another part of the island, lie low for a few weeks; as only a Veddah can being nomadic and expertly self-reliant. The savage could survive on his wits in the wilderness of Sri Lanka without any need of support from others. As he crept through the undergrowth towards the Mercedes his thoughts were dark and menacing. Not since his military days had he felt such a flow of adrenalin into his guts, heightening his senses and tensing his muscles. There was no question of flight, this was an outright fight for vengeance.

He quietly opened the boot of the car and swore as the light shone out illuminating his surroundings with an eerie glow. The small bulb shattered as Ziyad hit it with a clenched fist. He looked around into the heavy dusk, fearful that it had been seen by anyone, including in the bungalow close by. The pain from slivers of glass lacerating the taught skin of his knuckles was dismissed as collateral damage.

He wiped off as much as he could onto the leg of his trousers and returned to the task of finding some sort of a weapon. All that was available to him was a heavy tyre brace.

Ziyad shut the boot lid with care, the click as it closed sounding to him like a gunshot in the silent forest. He remained crouched by the car until his good eye accustomed itself to the sudden dark. He needed to see clearly as he approached the bungalow.

Stealthily he crept across open ground until he had some cover behind a lone tree that stood in front of the building. He was relieved to see that there was a dull light on inside and he tightened his grip on the cold metal in his hand.

The steps to the veranda creaked softly as Ziyad stepped up to the front door. It was ajar and he could hear movement inside. He stretched out his hand and gently pushed the door. It swung smoothly open, the hinges well oiled, to slowly reveal the interior of the room. The light spilled out across the veranda until the door bumped softly against something that lay within its arc of travel.

Randul was on his knees, his shoulder close to the floorboards as he felt round in the underfloor void for the last pouch. The others lay on the floor by his side.

Framed in the entrance, Ziyad eyed them covetously.

Randul whirled round and in his haste to free himself felt the rough wood scrape across the flesh of his arm. He jumped to his feet and the two men stood watching each other. Randul unintentionally glanced across to the table and the wrapped object that lay well out of reach. Ziyad followed his line of sight and his eye lit upon the roughly covered package. The oily cloth alone was enough to tell him that it was a pistol.

Thinuka's pistol.

His pistol.

Before Randul could move, Ziyad was already at the table, the tyre wrench held at a threatening angle, his knuckles smeared with a thin sheen of blood. The

Arab's jaw was clenched tight, the muscles bunched tightly, his single eye blazing with rage. He flicked open the oiled cloth to confirm what he already knew.

Ziyad did not speak, could not speak. The blood thumped in his ears, overwhelming what little noise there was in the room. He knew what he was going to do without any thought for the consequences of his actions. Randul stood like a statue, unable to move, unable to think. Ziyad had passed beyond rational thought and the hunted recognised the bloodlust in the eye of the hunter. Ziyad used the time to settle his breathing into a deeper, more regular pattern, and a strange calmness prevailed as he looked at the youth before him. He had killed before and he would again. He had no compunction whatsoever over the fate of this vermin.

Randul was terrified. He had never seen a man with such murderous intent. The adrenalin that was pumping around his own veins screamed for him to run, escape, get as far away from this madman as he could, as quickly as he could. His voice pleaded with a tremor that he could not disguise.

"You've got to believe me; I didn't kill him. He fell, I swear. I admit that I did find his body, and the gun and, yes, I took it. Why, I really don't know…" The words tumbled out of his mouth and then faded into a whisper until he fell silent. There was nothing more to say. Randul knew what the truth was, pure and simple. From the body language and the look on the face of the Arab, it would not have mattered what Randul had said, his ears were deaf to explanations or excuses.

The Arab took up the gun and placed the tyre brace on the table in its place. He pointed the pistol at Randul's stomach and flicked it to tell Randul to move away from the chamois pouches on the floor. Randul shuffled into the far corner of the room. Ziyad slowly and deliberately advanced to look at the soft bags that lay at his feet, constantly keeping half an eye on the savage. Randul stared at his own scratched and bleeding arm. He wiped the wound, leaving a smear of red on his skin that glistened in the poor light.

"Is this all, you piece of Veddah khara?" Ziyad snarled.

Randul winced at the insult but did not reply. Ziyad lifted the barrel of the gun so that Randul could see down the black tunnel into the chamber. His lower lip quivered as if he was about to weep. Ziyad felt a deep sense of satisfaction that the boy was paralysed with fear.

Such power had been absent from his life in Sri Lanka and its resurgence made him feel good.

"I'll ask once, and only once. Is this all? Where are the Padparadscha?"

It would make little difference if Randul responded or not, he was a dead man standing. If there were any gems remained in the void, Ziyad had decided that it would be simpler to let Randul get down on his knees to ferret around for them beneath the floor.

It would be the boy's last act.

"There is one more pouch," Randul grimly admitted.

"Go on, then, you filth. Get it." Ziyad indicated with a further flick of the barrel of the gun for Randul to get on his knees and retrieve it.

Randul looked down and took the few steps forward to tentatively pass between Ziyad and the sink. Randul knew that it was now or never. Ziyad stepped smartly back but in doing so briefly lost balance and focus. He missed the sleight of hand.

The boy had got too close.

Randul had seen the old boning knife lying in the sink and moved too swiftly for Ziyad. The Veddah was in close combat before he could re-aim the gun, let alone fire it. Randul's body crashed into Ziyad while simultaneously he slashed the knife in an upward arc. Ziyad felt the narrow blade puncture him just below his ribs and he let out a rasping gasp of air. He gulped to replenish the oxygen forced from his body by the impact, but something was not right; his lungs did not respond. Randul was unable to land any further blows before they both crashed to the ground and the gun skittered across the floor out of Ziyad's weakened grip.

Randul's hand felt sticky with the warm liquid that was oozing onto Ziyad's shirt. His one eye looked up at Randul, initially in dazed confusion, followed by alarm. His mouth open and closed like a fish out of water, as he tried to draw air into his deflated lung. Randul had recovered to a squatting position alert to any counterattack from Ziyad. None was forthcoming, and he looked on with a morbid fascination as Ziyad's eye lost focus and he seemed to slip into semi-consciousness, gulping noisily through his open mouth.

Suddenly Ziyad twitched and raised a hand in supplication, realising that he had lost the initiative and was now the victim. Air was in short supply, and he felt lightheaded. The boy floated in front of him as if viewed from beneath the surface of an engulfing sea. Waves of light swept across his field of vision and the sound of someone fighting for air was remote and unattached to his body.

Randul shook himself out of his own morbid stupor. The knife handle was protruding from the side of the injured man on the floor, blood smudged across its handle, soaking into the dry boards. Something told him that to remove the knife might hasten the loss of blood and while he felt little sympathy for his victim, he did not want to make the mistake that Ziyad had made by getting too close.

Satisfied that the Arab was incapable of taking any action against him, Randul shuffled over to the void and stretched down into the furthest recess to recover the last bag. It was catching on the joist and, despite the need for haste, he suppressed any waves of panic as he wriggled it too and fro to release it. Ziyad lay watching him, his breathing very shallow, but his good eye managing to refocus on the now freed bag. So close. So very close.

That little Veddah shit had outsmarted him yet again.

How had he allowed that to happen?

Randul did not linger. He placed the bag by the sink and rinsed the blood from his hands. Once clean, he took up the other pouches from the floor and packed them all in his rucksack. Ziyad continued helplessly to follow his every movement. Randul glanced down at the stricken Ziyad, his patch had slipped up to his forehead to reveal the empty eye socket. His good eye seemed to beg an answer to an unasked question.

Randul silently took up the last pouch from where it lay by the sink and opened it. He tipped it until three large stones fell into his open palm. He took the largest between the forefinger and thumb of his other hand, rotating it in front of Ziyad's eye. The light from the lamp sent sparkling shadows dancing across his ashen face.

It was torment for Ziyad. It was huge, a delicately pale lotus blossom hue, must have weighed at least one hundred grammes, around 500 carats. Ziyad lay in awe, gasping for air, his eye bright and attentive despite the lack of oxygen.

The pain insidiously spread, throbbing in his ribs, drifting inexorably towards his shoulder. Ziyad attempted to speak but was unable to do so. One small error was to deny him possession of a dream.

And now it was too late.

Randul looked down at Ziyad whose skin had taken on a bluey-grey hue. He lay vanquished. Randul briefly wondered if he should alert anyone to come to the aid of the dying man prostrated before him. Then he remembered that it could all too easily have been him with a bloodied bullet lodged in the boarded wall, having blasted its way through the back of his skull. Pity quickly gave way to a renewed sense of urgency for him to depart and put as much distance between him, the bungalow and Ziyad as was possible. There was no turning back. Randul had to run.

To disappear, far away.

He did not know where. The North of the island would not be far enough. He needed to disappear, to get right away from Ziyad. From the Sinharaja. From Sri Lanka.

He stopped as he reached the door and, almost as an afterthought, returned to the prone Ziyad. He slipped the backpack from his shoulders and dug deep into its interior. A well filled pouch emerged, and he deftly untied the cord around the neck.

He scattered some small blue stones over Ziyad before patting down his trouser pockets and removing his car keys.

"For the car."

Ziyad made no sign of hearing him, he just stared at the small, glittering blue gems that littered him and the floor around him. Randul picked up the revolver and thought about turning out the lights. As he passed the threshold he decided against it, the sum of his mercy. He did not bother to close the door, there was no point.

It took Randul no time at all to discover the parked Mercedes and he returned the brace to the boot of the car before opening the passenger door and slinging his backpack onto the seat. As he was about to slam the door shut, he spotted the leather briefcase in the shadow of the footwell. He leant across and popped the catches to lift the flaps.

He whistled quietly as he saw its contents and then smiled to himself before climbing into the driver's seat and starting the engine.

*

It was three weeks later when a blue Mercedes was found abandoned in the car park at Bandaranaike International Airport.

PART TWO

England

Twenty Years Later

I have reviewed The Sauceror's Apprentice on two previous occasions during my career as a restaurant critic and it is sad to witness the downfall of one of the most innovative dining establishments that London has seen since it first opened in 2001. Anyone who wants to compare my earlier visits should refer to my report for this newspaper on 23rd January 2001 on the occasion of the grand opening, or my piece for The Good Restaurant Guide of 2001.

In those heady days, Stephen Silchester had been the doyen of the culinary world. A Young Chef of the Year and the creator of a truly innovative fusion of Sri Lankan cuisine tinged with subtle influences from the Mediterranean. Silchester had no competition, he left his peers in his wake with imagination and creativity that was second to none. This ingenuity was inspired when he travelled to Sri Lanka and met a young local man who he referred to in those frivolous day as his "Consultant Herbologist". Their short partnership inspired an amalgamation of traditional ethnic ingredients to create dishes of extraordinary complexity, all foraged from the forests of that island and extracted or processed in a manner that remains a secret of the reclusive chef to this day. He developed a style of culinary excellence that only appears once or, if you are lucky, twice in the life of a humble restaurant critic.

But, oh, how the mighty are fallen. I had the great misfortune to dine with a friend at the newly refurbished premises on the site of the first Sauceror's Apprentice on fashionable Mayfair's Brook Street. Great expense has been lavished on the interior design and decorations but, bearing in mind that this venue has been closed for over a year, the results disappoint and add nothing to the experience. The long-awaited reopening was eagerly anticipated by gastronomes, and I include myself amongst their number, who circumnavigate the globe to seek out a much-anticipated reincarnation of this culinary holy grail.

What a travesty of descriptive puff from the PR people. There was little that was new, in fact the offering was decidedly old hat without the mystique of its original concept.

What was so extraordinary about Stephen Silchester's cooking when he set up his establishment as part of the prize for winning Young British Chef of the Year back in 2001 was the exquisite if transient taste of his food. That might sound trite but anyone who was anyone fought for a place at the Sauceror's Apprentice to experience this gifted individual's first tasting menus. Each diner came away convinced that they had had a personal epiphany of tastes and textures that were unique to them. They might have ordered the same dish as their companions or other diners, but the experience was completely different for everyone. How this was achieved remains a mystery. Alchemy was undoubtedly at play, and I suspect that this had a great deal to do with the short-lived partnership with the young Sri Lankan who he met all those years ago. If so, where is this maestro today? If it was he who was the catalyst behind Silchester's early success, then there is no more important time for him to re-emerge. It is obvious that he had nothing to do with Silchester's latest phoenix moment. The ashes remain unrevived.

I have only one word for the dismal meal. Bland.

There is no other word for it, and it is, I regret to say, the deepest insult you can give any chef. But I am unapologetic and would say it to his face were he anywhere to be seen when we visited his establishment. My guest and I came with great expectation and left in deep depression. How can someone so stratospherically talented descend to these depths? Arrogance? Apathy? Conceit? I do not know, but I mourn his culinary demise.

If he was, as we were assured (but could not believe), personally responsible for the preparation and heating (I cannot bring myself to write cooking, for it did not strike me that the art of gastronomy had been applied to the offering) of the dishes presented then he should be ashamed. Each plate of food was insipid with accompaniments that did little to assuage our disenchantment. If this is what Silchester now has to offer, then he needs to return to Sri Lanka as swiftly as possible to rekindle the sorcery that inspired the name of his establishment and wowed so many gastronomes the world over.

Where was the individuality, the imagination, the flair, the expertise? Silchester is a shadow of his former self, a faded star of the past, an imploding culinary black hole, a has-been who, having ascended to his zenith on the turn of the millennium, has been on the wane ever since.

I may be transgressing some unwritten rule of the guild of restaurant critics, but I cannot bring myself to describe any of the dishes we chose to eat because I would not recommend anyone even to visit this restaurant, let alone to dine at it. This once mighty emporium of gastronomic and nutritional excellence is now a dying swan that will decay, its bloated carcase being deservedly flushed away on the tide of obscurity, ultimately to sink from consciousness.

Tom De Pietro - Restaurant Critic of the Year

13th August

Chapter 21

Stephen Silchester stumbled across the small living room in his miserable apartment just off the Shepherds Bush Road to collect another bottle of vodka from the sideboard. He was unshaven, his shirt creased, untucked and in need of a wash, as was the body that occupied it. A crumpled newspaper lay on the floor by the sofa, the page with the article by the renowned restaurant critic, Tom De Pietro, shredded in petulant anger. The first empty bottle of the day was on the low coffee table that was stained with rings from a collection of glasses and cups that remained on its surface.

He held his last clean cut-glass tumbler in a vice-like grip while trying to twist the top off the bottle with the other, resulting in a contortion of fingers and thumbs. The seal finally cracked and shakily the top was unwound and tossed aside. He enthusiastically filled his glass half full of the clear liquor, dribbling it down the side as the vodka was shakily slopped in. Taking a huge draught, he swilled it around his mouth both to wash away the slimy film that had adhered to the surface of his uncleaned teeth and to diminish the lingering aftertaste of garlic. He swallowed and then, almost as an afterthought, threw the glass across the room so that it smashed and liquor-patterned the emulsion painted wall. Neat vodka ran down the surface in rivulets and collected on the top of the skirting board. The wall sparkled with slivers of glass that caught in the limited morning sunlight that struggled its way through the filthy window, competing with the table lamps that were dotted around the room and remained alight from the night before.

The critic was right, and Stephen knew it. That was what was so bloody unfair, he thought. The revamping of The Sauceror's Apprentice was the last throw of the dice. He had pulled in all the favours that he could and mortgaged himself up to his neck, and beyond. The critique from Tom De Pietro, once a close friend, had been devastating – worse still, it hammered home the last nail into the coffin of his reputation and any opportunity to fight his way back into the higher echelons of the restaurant elite. In his heart Stephen had to accept that it was a failure, he was a failure. It was the latest in a catalogue of disasters to have befallen him over the last few years and he had resorted to his sole source of consolation, the bottom of a bottle.

Alcoholism had perniciously crept up on him until he was in its firm embrace. The wealth that he had built up over the early years of his success had been frittered away by the consumption of increasing quantities of liquor and cocaine. The house in the country had gone, as had the gite in France, the Aston Martin together with the glitz of being a feted celebrity. The television show flopped eventually as his presentation became increasingly erratic and the production team lost patience with the culinary genius who had taken a self-destructive path, ostracising sponsors, friends and colleagues. He had become a laughingstock without the affection or respect held for his forerunners such as Keith Floyd, Gordon Ramsey, Rick Stein or Jamie Oliver. He was the pariah of the restaurant world.

Stephen had no-one to blame but himself. However, there remained an underlying resentment that gnawed away at him and was levelled directly at the Veddah, Randul Ranatunga, who had promised to continue to support him with his unique botanicals - and almost immediately had failed to do so. In the early years he had continued eking out the contents of the box that he had brought back from his trip. When that ran out, he had ended up paying ridiculous prices to importers for some of the more common raw materials that he could name. What he could not replicate was the alchemy necessary to process or blend them to the exceptional quality that Ranatunga achieved.

In desperation, he had made one return trip to Sri Lanka to try to find Randul, but he had disappeared. There were local rumours about a vendetta and that he had been responsible for a vicious attack on a businessman over a deal that had gone wrong. It was thought that he had fled the country and he had never been heard of since.

Stephen had even driven out into the Sinharaja Forest to visit his bungalow, but it was overgrown and deserted. The doors were unlocked and the interior remained in a time warp. His small laboratory behind the house was untouched and there were some items that Stephen managed to retrieve but their quality was far from ideal compared to the fresh material that Randul had supplied and that had become the basis of Stephen's unique and revered cooking style.

Upon his return to the UK, Stephen started to slip in the eyes of his ever more demanding but only transiently loyal devotees. His disciples needed an everchanging diet of culinary wonders and surprises from their Master and in the absence of such constant gratification would not tolerate, or accept, any limitation on his innovation, or any sign of imperfection. Support slipped away like shadows in the morning until the blinding light of criticism stung his ego and pushed him into the solace that he imbibed this morning.

The insistent buzz from a mobile telephone made Stephen vaguely look around the room for the source of the irritating noise. Lumbering over to an antique writing desk in one corner of the room, strewn with unpaid bills and solicitors' letters, Stephen rummaged under the detritus and eventually located his mobile. Fumbling to get the screen uppermost he myopically tried to read the legend to decide if he should take the call or not.

His lawyer.

Contemplating whether to ignore it, he inadvertently pressed the green button instead of the red and heard the voice of Peter Asquith tentatively ask, "Stephen? Stephen, are you there?"

Stephen unstuck his tongue from the roof of his mouth and spoke with a thick unclear voice, "I'm here."

"Are you alright? You are a bit muffled." Asquith almost sounded genuinely concerned, as well he might, bearing in mind the amount of fees that Stephen Silchester owed his firm. The news that he was about to impart to his client was not going to ease the situation, but there was no possible alternative open to him.

"What do you want, Peter? I'm not feeling too good this morning." The slurring of his words immediately told the solicitor what he had suspected, having had no response from a call that he made to Stephen an hour or so earlier.

"It's not good, I'm afraid."

"It never is," Stephen pulled out the chair that was in front of the desk and sat heavily. "Get on with it and let me get back to something worthwhile."

Asquith took a deep breath before speaking,

"Your landlord has refused to accept any arrangement to pay off the back rent."

"That's not a surprise. Anything else?"

Asquith took a second deep breath. Over the years of their acquaintance Silchester had become an increasingly volatile client, and the solicitor was glad that he was speaking to him from a distance rather than face to face. Stephen sat waiting for the next revelation, his shirt pulling tightly across his distended stomach, the buttons tautly restraining the fat from breaking free. Darkened sweat stains formed arcs beneath his armpits and even Stephen could detect the smell of stale body odour that wafted from his body. His nose wrinkled in distaste, and he lifted his arm to confirm more precisely, if confirmation was necessary, as to where the odour was emanating. He puffed out his cheeks and exhaled as his solicitor continued with his unwelcome update.

"As the registered office of your company, we have also received final demands, or more explicitly, ultimatums from HMRC, several suppliers and your bank. Stephen, they are going to make you a bankrupt and there is nothing I can do to avoid this."

There was a silence at the end of the phone and Asquith wondered if his client had walked away, hung up or passed out.

"Stephen? Stephen? Are you there?"

After a pause, Stephen answered wearily.

"Anything else?" His voice had a resignation to it that indicated that he was ready to capitulate to the forces that were ranged against him. Asquith decided to push on regardless.

"Yes, as it happens. There's one further thing."

"Go on then."

"Stephen, as you are only too well aware, you owe my firm a great deal of money in back fees. My partners have discussed this, and we can no longer offer you legal services until you've paid off at least…."

"Kick a man when he's down, why don't you?" Stephen commented listlessly. The solicitor started to justify his point of view, but Stephen was quietly succinct.

"Fuck off, Peter," and terminated the call before tossing the 'phone back amongst the papers littering his desk.

With a grunt, he lifted his overweight body from the chair and took up the bottle once again. Without bothering to find a glass, clean or dirty (he knew there were none clean), he lifted the top to his lips and poured until his mouth was full. The excess trickled down the side of his jowls onto his already soiled shirt.

The 'phone rang again.

"Oh, for Christ's sake", the bottle banged down onto the table and Stephen grabbed the irritating machine.

"I told you to fuck off, Asquith."

There was a long pause on the line and Stephen was about to reject the call when he heard a calm, sophisticated male voice.

"Mr Silchester? Mr Stephen Silchester?"

Stephen was wary. Was this another creditor about to add to his woes? However, there was something about the assured sound of this person's voice that made Stephen relent and acknowledge that it was indeed him.

"I apologise for disturbing you, but I believe that I might be able to be of assistance to you."

Silence once again. Stephen was weighing up if this was some sort of hoax call or really someone who was prepared to dig him out of the ever-deepening hole that he found himself in. What had he got to lose – he had lost everything already?

"Who are you?"

The person at the other end seemed to consider the question for a moment before responding.

"My name is Randolph Curran."

Stephen wracked his brain to see if the name meant anything to him and drew a blank.

"And why, Mr Curran, would you want to assist me and, more to the point, how do you know that I need any assistance?" Stephen sounded irritable but Curran remained implacable to the suspicion levelled at him

"Well, I suppose that I feel that you might not have been the architect of your own downfall." His diction was very precise and even in his intoxication Stephen perceived a hint of an accent to the clipped English.

"Downfall? Bugger off. I have just relaunched my restaurant and everything is looking good…" Stephen was damned if he was going to accept failure to a stranger. However, his bluster was cut short by a slightly firmer tone from Curran,

"If you have read Tom De Peitro's critique of the meal he recently took at your establishment, you cannot seriously believe that you can survive such an excoriating review?" Curran allowed his observation to sink in and Stephen was starting to sober up by the minute. The caller continued,

"You are heavily in debt, and you will be declared bankrupt at any moment. Do you have an alternative solution or anyone else to play the white knight? Is someone waiting in the wings to pick up the pieces?"

Stephen was perspiring profusely as the alcohol oozed through the pores of his skin and dampened his grimy collar. Curran obviously knew a great deal about his circumstances, and Stephen grumpily asked how he was so well informed.

"Mr Silchester, I am a businessman and I keep my finger on several pulses. I have dined at your table on a few occasions. I must acknowledge that once you were a master of your art. I believe that your gift can be restored to its former glory, but only with my assistance."

Stephen listened, incredulous at the arrogance of the man. He did not need anyone to teach him how to run his business. With his head thumping he could only conclude that this idiot was an affluent fan who might be foolish enough to offer financial support. Even at this late stage it was possible that a substantial injection of capital might hold off the wolves circling his restaurant.

"What are you proposing?" Stephen slumped back into a chair behind his desk and stretched across for the half full bottle.

The line was quiet and then the voice at the other end spoke.

"I am not willing to make any cash available to you, Mr Silchester, if that is what you were expecting."

"What then?" Stephen took another swig from the bottle.

"Your financial affairs are your own business and are neither the object of my interest, nor this call." There was silence again.

"Go on." Stephen sat with his head in his hands, the telephone lying on the desk.

"You will have to accept that you will be a bankrupt by this time next month with a huge weight of debt around your neck. Credit will not be available to you, your already damaged credibility as a restaurateur will be impossible to restore to the same level again. I know that some bankrupts rise from the ashes, but they have skills that are not at your disposal. You are ostensibly finished as an entrepreneurial chef and restaurateur. Finished unless you take up my invitation."

Stephen did not take kindly to either the clarity of the lecture or the cold truth that it held.

"Well in that case, I don't think we have anything further to discuss."

Curran was not to be dismissed so easily,

"Why don't you come to my house and we can discuss my proposal over lunch? Shall we say, Monday?"

This was not so much an invitation but a confirmation of the arrangements.

"I will send my car for you at 11:00am."

Stephen was about to object when the telephone line went dead.

Chapter 22

Every night for the last twenty years Ziyad relived the horror that had almost terminated his existence. In some respects, he wished that it had. Sleep was impossible when darkness fell and so he lay in his bed and watched the ceiling. An insect scurried across the inverted surface defying gravity. Oh, how he envied it.

He had been lying by the doorway of the Veddah's bungalow for an hour before there was any sound of life outside. His breathing remaining impossibly ragged and shallow. Somehow, he had managed to drag himself to the front door, but any further exertion was impossible. There he lay, slumped over the threshold hoping that, in the unlikely event of someone passing, they would see him and come to his aid. Any expectation of surviving the wound inflicted by the Veddah was dwindling by the minute.

But then, to his disbelief, he heard a car stop and the doors open. He tried to turn his head so that he could look across the worn boarding of the veranda or to cry out for assistance, but both were impossible. He was prostrate, face down in the doorway, his view restricted to a strip of bare ground at the base of the steps and little more.

The footsteps moved closer, and two pairs of dusty, leather boots entered his peripheral vision. The boots were of a specific design and the style was familiar to Ziyad, but out of place in the jungle. Whoever they were paused and surveyed the scene. There was no conversation and after a moment they ascended the short flight of steps and stood either side of his prone body.

Ziyad could neither move nor lift his head. The two men, the size of their boots gave this away, lowered themselves onto their haunches. Large hands on his right side rolled him over and for the first time he could see his saviours. He quaked at the realisation that these were no saints. He had moved from one hell to another. The smell of quat on the breath of one of the men was unmistakeable and provided a flashback to the war-torn land of his birth. He had sat alongside scared men and boys before battle, chewing the tart green leaves picked just minutes before to deaden the fear and inject a brief euphoria before the reality of battle took over.

The second man, still out of sight to the stricken Ziyad, rose and walked into the house and slowly inspected the interior, presumably to check that Ziyad was alone. There was the sound of running water and then the steps returned.

The one who had turned him over was young with prominent ears and short black hair, slightly curly on the top. A shemagh scarf, or keffiyeh, was loosely wound around his neck obscuring the lower half of his face. He wore a collarless cotton shirt and khaki combat trousers. His eyes creased around the edges as he bent lower to reveal his face and smiled down at Ziyad. Stained teeth protruded below a thin straggly moustache, his skin was sallow, and weather worn, with bright beady eyes that lay sunken in the sockets with darkened folds of skin below each one.

"You are a hard man to find, brother." His voice was silky soft and defied the hard edge to his glinting eyes.

Ziyad tried to speak but his tongue felt swollen, and his lips had stuck to his teeth, so he just mouthed silently. The second man appeared by the side of the first and lowered himself onto his haunches. He was older and dressed in a grey cotton jacket and loose blouson shirt open at the chest to reveal a mass of chest hair. He was of a swarthy build, and he looked tired, also with dark bags under his black soulless eyes. His mouth was not smiling, he had not smiled for a long time. He proffered a glass half full of water before realising that Ziyad was in no position to take it. He carefully placed it to the upper side of Ziyad's lips and poured until the cool liquid trickled into Ziyad's mouth. He swallowed gratefully.

The relief was only momentary as the glass was removed.

Both men squatted silently by him and watched the water partially resuscitate their charge.

"Do you know why we are here? Why we followed you?" The man with the water spoke in guttural Arabic and Ziyad feigned incomprehension.

"Don't tell me you have forgotten your native tongue. Come Al-Jabri, you cannot fool us."

At the sound of his former name, Al-Jabri, Ziyad's eye flickered and the two men knew instantly that they had tracked down their man.

"There, I thought it would come back." He reoffered the water and Ziyad gulped trying not to choke between the twin efforts of drinking and breathing.

"It has taken many years to track you down and now we find that you are at death's door." The water was removed once again and Ziyad alternated his gaze between the two men.

"Your death, while a delightful and deserved possibility, is not quite what we want…yet." The older man put his head to one side and bent lower to see the extent of the wound. "That looks serious, brother. A punctured lung I suspect, but cleanly inflicted. You might live - if we get an ambulance to you swiftly. Would you like us to do that for you?"

Ziyad nodded his head, but the movement was so small that it was difficult to detect.

"If we did that, you would have to do something for us. Can you do that?"

Another infinitesimal nod.

"Many years ago, you disappeared with something that was not yours. Something that made you a wealthy man and has provided for you in your new life. We see that you have invested wisely to grow this windfall still larger. Now it is time for this to be returned to those from whom you stole it. With interest."

Ziyad was moving in and out of consciousness but understood the message. It could not have been clearer. It was useless to get into any detail as to how and when he could liquidate his complex network of investments but liquidate it he would in exchange for the life that was gradually slipping from his grasp.

Ziyad uttered a gurgle and the older man looked content.

"I shall take that to be an affirmation of your cooperation. But tell me, were you about to run again? Judging by the empty state of your safe in your shop I would conclude that you were. By the way, your assistant was extremely cooperative…eventually."

Ziyad wanted him to stop talking. He would do whatever was asked of him. He needed immediate medical attention. He had had a good run and if they wanted the money that he had embezzled returned to them, then that was fine with Ziyad. Just get him some help!

"We can't risk you vanishing again. I think we shall need to slow you down."

The younger man had repositioned himself behind Ziyad and was massaging the base of his skull, running his fingers and thumb down the top of his spine. Ziyad lay unsure as to what he was doing but misgivings built in his mind as time and life slipped away.

"We will return to make the arrangements for the repatriation of our funds when you are feeling a little better." The older man stood and Ziyad felt a sense of relief. They were going to assist him.

"Now, let's see if we can help relieve that pain for you?" The second man had stopped moving his finger and thumb on the back of Ziyad's neck, just beneath his skull. They pulsed, gently feeling the gaps in the vertebra, trying to detect a specific point in his neck. The first man returned to his haunches so that Ziyad could see him. He looked passed Ziyad at the invisible man behind and gave a silent nod. Ziyad heard a metallic click. The fingers moved again and felt their way down the first three joints to his spinal cord and then stopped. He felt a sharp prick to his skin and a slipping sensation. Something warm ran round his neck, a warm wadi of blood. The young man worked with such speed and certainty until suddenly all sensation ceased for Ziyad. He could see, hear and feel the boards against his cheek.

Otherwise, nothing.

No pain in his ribs. No sensation whatsoever below his neck. The older man watched with interest and took hold of Ziyad's limp hand and lifted it. Ziyad observed but did not acknowledge the action, his view was separate from the limb that was being moved by another. The hand fell back onto the veranda. Ziyad wanted to scream but he could not, his breathing became even more ragged with fear. Black motes and bright flashes flitted across his vision, and he vaguely heard a distant voice say with assurance,

"I don't think you will be slipping away from us again." And then, as an afterthought, the drifting voice added, "Help is on its way." The two men retreated to their car, but Ziyad did not hear them drive off.

Every moment of that evening so many years ago remained etched into his memory and, as he experienced most nights when it was quiet and dark, his body became drenched in sweat. The insect that he had been watching had reached the corner of the room where the ceiling met the two walls. It rested. The wet bed that Ziyad lay in smelt of urine that had leaked from his incontinence pants. Not that he had any sensation of dampness. Below his third cervical nerve he had no sensation at all. Before they left him, his supposed saviours had guaranteed that, with expert efficiency. He would never be able to run again or do much else. It had been a neat incision of a thin, keen blade between the blocks of bone that formed his upper spine, done with surgical precision.

And so, the years had agonisingly passed. Slowly and with infinite monotony. He had had to endure the ignominy of having every simple task performed for him by a series of impersonal carers who dealt with his bodily functions with lifeless efficiency. Slowly and insidiously his vast intertwined portfolio of investments had been unwound and gradually liquidated for repatriation. The two men who had imposed on him the life of a quadriplegic appeared at regular intervals. Initially, he had told Ameesha that they were business associates, but the younger man was taking too much interest in his daughter and so he had had to tell her what had happened, and how his reallocation of funds from the militia to his private account had finally come to haunt him.

To his surprise, Ameesha rose to the challenge and, with maturity she became an adept, shrewd and cunning businesswoman dealing with his affairs with a toughness and skill that impressed him. His former reticence in agreeing to her having any involvement in his financial affairs was swept away. He accepted that he was foolish to dismiss her desire to become involved but now through necessity he had to rely upon her. She would have enriched them both, if there had not been such a dramatic turn of events. Now they worked for the benefit of others. His lack of freedom of movement made him cantankerous and bitter. Slowly the assets that had been under their control were liquidated and the considerable wealth that Ziyad had built up over the years was being dissipated.

However, Ameesha was her father's daughter, both smart and devious. She managed to ensure that certain items were kept out of sight of the two Arabs who appeared at regular intervals to monitor progress and check that money continued to flow through to their paymasters. Despite the intricate web that Ziyad had woven around his fortune, the older Arab seemed to have a more than passing knowledge of the details of Ziyad's affairs. Someone somewhere had not been as discreet as Ziyad would have expected or wished. But where money was concerned, he knew that you could trust nobody.

Not even your wife.

His faith in family loyalty had been further dented shortly after he was released from hospital. It was when he was at his lowest ebb that his wife announced that she was unable to live with a quadriplegic. She boldly admitted to his face that she had been having an affair with a younger man who ran his own successful business. Ironically, he was the salesman who had sold Ziyad the Mercedes that he had given Thinuka. The car was eventually found abandoned at the airport following the disappearance of the Veddah. The large quantity of precious stones and cash removed by Ziyad from his safe had also disappeared, presumably with the Veddah. There was a certain irony in Ziyad's misfortune, not that the authorities were made aware of the existence of the lost riches. Ziyad seethed at the recurring image of the obvious delight on the filthy savage's face when he discovered his additional good fortune. Neither the savage, nor Ziyad's bulging briefcase had been seen since.

The only revenge that Ziyad could exact was to ensure that the full blame for his injuries were placed firmly at the door of the Veddah boy. While the police made a half-hearted attempt to trace him, it was all to no avail. They swiftly concluded that he had taken a flight out of the country and would never be seen again. Ziyad knew that the airport was too secure for anyone, let alone a Veddah, to secretly export either himself or the quantity of gems and money that he would have had in his possession. And anyway, he had elicited the fact that no airline had a record of Randul having flown that day.

So much for Sri Lankan police efficiency. For the amount that Ziyad had paid them over the years he would have expected more.

"Good morning, Baba." Ameesha, his daughter, entered the room with a cheery smile and dressed in a flowing summer dress. The formalities of the morning had been completed by his carers, the windows opened, and fresh flowers placed on the table at the end of his bed to mask the lingering odour from his night's incarceration. The orthopaedic bed had been set so that Ziyad was in a half-seated position and could focus on his daughter.

Ziyad could speak, but his voice was weak, and his breathing remained laboured. When there was no need, he would just nod or use his grey eyebrows, deeply lined mouth or hooked, bony nose to express any opinion that he wished to convey through the use of facial contortions. As he had no use of any other part of his body, his face had become much more flexible and expressive, and he had to take some form of satisfaction from the wide range of visual signs that were capable of being interpreted by his audience. Not that he saw many people nowadays. His life had been secretive before he had had the misfortune of being selected by that Veddah filth as his chosen dealer. Now the two Arabs had discovered and punished him, his life was positively monastic.

He was a shadow of his former self, aged and wizen, bitter and wracked with a deep and lasting hatred for the Veddah.

Ameesha breezily lent over his bed and, holding her breath, gave Ziyad a peck on both cheeks before drawing up a chair to sit beside him. Without any preamble, she went into the day's agenda.

"I have spoken to the lawyers in the Cayman Islands, and we have completed on the sale of the warehouse in Toronto. There is a conditional agreement to sell the land in California, but the development permit has still been delayed." Ziyad hissed and his mouth was tight to inform Ameesha that this was unacceptable.

"I know, Baba, but we have little alternative. Your associates," when discussing repayments, Ameesha always referred to the two Arabs as Ziyad's 'associates'. It galled him every time she used the word.

"Your associates have set the timetable for the next repayment and we are behind unless we can get these deals completed. We are so close to getting them off our back, surely it is worth the sacrifice of a few hundred thousand dollars?"

The mouth slackened and eyebrows twitched upwards in capitulation. Ameesha patted his slack arm and continued in a softer voice, even though there was no one else around to overhear.

"The upside is that I have managed to get a side agreement with the US purchasers that will secure us an uplift when the development permit is eventually given. So, the overage is completely protected and comes to our account, not your little Arab friends."

Ziyad grunted and then sucked in air spasmodically. He hated the way she patronisingly referred to the Arabs as his associates or his friends. It was an irritating habit and each time it was used as an accusatory reminder of the reason for their current predicament. The draining of their capital and the obliteration of years of diligent and shrewd investment was the fault of that savage. If he had not appeared, Ziyad and his family would be continuing in a state of affluent bliss.

"What about London?" rasped Ziyad, each word punctuated by a sharp suck of air.

"Mmmm." Ameesha crossed her legs and shuffled the papers on her knees. "I spoke to the agent, who I have to say sounds quite dishy."

Now she was taunting him with her preference for western man rather than someone more suitable, someone chosen by her father.

"You know the type, that rounded English public-school voice, floppy hair and slightly fey – a Hugh Grant or a young Bill Nighy."

Ziyad rolled his eyes but smiled wanly to show his exasperation was partly in jest. Ameesha had become a fan of English movies and TV series and spent many hours watching box sets in a room she had set up in the house as a home cinema. She had cocooned herself into the house and, like her father, eschewed any normal social life preferring to immerse herself in her father's business affairs. Whether this was solely as a result of the financial demands placed upon them by the Arabs or out of filial duty was unclear, but whatever the reason, it meant that she had control of the empire that Ziyad had amassed, and that was being systematically dismantled without undue interference from anyone beyond the two of them.

"I shall look him up on the 'net and see if the reality matches my fantasy." She laughed at her shamelessness, noting the wince that flashed across her father's face. Some years ago, Baba had tried to marry Ameesha off to an elderly Indian who ran a successful private banking business in Colombo. She had fought against the union, and it was only after the police raided the man's home that it turned out that he was laundering money for an organised crime gang from Kolkata.

Baba had relented and Ameesha subsequently used her own judgement, usually expressing interest in those that Ziyad would not approve of, but he was powerless having himself made such an error of marital judgement. Not that any men really featured much in her life. She found the challenge and the thrill of her business activities quite satisfying enough. The real exhilaration, however, was outwitting the Arabs. The older man had never given her a name and she called him somewhat unimaginatively, Ali. The younger was too stupid to be of real concern, save for the fact that he had a sadistic trait that had to be watched. He assumed that, as an attractive young woman, she was fair game and had tried on more than one occasion to take advantage of her. Ameesha had rebuffed him by telling him that she preferred women to men. From his reaction she thought she had made a terrible mistake and that he saw her preference as a challenge. To her surprise, however, his apparent response was one of horror and disgust. However, he remained a constant threat as he continued to make it clear that if he wanted her, he would be justified in taking her, part of the price to be paid for the dishonesty of her father.

Her diligence and commercial acumen had meant that she had slowly liquidated most of the assets to enable them to repay the Arabs, while simultaneously accruing some profits on the side. Each quarter she would meet with Ali and provide an audit, albeit somewhat abridged, of her activities. If approved, arrangements were made for a transfer of funds from one of Ziyad's anonymous accounts in the Cayman Islands to a nominated account that was supplied by Ali. On each occasion the details applied solely to that particular quarter's payment. Always different, and always untraceable a few minutes after the transfer had been made.

The hidden top slice was spirited away into a separate account from the one making the transfer to Ali's nominated account and held in the name of Ameesha rather than her father – better to be safe than sorry. Her father was a marked man, and she had no intention of being seen as anything other than a catalyst in the liquidation of the assets. She suspected that once the final repayments had been made that her father would be surplus to requirements. She was young and had her whole life ahead of her, while Baba was a shell that had no future, merely an empty vessel waiting for the breakers yard, wallowing between life and death. She had no intention of being around to become collateral damage.

"What about London?" Ziyad repeated.

"Well, as suspected, the restaurant, what was it called?" She fumbled amongst her papers to find the name, but Ziyad knew it from memory,

"The Sauceror's Apprentice," Ziyad shook with a fit of coughing that wracked his weakened body.

"That's right, Baba." Ameesha patted his arm again, "How clever of you. The old grey cells are still in full working order, at least." Ziyad scowled at his daughter, but she ignored the reproach.

"The tenant's lawyers tried to make a derisory offer to settle the outstanding rent, but I rejected this as I understand that the business is on the verge of bankruptcy. I did suggest that we take a surrender of the lease and include their fixtures and fittings, all of which are newly installed and must have cost a fortune. They have a good resale value which will make us a profit. I have located an art gallery that will take the restaurant premises, once vacant, offering a ten percent uplift in rent which together with a sale of the fixtures and fitting will provide a more than acceptable return. We can sell a long lease on the gallery and I think I have an investor for that."

Ziyad nodded his approval to Ameesha's report and started to ask about the apartments above the restaurant, but Ameesha was ahead of him.

"We have sold long leases on all the refurbished apartments and deals are in solicitor's hands for the disposal of the rental units. We should clear twenty million, net of fees and costs. I have transferred the headlease into one of my shell companies and so the transaction will be invisible to our friends as will the retention of the penthouse apartment on the top floor." She looked self-satisfied with her work and Ziyad acknowledged his admiration by slowly shaking his head up and down with a half-smile and a half grimace of his mouth. His eyes were as encouraging as he could make them, and he hoped that his daughter understood his appreciation, but not his apprehension.

"In fact," she continued, "I am proposing to go to London to sort out the final details and have a bit of a holiday. You will be alright here without me, won't you?" Ziyad was not given the opportunity to give any expression or utterance on the decision. Ameesha had already given her father a final peck on each cheek and left the room.

Twenty million pounds would easily cover the final payment due to the Arabs while leaving a reasonable invisible balance to pay for her trip to London. Once the final payment had been made, she assumed she would find out what Ali and his companion had in mind for her father, and for her. She was fearful that it would not end well for Baba. As for her immediate future, she would be much safer in London than in Kandy or even Sri Lanka.

Besides, she wanted to meet with Stephen Silchester as he was the one possible link to the missing Randul Ranatunga, with whom she had some unfinished business, if only she could find him.

Aloka had told her of the visit to her father's shop by the Veddah all those years ago and the story of Padparadscha sapphires the size of which would dwarf the largest recorded stone currently held in a museum in New York. Her father had craved possession of those stones, even keeping them a secret from his beloved Ameesha. Aloka, on the other hand, had not been anything like as reticent about regaling her with what he had seen and heard. She had to accept that the story may have become embellished in both the telling and with the passage of time.

However, if the story was even half true then she wanted to avenge her brother's death and her father's fall from grace by dispossessing the boy of the sapphires. She avariciously coveted their ownership, not for financial gain but for her own enjoyment. Certain art collectors will pay massive sums for illegally obtained old masters or contemporary paintings purely for their private delectation. Well, Ameesha felt the same about those Padparadscha. She desired them, to be admired by her in solitude, comforted by possession as opposed to any sense of preservation or guardianship for the benefit of future generations.

Her father had been the last to see Randul, but Silchester, in his early years as a restaurateur, was the one who had benefitted from the special botanicals that the boy had created and supplied. A year or so ago, she had been up to the bungalow and had found it deserted but she knew that someone had been before her and removed any remaining stock. She had tried to see him then, but his visit was too fleeting for her to make contact. Of course, he was totally unaware that a company controlled by her family was his Brook Street landlord.

It was time for Ameesha to travel to London and take advantage of his commercial decline to discover if he knew where Randul might be. His reported ruin would make him vulnerable and, hopefully, bitter towards anyone who had had a hand in his downfall. Surely by now, any false loyalty towards the Veddah must have dissolved into spiteful revenge.

Ameesha returned to Ziyad's study, that she had refurnished in a more lavish style to suit her own tastes and contacted her travel agent to make the necessary arrangements. She would fly into Heathrow and get a car to pick her up and deliver her to Claridge's Hotel. She sat back in her ergonomically designed chair relishing the anticipated break from the tedium of Sri Lanka and living in the shadow of her incapacitated father. Everything was now in her name, and she was a wealthy woman. If she did not return, her father would be destitute within a month and the house repossessed by the bank that had, at her instigation, lent ninety five percent of its value to another of the shell companies she had created. This one had Ziyad registered as the sole beneficiary, but the money had evaporated long ago into a web of transactions ending in a deposit into her account held with Coutts Bank in London.

Her years of self-imposed solitude and the single-minded pursuit of her father's wealth, all on the pretence of taking his instructions in order to satisfy the demands of the Arabs, had taken its toll. She was in her late-thirties and, finally, she saw that the end was in sight. A new life beckoned, prosperous and even a little hedonistic. Why not? She deserved it.

Baba lay deep thought. He recognised certain family traits in Ameesha that served to reinforce his misgivings.

Misgiving that were well founded.

Chapter 23

Stephen popped four paracetamol pills into his mouth and washed them down with lukewarm coffee, a meniscus having congealed to the side of the mug. A milky skin attached itself to his top lip and he wiped it away with the back of his hand. Shaving that morning had proved to be a challenge and he had a couple of small pieces of toilet tissue stuck over cuts, the blood having congealed in the weft of the soft paper. His pyjama top was open at the front and the soft white flesh of his belly hung over the draw string of his trousers.

He trudged barefoot back to the bathroom and showered, the tissue becoming dislodged from his face and floating round the plug until it disappeared with a diluted red wake chasing its progress. Hastily drying himself, Stephen looked across at the pile of clothes that had been piled onto his unmade bed. More garments were outside his wardrobe than remained hung up within, indecision having plagued him as to what he should wear for his lunch with the mysterious Mr Curran.

He had spent time searching the internet for Mr Randolph Curran. All that he could piece together was that Curran was a refugee who had arrived in Britain some twelve years ago. Business success as an up-market jewellery designer swiftly followed, as did the shop in Bond Street. Any one of the items displayed in the window were too rich for Stephen's pocket. Besides, the security man positioned at the entrance was far too intimidating to allow him to have the courage to enter the shop.

The nerve centre of his empire was an estate in Oxfordshire that he had bought eight years ago and set about rewilding, to the dismay of his tenant farmers who were forced to adapt traditional practices to a new regime or find themselves dispossessed. He had compensated each of the latter handsomely, but the loss of productive farmland did not go down well with the National Farmers Union or the locals. Fences were erected and footpaths diverted, all done in strict accordance with the law, but feelings ran high, and the local press focussed on his disruption to the balance of life in this rural idyll.

However, gradually, animosity and interest waned. Whatever he was doing behind the high stock-fencing and restored soft-brick walls that enclosed the estate was not seen as of immediate importance to the neighbouring inhabitants who lived beyond its boundary. Should they have been of a mind to find out, the eight years of ownership had seen a transformation of the landscape. Ancient woodland was brought back to life through careful and intensive management, new woods were planted and acres of multicoloured hay meadows prevailed on the previously monocultured fields. The estate employed local firms and contractors, paid them promptly and thereby created a loyalty towards the foreigner who took such a personal interest in all that was undertaken on the estate.

The main residence, a Queen Anne house that had been allowed to fall into a state of sedate dereliction by the former cash-starved owners was refurbished and fitted with a myriad of energy saving devices that made it carbon neutral. The building and its outbuildings became a model of energy efficiency and its acres a haven for all species of indigenous wildlife that thrived in the restored ecological oasis. The locals saw that the limited staff who lived within the estate curtilage were, like Mr Curran, all Asians. Despite being subject to periodic enquiries, they remained resolutely polite but evasive, merely confirming that their employer was wonderful and his home very beautiful. It was not for them to betray their master's right to privacy or to question the commercial viability of his enterprise. The 'County-set', comprising of other landowners, including a deputy Lord Lieutenants, the High Sheriff, some local magistrates, hospital consultants, farmers and investment managers all considered him to be a maverick. Polite and charming though he was, they dismissed his rewilding of the estate as the plaything of a wealthy idealist.

Eventually, when Randolph Curran was satisfied that the foundations of his vision had been set firm, he agreed to the estate being opened to the public once a year, which appeased even his most vociferous critics. When the locals stormed the open gates and strode up the long drive ("Mr Curran does not permit cars with combustion engines to enter onto the estate lands"), they begrudgingly had to acknowledge that what had been created was particularly special. The more elderly visitors harked back to their childhood and, with rheumy eyes, regaled their grandchildren, and anyone else who would listen, with reminiscences of the bucolic countryside of their youth. They had to concede that in the short period of his stewardship, Mr Curran had managed to recreate those halcyon days that were recalled with such affection.

Otherwise, Stephen had found little more about the man. There were some grainy photographs, but none gave a really good image of the man who seemed to avoid cameras and surprisingly maintained an unaccustomed privacy in these days of celebrity culture and vacuous media influencers.

After a number of false starts, Stephen chose a red checked shirt with a blue suit but rejected the tie. The shirt was roughly ironed and the collar no longer able to encompass his neck with any degree of comfort. He had roughly polished his only pair of scuffed, brown leather shoes. Once his attire was complete, he stood in front of a full-length mirror and studied the man before him. It was not an encouraging sight. The degree of weight-gain was a shock even though he saw it every day. The loose double chin, the drooping jowls, the distended stomach, the pasty complexion and the dark bags under his eyes made him appear much older than his forty-five years. Donning more formal clothing seemed to emphasis his expansion and he vowed to himself that, starting tomorrow, he would do something about it. To complete his ensemble, he stuffed a bright green silk handkerchief flamboyantly into his breast pocket. It stood briefly erect before flopping over the edge to hang languidly down.

As promised, a sparkling, black Tesla saloon arrived on the dot of 11:00am. The smartly uniformed Asian driver stood by the open back door as Stephen squeezed himself into the vehicle. The front passenger seat had been pushed forward to allow the person in the rear to have plenty of legroom, but for Stephen it was getting in that posed so much trouble. Finally, he settled himself, straightened his jacket and pulled his seatbelt across his bulk.

The driving was fast and competent, the driver meticulously signalling at each junction and maintaining a strict lane discipline as they sped along the M40 motorway. There was no conversation, but now and again the driver glanced in the rear-view mirror at Silchester, as if to check that he had not bailed out of the car en-route. The miles slipped by, until they exited from the motorway on the far side of the Chilterns and sedately wound through country lanes, slowing for the odd horse rider out for a late morning hack prior to lunch.

Stephen did manage to ask the driver how long he had worked for Mr Curran.

"We have been together since we came to England, Sir."

"Where did you both come from?" Stephen could not really care less but felt he had to ask.

"Many countries," the driver responded unhelpfully.

Stephen's head still ached and so he could not be bothered to pursue the point. Eventually, they arrived at two high brick-built gate posts each crowned with a stone lion standing sentinel holding a sword. The ornate wrought iron gates silently opened as they approached. A long straight gravel drive lined with lime trees stretched out before them, and the car crunched over the surface at a sedate pace. It gave Stephen time to take in his surroundings which were impatiently fashioned by man in a form that nature would have adopted given time. It was not manicured but equally, there was nothing overtly out of place. Windfall branches had been carefully cut to length and then piled up to provide cover for birds and small vertebrates. Beyond the rank of limes was parkland with mature and semi mature trees all of which had space to breath and spread their canopy. Leaves, such as were visible had been swept into neat piles and lay in carefully placed leaf clamps.

The trees slowly gave way to an open wild-flower meadow that stretched to the brow of a hill where the land fell away to expose the main house, that had just come into view, set in a broad vista across the open countryside. The drive became a semicircle of swept gravel that was surrounded by a low stone retaining wall. Tall grasses swayed as the wind gently drifted across the meadow, setting up long, mesmerising waves of movement.

The car pulled up smoothly in front of the black painted doors, the sheen from the perfect finish reflected the view and the stationary vehicle. The driver hurried round to let Stephen out of the car. Simultaneously the front door opened as if his arrival had been choreographed.

Stephen struggled to extricate himself from the low-slung saloon car and the driver offered him a hand. He refused the proffered assistance and leant heavily on the door to heave himself out of his seat. The car lifted marginally as his weight was transferred from the leather upholstery to his feet. Pulling himself upright and sweeping his hand down his crumpled jacket, Stephen had the opportunity to inspect the man, who he assumed to be his host, standing on the threshold.

Randolph Curran was tall, darkly tanned and had the look of a man who took care to keep himself in shape. Stephen estimated that he was of a similar age to himself, but with a thick head of long hair that was steel grey and swept back off his forehead to be held in a bun at the back of his head. While Stephen had always thought this an affectation favoured by moronic footballers trying to be fashionably individual, the style sat entirely naturally with Curran and imparted on him an air of distinction. The hirsute Curran also sported a full beard that was immaculately fashioned. His soft brown eyes were bright and welcoming, the warm smile of greeting showing off perfectly regular white teeth.

Mr Randolph Curran, Stephen thought, had one of those faces that you recognised but could not place. The familiarity of someone that you feel that you should know but have probably never met. He stared at Randolph slightly too long, unsure if he had seen him before. His memory, befuddled by alcohol and drugs, failed him and he shrugged his shoulders in defeat.

Stephen's suit was creased after having been crushed by the overly tight seatbelt for the past hour. Conversely, Curran's clothing was relaxed in style, but discreetly expensive and tailored by a master. The country suit, the crisp, flawlessly ironed light blue shirt and the club tie of maroon, with green and saffron stripes, were impressive and denoted a man at ease with himself, self-assured, wealthy and of impeccable taste. Gold cufflinks caught in the sunlight as Curran extended his hand in greeting.

"Mr Silchester, may I call you Stephen? Welcome to Wykeford Manor." The voice was silky and the clipped English was well spoken and precise, but with the hint of the underlying accent that Stephen had heard in their telephone conversation.

"Thank you for the invitation." Looking around generally but focusing on nothing in particular, Stephen waved his hand vaguely to encompass all that he could see. "Quite a place you have here."

"I'm glad you like it. Shall we go through and have a drink before lunch?"

As usual, when Stephen had dragged himself from his bed earlier that morning, he was suffering from another hang-over from hell and, consequently, had vowed that he would not drink for a couple of days. His consumption had got out of hand and he needed to rein it in before he became completely hooked. Those who knew him well might have said that this conclusion was a tad too late.

"A gin and tonic would be good."

Curran was slightly taken aback by the premature request but managed to smile congenially.

"Certainly. We'll go out on to the terrace."

His host led the way into the spacious entrance hall that was approached through a more modest vestibule with glass doors to keep out the draught. On his left were closed double doors to unseen rooms while to the right there were several other doors, one to the front being left ajar to reveal a large dining room with a long, polished table that must have been able to accommodate twenty or thirty people at a sitting. Stephen craned his neck to try to see more but was interrupted as a staff member appeared from one of the other doors. His order must have been heard from beyond the hall and the young Asian in a smart informal uniform asked if he would like lime, lemon or cucumber in his gin.

"Oh, I don't care really. Surprise me."

The attentive member of staff bowed with his hands held together as if in prayer and Stephen found himself automatically reciprocating. He followed along behind Curran who occasionally glanced over his shoulder to make sure that his guest had not got lost. They entered a comfortable drawing room. The focal point was an enormous fireplace with an intricately carved, marble mantlepiece. A gilt clock sat in the centre and the walls were covered in paintings, mostly landscapes but with a few portraits of bewigged gentlemen and their ladies.

Curran noticed Silchester pause to study the paintings.

"A lot of the contents came with the house when I purchased the estate. A large amount of it was rubbish and beyond restoration but a few items were amusing and worth keeping."

Stephen looked around again and thought that if this was only a few items then he shuddered to think what the volume of the complete contents of the house had been.

Tall French doors opened onto a paved terrace with a pagoda over, providing dappled shade and supporting an old vine that had small, immature bunches of grapes dotted along its gnarled stem. Two comfortably upholstered chairs had been set up to look out over another wide, open vista. A trestle table was positioned between the chairs, covered in a white tablecloth and two coasters waited to receive their drinks that arrived as they stood admiring the view. Curran guided Stephen to one of the chairs and then he sat and held his glass of elderflower cordial in his slender, artistic fingers, a thick gold signet ring on his left hand being the only sign of adornment.

"Forgive my impertinence, Mr Curran, but why am I here?"

"Please, call me Randolph. As to why you are here, let us discuss that after we have eaten. I have something else I would like to show you which might enlighten you."

Stephen settled for the brush off and took a huge gulp from his drink and swallowed gratefully. He would start his abstinence tomorrow.

*

Lunch at one end of the large dining room table proved to be a somewhat stilted affair, conversation being spasmodic and, at times contrived. Excellent wines were produced and served to Stephen, who gulped rather than savoured the refined quality. Curran held his hand up to refuse at each pouring, preferring to sip on a cut glass tumbler of tap water. Stephen noted that the food was adequately cooked, but unexceptional to his trained palate. There were at times, hints of some indefinable flavours that seem to fight for recognition with the other ingredients. Try as he may, he could not quite recognise these competing minor elements of the dishes and, refilling his empty glass, satisfied himself with a further mouthful of the delicious wine.

The meal concluded with coffee and some sweetmeats. The copious quantity of wine that Stephen had consumed did not help in his analysis of the exquisite morsels that he ate. As to how they had been made and what had been used to give them their unique flavour, he was beyond caring.

Curran delicately wiped his mouth and carefully folded his napkin, placing it by the side of his glass of water. Stephen took this as a prompt for him to cease picking at the crumbs on his plate and he removed his napkin from where he had tucked it into the neck of his shirt. Specks of food tumbled from the damask material onto the floor and Stephen thoughtlessly scrubbed them with his feet into the Persian rug that covered the oak floorboarding beneath his chair and the dining room table.

Rising from his seat, Randolph indicated that Stephen should follow him.

"I thought that you might like to have a look around?"

Stephen hauled himself upright and steadied himself against the side of the table.

"I'd like to know why I am here? Nice lunch and all that, but I do have things to do this afternoon."

Randolph smiled knowingly, "I'm sure you are a very busy man, but I think you might find it worthwhile to spare me just a few more minutes of your valuable time. If you then wish to hurry back to your flat, I'll get my driver to take you."

Stephen sighed indulgently, as if satisfying a child's request for his attention, and followed in the wake of his host. They walked to the rear of the house and into a boot room. There was an array of waxed coats and hats hanging on pegs above a line of walking boots and wellington boots, all cleaned of any signs of mud and neatly lined up by size. Stephen did not know how many people lived in the house, but the selection seemed excessive for even a large family.

During the desultory conversation over lunch, he had discovered that Randolph was unmarried and did not have a partner, either male or female. He was an attractive, eligible man who seemed to spend his life in some degree of isolation. Stephen was becoming oddly fascinated by Randolph Curran and found him attractive, in fact, very attractive. His affable disposition was almost imperceptibly flirtatious.

From the back door they entered a York stone, paved yard with climbing roses hung against high walls that enclosed the small courtyard. On the far side was another stone-built outbuilding that was rustic in character but carefully maintained with recently painted timberwork and sparkling panes of glass in every casement. Randolph led the way without checking if Stephen was still with him, he knew that the chef's curiosity would hold him close.

He stopped at the close-boarded door, painted a pastel green that reminded Stephen of moss hanging from the branches of ancient oak trees. Curran took a large metal key from his pocket and slipped the escutcheon plate aside before inserting it into the keyhole. Stephen watched the long slender fingers twist the key in the lock and then push the door open. A thick, heady aroma wafted out to greet them and it was then that a dawning occurred, a transformation, a sudden jolt in his alcohol impaired memory. Instantly, he was returned to a shack to the rear of a bungalow in Sri Lanka.

He stood and looked into Randolph Curran's beautiful, soft, brown eyes, trying to strip away the years, erasing the wrinkles from the face that watched him with undisguised amusement. Stephen mouthed silently all the questions that had never occurred to him over lunch. His disbelief rendered him a mute as his mind wrestled with the impossibility of the situation in which he found himself. He stuttered a stupidly obvious question.

"Who? I mean, can you be, are you really?"

"Ah, now I think you know who I am." Randolph flicked on a light switch and Stephen stumbled into the building still not believing what he was seeing before him. He could not take his eyes from the face that looked knowingly at him. He shook his head to clear the accumulated alcohol from his brain. Curran stood and held his arm open as if to invite Stephen to look around at his surroundings, but Stephen only had eyes for his host.

Were he to look, he would have seen that the room was devoted to a long bench. The walls were shelved and held more reagents, powders, liquids, glass containers, tubes, and equipment than would be found in the best chemistry research laboratories anywhere. A smoke cupboard was positioned to one side and a double sink with high standing taps each with long extended arms such as those used by surgeons when scrubbing up. Somewhat incongruously, against the far wall was a top-of-the-range commercial oven with a range of different sized hobs over. The shelving above that was stacked with cooking pots and implements hung from a rail to the front of the wide extractor hood.

Stephen walked around the room in a daze, in awe of what had suddenly been revealed to him by the simple act of unlocking the timber door to this apothecaries' workshop. Above all, what was more overpowering than the array of equipment was the powerful aroma that suffused every part of the laboratory, surrounding him, bathing every fibre of his clothes, his hair, his skin, the open pores inhaling every molecule that touched its surface. It was strong but wonderful. It invaded his olfactory passages, transporting him back to the years of his youth, the unforgettable visit to Sri Lanka, the young man who foraged for those magnificent botanicals, the food that he had created in the basic kitchen of that simple bungalow in the forest with his friend Randul. Everything from that magical period of his life flooded into his head, he was carried back to the genesis of his career. All the hopes and aspirations of an ambitious chef at the start of his journey to fame and fortune. How those dreams had withered and died, slipped from his hold and left him a broken pathetic specimen of a human being. Weak, washed up and defeated.

Without any sense of shame, Stephen found himself silently weeping, his big shoulders convulsing in self-pity at the recognition of his own abject failure in the presence of this man, and his obvious success in life. He revealed to his host his despair, even though he had turned away to hide the wave of unexpected emotion that sweep through him.

A hand gently rested on his shoulder and Stephen sniffed and faced his erstwhile friend from all those years ago. Stephen sank into Randolph's enfolding arms and wept unashamedly, drenched in self-pity.

"Why?" He sobbed.

Randolph stepped back and leant against the long bench, seemingly unrepentant but not without sympathy for the crumpled figure before him.

He answered softly.

"It's a long story, but I had to leave Sri Lanka rather swiftly."

"Are you really Randul?" Stephen asked hesitantly, wiping away tears that streaked his cheeks, still doubting his own eyes.

"I was once, but now I am Randolph Curran."

Stephen shook his head from side to side in disbelief. How different could his life have been if it were not for the mysterious circumstances that had forced Randul to leave the Sinharaja Forest, to flee Sri Lanka.

He stared hard at the suave man before him and tried to superimpose the features of the fresh-faced young Veddah who he had met and formed such an intense friendship with all those years ago. How was it possible that he should show up in his life at the time of his lowest ebb? At a period when his catastrophic failure was going to be exposed publicly for all to see.

Slowly and insidiously, Stephen's mood started to turn more malevolent. Why had Randul, Randolph, or whatever the hell he chose to call himself, left Stephen to flounder alone in his desperate attempts to preserve the initial magic that had raised his cuisine above that of all his competitors. Was he sitting in the luxury of his expensive estate observing from afar the ignominy of being berated by the harsh critics who catalogued Stephen's loss of status, his loss of confidence, ability, innovation? His culinary artistry deserting him, the accolades and fame having touched him too early, causing his life and his talent to implode into an abusive fog of alcohol and drugs. Did the downfall of Stephen Silchester serve some obscure purpose that Randul was now seeking to exploit?

"This has been a shock for you. I had not intended it to be so and should have tried to make it easier for you." Randolph looked down at his shoes while Stephen blew his nose loudly on his silk handkerchief and stuffed it back into his trouser pocket. Randolph looked up.

"I lost all that I lived for in Sri Lanka."

Stephen let out a short snort of derision to indicate that he had lost more. Randolph continued, ignoring the interruption.

"I've continued with my research and restore this estate to its original form in order to recreate the right conditions for the return of the ancient flora and fauna that was so prevalent in England in the Middle Ages. It has taken some years, during which I have continued to study and utilise the properties that such indigenous herbs and vegetation."

Randolph emphasised his point by lifting jars, showing them to Stephen and then replacing them gently on the shelf.

"The results have been very interesting but, despite many attempts, I have not found anyone who can contribute the necessary culinary skills to match those you demonstrated in Sri Lanka when utilising my botanicals and additives. The proof was in the lunch that you ate today. I watched your reactions closely and, at no time, were you showing any sense of rapture by what was presented to you. Confusion, perhaps, but not rapture. Not the experience that you had when Ranjid cooked for you all those years ago. My chef, despite being well trained, is still not able to recreate the culinary excitement that seems to come to you so naturally."

Stephen listened and allowed the information to sink in before he responded with unexpected anger.

"So, you left me to stew. You knew that without your ingredients it would be impossible for me to produce the dishes that were my intrinsic trademark. Oh, how you must have laughed as you sat up here in your ivory castle, surrounded by your rewilding and your wealth, to watch me struggle and ultimately fail. How could you do that? I thought we were friends."

Randolph looked sympathetically at his friend and nodded his head in agreement.

"You're right. I deserted you. I had to for reasons that you need not concern yourself with, but you must believe me, I had no alternative."

Stephen looked unconvinced, silently wondering if the rumours that he had heard about the vendetta during his short return trip to Sri Lanka were true. Whatever had occurred must have been pretty serious for Randul to flee his homeland.

"When I arrived in England I had to build a new life for myself. I had no time for my research and no foraging upon which to base it. When I bought this place, I spent years re-establishing the local flora and fauna. I knew that I could not replicate my work in Sri Lanka and had to start again with the indigenous ingredients that appeared on the estate. It is only now that I have been in any position to pick-up from where I left off."

"OK, so now you come to me to enable you to continue with your little hobby. Christ, you've got a bloody nerve." Stephen turned to leave but hesitated as Randolph said,

"Are you not still curious as to why I have invited you here? It was not to gloat, nor was it to apologise. I have a suggestion to make if you would just wait a while."

His voice was gently entreating Stephen to stay, and Stephen could not resist. He huffed in apparent exasperation but felt in his heart that he had nothing to lose by hearing what Randolph had to say.

The gap between the two men had closed and Stephen stood a foot or so from Randolph. He could smell his cologne, see into his clear eyes, the softness of his hair and the smoothness of his skin. Something stirred deep within Stephen, he felt a desire to put his hand to Randolph's cheek, to feel his warm skin, but he resisted. Before him stood the proud young Veddah as a mature man. His mouth was dry as he attempted to cover his embarrassment.

"You're right." Stephen suddenly felt a need to unburden himself to Randolph, to face up his failure. "I came because I have my back to the wall. I am desperate and would grasp at any help that you, or anyone else, might have to offer."

Randolph maintained an unblinking watch on his companion as Stephen struggled for the words that would bridge the divide that the last twenty years had opened up between them. He still felt resentful at Randul's disappearance, and his failure to fulfil his promise to keep The Sauceror's Apprentice stocked with his fantastical potions.

What he had tasted at lunch did not excite him in the same way that he had been excited by the dinner served in the scruffy little lodging house in Kandy. He wanted to recapture that magic. He wanted to rekindle their friendship, to grasp the peace offering made by Randolph. Stephen was unsure if he could trust the beautifully elegant man who had thrown him the lifeline, but as he swirled into a vortex of financial and reputational ruin, he had little viable alternative.

"I'm sorry. This is all a bit too much to take in." A sudden wave of honest realism swept over Stephen. "I'm a washed-up restaurateur, dependent upon drugs and alcohol to keep my head together. What do you want of me? You appear as if a guardian angel, to do what? Save me? Wallow in my decline into…into…?" Words failed him as to where his future was heading. "God, I don't know what."

Stephen turned from facing Randolph and slumped onto a stool staring unseeing at the selection of chemical bottles in front of him. He suddenly felt very tired. He had admitted to this comparative stranger who had reappeared into his life, his dependency on stimulants to live his life. Previously, he had never managed to do that to anyone. Sporadic attendance at Alcoholic Anonymous and a couple of drug rehabilitation clinics had not achieved the degree of self-realisation that the last twenty minutes had produced.

Stephen sat silently with Randolph, neither man speaking, both absorbed in their own thoughts. Stephen finally admitting that he had messed up his life, suddenly felt an overwhelming sense of release. Something in him had popped. It was as if he had had a weight that had hung round his neck removed. He felt sharper of mind and freed from the depression that had been dragging him further and further into the clutches of his addiction. Hardly a Damascene revelation, but certainly a sense of enlightenment.

Perhaps the man who was perched in his relaxed manner against the bench looking down at him was some sort of saviour. Would he restore Stephen's love for cooking, his imagination for new and daring mélanges of tastes, textures and smells that would stimulate people's senses, exciting, challenging, and refreshing.

Without thinking, Stephen got up from his stool and wandered over to the shelves that were weighted down with Kilner jars full of the harvest that Randolph had processed and stored. Each one was carefully labelled and many had names unknown to Stephen. He randomly took down bottles and containers and inhaled deeply or tasted pinches of each. The variety was enormous, and his mind began to put together ingredients that would add to or be enhanced by the tastes and smells that he was experiencing. He became more animated, moving around the room with greater fluidity.

Randolph watched as Stephen opened the fridge that stood to one side of the cooker. Ignoring Randolph, he started to take out various simple ingredients. From a bowl he chose tomatoes, fennel, sweet potato. He took down a wok from one of the shelves. Stephen found his hands moving automatically between the various items that he required, his brain having memorised almost instantly each flavour and aroma that he required.

Stephen was like a child in a playroom full of his favourite toys, almost spoilt for choice but focused on the creation of his ad hoc dishes. Randolph sat on the stool vacated by Stephen and just observed as the chef busily worked away. Each dish was tasted and then started again if it did not find the level of perfection he was seeking. Sometimes he would ask Randolph's opinion, but for most of the time he was totally self-absorbed. Gradually, his demands for specific items became more obscure. Randolph would hunt through the specimens held in jars on the shelves to try to match the requirements or offer an alternative that might add something unique to the flavour.

On a couple of occasions, he rang through to his kitchen asking someone to deliver an ingredient to the laboratory. Each time he took delivery of it at the door without letting anyone into the hallowed space. The speed of production of dishes accelerated as Stephen worked away. He was hot and stripped off his jacket. His work rate accelerated.

The building was awash with different smells, all of which transported the two men back to a sweltering kitchen in Kandy, dissolving twenty years of separation, replacing despair with an almost ecstatic level of joy. The range of ingredients that Randolph had made available to Stephen was even more diverse than those he had used in Sri Lanka and the effects on the senses infinitely more enchanting.

After nearly four hours of frantic cooking, the two men collapsed into an excited exhaustion. Each was on a high that was inexplicable given that nothing that Stephen had used to create the dishes had any opioid characteristics. They were the product of an organic growing environment, a knowledgeable botanical chemist and a talented chef.

The combination was sublime, the potential was formidable.

It was late by the time Randolph and Stephen had completed their discussions and both made copious notes in accordance with their individual disciplines. This time the conversation flowed in a torrent, each trying to better the ideas of the other. It became clear that Randolph was not going to assist financially in stopping the existing restaurant premises being repossessed by the landlord. However, he would protect the name and domain name from opportunistic investors or potential impostors.

There was an inevitability to the loss of the Mayfair premises that Stephen swept inconsequentially aside with a wave of his hand. The prospect of a different kind of offering had him galvanised into a heightened sense of creative exhilaration.

Randolph's usual cook was dismissed for the night and while they continued to talk Stephen worked like a demon in the main kitchen within the body of the house. Dishes appeared and were tasted, considered and, where successfully, consumed with delight. Equally, any offerings that did not reach the correct degree of perfection received harsh criticism and were binned, the reason for such failure being carefully noted down by both men for future reference.

Dinner was eaten sporadically at the kitchen table as each new offering was completed, and the talking did not cease for the whole duration. The meal catapulted Stephen back to his more creative days, while Randolph realised that his restraint over the past few years to expose his real identity to Stephen was a mistake. The two men gradually slipped back into a rekindled youthful enthusiasm that had enveloped them when they first met. What the intervening period had confirmed to them both was that neither could achieve their respective objectives without the other.

As they sat with mugs of Sri Lankan green tea on the table before them, Stephen asked the question that had been gnawing away at him since he discovered that Randolph and Randul were one in the same.

"I know what the press said happened in Sri Lanka before you ran, but how did you escape and how did you end up here?"

Randolph placed his hands around his mug and sat staring at the steam as it rose as a wisp towards the ceiling, the light catching the individual minute droplets of vapour.

"It's a long story and not one I choose to recall too often." He lifted the tea to his lips and blew gently across the surface of the hot liquid. "I basically made my way to the north of the island, took a boat across to Rameswaram in the Tamil Nadu province of India and thereafter followed the route that thousands of migrants have followed."

"You travelled overland to England?" Stephen asked incredulously.

"Yes. It was a hard time and all the while there were criminals preying on those who passed through their territories. Each taking a bit of whatever meagre possessions the migrants had left of their lives. It wasn't a good time, and I don't want to ever repeat the experience."

Randolph drifted into silence. He had no intention of describing any of the details of his experiences to anyone or the fact that he had had to fight through every stage of his journey. The hardships in themselves turned him from a naïve youth into a cunning and resourceful man capable of standing up for himself and defending the valuables that he was carrying with him on his journey. The cash from Ziyad's briefcase provided plenty of funds for judicious bribery and the purchase of transport over the most arduous sections of his exodus. He kept the size of his funds a closely guarded secret that meant that he existed as a loner, not making many friends and trusting no one.

He listened to whomsoever he encountered, keen to learn, to absorb the harsh ways of the streets that these characters displayed as badges of honour. He learnt about how you secreted valuables about your body as you progressed across the continents, how you avoided the most corrupt authorities and how you made pliable those who were open to the blandishments that supplemented their meagre government wages. The threats came from all sides, but mainly from his fellow travellers, those who had frittered away their modest sums of money and now sought to replenish their reserves by whatever means might be available to them. Desperate people in dire straits. Hyenas feeding from the stream of humankind that flowed across the countries between their past and the nirvana that was to be their future, be that England, or France, or America. Ever fortified by promises of wealth and security at the end of their trail, assurances given freely by those who had never been, to those who would probably never arrive at their true journey's end. All were sustained by dreams and visions that would evaporate in the harsh light of reality. The horrors that inhabited the overcrowded and undersized dinghies, that failed to stop the seawater slopping over the gunwales, failed to resuscitate the numb toes and fingers from the stinging spray, or stay the fear of capture when wading ashore through dark, freezing water onto the coast of who knows where.

Suffice it to say, Randolph had experienced every type of fear, misery and disappointment that could be heaped upon a person. But two years of nomadic life had left him with a sharp intuition, strong of body and mind as well as supremely self-assured. If he could survive the rigours of that period of his life, then his remaining years would be an evenly trod path that he would travel with astute equanimity. Unlike many of those who had arrived with him on a cold winter's morning in an unsafe RID from across the English Channel, he had stealthily repatriated a large amount of his acquired wealth to his chosen destination. Some was scattered around the country, secreted in tourists' belongings for innocent importation, all unaware of their cooperation to his cause. His only real social interaction during the two years of his journey was with such tourists. He used his ready cash to maintain a smart appearance and frequented the cafes, restaurants and tourist hotspots in the various cities or towns where he had temporarily resided before he commenced the next leg of his pilgrimage. Befriending them, sometimes with his charm, sometimes with his body, but always with the sole intention of offlaying his wealth across England for later collection, maintaining a steadfast belief that he would find those to whom he had secretly imparted a small part of his wealth for conveyance to his final haven. There would be losses, he knew that, but it was one of the accepted risks of his strategy. He figured that it was better to suffer some minor losses than to be continually feeding the outstretched, grasping hands of the traffickers who were constantly stealing or demanding money for little return from the dependent migrants.

His choice of targets was not quite as arbitrary as it might sound. Randolph was careful to cluster his carriers in the area around London which, while still vast, meant that the retrieval of his belongings was not as onerous as it might have been. He maintained a little dog-eared black book of addresses – "Oh, if you are in England then it would be great to see you," or "Do look us up when you are in England', or "Let me give you my details, it would be lovely to catch up when you are in London." All the entries were told that he was due to be in England in a few months, all unswervingly offered him hospitality when he arrived, but none really believed that he would materialise on their doorstep.

And when he did, there was an embarrassed, if not shocked, greeting from their suburban front doors, followed by an overly extravagant welcome. Randolph would never stay longer than was necessary to find the item in which he had secreted a trinket, some notes, or a stone or two. Sometimes it was difficult to establish where the item was but usually a reminder of its existence, a token that he might have given to a woman, a memento bought with him at a local market or a souvenir, elicited a search and recovery of the item to prove that it had been kept as a sentimental memory of a wonderful trip, of a liaison, of an adventure.

Slowly but surely, he re-amassed a large proportion of his belongings and fed them unobtrusively into the many bank accounts that he had opened immediately upon having been given refugee status under his new Anglicized name. Given the nature of his restored endowment, it was only natural that he would open and build-up his own jewellery business, culminating in the eventual acceptance by the establishment of Mr Randolph Curran as a British citizen and to promote himself as the model of an industrious and successful immigrant businessman.

One package that was never sought or recovered by Randolph was the one containing the blue sapphires that he had secreted in the boxes of herbs on the night of the gala dinner. They were intended as a gift from Randul to his English friend at the end of an adventure. Stephen had made no mention of the package either through embarrassment or purely a loss of memory as a result of fog inducing excesses. Whatever the reason, Randolph did not begrudge their loss or the use to which they were put by his friend. Stephen's needs were greater than those of Randolph. Perhaps it was a price that had to be paid for him abandoning his friend.

Throughout his long journey only the smallest of the Padparadscha sapphires travelled with him. At just over sixteen grammes it was easy to hide either on, or within, his body. At times it was difficult and dangerous. While making his way across the Ionian Sea to Italy, he nearly lost it when the boat he was on sank. He swam, floundered and floated in the water for a night and half a day before he was eventually found by three fishermen. They tried to strip him of his bag and its contents but underestimated the fight that Randolph had in him. After he had beaten two unconscious, the remaining fisherman reluctantly cooperated and landed him ashore on a deserted beach. The other refugees on the boat had not been so lucky. Randul found a number of bodies washed up on the shoreline, sandflies already starting their gruesome task.

Thankfully he had not been subjected to a more intimate body search. The seafarers on the migrant routes knew that amongst the desperate and despairing, there were those who still had items of hidden or disguised wealth with them. These made rich pickings in comparison to anything else they might catch in their nets. The bodies that lay on the soft sand had already been stripped of anything of value.

In the early days, before he was recognised as a reputable jeweller and dealer of gems, he had sold the smaller Padparadscha and a number of the yellow, pink and blue sapphires that he had recovered from his assorted and innocent mules. These had been auctioned in New York through an intermediary who took an extortionate fee for the privilege. Despite this, due to its exceptional quality and weight, the Padparadscha had made a substantial contribution towards the purchase of his home.

Together with the other stones, a number of those from Ziyad's briefcase proving to be treated and heated, so not as valuable as might have been expected, Randul found the means by which he could realise his dream of rewilding the estate through the reintroduction and nurturing of the native flora.

Thereafter it was relatively simple to slip other stones onto the market, normally through his own business that became the 'go-to' boutique jewellery destination for any well-heeled family seeking the unique or extravagant designs that he had to offer. Randolph's wealth increased exponentially. As his reputation grew, he spent less and less time at his place of business and more and more time in his extravagantly appointed laboratory, experimenting with the botanicals that thrived in the rejuvenated landscape that surrounded his home.

On his arrival in England, he had observed the young chef, Stephen Silchester, at his zenith. Then there was a period when the dream faded, the tabloid newspapers questioned why he had taken a break to travel back to Sri Lanka leaving his burgeoning business to stutter under the management of the extrovertly self-indulgent Armand. Upon Silchester's return from his trip there followed a dramatic slump in the popularity of The Sauceror's Apprentice. His unique skills seemed to evaporate and his reputation crashed.

Did Randolph feel any remorse? He was aware that his contribution to the success of the Sauceror's Apprentice was crucial, but he was too nervous to reveal his past to anyone. He wanted to forget his roots as a Veddah, the name of Randul, Ziyad the gems dealer and his former life. What he had achieved after his departure from Sri Lanka was infinitely preferable to the life that was destined for him as a wanted man from the Sinharaja Forest. Even in England, there remained the constant risk of the discovery of his real identity and arrest for the possible murder of the odious gem dealer. However, Randolph considered that risk to be more remote and therefore acceptable.

What had eventually changed his mind? Randolph knew that there was an ever-present desire to ascertain the true potential of his obsessive experimentation. To date he had had a series of unsuccessful attempts through the hiring of a succession of cooks and chefs who had tried and failed to emulate the gifts that were the preserve of Stephen Silchester. Randolph had tracked over the years the unravelling of Stephen's professional and personal life and finally decided that the time was right for him to step in, regardless of the potential risks.

Now, as he sat in front of his friend, replete with cuisine that defied explanation, he was sure that together they could set the gastronomic world alight once again. To re-establish Stephen was achievable. The satisfaction for Randolph was in the certainty that Stephen could not do it without him, being counterbalanced by the realisation that he could not do it without Stephen.

Stephen had finished his tea and was still reeling from the abridged story that Randolph had regaled of his escape and subsequent journey to England. In the light of the revelations, and the obvious hardships that his friend had suffered, he could not bring himself to blame Randolph for his own misfortunes. He should never have depended upon one brief acquaintance to shore up his whole business model. He had been so naïve. Now he realised that he should have expanded his own knowledge and contacts before he arrogantly took on the gastronomic world with the expectation of dominating it for longer than a nanosecond.

"So, what now?"

Randolph stood up from the table, walked across the kitchen and through the door into the entrance hall. Stephen was not sure if he was expected to follow but, due to his extreme fatigue from the events of the day, he remained seated. Randolph returned after a couple of minutes and handed a plain white envelope to Stephen. He weighed it in his hand and felt the thick contents.

"Don't open it now. It's late and I've a lot to do tomorrow. Take it with you and read it at your leisure. My driver will return you to your apartment and we can discuss it in a day or so, when you've had time to consider my proposal."

Randolph's arm was outstretched to indicate that it was time for Stephen to vacate the kitchen and return to London. The door opened and the driver materialised to accompany the visitor to the car.

Stephen hesitantly shook hands with Randolph and thanked him for a fascinating and enjoyable day. Randolph said that he would look froward to hearing from Stephen and the two men were once again parting as old friends. Stephen could not leave on a handshake and suddenly took Randolph into his arms and gave him a close hug. Randolph was initially taken aback and then put his arms around the bulky body and patted him softly on the back.

Stephen felt more complete than he had done for years, more positive, more alive. He spoke quietly into Randolph's ear, "Thank you."

The night air was chilly, and Stephen shivered as he hurried between the open front door and the car. The engine was ticking over and the heater already blowing warm air throughout the compartment.

The car crunched back down the drive at a sedate pace before gathering speed as it swung out through the open gates onto the main road. Stephen looked at the envelope but restrained himself from ripping it open to read the contents. He knew that car sickness would instantly afflict him, and he did not wish to risk that happening.

The M40 motorway was unusually quiet. Stephen lay with his head back against the headrest to doze and reflect on the day as another powerful limousine was speeding its way out of the Heathrow Airport tunnel towards central London.

Delayed, and subjected to an unnecessary customs search, a tired and irritable Ameesha headed for Claridge's Hotel.

Chapter 24

Wykeford House, Wykeford Estate, Oxfordshire

Dear Stephen,

It was a great pleasure to meet you again after so long and I hope that you enjoyed your visit. I told you that I wished to make a proposition to you, but equally made it clear that I was not prepared to provide any surety in respect to your premises in Brook Street. I would advise that you relinquish your lease on those premises and try to minimise any dilapidations claim that your landlord may seek to make against you. I do not think that this will be a problem as I believe that you are not able to make any such payment in any event. As for your other creditors, you will have to try to make an accommodation with them, although I suspect the HMRC claim will be more difficult to settle.

What I am proposing is a completely new start, albeit retaining your signature trade name of The Sauceror's Apprentice which you should hold onto at all costs. I believe that you are the registered owner of the internet domain name.

Today you will have seen that I have been continuing with my research that I started in the Sinharaja Forest in Sri Lanka. I have had to adapt that research to accommodate a different range of plants in my new home here in England. As you have seen, I have started to restore the natural ecosystem with the reintroduction of ancient and traditional species as well as a minority of non- indigenous species that I consider essential to my work. Generally, these have thrived. My current research has produced a new range of diverse, innovative and, I believe, unique ingredients for the enhancement of both flavours and textures.

However, despite my best efforts, I have been unable to find a chef that has your gifts and incomparable flair to maximise upon the potential of my discoveries.

This has caused me a particular frustration and despite my misgivings in reopening a connection with anyone who might have known me in my native country, I have decided that I have no alternative but to approach you in what I believe is your own time of need. I cannot allow your talents to be debased by alcohol and drugs. You have talents that have still to be fully realised and with my research I believe we can achieve something far greater than previously seen.

Forgive me for writing at such length and in such blunt terms but if what I am about to suggest finds favour with you, then I must insist that you cease any further abuse of your mind and body and focus your efforts unreservedly on my proposed joint venture.

In simple terms, I would like to back you in undertaking a tour of, initially, England with a pop-up restaurant concept serving a special taster dinner for invited guests who are inter-generationally influential. These events will be carefully managed and infrequent, with the intention of creating a mystical aura surrounding each one so that they become the "must have" invitation of the season. No other gimmicks are necessary, the whole enterprise relying upon my ingredients and your artistry in putting them together to create exquisite dishes for a discerning customer base.

I have included with this letter some additional material for your consideration. There is the specification for a mobile kitchen that I have commissioned from a firm in Hull together with some details of the venues upon which I have reservations provisionally held. You will no doubt have some observations to make, and any amendments can be accommodated.

Finally, you will find a suggested guest list for the first five venues. As I have mentioned, the invitees are a mixture of discerning influencers on social media along with society figures who will enhance the profile of The Sauceror's Apprentice. If our offering is acceptable to them, these people will be able to spread the word and the final venues will fill themselves from people clambering to take a place at our table. If you have any observations, particularly regarding the mobile kitchen, then please let me have these as soon as possible so that they can be incorporated into the build.

The financial arrangements will be on the basis that I shall fund the whole operation and amortise that cost over five years for repayment as a loan by the business. Any profits, and I believe that we can create a considerable return from our combined efforts, will be split 50:50 between us after expenses. I will take the role of silent partner as I do not want to be seen to have any overt involvement with the venture. My overriding interest is to continue and expand upon my research here at Wykeford to enable you to enhance your range of dishes and hence the culinary experiences for our guests.

I look forward to hearing from you when you have read this letter and the material enclosed herewith.

With best wishes

Randolph Curran

Stephen had read the letter and attached papers three times as well as poring over the design drawings and specification for the mobile kitchen. The latter was based upon one of those huge mobile homes used by Formula 1 teams or film companies for their stars on location. Not only did it have a fully fitted kitchen that would accommodate three chefs, but there were also areas for the transportation of any other fixtures or fittings that they may require for each separate destination. Freezers, fridges, hobs, ovens, work benches, vacuum packaging machines, water baths and so the list went on. The drawings of the layout had obviously been prepared by a professional kitchen designer with ergonomics paramount in the layout of each piece of equipment. Try as he may, Stephen could find no element that failed to satisfy his exacting standards.

When Stephen had first opened the envelope, his reaction was one of irritation. It was obvious that the letter had been prepared prior to his visit to the Wykeford Estate and there was a presumption on Randolph's part that Stephen would fall for his blandishments. The laboratory, the results of his research, the availability of ingredients, the lab kitchen, it had all been pre-planned and all that was required was for Stephen Silchester, the failing celebrity chef, to add his magic.

However, the more he read and studied the papers that Randolph had given to him, the more the idea started to appeal. Stephen had already had some outline ideas for dishes, and he could imagine the truck rolling into some of the locations garnering excited anticipation of the residents eager to be part of the adventure.

Stephen looked at his watch and suddenly jumped up from his seat. He was expected at the restaurant in Brook Street for a meeting with his solicitor, Peter Asquith, and someone from the landlord's company. Grabbing his phone and jacket he bustled out of the flat and walked as fast as his legs would carry his bulky frame. He puffed his way towards the underground station making yet another commitment to himself to get back in shape.

But this time he had an incentive to do so.

*

Stephen hurried down Davies Street and turned into Brook Street. Peter Asquith was standing outside looking at his watch and wondering where his client could have got to, or if he had forgotten altogether? Perhaps he was lying in his apartment in an alcoholic stupor, oblivious to this appointment with his landlord?

It was with considerable relief that he spied his overweight client turn into Brook Street and waddle across the road, waving a pudgy hand in greeting.

"Sorry, Peter." Stephen drew up to the solicitor and extended a hand which was taken and shaken briefly.

The restaurant looked abandoned and drab, having been closed for a week due to lack of funds and a lack of bookings following the crushingly harsh review by the food critic, Tom De Pietro. Customers had deserted his establishment, removed from the circuit of restaurants used to entertain and impress friends or business associates. It had become the place not to be seen.

"I thought you might have forgotten."

Stephen looked askance and proceeded to unlock the door into his premises. His for not much longer. Asquith watched him fumble with the keys and finally turn the lock. Inside, the temperature of the property was cold and the air smelt musty. Gone were the arresting aromas of succulent dishes waiting to satisfy the most demanding of appetites. Stephen went to the back of the dining room and switched on all the lights that brought a bit of life back into the vacant space. Forlorn tables and chairs yearned for the babble of conversation, the chink of glasses and the appreciative murmuring of happy diners, but the only sound was the rumble of traffic in the street outside and a distant siren echoing between the high facades of a congested Mayfair thoroughfare.

A hundred yards away, Ameesha emerged from Claridge's Hotel, refreshed having had a good night's sleep and a healthy breakfast in her suite. The delays to her flight and idiotic bureaucracy of the Border Control Officers at Heathrow had ebbed away and her mind was focused on the task ahead.

During her flight she had read the briefing papers from the managing agents for the property and her solicitor, both of which were tales of woe. The failure of The Sauceror's Apprentice had left her company owed nearly two hundred and fifty thousand pounds in service charges and rent. The property had recently been refitted which might be a blessing or a curse. If she could let it to another restaurant then the equipment might be of benefit, but if there was no demand for that use then the whole lot was going to have to be stripped out at a further cost of fifty thousand pounds. Her accountants had done a lot of work to assess the covenant strength of Silchester, the owner of the defunct restaurant, and found no assets of worth and discovered that the man was a degenerate, alcohol and drugs had crawled into his mind and body and, according to her advisors, left him virtually incapable of cooking an egg, let alone a gastronomic extravaganza.

She pulled her coat around her at the unaccustomed chill of the morning as she spied the frontage of the property further up the street. Ameesha had spurned the agent's offer to accompany her to the meeting. She had no need of anyone to hold her hand, particularly when she discovered that, despite his alluring voice on the telephone, he was a man in his mid-forties with a pockmarked face and greasy lank hair. Not the vision that she had conjured up in her mind, merely an awful disappointment. When accompanied by the news that the art gallery had pulled out of the deal that he had told her was a certainty, she lost faith in both the man and his professional capabilities.

Ameesha increased her pace to try to get some warmth into her body and stopped abruptly outside the door to The Sauceror's Apprentice. There were lights on inside and a couple of people appeared to be waiting for her. She assumed the larger of the two was Silchester, a man who obviously ate as much as he cooked. The second man was short, with thinning hair and wearing an expensive suit. He looked beaten before she had entered into any negotiations, and she suspected that he privately regretted having Silchester as one of his clients. This was going to be a piece of cake, she thought.

Peter Asquith was indeed regretting his association with the now failed Silchester. He was owed a huge amount of fees that even his successful practice could not afford to write off. To add to his woes, the landlord had said that they wanted a private meeting which meant that they had a proposition which, from experience, Stephen was going to reject and kick up a huge fuss. He was argumentative at the best of times but when forced into a corner he could be plain obnoxious. Peter felt that his role was going to be one of referee rather than advisor and he was not looking forward to the prospect.

When the door swung open to reveal an attractive young Asian woman dressed in a long coat, high heel shoes and carrying a slim, soft leather document case under her arm both men exchanged glances. This was not the landlord they were expecting, and Peter wondered, incorrectly, whether he might retrieve the situation slightly for his client. Surely his years of experience in the law of Landlord and Tenant would be more than enough to tie up this pretty young thing.

He was disabused at the first introduction. Ameesha had met men like Asquith before, and they had all underestimated her. The whole meeting lasted less than fifteen minutes and at the end Ameesha had taken back the lease, and all the new kitchen equipment, fixtures and fittings as well as the keys. Asquith had spoken no more than a dozen words, and the majority of those were while introducing himself. To his astonishment, Stephen listened quietly to the confident young woman who gave a well-informed analysis of his legal position, the alternatives that existed for both parties and her suggestion for resolution.

Stephen considered the offer for no more than a couple of seconds before unconditionally accepting her terms. She produced a document from her briefcase for Stephen to sign in duplicate. Stephen unsuccessfully searched in the pockets of his jacket for a non-existent writing implement. Ameesha swiftly handed him her Mont Blanc pen. Peter tried to justify his presence by asking to read the document on behalf of his client. Stephen rejected his unwanted advice with a dismissive wave of his hand and, signing on the spot, handed over the keys.

He looked around, taking in the surroundings that once, a long time ago, he had hoped would promise so much for the future. He was at the end of one era and the dawn of a new epoch. Naturally, he had regrets, but none that he was prepared to display to those around him. The young lady who represented the landlord was polite but firm. It made the whole affair so much easier. The last thing that had occurred to him was that she was not an agent but the owner of the building. Nor did he appreciate that she was pretty certain that she had already found a new tenant for the premises at an increased rent and who was prepared to pay a sizeable capital sum for all the equipment, as well as the fixtures and fittings.

Even if he had known, would it have made any difference? Not really.

"By the way," Ameesha asked, "whatever happened to your Consultant Herbologist?" She emphasised the title in a mocking voice. "Now, what was his name?"

Stephen stopped mid step and turned to face her, his mind racing as to how he should answer. Was it truly an innocent question, or did she know that only yesterday he had met with him? Coincidence or not, Stephen pulled off a masterly piece of bitter obfuscation.

"No idea. Bastard disappeared," he snapped and continued towards the door.

Stephen took one last look around and then was bundled out onto the street, his solicitor close behind.

All in all, Ameesha considered the morning to have been a particular success. Stephen had been dismissive of her question and for the moment she would accept his answer at face value. She had more pressing commitments. She was due to meet her new prospective tenant once she had ushered the last one out of the door

After that, she would visit one or two Bond Street stores to purchase some undeniably expensive bits and pieces and then she would treat herself to a light lunch in a small bistro off New Bond Street as recommended by one of the in-flight magazines that she had read on the aircraft.

"Well, I think that went rather well," Peter announced. Stephen just stared at him in disbelief.

"I'd forgotten you were there, Peter. I hope you're not expecting to be paid a fee for that?"

The lawyer snorted.

"Not much point really. You can't pay it anyway." He might as well get the inevitable over and done with.

"I am afraid that my firm can no longer act for you, Stephen, and we will have to take proceedings against you for our unpaid fees that now amount to," he paused as he drew a sheet of paper from his inside breast pocket and looked at the typed note, "over thirty-five thousand pounds."

"Ok." Stephen was beyond caring, "Thanks for letting me know. I wish you luck as I am going to declare myself bankrupt so you can put yourself in the queue, but I wouldn't hold out much hope of seeing more than a few coppers." Stephen started to take a couple of paces away before turning back to his solicitor and saying with heavy sarcasm,

"Thanks for your help."

Neither man noticed the Arab on the opposite side of the street dressed in a well-cut suit, lounging against a lamppost and lighting a cigarette. He made no effort to move as Stephen and Peter walked off in opposite directions, his gaze firmly fixed on the restaurant from where they had both emerged.

Stephen hurried off towards Hanover Square to find a café where he could have a resuscitating cup of coffee and telephone Randolph with his decision. Normally he would have retired to the Red Lion, The Blue Post or The Guinea but he intended to start his new regime immediately and so alcohol was off the menu.

Dialling the number that Randolph had given him, Stephen walked briskly through the Mayfair crowds, waiting impatiently for the call to be answered.

"Curran."

"Randolph, its Stephen. Stephen Silchester."

"Good morning, Stephen." Randolph sounded relaxed and friendly. "How are you today?"

"Sober," Stephen replied simply.

"Well, that's splendid." The words were genuinely meant, "Do you have a decision for me?"

"I've read through all the material you gave me and I'm up for it. When do we start?"

Stephen stopped and stood outside a small independently run cafe with the smell of freshly roasted coffee beans drifting out from the open doorway.

"Where are you?" Randolph asked.

"In London, where are you."

"Funnily enough, so am I. How about a spot of lunch?"

"Where?"

Randolph gave him an address and a time before ringing off. Stephen checked his watch and ordered a recuperative cappuccino from the Italian proprietor of the café. After his coffee, he wandered down to the Royal Academy to kill the hour before lunch.

Randolph replaced his mobile 'phone in the pocket of his suit, his tailor having cut the cloth so that such items did not spoil the line of his jacket. His morning had been spent in a meeting with his shop manager, a middle-aged Bangladeshi woman that he had met in the camp outside Calais. She was overqualified for the job, highly intelligent and wholly trustworthy. In fact, the majority of those Randolph employed had been the unfortunates who had made the same journey as him. Dispossessed, frightened and alone.

He vowed that if ever he made a success of his new life in England, he would seek to help those who did not have the same financial advantage that had endowed him. He was constantly surprised during his years of travelling along the refugee routes that there was so much displaced talent and professional expertise. He had rather simply assumed that all those seeking new frontiers were the uneducated and workshy, seeking easy pickings in the profligate West. But they were, in the main, family men and women who had lost everything, or almost everything. They were forced to desert their homeland to find a safer, more viable livelihood where murder, rape, corruption and destitution were not a part of everyday life. Aged relatives were left behind, too weak to make such an arduous trek, unwilling to leave the country of their birth; believing that the political aberration that subjugated their existence would be vanquished enabling them to return to a traditional normality that could never root itself in any modern state.

The upper floors of the New Bond Street store were for appointments with private clients to view major pieces of bespoke jewellery. The ground floor was a beautiful old shop that Randolph had restored with meticulous attention to detail and would have been readily recognisable by any late Victorian resident who should return to the street. The security guard outside the front door was a modern addition that had become a necessity due to the existence of a small cabal of thieves who, in broad daylight, used motorbikes to smash their way into jewellery stores knowing that even a small haul would be valuable, and the traffic congested enough to stack the odds of a two-wheeled escape in their favour.

Completing his business, he took a turn around the store and chatted to everyone, asking about the newly born, the sick relative or any exciting holiday plans. He prided himself on knowing every one of them by name and kept abreast of their circumstances and concerns. This paternalism was appreciated by all and never abused. Loyalty among his staff was absolute. They would die for him if required.

Randolph finished a brief conversation with the youngest member of his staff, a trainee who had shown great promise for the future. As he approached the door, he saw the security man had just completed the usual discreet search of an attractive young woman's slim leather briefcase and handbag prior to being granted admission. Satisfied that she had nothing of note, he pressed the bell and someone in the shop released the security catch. Randolph took the handle of the door and opened it for the woman.

She looked straight at him, flashing a most engaging smile with eyes that sparkled brightly. Her long coat camouflaged her figure, but he guessed that it was honed through hours spent with a personal trainer. Her hands were beautifully manicured, her fingers long and slender. Randolph always noticed hands as potential sites for his rings, a particular speciality in his range of jewellery. Expensive and beautifully crafted, he knew that there would be something in his store to tempt this elegant, and obviously wealthy customer. With some regret, he would have to leave it to others to satisfy her requirements.

She glided through the door maintaining eye contact with Randolph, the flicker of a smile playing on her lips.

"Thank you."

"You are most welcome." Randolph bowed slightly and still looked into her unblinking eyes. As she passed, she turned slightly to face him as if the doorway was too narrow, which it was not. She quickly appraised his attire and wrongly concluded that he was an affluent client leaving the premises. She would make discreet enquiries about him from the assistants while finding a bauble or two for herself.

Ameesha swept by and halfway across the shop floor turned her head for one final admiring glance. Randolph had remained holding the door, watching as she traversed the space between the entrance and the assistant waiting with anticipation behind the counter to serve her. You did not enter this shop unless you intended to purchase something, in much the same way that anyone who asked what the price of an item was, was unlikely to be able to afford it.

A minute nod of his head was reciprocated by the woman before they simultaneously turned to continue with their respective tasks.

Randolph strode out of the shop and, turning smartly right, almost knocked over a man who was standing at the shop front, peering in through the glass, observing the interior beyond the display shelves. Randolph danced to one side narrowly avoiding the man and apologised for his lack of attention. The man stepped away from the window and grinned to expose uneven teeth. A distinctive smell pervaded the space between them, a smell that Randolph recognised but could not name. Continuing on down the street, he looked back and saw that the stranger had reverted to looking into the window.

Randolph thought about backtracking but was relieved to see that his security officer was fully aware of the window-shoppers presence and had him under close surveillance. The guard nodded knowingly to Randolph.

Comforted, Randolph resumed his walk to his lunch engagement, the delights of the young woman who had passed him in the doorway lingering pleasantly in his memory.

Chapter 25

"It is rare that I have to offer my apologies for anything, let alone to someone that considered me to have slighted them in the past. But, in this instance I will be unreserved in my redaction of anything that I might have written in my column about Stephen Silchester. I do this not at the behest of a solicitor or as a result of a court judgement by an honourable judge citing libel or slander, but simply upon the evidence of my own palate at an occasion that I attended last Tuesday with great trepidation.

Visiting castles has not been my thing since I was seven years old and got locked in an underground cell in Lancaster Castle that once had housed the Pendle Witches. That was a mere two minutes of terror before the lights were turned back on and the steel door reopened. On this occasion, I spent nearly four hours in that same castle in raptures of delight.

Gone is the over-decorated boudoir in Brook Street, gone is the bland unimaginative fare, gone is any hint of complacency or lack of true talent. What has emerged from the wilderness years is a concept and a finesse that has taken the gastronomic world by storm. The majestic Lancaster Castle, once a prison and now a visitor attraction, had been dressed in such an understated fashion, comfortably furnished without being ostentatious or detracting from the inherent splendour of the Castle. The assembled company, and it was assembled as there is no method of making a booking, was by invitation only. We entered through the massive John O'Gaunt Gate into a subtly lit courtyard of epic proportions. The grandeur and gravitas of the building instilled in the guest a pent-up anticipation for something that you hoped would live up to the scale of the surroundings.

Let me assure you, dear readers, that the anticipation vastly underestimated the reality.

Should your postman arrive one morning to deliver a distinctive green edged envelope containing a heavily embossed invitation card, DO NOT treat it as unsolicited mail and toss it into the wastepaper basket. You will rue the day for the rest of your life. Such is the exclusivity of these dinners, that any invitation that is not formally accepted or is ignored guarantees that the recipient will be automatically excluded from any future event. To have had that opportunity and squandered it is tantamount to using a '61 Pomerol to clean your silver.

And any of you who are arrogant enough to think that your self-promoted or overblown celebrity status guarantees you a place at the table – forget it. You cannot book, inveigle or buy your way into this exclusive club. Each guest is carefully selected and that is it. Security is subtle but effective so that the most powerful in the land, if in receipt of an invitation, can attend without fear of an invasion of their privacy or risk to personal safety. The venues of future events are kept a closely guarded secret and mobile telephones must be surrendered upon arrival.

A select fifty people were at my dinner, and I have agreed, as have all the other guests to respect their individual privacy and anonymity. Oh, and just to make sure I do not transgress this rule, I have signed a banker's draft for £100,000 to be donated to a named charity in the event of my indiscretion. So, you will understand, as will my editor, why I am not at liberty to divulge to you who was at my side when we were seated along one long banqueting table. A pre-dinner reception served delicious English sparkling wine accompanied by canapes to die for. Small parcels of the most exquisite but indefinable mouthfuls, tinged with spices and herbs that, when combined, exploded in the mouth and sent the tastebuds into unrestrained ecstasy – and this was just the introduction to the evening's main event.

The taster menu was nothing short of faultless in terms of balance, taste, texture, aromas and flavours – all the senses were blown away with each wave of small dishes that kept flowing down the table like ripples of perfection. The source of these heavenly temptations was a state-of-the-art mobile kitchen, the proportions of which were to be seen to be believed.

Fish curries that were both sweet and sour, and chilli infused Parippu that was not just any dhal curry, a Polos curry that utilised the jackfruit as its base but imbued it with something indefinable that in all the years I have been tasting food I have never before experienced – and it did not stop there. Still the dishes kept coming, Gotukola Sambol, Beetroot curry, vegetarian Kottu, Egg or Cheese Kottu and a selection of flavoured Hoppers, each testing our tastebuds that were already suffering from a sensory overload but refusing to surrender, screaming for the gastronomic torture to linger on our tongues until the next explosion touched those physically exhausted cells.

I consulted with many of my fellow guests (who, as I said, must remain anonymous) and a game started all along the table whereby we tried to identify the individual or the blend of minor ingredients, each one of which punched way above its weight in the overall flavour of the dish. None of those present, and I do mean not one person, had any idea what Silchester had found but whatever these ingredients were, they gave every guest their own unique take on the exact nature of the plates of food presented to them. We might take a mouthful of the same dish, but we all experienced something entirely different.

Stephen Silchester is a culinary genius.

Nothing more.

Nothing less.

I do not believe that I have ever had an experience such as the one that I was fortunate enough to witness within the walls of that dour castle. I deem it a privilege to write here that I doubt that I ever will again – unless I am fortunate enough to receive another invitation. But, Dear Readers, may I state here and now that I have been told by the great man himself that this is a once in a lifetime opportunity for any of his guests.

This is fine by me as there is one small downside to being a member of this exclusive club. The cost. I am not going to tell you what I had to pay for my experience, but simply to say that it was worth every single penny.

Ambience	*****
Service	*****
Food	*Impossible to score too highly*
Price	*Impossible to afford more than once*

In Summary: Mortgage the house, sell the car, the spouse and the children...go at any cost."

Tom De Pietro

A Thoroughly Humbled Restaurant Critic

Chapter 26

There was silence in the house as Ameesha stretched her naked body under the soft cotton covered duvet and leant back against enfolding pillows to admire the view across the parkland in front of the bedroom window. Randolph had retired to his laboratory to work on whatever it was he did in there. He had started to explain it to her once, but she became bored and left him to it. Botany and science had never been one of her interests and she was not about to start now.

She slipped out of the bed and walked to the window, unashamed of her nakedness. The countryside was also naked, the trees leafless and the grass touched by a glistening frost that twinkled in the wan sunlight of an early winter morning. Ameesha walked across the room to the bathroom for a shower. She stood allowing the hot water to run down the full length of her slim body while she reflected on the whirlwind affair that had developed between herself and her lover.

Despite the late return to Wykeford House from dinner, Randolph had risen early and taken a solitary breakfast downstairs, leaving her to sleep on.

She detected that Randolph had been smitten at first sight when they passed in the doorway, her sashay across the floor of his shop emphasised her mysticism. The assistant had been helpful, if indiscreet, in telling Ameesha all about her employer as she exhibited some beautiful diamond necklaces and emerald rings. When Ameesha asked if they had any Padparadscha sapphires the young girl behind the counter became very animated. She called over her superior who had confirmed that there were a couple of items that madame might be interested in, but that she should return in the evening when they could entertain her to a private viewing.

She assumed that Randolph had been as curious about his new customer as she was about him because when she presented herself that evening, he was there to attend to her personally, showing her some of the most fantastic rings and pendants that she had ever seen. He was charming and attentive and when she chose a superb pendant with a delicate sunset coloured stone in a platinum setting and costing more than she had intended to spend, he had invited her to join him for dinner and the rest seemed to naturally fall into place.

She had spent a great deal of time with him since, either in London or staying at Wykeford House. All through this period, she had never lost focus on her business commitments and, having relet the restaurant in Brook Street, she put the building onto the investment market. Interest was strong, to the extent that she had instructed the agent to seek best bids, resulting in a minor frenzy of activity and culminating in an offer being accepted some fifteen percent above the agent's best estimate. This was the last asset that would be sold to pay off the balance of the 'debt' that Baba owed to the invisible bosses of the two Arabs who had cast such a shadow over them for the past two decades.

Ameesha was unsure as to whether they would acknowledge finality of the repayments. There was the ever-present threat that they would want more and more. She was confident that she had been careful to keep the secret excess profits separate, together with some of the more opaque investments. All that remained was to ensure that the last transfer was made without any mishap.

With all that had occurred over the past few weeks, Ameesha was acutely aware that she had neglected her father, having neither spoken nor contacted him for some time. She had found a sense of freedom that she was unwilling to sacrifice at the whim of her disabled father. She knew that eventually she would have to return to Sri Lanka, if only to finally rid herself and Baba of the two Arabs. As long as the money kept flowing in their direction, then they were content to leave them largely to their own devises. But now the debt was about to be repaid, she wondered what their true intentions were for them both.

The important thing was that the siphoning of the excess returns was to account in her sole control, rather than that of her father. He had created the chaos that they were only now emerging from, thanks in a large part to her ability and expertise, and so she felt it only reasonable that she should protect her own future. Her father was a paraplegic and would not live into old age. She had her whole life ahead of her and the wealth that she had accumulated gave her a lifestyle that enabled her to move in a bubble of sophisticated comfort no matter where she travelled. Poverty could be sympathetically observed, but not physically endured.

She dressed herself in a conservative trouser suit and silk blouse from a modest selection of clothes that remained at Wykeford House for those occasions when she stayed over. She had never suggested that she should move in as she wanted to maintain her independence while enjoying the benefits of a well-connected and attractive lover.

Her mobile telephone rang, and she quickly picked it up expecting the call. She listened and agreed that she would be at her solicitor's offices later that morning to sign the papers to complete the sale of the Brook Street building.

"The apportionment of the fixtures and fittings has been agreed as I wanted?"

The person on the other end of the line spoke for a minute and Ameesha listened intently,

"And the transfers of the completion monies are to be as I instructed?" She listened again, "Excellent. I shall be with you around eleven o'clock."

Ameesha tossed the phone onto the crumpled bed and picked up her pendant from the dressing table. She stroked the lustrous stone in its platinum setting. It was smooth to the touch and gave out a warmth that complimented its fiery colour. She closed the clasp at the back of her neck and smoothed the stone onto her blouse, admiring it and herself in the mirror. Breaking away from her reflection, Ameesha completed her preparations for the day and went down to the entrance hall where Randolph's driver was already standing to attention awaiting her arrival.

As she settled into the back of the Mercedes her phone shrilled again, and she looked at the screen. She quickly rejected the call before placing it out of sight in her small clutch bag.

*

Ziyad hoarsely cried out in frustration and a carer came rushing into his room thinking that he was in pain. And so he was, but not a physical pain. This was a mental anguish. His daughter had been in England for over eight weeks, and he had heard from her on only a handful of occasions. In the most recent weeks, she had not contacted him at all and now she was cutting off his calls.

He spat out the tube that enabled him to dial on the computer that hung suspended above him, within his eyeline, his only method of communication with the outside world. Yet again he sent an email urging her to call him. The deadline for the final transfer was imminent and, from past experience, he knew that Ali, the older Arab, would not allow any slippage in his exacting timeline.

Ziyad spent his days watching the balance of his wealth slowly diminish as accounts were closed, funds transferred, and investment managers dispatched. He had to be reliant upon Ameesha to protect his interests but try as he might, he was finding it increasingly difficult to locate, let alone access, the stockpile of funds that she was skimming off from the deals that she was completing. A seed of dread had germinated in his mind and, the longer that Ameesha was away from his side, the stronger the roots of his mistrust grew.

Control appeared to have slipped from his grasp and he, more than most, knew how money could infect the consciousness of the young. In his youth it had wooed him to the point of having the audacity to defraud one of the most dangerous groups of people in the world. Not only had he stolen from the militia, but he had also stolen funds from those governments and corporations that had supported the militia.

Despite having covered his tracks and led a quiet, introverted life with his family, they had eventually tracked him down. They knew that they had to be patient in allowing Ziyad to unwind his complicated web of financial interests and they had shown that time was not an issue, as long as funds regularly flowed back into their coffers. Without his cooperation, restitution was impossible, but once the web had been destroyed, accounts emptied, assets realised, Ziyad knew that there had to be a physical price to pay. These people did not do things by half measures. Part of that price was manifest in his bodily incarceration. Every function had to be performed for him and each time a carer came to him, he suffered all the indignities that came with his incapacity.

Death would have been a welcome release, but that was not what was granted by those whom he had betrayed. Not yet. They wanted him to reflect upon his misdemeanours for the rest of his life. To dwell in the darkness of the night on the foolishness of his attempts to double-cross those whose wrath knew no limit. The passage of time did not dull the strength in their determination to exact a grim revenge. Ziyad could not even manufacture his own death, despite asking Ameesha and the carers on several occasions. He suspected that the carers were single minded in their task of keeping him alive. He employed them, he paid their wages, but it had become clear that he did not control them. They took their instructions from the infidels who inflicted this final torture on him, retribution for his disloyalty.

Ziyad rested his head back against the pillows and stared up at the ceiling, a spider repaired its web from the damage of the night before. He could not restore his web; he could not recreate the strands that had held his life together. A small fly erratically weaved through the air until it misjudged the expanse of the filaments and became entangled in the sticky threads. It paused in shock and then fought to escape, twisting and turning, become ever more entangled in that inescapable trap. Ziyad watched in morbid fascination. The insect rested briefly before returned to its ever more desperate writhing, slowly becoming aware of the spider's cautious approach for the final coup de grace.

Inevitable.

Indisputable.

A certain finality.

Ziyad envied that fly.

Chapter 27

"Who is this man that she has become romantically involved with?"

"He is not known to us. It appears that he is a successful businessman with a boutique jewellery shop in Mayfair, London. He obviously has considerable wealth, but its source is unclear. He lives in a country house in Oxfordshire. From what we can discover, he is a refugee made good in the land of plenty."

"Is he part of her business network? Is he involved or helping her in any way?"

"Not that we have seen. Our contacts in Cayman tell us that she seems to be acting on her own initiative. She has assumed control of all her father's wealth and managed the liquidation of the funds that we have submitted to you. The final tranche will be paid imminently. But she is a sharp one."

"So it would appear. Ziyad Al Jabri is of little further interest or use to us, but his daughter, this Ameesha woman, seems to think that she can out-fox us, that we are not as wily as she. Let me have a day or so to consider what might be an appropriate course of action. Keep watching her but do not make any contact or let her know that we are and monitoring her movements. In the meantime, I shall also do a little research into Mr Randolph Curran. Refugees usually have a past; it is just a case of digging it out of someone."

Ali smiled at the phraseology, knowing that it would probably be a literal description. He returned the phone to his jacket pocket and wandered back over to the café where his young accomplice had positioned himself on a seat in the window. He was intently watching the porticoed entrance to the solicitor's office that Ameesha had entered fifteen minutes ago.

Chapter 28

The "Pop-Up" tour was almost at an end for the season, and the Sauceror's Apprentice team were exhausted but elated at the success of the venture. Stephen had kept to his side of the bargain and been free of any form of intoxicant for the duration. The profits were satisfying and justified the hard work that had been put into the concept. Stephen enjoyed a lifestyle that was infinitely better than what he might have been expecting after the collapse of his Mayfair restaurant business.

The partnership with Randolph had worked well, with Stephen running the events and cooking with increasing flair and imagination. Randolph, in the meantime, remained in the background working at Wykeford House creating ingredients with ever more exotic flavours and increasingly spectacular properties.

Celebrities clamoured for invitations to fall on to their doormat and, surprisingly, the mystique that surrounded the whole enterprise had been maintained throughout. Journalists had attempted to infiltrate various dinners and even tried to join the team by applying for staff positions. Randolph vetted every one of the invitees and the staff with meticulous exactitude, rooting out fraudsters and imposters while maintaining the exclusivity of each event. They had travelled the length and breadth of Britain and venues vied for the opportunity to be hosting the events – in some cases offering to pay huge sums for the privilege. They had held dinners at some remarkable venues, but on each occasion the precise location was kept a secret until the very last minute. Guests had to travel swiftly to ensure a prompt arrival. If the doors had closed upon the commencement of an event, then no late access was available – or refund given.

The random nature and timing of each meal kept everyone on their toes and when a dinner was anticipated then speculation soared. The mobile kitchen was tracked to see where it was travelling next, and Randolph had created a shell vehicle as a decoy and had fun leading the media a merry dance around Ireland for example, while the real dinner was served in the centre of Stonehenge.

Randolph and Stephen kept in contact on Zoom but rarely met in person in order to maintain the anonymity of Randolph's contribution. Stephen was happy to take physical charge and merely referred all expenses or logistics other than those necessary for the preparation of the food to Randolph via a company set up for the purpose, the directors being a firm of accountants nominally separate from either Randolph or Stephen.

Randolph had attended only one of Stephen's dinners accompanied by his new girlfriend, Ameesha. Stephen was initially shocked to find Randolph in the company of his former landlady, but quickly developed a liking for the attractive and entertaining young woman. He warmed to her further when she sang his praises to all those who cared to listen. That and her beauty held most people's attention. Being the only Sri Lankan present, she could testify to the authenticity of the dishes while marvelling at the inclusion of a uniqueness that was, at times, both surprising and satisfying, without detracting from the ethnicity of each plate. Randolph made no mention of the source of the additions while Stephen was more than content to take all the credit.

After the meal, the guests mingled together, speaking to those who might have been at the other end of the banqueting table, or who they knew through business or separate social functions. Before he was accosted by the County's Lord Lieutenant, Randolph introduced Ameesha to Stephen and an elderly thespian who had just completed a run as Hamlet at The Old Vic.

The actor was monopolising the conversation in his deep baritone voice, but constantly looking over the shoulders of the small audience that had gathered around him to see if there was someone to whom it might be more advantageous to make himself known. He paused his monologue to take a card from a passing admirer and acknowledge the plaudits of the stranger.

Ameesha took advantage of the gap in the conversation to speak directly to Stephen.

"This was a wonderful evening, and the food was to die for. How long have you been doing this?"

Stephen welcomed the redirection of the exchange so that it focussed on him.

"Oh, ever since my landlady booted me out of my Mayfair premises." He twitched an eyebrow mischievously and Ameesha laughed loudly. Those nearby were not party to the joke and failed to see what was so amusing.

Stephen continued unabashed, "But it was probably the best thing possible at the time."

"For both of us," Ameesha had the grace to admit.

"I'm glad."

"How do you know Randolph, Stephen?" The question was innocently made, and Stephen was lulled by Ameesha's charm and apparent interest in his work.

"I was travelling, and we met by chance. If I remember correctly, I was lost, and he directed me to a hotel." The thespian lost interest in their exchange and drifted off to bore someone else.

"Where was that?" Ameesha asked. Stephen still failed to detect a certain persistence in her questioning and blurted out the answer before he had time to check himself.

"Kandy, in Sri Lanka." He bit his tongue as soon as he said it. Ameesha whirled her head round to see where Randolph was.

"That's amazing! I come from Kandy. He never told me." Stephen could not tell if she was offended or irritated by the fact that Randolph had withheld such a vital secret from her, "What was he doing there?"

Stephen stuttered a response that even he knew was contrived,

"I think he was travelling like me. Look, I had better see some of my other guests, would you excuse me?" He did not wait for an answer and hurried through the crowd to find Randolph and let him know of his mistake. He cursed himself for his carelessness and for betraying his friend's anonymity.

Ameesha stood considering what she had just learnt about her partner and then withdrew from those who surrounded her. She was surprised that Randolph had not mentioned that he had been to Sri Lanka. He had told her that he was a refugee and arrived in the UK when he was a boy but more than that she did not know. Conversely, she could not remember whether she had told him where she came from, it had never really come up in conversation, either because Randolph had not asked, or alternatively he did not care.

As an immigrant settled in a new country, accepted by that country and having made a success of his new life, perhaps his origins or that of those he had met were immaterial. Everyone taken at face value; for what they were. Their humanity measured by their present and future, rather than their past.

The more she mulled over the newly revealed fact about her lover, the more she recalled odd comments, an inflection in his voice, or a movement of his hands or head. She began to surmise as to whether Randolph was himself Sri Lankan. She wanted to ask him but knew that he was sensitive to any probing into his past. She had thought that this was because it was too painful for him. Perhaps there was more to his past than had initially occurred to her in the early days of their whirlwind romance.

Randolph extricated himself from a gaggle of guests and looked around for Ameesha. Strangely, she was standing alone to one side of the room as guests started to make their farewells and offer effusive thanks to the chef. It was rare that she was not feted by a crowd of young men seeking her attention and he made his way towards her with a concerned look on his face.

"Are you alright standing here all on your own?" He placed a protective arm around her shoulders and kissed the side of her head. A shiver ran down her spine, "You're cold. Let's get you out of here and go home."

She walked compliantly beside him, his arm still around her shoulder, guiding her to the exit and the coats. She banked, but did not dismiss, her earlier thoughts and snuggled against his warm body. She was cold, but also, she was curious.

*

While Randolph lay asleep, Ameesha slipped from his bed and wrapped a heavy dressing gown around her naked body. She padded down the stone stairs to the drawing room where the embers of a fire still glowed in the grate. Gripping the mobile phone in her hand she dialled as she curled herself into the deep armchair.

There were no more than two rings before an irascible Ziyad answered.

"Where have you been? Why do you not return my calls?" Ziyad was petulant that she should ring him at her convenience. Her lack of consideration and respect merely exacerbated his displeasure and made him increasingly ill tempered. The carer had arrived late, and it was not the usual man who dealt with his more personal needs, before the women entered his room to feed him and generally tidy him up for the day. Not that anyone came to visit him, but he still welcomed the attention and normally felt refreshed once the cold sweats of the night had been washed away and his face shaved. The unexpected call from Ameesha had interrupted these proceedings and thrown his morning's pattern into disarray.

"Have I disturbed you, Baba," Ameesha spoke with a soft deferential tone of voice. Ziyad had come to learn that this unctuous approach usually signalled a half-truth or even an outright lie. Whichever it was, he continued the conversation with care,

"Where are you? Still in London?"

"Yes, still in London." She tried to sound fatigued by her commercial exertions but Ziyad was not to be so easily fooled. "I have been so busy sorting out the sale of the Brook Street property, but this is now done. I have seen the solicitor and signed the necessary papers this morning. He says all will be completed this afternoon."

Ziyad felt a degree of relief mixed with an anticipation that there may be a 'but' to the final stages of the deal. "And they will make the transfer to our friends? Do you have the details of the bank they're using this time?"

Again, the soothing voice, "Yes, Baba, all is in hand. Hopefully by this time tomorrow you will at last be free of those terrible people. Your debt will have been repaid and they will be out of your life."

Ziyad growled, "Free to do what? Remain stranded in this house to be manhandled by people who clear up my shit, who wash me, feed me. I might as well be dead."

"Baba, don't speak so." Ameesha maintained the tones of a devoted daughter. "You know it upsets me. I shall be with you soon, but I would like to stay on here for another few days. I need a little down time."

Ziyad raised his eyes to the ceiling, one of the few means of communication left open to him. He resisted making any verbal objection. He felt bitter, but also slightly scared that his daughter was drifting away from him, and that she had too much control as to his future. While she remained remote from him, he knew that his influence was greatly diminished.

"Oh, yes. Why don't you go and have some fun? Don't worry about your crippled father," Ziyad said sarcastically. Ameesha listened and the line seemed to have been disconnected in the silence. Ziyad waited for a retort and willed her to speak because he could not abide her silences. They were more cutting than any rant.

Relenting, Ziyad eventually asked in a weakened voice, "Have you seen our friends recently? Do you know where they are?" Ziyad needed answers but gave little or no time between each question for his concerns to be allayed. He paused for breath, wanting to cough but without the strength to clear his throat. His breathing became laboured, and the muscles at the base of his skull ached in the effort of holding his head up from the pillow. He sank back and closed his eyes in exhaustion. He made no indication of having heard his daughter as she replied,

"I've not seen or heard from them since they provided me with the latest bank details for the final transfer. I hope they have returned to whatever sewer they came from." Ameesha hoped that what she had told Baba was true, but deep down she felt that it was not the last that she would see of her father's tormentors.

"Come home. Please, come home," Ziyad rasped, unable to disguise the fear in his plea. "Come home now so that I can see you. I'm weak and need to see my only child."

For once Ameesha was moved by the emotion in her father's quiet voice. But she was unsure if she ever wanted to return. She had succeeded in wresting control of the residual wealth that, through her own guile and efforts, she had amassed to her account without the knowledge of the Arabs, or her father. Her life could be joyously free with few responsibilities.

And there was a new love in her life.

In fact, though she could barely admit it to herself, Randolph was the first real love of her life. She had little experience of romantic, let alone sexual liaisons during her adolescence. Spoilt she may have been, overly endowed with baubles and luxuries, but the freedom to meet and interact with the opposite sex had been very much discouraged. She had slipped away with Thinuka on some occasions but even he had never let any of his male friends get too close. Her brother was merely judging others by his own standards of immorality, preferring to keep his baby sister away from such temptations - temptations that he was unable to resist.

Baba's motives for her virtual incarceration arose purely from his fear of detection by those whom he cheated. Those who did not forgive or forget, who had stayed with him since they eviscerated him. Twenty long years during which he had shrivelled to a shadow of his former self.

And that was the reason that Ameesha reluctantly concluded that she would have to return to Kandy. Not to appease her paralysed father, nor to protect him from his tormentors or, if it were possible, to save his skin. She needed to know that once the final repayment had been made then she would really be free. Not her father, but

Ameesha, his daughter. She needed to know that the shadow that had hung over them for the last twenty years was to be finally removed. The debt paid and the perpetrator of the crime, her Baba, punished.

What finally happened to Baba no longer concerned her. Probably he had good reason to fear the fate that would await him. He was the guilty party. The fool who thought he could cheat these violent men. His future was immaterial to her, his life was spent. If the Arabs were intent on exacting the ultimate retribution, it was probably a blessing. But she needed to know that she was finally absolved of all indebtedness, both financial and moral.

She had a life to lead. There was some catching up to do and Randolph seemed as good a vehicle as any to realise her ambitions. She needed a foundation and it seemed to her that England in general, and the Wykeford Estate in particular, was a pretty good starting point. She could envisage herself as Lady of the Manor, she and Randolph made a good couple. Randolph was wealthy, and she too was wealthy, once she had tidied up some minor loose ends. It was these final matters of detail that would also necessitate her return to Sri Lanka, but that would only be a temporary stay. Her long-term future, she decided, now lay at Wykeford.

"Just let me deal with these final few details and then I will return, I promise."

Could she hear a sigh of relief on the other end of the call or was it her imagination? She did not want to debate the matter further and so dispassionately declared her love for her father and blew an insincere kiss down the line before disconnecting the call.

Ameesha shivered in the darkness and pulled Randolph's dressing gown tightly around her naked body. Silently she climbed the stairs and returned to his bedroom, sliding beneath the covers to snuggle up to capture the warmth of the body beside her.

Randolph was fortunate to have preceded her back to bed by only a few seconds and lay controlling his breathing at a deep rhythm with his eyes shut, but his mind racing.

*

Ziyad had received Ameesha's declaration of love with equanimity and, if he were able, he would probably have shrugged his shoulders. He thought for a moment and voice-dialled the next number instinctively.

When the voice on the other end answered, Ziyad simply said,

"She's returning. We need to be ready."

Chapter 29

Randolph and Ameesha had slept in late and when they eventually came down for breakfast the sun was high and the air fresh as it wafted through the open sash windows into the dining room. Ameesha noted that Randolph appeared distracted, and when she broached the subject he blamed pressure of work before retreating behind the pages of the Financial Times.

The cook hurried in and asked if Ameesha would like fresh coffee. She deferred to Randolph who grunted positively but did not emerge from his newspaper.

"You need a holiday." Ameesha let the statement float across the table. She was unsure if he had heard or was too preoccupied with the financial affairs of the world.

"Uh huh." Randolph rustled the pages as he moved on.

"I am going to have to go back to Sri Lanka to complete some business," she paused and then added as an afterthought, "and to see my father. He's not very well."

Randolph lowered the top of the paper and peered over the edge that had flopped forward, narrowly missing some toast covered in marmalade that lay uneaten on his plate.

"I've never really asked you about your family, have I?" Randolph trod warily. His ignorance was one of intent rather than omission. He had avoided enquiring into her background to parry the fact that he had divulged virtually nothing of his own, apart from the backstory that he had created many years ago. He had used it for so long it had usurped the truth about his swift departure from Sri Lanka. Now that Ameesha had mentioned her sick father, he felt obliged to show at least a passing interest.

"What's wrong with him?" Randolph asked from the cover of the Financial Times.

"He's paralysed as the result of an accident some years ago. He gets depressed and misses me."

"Where does he live?"

"Our family home is outside Kandy." Ameesha watched Randolph closely for a reaction. Randolph shook the paper and turned to a new page, apparently intent on reading something that had caught his eye.

Ameesha was frustrated at not being able to assess Randolph's reactions.

"Can you come out from behind that paper for a moment?" She snapped and then added in a softer tone, "Please."

Randolph noisily closed the newspaper, folded it and placed it ostentatiously on the floor by the side of his chair. He fixed Ameesha with a slightly patronising stare as he waited for her to continue.

"As I said, he's ill and I need to go back to Kandy to see him. I also have some bits of business to deal with and then I intend to return to England, hopefully for some time." Randolph did not comment. Ameesha wondered if she dared try to elicit confirmation of what she had learnt the previous evening from her brief conversation with Stephen.

"I understand that you know Kandy?" She held her breath and observed closely. The handsome face before her almost succeeded in showing no reaction, but the faintest flicker of.... what? She could not tell what emotion was so very briefly expressed. Was it irritation, or concern, or fear?

With a decisive movement, Randolph picked up his newspaper, pushed back his chair and stood.

"When will you go?" He smiled with his lips but not his eyes.

"I will leave in a few days," Ameesha was deflated and felt that this was an apparent dismissal. "I shall return as soon as I can."

She did not want it to end like this but he was already moving towards the door.

"Why don't you come with me?" she blurted out, in hope rather than expectation. "You need a break, and you can reacquaint yourself with Kandy." She could not stop herself and quickly regretted it.

Randolph stopped and looked back at Ameesha, holding her gaze for an instant too long. His face had hardened.

"I've got a lot to do here. The estate needs me and then there's …."

Ameesha interrupted him before he could complete his excuses. She had come this far, so any further attempts to ensnare him seemed to be of little consequence.

"Rubbish. Everything on the estate runs perfectly smoothly without you having to be here. As for your silly laboratory work," she emphasised the last word to make it clear she did not consider his isolation in his lab was real work, "that can wait a few weeks."

She gave him what she hoped was her most winning and persuasive smile and Randolph found himself considering the suggestion almost against his will.

The cook interrupted the discussion with a cafetiere of fresh coffee, but on seeing that the master was standing and sensing a tension in the room, she silently withdrew. Randolph hardly noticed as he gazed out of the window deep in thought.

It would be an enormous risk, but after so long, would anyone really remember him by sight? He had changed dramatically from the callow young Veddah. Even Stephen had not recognised him when first he came to Wykeford.

Now he was a British citizen; he had a new name, and he had the wealth that enabled him to travel in a manner that would set him apart from any former acquaintances. Money, or a surfeit of money, had a way of anaesthetising the traveller from both the poverty and any other less endearing qualities of a country. You could move in a sanitised bubble floating above the flotsam and jetson of real lives, lives that scratched a living from whatever might be to hand, that fought for survival against squalid hygiene, decrepit housing and foetid ecosystems.

Not that the young Randul had suffered any such deprivations. The Sinharaja Forest had been an oasis of tranquillity and as he contemplated the life that he had before he discovered the Padparadscha gems, before he became Randolph Curran, the notion began to appeal. He would have liked to revisit his old haunts and to recapture some of his youth, even if in the guise of a tourist. He wondered if his old house was still standing or if it had been taken over by others. He could walk down to the river, even take a swim in its swirling waters.

Should he? Dare he?

"Let me think about it." His expression softened, "But now, my darling, I need to do some work and you need to get back to London. The car will come round and pick you up when you are ready." He walked over to her and, bending down, he kissed the top of her head.

"Is that ok for you?"

Ameesha looked up and took hold of his hand.

"I'm not asking you to come and meet my father as a prospective husband or anything like that." The thought had never occurred to Randolph, but it worried him that it might have to Ameesha. Her voice had become strangely persuasive, "Sri Lanka is beautiful at this time of the year, and we can do some of the sights that you did not do when you were there."

Randolph was not going to be drawn and strode to the door. As his hand gripped the brass door handle, she almost pleaded.

"I'll see Baba alone, but I'd like you to be there for me."

"As I say, let me think about it. I'll call you tonight. Are you going back to Claridge's?"

"Yes, just until I fly out."

He swung open the door to the hall.

"You could have bought a Mayfair apartment with the amount of money you have spent at that hotel." He passed through the door and said something to a member of staff. It seemed that one or other of his entourage was always close to hand.

The cook immediately returned and topped up Ameesha's cup.

She drank her coffee deep in thought as she planned her day, before returning to the bedroom to pack a small valise with her immediate requirements. The rest of her belongings had remained in the retained suite that lay empty in Claridge's during her sojourns with Randolph. These had increased in length over the last few weeks from a single night to two or three days. She enjoyed the lifestyle and the countryside, not forgetting the sex. She settled into her chair and smiled wickedly to herself. Let's not forget the sex.

She remained seated and took some deep breaths to settle herself once again. Randolph had infiltrated her affections more than she would have wished or planned. She had not come to London to be swept off her feet. She liked always to be in control, but this had proved an impossibility with Randolph. He was almost too good to be true and she wondered if her feelings for him could be kept under control should she ever have to do so.

It was not as if he was evasive when she mentioned Kandy, he just ignored her efforts to discover if he had ever visited. It was as if he wanted to forget his visit, because she could not accept that he did not recall being there. Stephen had remembered, so surely Randolph did.

Randolph heard the car crunch across the gravel to the front of the house and he went to say goodbye to Ameesha. On seeing his employer appear from behind the house, the driver wished him a jovial good morning and the two exchanged pleasantries as they stood waiting patiently for the passenger to arrive. The front door opened, and Ameesha walked out, smiling radiantly upon finding that Randolph was in attendance for her departure.

"I thought you would be too absorbed in your 'work' to see me off," she teased.

"Never too absorbed for you, Ameesha." He kissed her cheek as the driver loaded Ameesha's small bag into the boot of the car.

"You'll call me tonight with your decision?"

He feigned a puzzled look, "What decision?"

"Sri Lanka," she started, before realising that he was leading her on. She punched him playfully on his chest. "It could be fun, and I really would like to show you round the island. We can enjoy the sun, sea and…"

He lightly ran his fingers down her back and she quivered under his touch.

"That's quite enough of that, young lady."

Ameesha moved closer and he could smell a heady perfume rising from her body. She spoke with a husky voice, "Never enough. Never." She brushed her hand gently against the front of his trousers and he jumped back in surprise.

"Get in that car and go about your business, you wanton hussy."

The driver concentrated on the gravel at his feet and Ameesha laughed.

"Speak tonight?"

"Until tonight." Randolph waved as she climbed into the car.

Ameesha put the tips of her fingers to her lips and pouted a kiss in his direction. The driver jumped into the driver's seat and the car moved off towards London. Randolph watched it disappear down the drive and turned back towards the laboratory.

Sri Lanka. The home of his forefathers, the place of his childhood. It had been twenty years since he had left. He was a different man to the young tribesman that had fled from his past. With a new home, a new name, a successful business and a reputation; was it possible that the pull of his homeland was too great to resist? To revisit just once, to discover if there were any residual bonds that had not been severed, or was he a castaway, forever to be a stranger in his own country?

Randolph could think of a couple of other reasons for a return.

Chapter 30

"Has the last tranche of funds arrived in the nominated account?" Ali was talking to someone on his mobile phone seated outside a café on the Edgeware Road. He was surrounded by fellow customers chatting or sitting puffing on hookahs while they read Arabic newspapers and drank strong black coffee.

"Yes and moved on. There are no traces. Now you can tidy up the loose ends."

"What about this Curran man? The daughter's boyfriend?"

"Interesting you should ask. He has done a good job of covering his past."

"So, we are no nearer knowing who he is?"

"I didn't say that." The voice paused, whether for dramatic effect or to refer to notes, Ali was unable to deduce.

"It seems that Mr Randolph Curran is not quite the impoverished refugee that he portrayed to the British authorities. We believe that he is Sri Lankan, a Veddah."

"What's a Veddah?"

"Veddah's are the indigenous aboriginal tribe that inhabited Sri Lanka. Almost an endangered species. This one was a tourist guide from the Sinharaja Forest area."

"What has he to do with Al Jabri and his family?"

"We believe that he might have absconded with something that was rightfully ours. But more interestingly, we understand that he might have a couple of other items that could be of far greater interest to us. These items, if they still exist, are likely to be of enormous intrinsic value."

The Arab flicked his cigarette butt into the gutter, narrowly missing a woman who was walking by on the pavement. She gave him a disdainful look of censure, but he held her stare with an arrogant intensity until she looked away in discomfort. He continued with his conversation, unconcerned.

"Sounds interesting. What do you want me to do?"

"I think her father might like to know the true identity of his daughter's lover."

The Arab rubbed the stubble on his chin and lit another cigarette just as his accomplice arrived with a Playboy magazine tucked under his arm.

"And you know his true identity?" Ali enquired.

"Ask him if he knows a Veddah called Randul Ranatunga."

Chapter 31

All day Randolph was distracted, grappling with the dilemma of whether to travel with Ameesha back to Sri Lanka, and still he had not reached a definitive decision. He had never envisaged a return, not least for fear of being apprehended for the assault on the gem dealer, Ziyad - or would the charge be attempted murder? He did not know if he was still alive or if he had died in the intervening period since his flight from Sri Lanka. There was also the question of the contents of the briefcase that had provided Randolph with the funds to overcome several apparently insurmountable hurdles during his tortuous journey to Britain as a refugee. Why Ziyad had put the briefcase in his car and was travelling around with it was a mystery, but implied that what was in it was not wholly legitimate. Nonetheless, there was no doubting the fact that Randolph had stolen it.

The trouble was, the more he thought about a return, with all its inherent risks, the greater the desire grew to revisit the place of his birth. He had spent the whole day balancing the risks against the attraction of a return and the closer the time came to having to ring Ameesha with a decision, the more unsure he became that he had reached the sensible conclusion

*

With the completion of the sale of the Brook Street building, Ameesha had been in her solicitor's offices for most of the morning to ensure that the funds were correctly apportioned. The majority disappeared into the anonymous bank account as dictated by Ali, while the balance went into another of her private accounts in the Channel Islands. Once satisfied that everything had been done to her satisfaction, she thanked her advisors and left to find Randolph's driver who had remained outside. He was drumming his fingers on the edge of the door when she emerged.

"Claridge's, please."

He opened the door and wondered if his employer had envisaged him acting as his girlfriend's chauffeur for the day. It was not his place to question her and he drove on as requested.

They pulled up outside Claridge's and he was instructed to wait while she dropped off a bag in her suite and checked that there were no messages. He agreed to remain in the car and noted that the Audi that had been following them since they had left the solicitor's office was still in his rear-view mirror. He was trained to notice such things but did not react precipitously, merely keeping an eye on its presence. In Knightsbridge he had slowed slightly too quickly at traffic lights to close the gap and try to get a look at the driver. Unfortunately, the reflection off the windscreen was such that a clear view was impossible. All he could discern was that the driver was wearing a hoodie and baseball cap but that was the nearest he could get to seeing any useful features.

The doorman was immediately on hand to open the door for Ameesha who started to climb out as the Audi slowly passed and turned right into New Bond Street.

The doorman knocked on the chauffeur's window, "How long are you waiting, driver?"

"Only as long as it takes for madam to leave her bag and return to the car."

"OK. Don't be any longer, I need the space."

The driver raised the window and kept an eye on any movement behind him through the wing mirrors. The Audi did not do a circuit of Grosvenor and Davies Streets and reappear, but he remained alert and watchful. The street was unusually quiet and those pedestrians who did pass gave no indication of having an interest in either the car or the waiting chauffeur. This part of Mayfair was littered with chauffeurs waiting for their passengers.

Ameesha quickly entered her suite and picked up the telephone to ring her father.

"Baba, you're there." She was breathless from the brisk walk from the lift.

"Of course, I'm here. Where am I going to go?" His voice was heavy with sarcasm. "This is a surprise, to speak to you twice in twenty-four hours. What do you want?"

"Baba don't be harsh. I am ringing to tell you that I might be coming home with a friend." There was silence from the other end. "Baba? Are you there?"

"Who is this friend? Do I know her?" Ziyad assumed it was a girlfriend as he could not accept the possibility that his daughter would have a romantic liaison with a man that had not known to her father.

"It's a man I have met here. He is a Sri Lankan, or at least, I think he is Sri Lankan." Ziyad let out a contemptuous snort before she continued.

"Now he lives in England and has been very successful in business." She thought that the prospect of him being both Sri Lankan and prosperous would appeal to her father. One out of two was not bad, but Ziyad was eternally suspicious.

"What's this young man's name? What does he do? Am I going to meet him?"

"Whoa, whoa. Too many questions and I don't have time to give you all the details. You will have to wait until I see you. I am going to ask our booking agents to make the arrangements once I have spoken to him this evening." Ameesha knew that she was pre-empting Randolph's decision, but she was excited and eager to share her news with someone, even if it was only with her curmudgeonly father.

"You're paying for him to come with you. Sounds like a freeloader to me. You be careful, I know what men can be like around pretty, rich women."

Ameesha paid no heed to her father's warning and told him she would let him have the details when she could. He started to offer further advice but was cut short.

She gathered up her clutch bag and changed her court shoes for some trainers before hurrying back down to the car. The doorman touched the brim of his top hat as she exited the hotel. She thanked him and headed for the car. The chauffeur immediately spotted her appearance from the building and hopped out to open the rear passenger door.

"Where can I drop you, Madam?"

"Sloane Square to start with and then we will see."

The driver hesitated as he knew that his employer had not expected him to be her dedicated driver for the whole day.

Nor had the figure casually standing on the corner of Brook Street and Davies Street flipping through a copy of Playboy.

*

Ziyad sat in his motorised wheelchair thinking about what Ameesha had told him. His head was supported by a brace that was perpetually uncomfortable and his breathing was dependent upon the machinery and tubes that were connected to the oxygen bottle secured behind him. If there was a positive, Ziyad thought, then at least he was seated and vertical. He was able to look out over the courtyard of his house. It's proportions desecrated by the ugly lift that had been fitted to allow Ziyad and his wheelchair to pass from floor to floor. The water trickling from the small fountain brought some degree of calm to his irritable countenance.

A man.

Ameesha had found a man.

Or a man had found her.

And in London of all places. Ziyad had an increasingly low regard for London. Why? Because all his recent dealings had been with sharp witted bankers, lawyers, investment managers and real estate brokers. These parasites purported to operate according to the rules set by their regulatory authorities, while simultaneously offering services by which these rules could be circumvented. Admittedly, this was a convenience that had once suited his purposes, but when it came to liquidating his assets, such services were only available at an exorbitant cost in professional fees.

And all to what end?

He had had everything stripped from him. He was not confident that whatever Ameesha had managed to slice off the top was going to be to his benefit. His finances would be pitifully small in comparison to the incomparable fortune that he had amassed, and once controlled. When he had fraudulently stripped the militias of a vast proportion of their liquid assets, he could only marvel at the true scale of his achievement. It was far more than he needed, the embezzlement having become something of a mental, as well as a financial challenge. However, having successfully perpetrated the crime, it was impossible to go back and say 'I'm terribly sorry, I've taken far more than I intended. Would you like some back?'

So, he kept it. All of it. And because of its huge size, it had required considerable skill and dexterity to gradually allow it to seep into the legitimate financial system in a manner that did not draw attention to either its source or himself. By the same measure, it had taken even greater skills to liquidate the portfolio for repatriation to the Arabs. It was a complicated, but efficient web that Ziyad had created for himself. A web that was now a disintegrating filigree of loose strands drifting in the wind, the connections torn apart, the snapped ends of no purpose or value.

In some respects, Ziyad felt a strange sense of relief. The funds were now back where they had started, to be manipulated by his successor for the purposes of some ill-considered and inconclusive military adventure. Each bullet that rips into a son, every landmine that mutilates a daughter or a wife, each bomb that tears apart a family is paid for by those professional advisors who drink in the bars, eat in the expensive restaurants and travel in luxury to exotic destinations. The professionals that keep the financial markets around the world moving, devouring, absorbing and, ultimately, regurgitating capital. The profits from each deal spinning in concentric circles towards the top two or three percent who scrabble for its corrupting authority and power.

No longer could culpability be laid at his feet.

He was free of it. Or he hoped that he was free of it.

What was uppermost in Ziyad's thoughts, however, was the more immediate issue of the return of Ameesha. He hoped he had prepared adequately.

As if on cue, his housekeeper appeared and announced that his guest had arrived. He indicated that he would hold the meeting in his study. He sat quietly for a few minutes while his guest was ushered into the allotted room by the housekeeper, offered refreshment and generally settled comfortably to await his host's appearance.

Ziyad took a deep breath of bottled air to prepare himself. The electric motor whirred and using small head motions, Ziyad directed his wheelchair towards his study.

Chapter 32

The monsoon rain hammered on the roof of the house sending a haze of spray down from the eaves as the ripe drops exploded against the tiles. The view was misted due to the sheer volume of water that was falling from leaden clouds hanging low over the whole country. It had rained constantly since Ziyad had had the meeting in his study in anticipation of the return from England of his wilful daughter.

The humidity was high and Ziyad sat alone in his wheelchair by an open bedroom window trying to focus on individual raindrops as they hurtled earthwards. No matter how hard he tried; their speed was too fast for his eye to focus on their downward trajectory. Despite the noise of the rain, it was not so loud as to drown out the sudden commotion that rose from downstairs. Voices shouted orders in Arabic and others, higher pitched, responded. Someone screamed, and there was the sound of something hard crashing onto the marble floor, to be followed by dropped crockery shattering.

Ziyad nervously turned his wheelchair to face the disturbance as the door to his room was thrown open. Ali entered in front of a terrified housekeeper; the younger Arab had her arm twisted up between her shoulder blades. She winced in pain and a trickle of blood was just visible from a wound on her forehead. It was useless for Ziyad to order the two men who had invaded his house to get out. Ziyad was impotent. There was nothing he could do except seek the release of the frightened woman.

"There is no need for this. Let her go," Ziyad said quietly. "She is of no threat to you."

Ali turned and indicated for the younger man to release the woman. He seemed reluctant, but when the older man growled a command he relented and released her. The housekeeper hovered, rubbing her bruised arm, until Ziyad nodded his head that she should get out. As she passed the younger man he gave her a shove that sent her staggering down the stairs. The door closed and the young man insolently chewed khat and smirked as he slouched with his back to the architrave.

Ali sauntered around the room, inspecting the various pieces of medical equipment that had been fitted into the bedroom to facilitate Ziyad living as normal a life as was possible. He tugged on a pulley over the bed and inspected the rails attached to the ceiling that led into the bathroom.

Ziyad was not to be intimidated.

"I thought we were all done. You have had the final payment; my daughter has confirmed this from London." The words were heard by the man who slowly perused the room, but he merely nodded to acknowledge the fact. He was enjoying building the suspense.

"What do you want?" Ziyad hissed.

"Young Ameesha has done well." He continued to prowl, not making eye contact with Ziyad. "All work and no play makes your Ameesha a dull girl. But she is far from dull. In fact, she has been having a lot of fun in London." Now he looked at Ziyad to make sure he was listening. "Spent a lot of money, I guess. I mean, a lot of money." He emphasised the last four words.

There was a bowl of sweets on a side table, and he took one, carefully unwrapped it and put it into his mouth. He folded the wrapper and looked around for a rubbish bin. There was one in the bathroom, and he wandered over to dispose of the paper. As he opened the lid, he smelt the faecal waste and urine that were wrapped in an old incontinence pad that lay at its base. His face twisted in disgust, and he exhaled loudly as if to clear his lungs. Slamming the lid closed, he quickly left the bathroom and firmly shut the door. He tossed the sweet paper onto the floor at Ziyad's immobile feet.

"You are a foul old man. You smell of shit and piss."

"And whose fault is that?" Ziyad spat the words back at the man, spittle settling on his chin. It was ignored. The second man remained slouching with the perpetual sneer stuck to his face.

"In Allah's name, what do you want now?" Ziyad asked.

The older man was not to be hurried.

"She has a new boyfriend. Your Ameesha. Did you know that?"

"Yes, I had heard."

"Nice, good looking fellow. Rich as well. Has a successful business in the heart of London. Nice expensive shop dealing in nice expensive jewellery."

Ziyad's ears pricked at the mention of a jeweller.

"Big house in the country, lots of land. Still single. Very eligible. Would be quite a catch for any girl. A delicate English rose would have to accept the fact that he is an immigrant. A refugee, apparently, made good. Can you believe it? England, a land of opportunity."

Ziyad absorbed all the details but made no indication of particular interest.

"He must have had help getting started. Must have had a benefactor. You don't have that much of a success in such a short space of time without capital." He suddenly turned and faced Ziyad.

"You wouldn't know anything about that would you? Not another of your little side lines?"

Ziyad blanched slightly at the reference to side lines, but still managed to maintain his composure. He had no idea as to the identity of the mystery jeweller or where the Arab was leading. However, from his confident air, Ziyad was certain that he was about to find out.

"Are you sure you don't know him?" Ali took hold of the arms of the wheelchair and brought his face down close to Ziyad's, his eyes black and menacing, their noses almost touching. Ziyad could hardly focus on his features, but he did not need to in order to recognise the threat in the voice.

"I don't know any jewellers in London, certainly not of the type you're describing. Get to the point, will you?" Ziyad might have sounded brave, but inside he was quaking due to his obvious physical vulnerability, not to mention his previous experience with these two ruthless animals. Ali went down onto his haunches and fiddled with Ziyad's feet, gently straightening them on the footrests, fascinated with their flaccid feel.

"I'll give you a name. It might mean something to you." He studiously maintained his attention on Ziyad's feet.

Ziyad waited expectantly as the man below him suddenly looked up at his with a malicious intensity.

"Would Randul Rana….."

He stopped immediately when he saw the expression of horror and recollection flash across Ziyad's face.

"Ah, so you do know him."

Ziyad was speechless, his lower jaw shook uncontrollably, not with cold but with pent up fury.

"Of course, that's not his name in England," his interlocutor smoothly continued. "Too foreign sounding for the sensibilities of the English monied classes, and you certainly do need money to afford his goods. And it's not only the English that he serves."

The young Arab chortled from his position by the door.

"Serve, service. They're apposite words in the case of one such customer of his. He's giving a very personal service to her. Wouldn't you agree, Ahmed?"

Ahmed sniggered at the witticism as Ali continued to mock Ziyad.

"Innocent little Ameesha has been receiving a very personal service. Deflowered at the hands of your tormentor. What is more, his commercial success far outstrips your miserable little shop here in Kandy."

A seriously shaken Ziyad attempted to regain a modicum of self-control, sufficient at least to falteringly ask, "And my daughter has been seeing this man?"

"Seeing him? Seeing him?" Both men laugh cruelly at the naivety of a doting father. "She's been fucking him stupid, wherever and whenever she can. Can't get enough of it. In fact…"

"Enough!" Ziyad shouted. He could listen no longer. He spoke more softly, realising that it was unwise to antagonise either man.

"Enough, please." His breathing had become laboured, "Have you come here just to taunt me, or will you tell me what you want?"

Ali stood up and stepped back from Ziyad to recommence his perambulation around the room, inspecting photographs, picking up trinkets, turning them over in his hand and then replacing them. He stopped in front of a picture of Ameesha and looked at it closely.

"It's clear what he sees in her. She certainly is a beautiful girl. I suppose, in the circumstances, we should refer to her as a woman." He tossed the picture over to his companion who lasciviously ogled at the image of the girl imagining what lay beneath the rich fabrics that covered her naked body.

"I ask once again," Ziyad slowly voices each word pedantically. "What do you want?"

"One last service is all we require and then, I think, our business is complete." He looked over Ahmed as if seeking confirmation. There was a desultory nod, and Ali turned his attention back to Ziyad who sat exhausted and defeated, awaiting his final orders.

*

Stephen was alarmed when Randolph rang to tell him that he was going to go to Sri Lanka for a holiday. Stephen expressed his concerns and Randolph explained that after all the years that had passed, he needed to return to his homeland to visit the places that he yearned to see once more. The last time Randolph, or Randul, had taken a trip; Stephen's life had collapsed, and he was not going to allow that to happen again. He implored Randolph not to go but his friend had made up his mind and was not to be dissuaded.

"What if this gem dealer is still alive and waiting for you to return? Vendettas can be held in abeyance for a long time."

Randolph had already considered this, and he had placed several calls to the gem shop once owned by Ziyad Al-Quadi. Each time the call remained unanswered. He decided that either it had changed hands, or it was no longer run by Ziyad. It was a risky assumption but one that suited Randolph's decision.

Ever since Ameesha had raised the prospect of a return, he had found himself vividly recalling the night of his flight from the bungalow. The rising panic that he might have killed Ziyad, the wound that he had inflicted having proven fatal. When he took the car keys from Ziyad to borrow the Mercedes, Randul's only thought was to flee. The act of retrieving the gun from the floor did not register until he had driven away and joined the tarmac road.

Similarly, the car that was parked up on the verge did not register, nor did the two men who were seated in the front seats, their faces briefly lit by his headlights as the yellow beam swept across their windscreen.

All he wanted to do was to put as much distance as he could between the bungalow and himself before the police were called. As the road twisted through the forest he came to a familiar corner and slammed on the brakes. He took several deep breaths and looked around him to confirm his precise location. Grabbing his bag, he jumped from the car and, without looking back ran into the depths of the forest.

Twenty minutes later the Mercedes had disappeared, as had Randul.

The car was discovered eventually at the airport, as he knew it would be, but the person known as Randul would never be seen again.

Stephen tried another approach, "We only have two more dinners on the tour and one of those is Thursday night. Stay to see that through and then leave enough of your latest ingredients for me to then complete the final one." He waited, "Please?"

Randolph had already considered the final two dinners of the tour and did not want to let his friend down now that he had re-established his career. He told Stephen that everything was arranged and that he would ensure that there was no need for him to have any concerns. He was merely going for a few weeks and would be back before or shortly after the final dinner.

No matter how he tried, Stephen could not persuade Randolph to alter his arrangements further. Reluctantly he accepted the assurances that he was being given but remained fearful that history was about to repeat itself.

Randolph was immoveable because he had already told Ameesha that he would join her. Her initial excitement was to be tempered by disappointment when Randolph explained that he could not fly out with her as he had several things to tie up before he could get away. He arranged with her that they would meet up in Kandy four days after she had arrived so that she could see her father without him being around.

Unknown to Ameesha, he had already booked his flight together with an hotel. However, rather than four days later, it was a mere twenty-four hours later. This would give him three days to himself to enable him to return to the bungalow and the forest to relive some memories without any interruption or distraction. He did not want Randul to be resurrected, but there was one piece of house-keeping that remained to be completed, one part of him that was still to be erased. To see the sights and experience the sounds of the forest, to walk the paths and to forage one final time before casting aside his aboriginal past seemed to be an epiphany.

The modern Centauris Wild Hotel was of a large enough size for Randolph to be wholly inconspicuous as a holidaying guest. It was located on the shores of the

Uda Walawe reservoir and seemed perfect for his needs. Normally, he would have preferred a smaller boutique hotel but this was close enough to the Sinharaja Forest to make it accessible for his purposes. Although everything had happened very swiftly, the more he planned his return the more he felt the pull of the once familiar placenames. He had purchased a large-scale map and was marking up the various locations he wanted to revisit, including the peaceful glade on the fast-flowing riverbank where he, his father and his grandfather before him had once hunted for gemstones. One last visit, one last look.

*

Randolph stopped the Range Rover outside Claridge's Hotel and jumped out before the doorman had had time to cross the pavement to either stop or assist him.

"I shall be two minutes. I am just picking up…" he stopped as he realised for the first time in their brief relationship that he did not know Ameesha's surname. "A guest for the airport."

"Ok, sir. But don't be long, the wardens are everywhere." The doorman opened the entrance door for Randolph who immediately saw Ameesha standing at reception with her back to him.

He noted the array of luggage that was stacked on a trolley against which a young porter was lolling as he waited for Ameesha to settle her bill. She was a tall, willowy figure dressed expensively, her long black hair hanging down her back, shimmering under the lobby lighting. He felt a stab of emotion but steeled himself against any overt display of affection. It was not that he was not fond of Ameesha, but in every aspect of his new life, even now after years of comfortable living in a secure country, there was always an underlying caution. Randolph's approach to any relationship, be that social or business, was melded from his years on the refugee routes. Being preyed upon by every chancer, criminal and people trafficker drilled into him a sense of suspicion that was impossible to completely shake off.

And then there was that late night telephone call that he had overheard Ameesha make.

Caution prevailed.

Perhaps the trip to Sri Lanka and a brief respite before seeing her again might confirm in his mind whether this was to be a long-term relationship or not. He knew that Ameesha already considered him a suitable partner, but he had tried not to raise her hopes beyond their affair being a dalliance, a holiday fling, a life experience. But she radiated an innocence in matters of the heart - and the bed. She had energetically embraced her newfound freedoms.

He understood how stultifying life could be in Sri Lanka for a girl who was under the protection of a strict family. The practical expectations of any father would be very different to the romantic dreams or physical needs of a wilful daughter. Randolph had no idea what sort of man Ameesha's father was, she never spoke of him save to tell Randolph that he was a sick old man. It seemed to Randolph that she was hoping that she would be freed of the imposition of a forced marriage if her father should die before he had concluded any formal arrangements. However, these things were never certain, and it was always possible that her father was obliging her to return, not just to pay her last respects to a dying man. If that was the case, Randolph wanted to avoid any involvement in her attempts to defy her father. Randul knew how deep set such traditions were in an orthodox family and had his own good reason not to become embroiled in such disputes.

Ameesha turned and scanned the lobby before her eyes alighted on Randolph and she grinned in delight as she skipped over to give him a hug.

"Thank you for coming to see me off. I know you are busy, and I am so looking forwards to seeing you when you arrive."

She kept talking at a fast rate and Randolph half listened as she relayed what they were going to do and where they were going to go in Sri Lanka. She slipped her arm into his as they walked out of the hotel, her chattering away and Randolph thinking that her feelings for him were childishly touching. The porter dragged the heavy trolley in their wake and, when Randolph had remotely opened the rear door, he started loading the luggage into the back. Ameesha gave Randolph a peck on the cheek and slid into the passenger seat while he supervised the packing of the luggage.

He released the rear seats so that they could fold flat to allow the final pieces to be safely stowed.

Randolph generously tipped the porter and navigated through the traffic towards Heathrow Airport. Ameesha talked the whole way, not once mentioning her father or his condition. Randolph tried to enquire a couple of times and she just brushed it aside with a "much the same". Her excitement for their trip was infectious and Randolph found himself being swept up in her enthusiasm. Eventually she took a break from her ever-expanding itinerary to enquire of Randolph,

"What will you be doing before you fly out?"

"Oh, I have a mountain of things to do, so don't think I will give you a second thought." He casually glanced at her, and she gave him a hurt look before they both laughed. She placed her hand on his thigh,

"Don't you go finding comfort with any of those country wenches."

Randolph looked horrified, "Perish the thought. By the way, your English has become far too colloquial. Where on earth did you get 'wenches' from?"

"You'd be surprised what I've learnt from the rural landowners of Oxfordshire." She raised her eyebrows and looked at him with a coquettish leer.

Chapter 33

Ameesha exited the Sri Lankan Airways A380 at Bandaranaike International Airport. Despite the comfort offered by first class, the flight had become a tiresome necessity rather than an enjoyable luxury for her. As she crossed the threshold from the aircraft to her homeland, a wall of hot humid air hit her. It was in stark contrast to the dull, damp air of England that she had experienced over the last few weeks.

She passed relatively quickly through both Sri Lankan passport control and customs although the officers did take a long, hard look at her mountain of luggage. The young porter who was pushing the overladen trolley was being tested by wheels that fought his every effort to steer a straight path. The mirth of watching the small, wiry boy tussle with the wilful stack of cases distracted them from questioning her as to what was in all the bags.

The oppressive air enveloped her as soon as she passed through the automatic doors onto the sidewalk. A gaggle of taxi drivers touted for her attention as she looked around for the familiar Mercedes, but it was nowhere to be seen.

She took out her phone to see if there were any messages. It took a while for it to recognise her precise location before she heard the familiar pinging of messages arriving. She expected that it was to inform her that the driver had been delayed. On opening the text she was aghast to see a short message,

"Can't pick you up. Get a Taxi home."

The porter hovered at her shoulder keen to deposit her luggage and get back into the terminal to find a new customer. Waiting time was not cash time. Ameesha accosted an elderly, heavily moustachioed taxi driver and gave him an address. He looked sceptically at the cases and immediately concluded that there was no way he was going to get them all into his car, even if he packed them onto the back seat. He had seen the porter struggling to unload them from the trolley and he decided to pass on the fare. He hailed a colleague who had a larger people-carrier and gave the younger, fitter driver the destination. Ameesha tutted in frustration and took a seat in the vehicle as the porter and driver loaded all the cases into the rear compartment.

In her absence, albeit for only weeks rather than months, Ameesha expected to see changes in the familiar sights that passed her by on the journey home. But everything remained the same. The memories of her time in England were still fresh in her mind and the prospect of Randolph joining her in a few days gave her a twist of anticipatory excitement in the pit of her stomach. Perhaps she would discover where he had been and what he had done during his last trip to the island.

She still had no certainty as to whether he was born and brought up on Sri Lanka. His cosmopolitan demeanour, his sophistication, his maturity made her feel a bit of a rural bumpkin in his company. She was not as well travelled or as socially developed as Randolph; her upbringing having been so sheltered. The stay in London had opened her eyes to a wider and less introspective world. It was all as she had imagined and heard about, but never experienced.

Initially, her involvement in her father's affairs had been conducted under his watchful eye. As she became more adept and knowledgeable, Ziyad had had to admit that he had misjudged the entrepreneurial talents of his daughter. She proved to be a more than capable principal and gradually his advisors deferred to her more and more. Ziyad became a shadow to his daughter, but he remained alert to everything that she was doing. They jointly set up the vehicles that would be used to accumulate some of the proceeds from the liquidation of the assets on behalf of the Arabs.

Ameesha was as ambitious as her father had been when he was her age. The extra-curricular financial trades were astute and profitable, all being undertaken in her own time and increasingly out of the line of sight of Ziyad. The shop that she had assumed the management of, despite Ziyad having thought that he had delegated it to Aloka, provided the perfect front. Ameesha had inveigled the simple Aloka to assist her in tasks that did not tax what she considered to be his limited mental capacity.

Despite his apparent enthusiasm to learn from Ameesha, she noted that he remained in awe of her father.

It was, therefore, a more mature Ameesha that returned from England to see her father. Forever wily, still ambitious but with a new steely determination. Now she had no compunction about sealing her despotic father's fate. The prospect of remaining on the Island while her father slowly deteriorated and became ever more dependent upon her was not a future she would accept. She had other ideas that she had formulated over the period of restructuring of her father's financial empire. Now a wealthy woman in her own right, she had left Ziyad with a legacy that would hardly suffice in the short-term, let alone support him during years of dependency.

It was time to cut the apron strings and this meeting was going to finally break her free of his dominance. She was relishing revealing her achievements and seeing his shock on the realisation that she was clever and deceitful enough to have outwitted him. The man who had embezzled a fortune from one of the most dangerous militia groups in the world was about to feel what it was like to be the victim. She had little sympathy. In fact, she had not an ounce of sympathy for Baba. He was the instrument of their isolated childhood, their non-existent social integration with their peers - and the death of her beloved brother, Thinuka. He had tried to break free, to be his own man, and he had achieved that freedom to a degree, but at what cost? To him - his life. To her - a lost youth. Her father had compensated for the loss of a son by imposing an overbearingly defensive existence on his daughter, shielding her from anything and anyone who did not meet his standards and requirements.

His disability made him bad-tempered and demanding, exacerbated by the burdens placed upon him by the Arabs who sought restitution of the funds he had extorted. He had had to rely on Ameesha to carry out his wishes and it was at this point, with no friends and no contact with the outside world, that she formulated her plan for independence and revenge for his destructive impact on her life. She had felt bitterness, but this had been dissipated as she moved through London, as she took on her own personality and led her own life. Meeting Randolph had been a delightful bonus and she knew that she was fortunate that her first genuine sexual encounter was with a man who proved to be so gentle, caring and thoughtful.

Was she in love? She did not really know, but equally was hopeful. Randolph would be a good asset. She would wait and see what unfolded over the next week or so.

The taxi pulled up in front of her childhood home but the familiar gates remained steadfastly closed. Ameesha noticed that there was an intercom on a stalk that stretched from the kerb to the side of the driver's door. Now that was new.

The driver lowered his window and pressed a button that obviously rang inside the house. There was a long pause. Ameesha waited as light rain began to fall, gradually building in strength until it thumped on the metal roof of the vehicle. Leaning his arm out of the window, the rain darkening the driver's polo shirt as he struggled to hear what was being said to him. He turned towards her and impatiently enquired,

"He wants to know who you are? What is your name?"

"Oh, for fuck's sake," Ameesha had embraced cursing as another aspect of her emancipation, "It's Ameesha. His daughter."

The driver imparted the new information to the intercom and after a delay that made Ameesha push herself to the edge of her seat in irritation, the gates slowly opened. The windscreen wipers sloshed across the glass trying to clear the deluge that was now falling from the sky. Halfway up the drive a sodden man in an inadequate clear plastic cape stood beneath a canvas awning that was not doing much to protect him. The wind flapped the material into a dome over his head and water showered from the leading edge onto his feet. He bent low to confirm the identity of the occupant of the vehicle as it passed and then appeared to speak into a walkie-talkie.

Ameesha was slightly alarmed at the feeling of being a stranger in her own home. Since she had left it seemed that her father had become ever more paranoid over his security. Perhaps the fact that he was alone in the house, save for the hired help (help that he would not be able to afford soon), had made him upgrade the level of security. This was another service that would have to be terminated soon.

Ameesha had neither seen nor heard from the Arabs since her departure for London. The English solicitors had made the final transfer successfully and while she hoped that they might have been recalled to where they came from, she was not so naïve as to assume that they were satisfied and truly had melted away.

The car pulled up at the front door beneath the overhanging portico. The sudden cessation of the thrumming of the rain on the car roof was a relief, although the driver did not seem to notice as he shouted unnecessarily that they had arrived and that she should get out. He made no attempt to open the door for her and merely asked for payment of his fare.

"Unload my luggage and put it by the door." Ameesha was not taking such impudence from a mere driver. His annoyance at being ordered to do something by a woman was evident, but she was impervious to his exasperation. He grumpily extracted himself from his dry vehicle and started to unload her luggage as instructed, having walked past the car door that Ameesha was waiting for him to open for her.

Every one of the cases was too heavy for the slight man to handle on his own. He was struggling as he part lifted and part dragged the bags to the front door. Ameesha dug around in her clutch bag for some money and, when she had alighted from the vehicle, she silently handed it to him. He quickly scrutinised the notes and grunted at the insultingly modest tip. He held out his hand for more, but Ameesha held him with a withering scowl and he reluctantly withdrew his demand.

Another man opened the front door to the house and gave a perfunctory welcome before telling Ameesha that her father was waiting for her in his study. She neither recognised nor acknowledged him and swept past into the hallway. She swiftly looked around and was comforted by the fact that at least everything here was as it had been when she left.

She wondered if she should have asked the driver to wait while she had her meeting with Baba, and then to take her back to a hotel. She did not imagine that

Baba was going to want her under the same roof as him once she had made her intentions for his future known to him. She was thankful that he would be unable to physically assault her from his wheelchair, but she worried that the new staff might come to his aid. Without relying on any physical intervention, she knew that he still had the ability to cut her with his tongue.

The door to the study was open and Ziyad was seated with his back to her, outlined in silhouette, a table light illuminated behind him. As she entered and walked across the room, she could see that he had a straw to his lips and his regular glass of malt whisky sat on the detachable table over his immobile knees. Ziyad made no effort to turn his chair to face her but waited in silence until she was at his side and had perfunctorily kissed his forehead.

"Hi, Baba. How are you?"

Ziyad took a sip through the straw and swallowing, he wriggled his mouth to free the end that had lightly stuck to his dry lips.

"As before." His head was supported by the framework that rose from the back of the chair, so he merely shifted the gaze of his one operational eye to focus on his daughter. There was something indefinably different about her stance. Her figure was fuller, she stood more erect, appeared more confident, verging on confrontational.

"How was your trip?"

"Wonderful. I never knew that London could be so fabulous." She enthused but her father did not move his eye from her face.

"And what of Oxfordshire? Was that equally 'fabulous'?" Ziyad imitated an overly English accent.

Ameesha was taken aback by the question so early in the conversation. She attempted to maintain her poise, but she was her father's daughter and her discomfort was evident to Ziyad.

"It was beautiful, but how do you know about Oxfordshire?"

"I am not a fool, Ameesha, and neither are our friends."

On the mention of their 'friends' Ameesha's expression changed to one of shock, tinged with a little fear.

"They've been here?" She stammered, "What do they want?"

"Well, we'll get to that, but from what they told me they know a great deal about your activities. Your Randolph, if that's his name, has been enjoying your visit as well – and in more ways than one!" Ziyad spat out the last phrase in disgust and in her surprise, Ameesha tried to defend herself.

"Please, Baba!" She was flustered and exasperated that she was unable to dominate the conversation as she had intended. It was typical of Baba to take control and undermine her immediately upon her return. It was as if he had been rehearsing these opening sentences before her arrival with the express purpose of throwing her off-guard.

"We will come back to him in a moment," Ziyad craned his neck and took up the straw that had been just out of reach to suck a further dram of his drink. It caught in his throat, and he coughed, the straw flying out of his mouth and settling lopsidedly over the rim of the glass, its end out of the liquid. Without thinking, Ameesha leant forward and repositioned it so that he could sip again once his convulsions had ceased.

"You have been busy as well, I see." Ziyad had recovered. His eye narrowed, and his mouth tightened. Ameesha was once again on the back foot.

"What do you mean?"

"Why do you insist on treating me like a simpleton?" Ziyad's voice gave way to exasperation before he reverted to one that was calm and steely. "I have watched as you unwound my business interests and I must admit that you were very competent in all that you undertook on my behalf. But it appears that you have been a bit too creative with some of the accounts. I suppose that you thought that as I was confined to this contraption…"

If he could have done so, Ziyad would have slapped his hand against the black armrest to emphasise his point.

"My body might be broken and useless, but my brain is not." He turned his chair to better face Ameesha.

"Did you really think that I would not maintain my contacts? Contacts that you may have overlooked or been unaware of and who still hold a loyalty to me." Ziyad took another small sip of whisky and seemed to savour the flavour before continuing.

"Loyalty. I value loyalty very highly. Don't you?"

Ameesha did not offer an answer as she did not like the direction the conversation was travelling.

"I'm prepared to pay generously for it."

Ameesha was feeling weak and tired as she sank into a seat to the side of Ziyad's desk. She thought that she should say something, to try and wrest control of the exchange back from her father, but as she opened her mouth, he raised his eyebrows and opened the eyelids to his one eye as if in surprise. She knew this of old to be a sign that she should not interrupt him. Her carefully laid plan that seemed so clear on the aircraft appeared to be unravelling.

"Please allow me to continue," Ziyad paused to ensure that she understood that he had not finished. She sank back into her chair and wished that she could get herself a drink, but she was rooted to the spot.

"Your efforts to siphon a percentage of what you were liquidating on behalf of our friends was well conceived and the execution has been exemplary. Your only mistake was to underestimate the fact that those with whom I have worked for many years have my interests and, I suppose, their own at heart."

"No, Baba, you've got this all wrong."

"Quiet!" Ziyad snapped as strongly as he could before allowing his breathing to return to an even rhythm before continuing. Ameesha sat silently like she was a teenager discovered in her room with a boy.

"The error is entirely yours. You didn't really think that you could outsmart me, to embezzle the master embezzler? Don't answer that! I will do it for you. You can't, you never could and you never will." Ziyad's breathing had become laboured again, and he panted between each word as he continued.

"You can't deny it and you will have to live with the consequences. All the little side deals that you have been sticking into your collection of accounts and investing with eager new managers have been recorded meticulously."

Ameesha could not help herself, "By who? This is a bluff, its rubbish."

She had been so careful to ensure that everything was kept separate. She had purposely never used the computers in the house. All her meticulous records had been stored on a new laptop that she had bought and kept secreted in the safe at the shop. After hours, when her father thought she was diligently running his business affairs, she was transferring what she felt was her rightful share of each transaction to remote and secure accounts. She had constructed a new web of brokers and bankers that she had carefully groomed for the purpose, and she assumed were her people. How could her father possibly know about all her activities? Which of her appointees had betrayed her?

Ziyad sat sipping his drink, watching the impact of his revelations. He was enjoying his position of power over his conniving daughter.

"Why don't you join us?" Ziyad spoke out into the gloom that had enveloped the room beyond the arc of light that surrounded Ziyad.

Ameesha looked expectantly around as the door to the study swung open and a figure entered that she immediately recognised.

"Aloka!"

The shop assistant walked slowly and silently across the carpet maintaining a wary eye on Ameesha, ready to retreat should she spring at him. He knew that this was unlikely because the damage was done. Under his arm he carried a laptop that earlier in the afternoon he had taken from the safe, as he did every morning before Ameesha appeared at the shop. It was identical to the one in Ameesha's hand luggage that was stacked by the front door. Involuntarily she looked towards the hall but could not see if any of the cases had been opened. The computer cradled under Aloka's arm was identical to hers and she immediately assumed that he had taken in out of her bag.

"How dare you go into my luggage!" she yelled. Aloka looked across to Ziyad for support and he nodded to confirm that Aloka had nothing to fear from a now flustered and angry Ameesha.

"It was not difficult to arrange for a duplicate machine to follow your activities, Ameesha. Of course, we ensured that you were blind to our monitoring of your little game, as you were ignorant of the amendments that we incorporated into each of your instructions – all done through the wonders of Aloka's laptop here."

Ziyad waited to see if his daughter was going to try to argue her case but there was silence. The rush of colour to her face had waned, she just listened as Ziyad continued.

"My loyal colleague, Aloka here," Ziyad raised his chin towards Aloka as if introducing him to Ameesha, "watched and once we knew what you were doing, we issued the necessary instructions and paid the necessary additional 'fees' to those who had to be party to my annulment of your every move. As far as you were concerned, my dear Ameesha, all your newly appointed acolytes were acting on your behalf. But you forget that I have moved silently through this twilight financial world for a long time. These young men and women that you thought you had under your control ultimately answer to me. Me, Ziyad, who has earnt them huge sums from my various business transactions over many years. An upstart like you is not appreciated, particularly if your intentions are solely to cheat one of their most esteemed clients – let alone cheat your own father."

Ameesha started to object but was silenced once again by a single, vicious glare from her father.

"Ameesha, my darling girl, you are a novice. Quite a talented novice, but none the less, a novice. And now it is clear that you are a cheating novice. Your old Baba was always one step ahead of you, though. It wasn't difficult to turn every one of your young advisors to be within my grip." Ziyad grinned mirthlessly with triumph. This was a victory that he shared with Aloka, who had served Ziyad well and in return Ziyad had rewarded him well.

Ameesha felt crushed and desperately tried to think of a way to restore her credibility but realised that the damage was irreparable. Her deception had been uncovered, and Ziyad had easily routed her from what she had perceived as a position of strength. She found herself a victim of her own conspiracy.

"Do you have anything to say for yourself?"

Ziyad sounded like a judge about to pass sentence, which in a way he was. Ameesha considered weeping or shouting, but neither were going to work on her father this time. The set of his mouth, the hard unforgiving eye told her all she needed to know. She silently shook her head which her father took as an admission of guilt. In his world, she was guilty of the most heinous of crimes, that of family disloyalty and her sentence was going to be long.

Ziyad indicated to Aloka that he should leave them so that he could pass judgement on his offspring. Ameesha could see that even though he had left the room, Aloka hovered at the threshold, out of Ziyad's line of sight, but within earshot.

"I have made arrangements that none of the funds will be accessible to you until I die, and possibly not even then."

Ameesha stared open mouthed at her father, unable to take in exactly what he was saying. Her mind was in such a state of turmoil that she could hardly understand the words that flowed from her father's mouth. It was as if he was speaking in a foreign language. She tried to both listen and formulate her own strategy for the banishment that was sure to follow.

"Should I die in a mysterious or unnatural manner, then my lawyer in Colombo will place all the funds into a trust that Aloka will oversee for the benefit of him and his family. You will have no benefit from this trust. Ever."

Ameesha looked across to Aloka who was triumphantly studying her reaction. She could not grasp what she was hearing.

"If, however, I live a long life and die as Allah permits then it is possible that you will reap half the benefit, the other half going to Aloka as my trusted confidante."

Ameesha could remain silent no longer, "Baba you can't do this. I shall overturn the will in court." She turned to where Aloka stood, partially concealed by the door and shouted, "Aloka, you snake, have you been planning this all along. I trusted you; I gave you responsibility for the shop, I…"

"You betrayed your father," Ziyad interrupted with a voice as cold as ice. Ameesha sank back sulkily and resigned herself to an unjust and unexpected defeat.

"What's to stop Aloka seeing to your early demise. Look at him, smirking at the door." She raised her voice again so that Aloka could hear, "He planned this all along and now is within a whisker of taking everything from me." She continued to sound petulant, a spoilt child denied her own whims and desires.

"If I may continue?" Ziyad silenced her whining, "My lawyer has specific instruction should anything untoward happen to me - at anyone's hands. Your fifty percent is dependent upon you remaining here and providing care for me in a diligent and loving manner as befits a daughter to her father. You will receive a modest allowance for as long as you perform your duties. It will certainly not give you a lavish lifestyle, but it will be perfectly adequate for your everyday needs. Of course, you could leave now," a dramatic pause, perfectly timed, "with nothing. The choice is entirely yours." Ziyad fixed his gaze on his daughter who slowly shook her head in shock and disbelief.

Ameesha thought for a moment and suddenly inspiration hit her. Of course. It was obvious.

"In that case, I shall leave now," she blurted out, without thinking. "I shall marry Randolph. He is very rich and can well afford to keep me, and love me, and care for me."

She had no idea if Randolph would consider marrying her, but it was the first thing that she could think of on the spur of the moment. She would have to work on him to get her will, but it was not beyond her capabilities.

Ziyad smiled cruelly, "Ah yes, your beloved Randolph. I said that we would return to him and as you have raised the subject, I think the time is right."

Ameesha felt a hollow sensation in her chest, her heart fluttered irregularly, and her breathing was shallow in anticipation of further trickery from her father.

"What about Randolph?" She asked quietly.

"When he knows who you are, I think it very unlikely that he will have anything more to do with you."

"What do you mean?" Ameesha stood up and looked indolently down at her father.

"He might not be quite the person you think he is."

Ziyad was enjoying the discomfort that he was inflicting on the traitor who sadly was his own flesh and blood. She tried to look defiant, but he could see that her defences had crumbled, as had her future. The world that she had expectantly promised herself when she walked back into this house had suddenly been whisked away from beneath her.

"Who do you think he is?" she asked.

"That is awaiting final confirmation, but I have my suspicions." Ameesha was confused and stood waiting for Ziyad to elucidate but he remained taciturn. He took a victorious sip from his whisky. A dribble escaped the straw and ran down the side of his chin. Ziyad looked across to his daughter and his expression made her involuntarily go over and mop the liquid away with a tissue.

"Thank you. You will soon get the hang of it."

Ameesha sat down again.

"Now, I think it would be appropriate for," he hesitated before uttering the name as if questioning its validity, "Randolph, to meet me."

"Why?" Ameesha asked, her voice flat, filled with a sense of resignation that she would ultimately do her father's bidding.

"Well, if he is to be the man for you, and I am to approve of him, then it is possible that I should pay him a dowry."

Ameesha studied her father and, as his face gave nothing away, took the bribe for the attendance of Randolph as a small compensatory positive. In fact, she suddenly felt that there may just be an escape from the prospect of spinsterhood and a life as a carer for a vengeful, unappreciative paraplegic parent during his declining years. If she was going to be given a chance, however slim, to abandon her father, then perhaps Ziyad should be given the opportunity to meet Randolph, particularly if a dowry, however modest, was on offer. Surely, with this last grain of financial hope, she would be able to soften the harshness of her father's heart. She would outwardly agree to his terms and play the dutiful, caring daughter for the time being, at least until Randolph was due to arrive. That may further loosen the tightly knotted purse strings that Baba had secured around her future.

"He may not want to come."

"Oh, my darling daughter," there was no hint of affection in his voice, "I'm sure you will find a way to convince him." Ziyad stared hard and his daughter took a deep breath and exhaled in exasperation.

"Now, run along and get unpacked. I will need a commode in a while, so come back once I have had a private word with Aloka."

Ziyad tilted his head to one side to indicate that her audience of him was terminated. He called for Aloka, who was still hovering by the door, to return.

As Ameesha swept from the room, she passed Aloka who quickly stepped back from her furious approach. Once she had passed, shooting him a withering look as she did so, he hurriedly disappeared into the relative safety of Ziyad's study. The laptop was still held tightly under his arm, as if he anticipated that Ameesha might try to make a grab for it.

Someone appeared to have taken her bags to her room and so she climbed the stairs deep in thought. Randolph had suddenly taken on a new importance in her life, he was her lifeline, and she could not need him more than she did now.

Chapter 34

Randolph arrived at the Centauria Wild Hotel around twenty-four hours after Ameesha had thrown herself on her bed and screamed into her pillow following the unveiling of her duplicity by her father.

The monsoon rain had abated for a while and a weak sun cast an eerie light across the Uda Walawe reservoir, the water glistening as ripples were lifted by a soft breeze that drifted across its surface. Randolph stood on his balcony and filled his lungs with the fresh, rain-washed air. On the flight he had planned out his itinerary for the three days that he had in isolation before meeting up with Ameesha. He expected that she would call him at some point, and he was mindful that he had been ambiguous as to his precise arrival date in Sri Lanka.

He fretted throughout the flight back to Sri Lanka that he would be recognised, and his past would catch up with him. His concerns proved unnecessary when, upon his arrival at Bandaranaike Airport, immigration and customs paid him no attention whatsoever. The driver that was allotted to him for the transfer to the hotel had chatted excitedly all the way, informing him of all the temples, wildlife reserves and the beach life available to tourists at this time of the year. Randolph listened as if he were a tourist to the Island, feigning ignorance of all that was on offer but overtly aware that the monsoon season was not the time for many of the attractions that were being extolled. The driver took the opportunity to find out if the well-dressed Englishman had already booked his own personal driver, in the hope of a lucrative hire if such arrangements had been overlooked.

"Thank you for the offer, but I will probably hire a car and drive myself around."

The driver looked askance and waggled his head from side to side.

"That is very unwise, sir. We are all terrible drivers. It would be very unsafe for you to drive. Many accidents occur on this road. I can do you a very good price. How long did you say you were staying?"

Dark eyes stared back at Randolph from the rear-view mirror and the driver proved his point by narrowly missing a handcart being pushed along the side of the road by a small boy who struggled to keep it moving though the ruts and bumps.

"Don't worry, I can deal with it, but thank you again for your offer."

The driver shrugged his shoulders and accelerated through a narrow gap between a truck and a tuk-tuk. He had obviously decided to show Randolph just how dangerous driving could be in Sri Lanka. His arm hung out of the side window, and he continued to steer one-handed around slow-moving traffic and trucks spewing out plumes of acrid exhaust fumes.

The smells and sounds of his homeland infused the interior of the car and recalled an earlier life that had been simple and carefree. Randul let the breeze blow in his face with his eyes closed and allowed his mind to reacquaint itself with an environment that had once been so familiar to him. As Randul observed the passing urban and rural scenery, the latter appeared to have changed very little. The roads were wider, marginally better surfaced and much busier with traffic than they had been when he had been living in the Sinharaja. The towns and villages that he recognised were congested and the amount of construction on the edges was expansive. But he was pleased that he was still able to identify a great many of the sights as the miles slipped by.

His driver, foreseeing no likely prospects of work from the dark-skinned Englishman, had taken to lengthy conversations on his mobile phone that was precariously balanced on his lap. No attempt was made to use an earpiece and Randul listened with amusement to a sister regaling the driver with the failings of her children, the woes of her marriage and the stresses of looking after their ailing parents. The driver gave plenty of advice to his sister but made no attempt to offer any assistance of a practical nature. Unaware that Randul could understand what was being said, he cut his sister short to tell her that he had a rich but mad Englishman in the car who looked more local than English. He spoke of his incredulity that his passenger was proposing to hire a car and drive himself, so was probably going die.

"He does not realise just how bad we are at driving." His sister laughed and Randul let the ensuing conversation drift into the background as he reverted to watching the scenery flash by, desperate to arrive, check-in to the hotel and finally get some sleep.

The next day the expected telephone calls came from Ameesha. She had rung his mobile number, but Randul had slept late or was in the shower and so the five attempted calls were shown unanswered on the screen. He decided to have a quick lunch and then he would call her. He had to factor in the time difference of five and a half hours between where Ameesha thought Randolph was, and where Randul really was, namely some sixty miles as the crow flies to the South of her home in Kandy. He would have to remember to feign a sleepy early morning conversation as if he were still at Wykeford House in Oxfordshire.

When he eventually did call her, she answered swiftly but sounded different. She was morose rather than her usual garrulous self. At the sound of his voice, she seemed to perk up and asked what he had been doing in her absence and whether he was missing her. He tried to stick to as near to the truth as he could and confirmed that he missed her terribly, although he had to admit to himself that he did not feel the absence as much as she obviously did. He dutifully enquired after her father's health, and she dismissed any concerns as being unfounded and that he was fine.

"In fact, he would love to meet you as I have told him so much about you and Wykeford, and London and everything." By this point her voice had resumed its usual enthusiastic tone, but Randolph was wary.

"What have you told him?"

"Oh, you know. About your estate and the rewilding. Your business in London and how much in love we are."

She dropped the final element of the sentence in as naturally as if it were true. Randul did have a fondness for Ameesha and enjoyed her company, both in and out of bed. However, whether his feelings extended to that short word 'love', he was not sure. It seemed that with her return to Sri Lanka, she had assumed a deepening of their relationship beyond that felt by Randul. He suspected that she might have exaggerated the nature of their relationship to her father and perhaps now her father saw impending nuptials. Since he had overheard her nocturnal telephone conversation in Wykeford House, he was certainly not convinced that Ameesha was being completely honest with him. Without a sense of complete trust he would never commit to such a course.

"I'm not sure about that. Let's wait until I'm there and decide then." Randul hoped that by the time they met in a couple of days, his deferral would calm her enthusiasm. It seemed from her response that that might be wishful thinking.

"He won't bite, he just wants to meet the man his daughter is besotted with."

Randul brushed this off with another "Let's see." Things were moving too fast, and he was nervous about being in an environment where relationships between eligible men and women could be so easily misconstrued. He had no desire to become an external competitor for Ameesha if her father had already entered into a marriage agreement with a local family. While arranged marriages were becoming less popular, some traditionalists remained and to interfere with such arrangements was very unwise. Randul had no wish to do anything that might draw undue attention or start people asking unwanted questions. Not for the first time, Randul wondered whether his return was wise and if he should have let the shadows of a past life remain unlit.

They chatted for a few more minutes and Randul parried the questions about what he was planning for the day and who he might see. Some specifics were left unanswered and finally he found an excuse to have to ring off,

"I've got to go, there's someone at the door and I have a meeting starting in a few moments."

She continued speaking for a few seconds, confirming her love for him, how much she was looking forward to seeing him and what she was going to do to him when they did meet.

"That's quite enough of that sort of talk, you are a very smutty girl," he rebuked her playfully.

She purred on the other end of the line and then the line went dead. Randul sighed, unsure quite what had happened between her leaving Heathrow and arriving in Sri Lanka. She was far more affectionate and almost overbearing with her keenness for him to meet her father. She had hardly mentioned her father when they were together in London. In fact, Randul believed him to be dead until she had suddenly announced that she had to return to see him because he was ill. It was only subsequently that she had revealed that he was severely disabled. Randul merely thought that by returning she was doing her duty as a devoted daughter. But it seems that her father was not as ill as she might have implied and was perfectly capable of fulfilling his traditional protective role, scrutinizing the suitability of any man who might have purported designs on his daughter.

Randul mulled over the position he found himself in and took his own advice, namely, to wait until he and Ameesha met in a couple of days. In the meantime, he had to arrange to hire a car and use his time to best effect before he formally 'arrived' in Sri Lanka.

After an hour and a half of tedious bureaucracy, he sat behind the wheel of the Audi on his way towards the Sinharaja Forest and his former home. He was filled with a mixture of apprehension and excitement. Apprehension at the possibility that the bungalow had collapsed or was being squatted in by another family, and excitement to be back on such familiar ground in such familiar surroundings.

The road was much as he recollected, although there seemed to be more vehicles travelling at higher speeds. Quite a few new buildings had been constructed in areas that he remembered as wide, open country. Gradually the forest closed in around the car and the way became narrower and more potholed. The Audi's suspension crashed against the edges of deep holes and Randul began to understand the exemption of insurance cover on the hire car for tyres and wheels.

As Randul approached the final corner he stopped the car slightly distant from the bungalow. He gathered his day-bag and approached his former home. It appeared to have been left abandoned and the vegetation had overrun the building. The fact that another family had not taken it over was a relief. Randolph sat for a moment and watched the silent structure. There was an air of deserted melancholy that hung over the clearing as if the house mourned his departure and had lost hope of him returning. The veranda railing had collapsed, and the corrugated iron roof sagged slightly at one end. The metal table was upturned and lay like a corpse against the corroded feet of the two chairs stationed either side of the void. The front door was closed and the windows grimy with years of neglect.

Randul slowly walked around the site. The place looked so small and vulnerable to him now. Upon completing his circumnavigation, he ambled slowly, almost guardedly towards the entrance, as if expecting someone to suddenly call out and challenge his arrival. To question his presence in the past.

The steps up to the veranda groaned under his weight and he trod carefully, aware that the timber could give way at any time. His hand closed around and turned the door handle. The lock was stiff and unyielding. It took a firmer grip and a more concerted effort to release the catch and free the door from its swollen frame. Randul could not restrain a smile when the door creaked open like a sound effect from some gothic ghost story. He pushed harder as the bottom edge of the door caught against the floorboards that had buckled slightly in the humidity that had invaded the interior and been absorbed by the aged timber.

Everything smelt musty and a thick layer of dust and pollen covered all the surfaces. Randul's footprints tracked his progress around his former home, the soft detritus from the floor sticking to the damp soles of his boots. A couple of cupboard doors were open, as if someone had hastily collected something and left. For all Randul knew, they had remained unmoved since his own hasty departure. Water had managed to seep through the roof at the end of the living room and decay was spreading out across one wall. A dark filamentous growth expanded in an arc from the top corner, gradually devouring the fibres of the timber as it progressed its downward path.

The structure was probably too far gone to be capable of restoration, but Randul was already wondering if he should rebuild the house, keep it for future trips. Let it out for others to enjoy. Then he realised quickly that his repossession of this land would draw attention to his true identity. The return of Randul Ranatunga to his birthplace and the ramifications for his liberty were not worth the physical reality of his vain daydreams. He would consult with his lawyers to see what could be done; it was possible that over the intervening years the State had assumed the title to the apparently abandoned property. Perhaps he could buy it back in his new persona?

Whatever the outcome, Randul was unprepared for the strong affinity he felt for the building in which he stood. The desire to return grew in his chest, the chance to revert to living a simpler life, but with some of the comforts and benefits that Randolph might be able to provide. He took another careful look around the room and then left the house by the rear door that opened surprisingly easily. It swung idly on its hinges in a slight breeze that swept in from the front door collecting dry leaves that rustled across the floor. It was not sufficiently strong to close the rear door, but enough to flick at the dust, roll it gently across the floor, allowing the building to breathe again, to clear its interior of years of mustiness.

The shed that had formed his rudimentary laboratory for processing his foraging had suffered to a far greater extent and the roof had collapse down one side. The door was hanging by only one hinge, and he bent down to look in under a thick growth of vegetation that formed a canopy in substitution for the tin roof. There was little to be seen apart from a few glass flagons, some tubing, phials and other unrecognisable items lying broken on the floor. Another thick layer of dirt and vegetation carpeted the rotting boards that sagged under the weight and decay of the years of exposure to the elements. The quiet that imbued the derelict building competed with the sounds of the forest that seemed to increase in volume until they had captured Randul's attention. Countless memories swirled around him as he crouched in the clearing, touching him briefly before softly drifting away as if released by his presence, to fade away into the trees accompanied by the birdsong.

Randul looked back at the house while remaining on his haunches, listening to the voices of the forest. The undergrowth had crept in to enclose the house within its embrace, to envelope it back into the body of the Sinharaja where it would eventually decay and be absorbed to provide sustenance for future generations of plants. Was it a form of sacrilege to fight back against the encroachment? Should he leave the plot to disappear, for the seeds of foraged plants to germinate and flood the area as a memorial to his attempts to exploit the forest?

As Randolph, he had tried to recreate a wilderness in a foreign land but here before him, no effort was required. Nature was the dominant force, having no need for the assistance of man to rewild a habitat that had yet to be stripped of its natural flora and fauna. Randolph had sought to reverse the monoculture prevalent of English farming. There the land had been commercially exploited to produce food, starved of natural nutrients and then, to increase productivity, flooded with chemicals that leached through the soil, polluted watercourses and denuded the earth of any structure or form. His intervention had meaning, it was a cause that he would not abandon.

Randul looked around him with a sense of awe and he wondered how he could possibly desert this place again. Here he was witnessing the process of the natural environment managing its own affairs and doing so with consummate efficiency. It was only when man sought to interfere that nature paid the price.

He rose stiffly and very slowly rotated on the spot to fully observe how his surroundings had evolved, to bear witness to the restoration of the balance of nature's forces that accompanied the slow erosion of any veneer of his family's former presence. He felt a certain sadness, but also a certain satisfaction that his interference in the status quo was to be abandoned. His decision was final, he would not return, he would not seek to reinstate the house or perpetuate the scar on the forest, everything would be allowed to return to normality under his protection.

Randul walked decisively back round to the front of the house and picked up his small day-bag from the veranda. He slipped his arms through the straps, shrugging his shoulders so that it sat comfortably on his back.

Progress through the forest was slow, the paths that he had regularly trodden were overgrown and not easily discernible. This was an area where tourist guides did not bring their visitors and Randolph was able to linger in the sure knowledge that he was alone. He recognised several species that he had collected in his previous life, but they seemed to be in less profusion than he remembered. Some, out of habit, he picked and popped into his bag, others he merely rubbed between his fingers for the memory of a scent, aromas that in some instances he had not experienced since he left. The purchase of dried products or vacuum-packed material never held the same sense of freshness or intensity as those used within hours of having been harvested from the forest.

Gradually the land became more undulating, and Randul started to climb, the vegetation around him defining the height he had achieved better than any altimeter. The humidity had also increased, and the clouds above the Sinharaja had darkened. Drops of water were just beginning to infiltrate through the thick canopy of leaves indicating that the rain had started in earnest but had yet to beat its way through to the understorey of the forest. It was not long before his shirt was soaked, the water running down his face and neck. It was not uncomfortable or unpleasant, and Randul maintained his pace until he reached a ridge that overlooked the river where first he had found the Padparadscha sapphires.

The view was breath-taking, with peaks rising beyond the valley along which the water flowed. The ridge was of broad slabs of rock with hundreds of little rivulets cut into the surface. Each was filled with water that raced to join the river below. From his vantage point Randul saw, unsurprisingly, that the river appeared unchanged.

The path down was steeper and more slippery than he recalled as he gingerly edged his way towards the clearing from where he used to swim and bath. The river was high and the water moving very angrily around the rocks that stuck above its foaming surface. Randul knew that the river was far too high to swim in even the most protected pool. He wondered if the force of the flow was going to be too strong for him to have one last wander across the exposed islands of rock that remained above the torrent of water.

He stripped off his wet shirt and removed his boots. He waded tentatively out into the water and placed his feet firmly in the shifting shingle. He could feel the pebbles scratch and bump his soft skin and he braced himself against the strong pull of the river. The water was up to just above his knees but the movement around his feet and the swirling water tugging at the fabric of his trousers gave him a sense of instability that would never have existed in his youth. If he lost his footing and stumbled, then he would almost certainly be swept out of the lee of the rocks and off down the river.

For approximately fifteen minutes he managed to shuffle from rocky outcrop to rocky outcrop, all the while his weakened calf muscles urged him to cease, and the soft soles of his feet ached from the abrasive shingle. He had searched some of the smooth holes in the rock surface but had not expected to find anything. That was not the purpose of the exercise. It had been a form of exorcism, to experience the sense of place rather than the act of reconstruction. He wanted to fix the memory in his mind as he would never return after today. The unrelenting struggle to scrape a living from this land had faded from his memory, been romanticised over the years of recollection. He was far removed from the young man who had found his fortune in these waters, a fortune that had not always brought him joy. He had been exploited and abused as he hid behind the disguise of a refugee. But his exile had never been with the serious intent of returning, to reinstating his former life.

Randul was dead.

He perished on the desiccated dunes of the Arabian Peninsula, he drowned in the peaks and troughs of a Mediterranean storm, he was murdered at the hands of the organised criminals who exploited and destroyed the lives of those they purported to assist.

Randolph put his shirt and boots back on, took up his day-bag and left the river without looking back. He had done what he intended to do. He had proved to himself that his life had moved on from this Island and that he should return to his true home and continue to build his future there.

However, there was still one final place that he had to visit to complete the cycle. He took a different, more indirect route away from the river and again the path led him upwards. He kept up a pace that a Veddah could maintain for a day without over exertion, enjoying the walk, his mind now clear and decisive, reinvigorated, eager to concentrate on projects on his Estate. He marched purposefully, the path well known to him, and allowed his mind to wander as he prepared a checklist of tasks that he would put into motion immediately upon his return to England.

He climbed a sharp incline with a cliff to one side and slowly made his way along the ridge. He stood at the highest point and looked down. The crumpled body at its base had long been removed, but the memory remained. Thinuka had been foolish to follow Randul, but at the same time, Randul still held the sense of guilt that if he had led him on a different path to a different part of the forest, he might have avoided the death of Ziyad's son. His mind turned to the gem dealer. His name was a distant memory, but unforgettable just the same.

He did not think he ever knew his surname, but he could remember the scrubby little shop in the backstreet of Kandy. He thought he might take a quick look when there and see if it still existed. He doubted that it would but somehow felt drawn to complete his pilgrimage. He pulled himself away from the spot and continued his journey along the ridge as it meandered downwards. He scanned the rock formations jutting up from the ground and started to think that he would have to retrace his steps.

Suddenly he spied a round topped rock that he had unexpectedly approached from the rear. He skirted around the formation until the weather eroded face with its deep eye sockets, snub nose and open mouth was clearly visible. As he faced Monkey Head Rock it was as recognisable now as it had been when he had stumbled in a panic-stricken daze through the dark forest after his altercation with Ziyad.

Randolph placed one hand on the top of the head of the monkey and leant down to push his other hand into the smooth opening that formed the monkey's mouth. Something moved to the touch of his fingers, and he involuntarily jumped back. Tentatively he reinserted his hand before feeling deeper into the void.

Under the litter of decomposed leaves, he felt the unyielding irregular shape that he had deposited there so many years ago. The upper edge of the hole over hung the lower and so had protected the interior from the worst of the rain. He dug his fingers into the surrounding dirt and closed them around the package. Gradually he pulled it up towards the opening. The lips of the open mouth seem to be too narrow, and Randolph had to rotate and manipulate the package until it was free. The oiled cloth appeared untouched by time and Randolph gently placed it onto the grass at the base of the rock as if it were a divine relic.

There was a reluctance to unfold the material around the parcel. What demons would be released once the contents was revealed? Randolph took the edges and meticulously unfurled the cloth, its footprint expanding across the grass as the contents came closer to the surface. A glint of bluish metal and then, suddenly, a small canvas bag rolled out to one side and settled onto the grass. He lifted the last flap of oiled cloth from the revolver and left it untouched at the centre of the material. He picked up the small canvas bag and felt its weight. The objects within softly clinked together and Randolph carefully undid the ties around the neck of the bag before shaking the contents onto the cloth.

Two large stones dropped silently out and settled separately from one another. Randolph had not seen these stones since that fateful night and once again he was awestruck with their size and beauty.

He knew, even in his frenzied state of mind that fateful night that he would never be able to take these stones with him. They were too valuable and would be infamous as soon as they were released onto the market. To have one giant Padparadscha was extraordinary, but to own two was, well exceptional.

Unlike Randul, Randolph had a very good idea of what the true value would be if they were to be offered as a pair onto the open market. Currently, the largest known cut stone remained at around one hundred carats and continued to reside in The Museum of Natural History in New York. These two huge stones retained their mesmerising beauty. Even now he found it difficult to precisely define the colour. It was a certainty that both stones would cut to reveal the most perfect pale salmon pink of the lotus flower after which they were named. The juxtaposition of the stones and the weapon was surreal in Randolph's eyes, and he replaced the gems into the bag to separate beauty from violence.

He pushed the stones deep into his day-bag and then returned his attention to the gun. What was he to do with it? Return it into the monkey's mouth and forget about it? It had not been found since he had deposited it there all those years ago and so this seemed to be the best solution. Without thinking, Randolph checked the chamber of the ancient weapon and saw that the bullets remained in their allotted position, the oil cloth and the deep recess in the rock having protected them from corrosion. He wiped the metal of any fingerprints and carefully wrapped the gun in the cloth once again before replacing it from where it had been hidden, hopefully never to be seen or used again.

Chapter 35

Aloka raised the shutters to the shop front as usual. He took a moment to stand back on the side of the street and admire the premises, built a couple of years ago and nestled in the main retail area close to the Bank of Ceylon, The Peoples Bank, electrical shops and a few competing jewellers. His window display was the largest and brightest, pulling in much of the tourist trade that either was staying in the town or just passing through.

Ziyad had left him to his own devises, and he had expanded the business, paying over to Ziyad the agreed percentage of takings while simultaneously monitoring the activities of Ameesha, who came and went in the mistaken belief that she was running the shop on behalf of her father. They all performed their individual roles, players in a theatre of deceit. Each pursuing their own specific agenda, each unaware that their duplicitous lives had succeeded in spinning a web that would eventually inextricably entangle them all.

Aloka satisfied himself that his shop was prepared for the day's trade and that the window was set to his satisfaction. He hurried into the premises and was greeted by his staff; the numbers having expanded as a direct result of the success of the business.

But this morning Aloka had little time to exchange pleasantries.

Today was the day that Aloka returned to the old shop, as he did every two weeks. Not for any nostalgic reason but instead for a clandestine meeting to receive any specific instructions and impart information that would assist those to whom he had become beholden.

Meanwhile, as she ate a solitary breakfast at home, Ameesha was excited at the prospect of the arrival of Randolph. She had spoken to him regularly on the telephone over the days of their separation but had not heard from him for the last twenty-four hours as he flew from England towards her welcome embrace. The shock of her father's reproach and the venal punishment that he had imposed on her had boosted her determination to use Randolph as her liberator. She knew that like a hungry panther, she had to stalk him with care. He was still an unpredictable prey, canny and cautious. If she acted peremptorily, he would take fright and flee. She thought that when she left him at Heathrow Airport, she had effectively inveigled herself into his life to ensure her success. But, having been so ignominiously outwitted by her father, she had developed self-doubts as to her own aptitude to irrevocably ensnare the affections of Randolph. Marriage to Randolph was her sole objective and infinitely preferable to the unedifying vision of her future offered by Ziyad.

Ameesha visualised that a life as the mistress of the Wykeford Estate was one that she could easily find very acceptable. Randolph had the wealth to be able to keep her in a manner she felt was beholden to her. His business and social standing would enable her to mix with a level of society that might provide new opportunities for her to build on her own financial independence, should there be a need to leave Randolph for pastures new. Who knows what might become accessible to her once she was ensconced in Wykeford House? The prospects became rosier the more that she dreamt of her future in England. However, the priority above all else was to escape the clutches of her vindictive father.

The possibility of a dowry was a surprise and never strayed far from her thoughts. She mistrusted the reliability of her father's offer, but on the other hand the chances of something were better than the certainty of nothing. The ability to convince Randolph to meet her father was still going to be a challenge, one that had been troubling her since Ziyad had made his demand. The only way that she could see of persuading Randolph to attend was to be honest - to a degree. She had decided that she would explain that her father was a caring parent who wished to meet and approve of her daughter's choice of boyfriend. His character would have to be massaged to portray an affectionate old softy who doted on his strong and wilful, but dutiful, daughter.

She was similarly troubled by the strong impression given by her father that he knew more about Randolph than she did. What had he meant when he stated that he might not be who she thought he was? Surely, she had got close enough to Randolph not to have misjudged him. She knew that he was a refugee but that was many years ago and resulted from the need for him to flee from persecution. But from where had he fled? She had never been told. In fact, the more she thought about it, the less she did know about his past, apart from the brief and very scant details that he had imparted at moments of his making. She had put this down to the pain of recollection as opposed to a resolute evasion of the truth. The fact that he had been keeping some elements of his past from her was no worse than her omission in revealing everything about her life to him. If, in time, she discovered any unpalatable details about Randolph then she would deal with them at that point. The priority was to establish herself in the safety of the English countryside under the protection of Randolph, whether that be permanent or temporary.

*

Randolph had packed up his belongings some hours earlier and they were loaded into the taxi for the journey to the airport. He was probably being overly cautious, but he did not want to risk the chance of either being seen arriving in Kandy from the wrong direction, or his driver inadvertently revealing where he had picked up his fare. His short break at Uda Walawe had been enjoyable and had served a purpose. The solitary homecoming to his tribal lands emphasised the gulf that existed between his former aboriginal life and his new life, a gulf that was too wide to bridge. He recognised that realistically there was no future for him in Sri Lanka.

In England he had retained a faint desire to return but as the years passed that desire became an itch that he could not scratch. The opportunity presented by Ameesha had been the catalyst that had made that itch insufferable but, truth be known, he had found that the trip had been cathartic. It had established that his life on the Island had ended when he took flight following a brawl that had not been of his instigation. The dealer, whose shattered features he could recall clearly, was a speck of grit in his memory. An irritant that he had surrounded with more palatable reminiscences. The recollection smoothly encased like a pearl in the body of an oyster, ever present but desensitised. An invasive entity that had touched his life and set in train a series of events that had, in most aspects, transformed his life for the better.

In truth, he was indebted to the dealer, but it was one debt that he had no desire to honour.

It had been a long day and Randolph wondered if the subterfuge was worth the effort. He arrived at Bandaranaike Airport prior to the landing of the flight from London and waited an hour to allow for the passengers to pass through immigration and collect their luggage. Nobody was interested in his presence and when he emerged from the arrivals area, he was pounced upon by several enterprising taxi drivers who recognised a wealthy tourist when they saw one. He chose the oldest who looked most in need of business and helped him to load his limited amount of luggage into the boot.

Randolph sat back in the car and allowed this second driver to yet again regale him with the wonders of Sri Lanka until he drifted off to sleep. He awoke as they approached the outskirts of Kandy and Randolph unexpectantly found himself asking the driver if he could make a short detour. Naturally, the driver was content to do so once Randolph agreed the additional fare. Almost out of habit, Randolph kept his face partially obscured from any inquisitive passers-by. He knew that he was being paranoid as no one seemed to be interested in the unexceptional passenger in the unexceptional car.

The driver wound their way along the back streets until Randolph asked him to stop at the head of a mean alley. The buildings either side were more dilapidated than he remembered but up on the left-hand side was the ramshackle shop that Randul had visited on his first meeting with Ziyad. It appeared even worse for wear and unoccupied. Randolph resisted the urge to get out and walk down to take a closer look. There seemed little point.

The car engine ticked over, and the driver watched Randolph with interest, wondering why his passenger would want to come to this squalid part of town. Most of the shops had moved to around the more popular retail centre. It was a curiosity of little consequence to the driver, the additional fare more than compensating for his time and effort.

After a minute or so, Randolph realised that there was nothing further to be gained from staying and told the driver to continue. The driver pushed the gear lever into drive and the car started to move as Randolph took one last look down towards the shop.

Just as he was about to lose sight of the frontage of the shop, the door opened and Randolph shouted for the car to stop. The driver thought that there was a major problem and slammed on the brakes, the wheels sliding and squealing on the warm, dust strewn tarmac. The sudden halt propelled Randolph forward and he steadied himself on one knee and watched as two men emerged from the shop followed by a third who turned and locked the door. They exchanged adieus, and Randolph thought that one of the first two men looked familiar. But from where?

Both men headed towards the car, walking with self-confident swaggers. The third man turned away and disappeared in the opposite direction up the street towards the centre of town.

Randolph watched them approach, one noticeable older than the other. It was the younger man that Randolph thought he had seen before, but from where was still eluding him. He looked directly at the car as he chewed gum and appeared to gag before he spat a large globule of greenish phlegm onto the side of the road. The older man took a cigarette out of a crumpled packet and lit it with a plastic lighter, inhaling deeply. There was no reason to wait until these two came past the car and Randolph settled back into his seat and instructed the driver to move on.

From a distance, Ahmed peered into the car that had suddenly screeched to a halt at the end of the alley. He would not have noticed it save for the impromptu sound of the tyres sliding on the dusty road. The passenger must have been thrown forward by the momentum and was on his knees looking straight down the alley at him. Their eyes met for an instant and, unlike Randolph, the younger Arab had an immediate recollection of where he had seen the smartly dressed gentleman crouched at the rear car window. He almost choked before he quickly spat the khat filled saliva from his mouth in order to alert Ali. The car edged forward and disappeared out from sight as Ahmed harshly grabbed Ali's arm, causing him to cough in surprise from the unexpected inhalation of the acrid smoke from his newly lit cheroot.

*

Even allowing for the minor detour, the journey to the airport and then to Kandy had taken longer than Randolph had anticipated, and he did not arrive at his hotel until early evening. He was dusty and tired, much as he would have been if he had endured a thirteen-hour flight from London. His driver unloaded his luggage, and the porter took charge of delivering it to his room.

The interior of the hotel was still recognisable from when he had sat in the lobby drinking coffee with Stephen all those years ago. However, the decoration and ambiance had become much more lavish, the hotel having been bought in the interim by a local businessman who had bestowed both love and money on the property. The interior was plush and the staff smartly uniformed, well trained and attentive without being overbearing or obsequious.

A receptionist had been expecting his arrival and handed him a note that had been left for him. He recognised the writing as that of Ameesha and quickly read the brief welcome. She had wanted to join him that evening but due to family matters she would give him the opportunity to rest before seeing him in the morning. He was relieved that she did not insist on joining him that night. He had no energy for the undoubtedly strenuous demands that she would place on his body on being reunited.

Once in his room he stripped, showered, fell into bed and slept deeply.

*

Ziyad, however, was not sleeping. As usual, he spent the night hours lying on his bed, an inanimate body imprisoning a frenzied mind that reviewed the events of the day and contemplated those of the day to come. Ameesha was too attentive, and that told him that she was planning something. She was not the sort of woman who took defeat lying down and he knew that he had to be on his most alert over the next few days. She assured him that she would bring Randolph to meet him, and he eagerly anticipated their final reunion. What he bitterly regretted was the fact that his long-awaited revenge would have to be at the hands of others. His broken body was incapable of exacting anything other than a verbal assassination and that was not enough.

Nothing like enough.

In the darkness he regularly saw the diffused orange-pink hue from the Padparadscha sapphires that the savage had taunted him with as he lay in his own blood, breathlessly willing air into his punctured lung. He could visualise the unique colour and clarity of each stone as they slowly spun weightlessly in the void above his head, exuding their own luminosity into his foetid chamber. He had to endure the smell of his own excrement until Ameesha returned in the morning. The final indignity, his body useless but his senses alert to witness every uncontrolled bodily function.

He pushed the foul odour from his mind and concentrated on his vision of the stones. The final act of revenge would be to take possession of the raw gemstones, the like of which he had never seen before. The cost to him was the enforced division of the spoils.

In the circumstances, he did not feel that the barter was unreasonable. He very much doubted whether the true worth of the stones was appreciated, and he wondered if he would be able to spirit both stones into his ownership with the promise of something more appealing to the needs and desires of his accomplices.

The raw Padparadscha gems of his dreams delighted him. They soothed him. They seduced him. At last, they were to be his. He had monitored the market over the years and had the savage tried to sell any of them on the primary or secondary market he would have known. You could not dispose of stones of that size and quality without drawing attention to yourself. Of course, Randul could have broken them up into smaller jewels, but Ziyad had seen in the aborigine's eyes the same lust for them to remain intact. Once touched, caressed, raised to the light to reveal the magnificence of the colour, it would be tantamount to a sacrilege to break the stones into smaller, less valuable baubles. These were gems of global significance, and no one possessed with the knowledge and appreciation of the intrinsic importance of these stones would permit them to be so cruelly violated.

They were so nearly within his grasp.

All it required was for Ameesha to lure the savage to his home, into his lair so that he could verify that Randolph was indeed the elusive Randul.

Chapter 36

Randolph ordered hoppers, fresh fruit and coffee while Ameesha sat opposite him with a dreamy smile that spread from her lips to her smoky eyes. She studied the man before her, his swept back greying hair, the tightly formed bun, the carefully trimmed beard. His dark eyes were clear after a long night's sleep and light creases formed at the outer corners as he smiled across the table at her.

He was woken just before dawn by a warm body sliding into his bed and a pair of hands eagerly exploring his skin. Ameesha had managed to gain access to his room from a sleepy porter by pretending to be his wife.

If only.

She quietly undressed leaving her clothes discarded on the floor. As welcomes go, it was both enthusiastic and energetic, and testing of his physical stamina. Ameesha was eager to please and willing to experiment in ways that he found surprising. She had been such an innocent and shy lover when he first met her. There was a reserved approach to sex that he saw as one of her charms. That morning she had displayed a voracious appetite that had taken him aback. It was as if she had studied the Kama Sutra in detail and was now demonstrating as many of the alternatives as was possible.

Her whole demeanour had changed. She was visibly more accommodating, less argumentative. So much so that Randolph was unprepared and became apprehensive as to her motives. Whether this was because she was in her home country and therefore more confident, he was unable to determine. Certainly, she was unsure of her surroundings when she had arrived in London, preferring to frequent well known shops and restaurants that were recommended in the tourist guides. Her adventurous side only materialised when she met Randolph, and he could provide a cultural support for her. He was unsure if the 'new' Ameesha was one that he found as delightful as the rather naïve and childlike woman he had met and taken as his lover in England.

Once his breakfast had been delivered to his table, along with a pot of black tea for Ameesha, she concentrated her green eyes on his and leant closer across the table.

"Will you do something for me?"

"I thought I already had." He winked at her, and she feigned shock.

"Not that, although it was delicious." She simpered and raised her eyebrows causing her irises to be fully visible, the lights of the dining room catching their emerald colour to great effect.

"My father has asked to meet you and…," She immediately saw his face fall and the mouth harden. "I know, I know. You said you just wanted to spend the time with me, but he is an old man and loves me so much that he wants to meet the man I have fallen in love with."

Her face implored his acquiescence, and he allowed his hostility at the suggestion to soften.

"Ameesha, I am not ready to meet your father. You know that I'm very fond of you," Randolph avoided any mention of love, and Ameesha noted it, "but I know that in your culture such things can be," he searched for the right word, "misconstrued."

Ameesha looked crestfallen and hurt, "I do love you, Randolph. I accept that you may not have quite reached the same stage in our relationship, but he is an old man. I don't know how much longer he has to live." Randolph looked sceptical and Ameesha quickly added, "I've not mentioned it before, but he is a paraplegic." Randolph was taken aback by the revelation, not so much by the fact that her father was paralysed but by the realisation that life in Sri Lanka as a disabled person was hard at the best of times.

"How long for?"

"Some years. He has carers. Although I do try to do all that I can for him," she lied. "I'm all he has. I am the apple of his eye. It would be wonderful if he could meet you and see what a fine man I have found for myself."

Randolph thought long and hard as he sipped his coffee. Ameesha pursued her cause.

"He loves me so very much and cares for my wellbeing. Knowing that I am cared for by a successful and handsome man will give him great comfort in his last moments."

This implication of imminent death was unexpected and, while he saw no particular risk in satisfying the wishes of a dying old man, something was gnawing away at him, silently warning him.

"Let me think about it, will you?" He watched her reaction closely and her eyes lowered, and she allowed her mouth to slacken into a downward curve. He knew that she was not used to him denying her any normal requests, but this went beyond the bounds of normality. Her bottom lip quivered as she appeared to fight back her tears.

"I have never begged you for anything, well almost anything," she looked up through her lashes at him, unable to resist the innuendo, "but would you please do this one little favour for me?" She saw him relent slightly and pushed home her advantage, "It need only be for a short time, he tires quickly. Just so he can see you and give his approval. That's all, I promise."

Randolph allowed the air that he had been holding unwittingly in his lungs to escape in a long sigh of capitulation.

"OK, but just a quick visit. I want you to show me around before I return to England. We only have a few days before I must be back."

Ameesha immediately cheered up and impatiently arranged for the visit to take place that afternoon. Randolph was more than happy to get it out of the way as soon as was possible. She excitedly assured him that for the rest of the time she would give him the time of his life, in every way possible and giggled salaciously.

Randolph had wondered what they were going to do for the morning as he had no desire to aimlessly wander around Kandy in case he was recognised. Ameesha dealt with that quandary by following him back up to his room and providing sufficient distraction to keep him occupied until it was time for a late lunch.

*

The drive out to Ameesha's home was silently tense but uneventful. Randolph watched the scenery slide by, recognising some of the roads, but more modern designs of housing had appeared along their edges denoting a suburb of increasing affluence. These buildings were constructed for the wealthy, not the poor. High walls maintained the owner's privacy and security. The grounds, when they could be seen, were well tended with a profusion of diverse plants and flowering shrubs. Each one had ornate, automated, wrought iron gates of varying designs, with entry phone panels set in pillars or at the end of metal poles that protruded from the neatly cut verges.

Ameesha sat tight to the side of Randolph; her hand placed lightly on his knee. She knew that he was uncomfortable at the prospect of meeting her father, but the possibility of a dowry, even if she did not actually marry Randolph was too tempting to forego.

"What do I call your father?" Randolph did not intend to play the prospective husband and refer to him as Dad or Father, or even PaPa. "What do you call him?"

Ameesha quickly responded, "I call him Baba but you should probably use his first name."

"Which is?"

"Ziyad."

The word sent a chill down Randolph's spine, and he felt the colour drain from his face. He tried to keep his voice as neutral as possible, not wishing to alert Ameesha to his anxiety.

"What did you say your father did for a living?"

"I told you. He is an entrepreneur, a trader. His interests extend far and wide. That is why I was in London, to oversee the sale of some of his properties. He has been liquidating a large part of his portfolio." Ameesha remained suitable vague, thinking that the precise reason for the liquidation would scare Randolph off immediately.

The mere mention of Ziyad had already started alarm bells ringing.

Randolph was not put at his ease. Ziyad is not an uncommon name but a name that resonated with his past. A name that he had no desire to be reacquainted with. He felt foolish for not having taken more interest in Ameesha's family and upbringing. She had never proffered the information and he had never thought to quiz her. He had the impression that her parents were dead, she never mentioned them and always seemed to be acting on her own behalf. He was certain that she had not revealed that her trip to London was anything other than one of personal choice. Certainly, there was no hint of working on behalf of a successful father, or that the wealth that she displayed was dependent upon the generosity of her father.

"What is his family name?" Randolph was not sure if he could remember Ziyad's name but was sure that he would recognise it if he heard it. Ameesha was becoming nervous at the questions that Randolph was pointedly asking at her, as if he was seeking confirmation of some fact that had eluded him for a long time. She did not want to admit to her adopted name, the pseudonym they had used in Sri Lanka. She felt with some sense of dread that somehow her father's name might be known or represent a threat to Randolph. She did not need to scare him away. She saw no reason for Randolph to fear her father, a paraplegic who had a sharp tongue but no ability to threaten anyone now. In the past, Ameesha was sure that Baba could be fierce and harsh, but now he was a shadow, a husk of the man he once was.

Ameesha made a split-second judgement and gave him their true name, "Al Jabri." Randolph made no show of recognition, and she continued, "It's Yemeni. We emigrated to Sri Lanka when I was a little girl, much the same age as you must have been when your parents arrived in England."

Randolph did not react to the reference to his own fictional past, he was thinking hard but could find no link with the name. Perhaps he was worrying over nothing. He comforted himself with the fact that the meeting would hopefully not last long. By way of an assurance he instructed the driver to wait for the duration. Ameesha quickly glanced at Randolph but felt that it would be unwise to question his orders.

They sat in silence as the car drew up to the gates to Ameesha's home.

"Do you want me to go in, sir?" The driver asked via the rear-view mirror.

"Yes."

"No."

Ameesha responded just a millisecond after Randolph. He turned and faced her, his expression no longer affectionate, a tight mouth beneath cold eyes.

"I am doing this for you, but don't think I am happy about it. The car and driver stay and when I have decided that the meeting is over, I shall leave." He stared her down and any rejection or objection to his conditions evaporated. For the first time Ameesha saw a harder more determined look in his eyes and did not doubt that Randolph would conduct the meeting firmly on his terms.

"Drive on and wait for me." The driver pushed the keypad and waited, flicking his eyes between the gates and his passengers seated in the back of his car. This was a lover's tiff, and he admired the fortitude of the man. He was correct to demand obedience from his woman and the woman needed to respect his dominance. This was the way things were and should remain without any Western sensitivities diluting the traditional customs. The driver was proud to be Sri Lankan and suspected that the man seated behind him also had Sri Lankan blood in his veins. The intercom crackled into life and a voice asked who was at the gate.

"Who shall I say it is?" the driver asked.

"Ameesha." Her voice was sullen, and her hand had been removed from Randolph's knee. The driver repeated the name and almost immediately a man materialised from behind one of the pillars and peer through the gates into the car. Ameesha paled and her hand twitched on Randolph's knee. The man nodded an acknowledgement as the gates juddered into motion and slowly swung open.

Randolph looked around as the car proceeded up the curved drive towards the front of a colonial style house. The covered entrance was as wide as Randul's whole bungalow, and the bougainvillea hung in ropes from an upper balcony.

Ameesha was not noticing any of the details that Randolph was absorbing as they drew up outside the house. She was wondering where the security men were, why there were no gardeners in evidence. Her father always kept a good compliment of men around for his protection and support but this afternoon the property appeared to be deserted from the usual daily activity.

As they drew to a halt in front of the steps up to the house there was no one to meet them and the driver had to get out and open her door. Randolph saw nothing unusual as he knew no different, but she had a cold elliptical thread of fear spiralling from her stomach to her heart. Had she misjudged her father yet again? Was Baba's insistence that she brought Randolph another twist to a fragmented seam of intrigue?

Randolph detected her hesitancy and held back from getting out of the car, as if he was absorbing his surroundings. The atmosphere had changed and he felt uncomfortable with his decision that had been made at Ameesha's insistence and against his better judgement. Ameesha bent down to look back into the car to try to reassure him, but his face betrayed his reluctance to move.

This was a mistake. Randolph had allowed his judgement to be clouded by Ameesha's persuasion that her father was both doting and doddering. During all the time Randolph had moved across countries as a refugee he had relied upon his innate ability to assess any situation in terms of its risk. On this occasion he had not listened to his common sense and, although he did not know what the risk was, here at the house of Ameesha's family, there was an undoubted feeling of dread building in his mind. Indecision fluttered around him as he tried to reach a conclusion as to whether he should instruct the driver to turn round and take him straight back down the drive. If his apprehension was unfounded then the gates would open, but if they did not…

The driver innocently assumed that Randolph expected him to open the door for him and he hurried round to do so, first collecting from the boot the daypack that Randolph had handed to him at the hotel. Ameesha followed him and stood with her hand out as a welcome to her home.

It was too late; the decision had been made for him.

Randolph pulled himself forward out of his seat and took her hand in his, the daypack held in his free hand. They walked together up the steps and into the entrance hall. Randolph was now alert and wary, Ameesha's grip tight and insistent that he should continue moving forward. There was a heavy silence in the hall and Ameesha seemed reluctant to shout to see whether there was anyone around. Still there was no sign of any staff or carers.

Randolph placed his pack by the door and looked around as Ameesha called out weakly, her mouth dry and her vocal cords stretched taut. The second attempt was louder and echoed around the space. A whirring sound came softly from a side room and Ameesha turned to see her father in his motorised wheelchair roll into view from his study.

The identification of Ziyad took Randolph no time at all. Panic gripped his stomach and his years of dread was brought alive by the shrunken body that sat strapped to the chair.

"This is a mistake, and I must go." Randolph turned to leave but the man from the gate had stepped through the door and closed it firmly behind him. Ameesha looked alarmed and gripped his hand tighter, whether for his benefit or her own he could not tell.

"What's going on?" Her face turned from Randolph to her father and then to the man at the door who stood firm with his arms crossed, obviously having no intention of moving.

Ziyad approached them both and stopped in front of Randolph. He stared long and hard into his eyes and absorbed the features that now obscured the once young face that disarmed him and then gloated at him in the bungalow.

Nobody spoke. Ziyad continued to study the man who stood uncomfortably in front of him. He wasn't totally certain and needed to be sure that this Randolph was truly the savage Randul. The man before him was broader than the skinny little filth that had stabbed him in the lung, but a life of good living did that to a man. His hair was thicker, the trimmed beard an addition in maturity, but the eyes were unmistakable, and confirmation, if such confirmation was needed, was evidenced by the fact that Randul was avoiding looking at Ziyad. There was an expression of unsuppressed dread, his eyes flickering around the hall to assess the feasibility of an escape from his situation.

Eventually, Randul did look directly down at Ziyad and evaluated the extent of the disability of his nemesis. He was comforted in the realisation that the man was really no physical threat. A punctured lung might cause some lasting ill effects, but it would not turn a man into a paraplegic. Some other misfortune must have befallen him. Randolph relaxed imperceptibly and might even have experienced a modicum of compassion for the gem dealer if it were not for the man guarding the door.

Ziyad could stand any emotion from this filth, except pity. He thought he fleetingly detected it in the savage's eyes and that was unacceptable, even contemptable. The anger rose in his throat, but he suppressed the urge to hurl insults and abuse at this sophisticated imposter.

Instead, he turned back towards his study and quietly asked them to follow him. Ameesha hesitated and then obeyed, taking Randolph's hand again. This time he knew that she was as apprehensive, if not scared, judging from the strength of her grip. He walked into the room and was offered a seat in a bay window overlooking a colourful rose garden. It was reminiscent of England, Randolph thought as he sat in the chair and crossed his legs, trying to remain aloof from the threat that he felt surrounded him. The light was fading already, and Randolph could not work out if it was signalling another monsoon downpour or that twilight had arrived. Table lamps were lit around the room, but the austerity stripped the study of any character or charm, it was not a room for entertaining or chatting with family and friends.

This was a space for an inquisition. Ziyad continued to watch Randolph until Ameesha broke the silence and unnecessarily introduced Randolph to her father. Ziyad moved his head in a small up and down motion. Randolph saw little to be gained by perpetuating any pretence,

"Your father and I have met before."

Ameesha sat on the window seat next to Randolph, her mouth slack jawed.

Ziyad smiled in triumph. "I really wasn't sure. You've changed a lot in the intervening years." He spoke quietly still controlling his indignation.

The atmosphere remained electric, and Randolph wondered if this was merely a case of Ziyad satisfying his curiosity. He had his doubts but needed to clarify, if for Ameesha's benefit alone, that he was not the cause of her father's misfortunes.

"I don't know why you want me here, but you know that I'm not responsible for your present situation." Randolph nodded towards the wheelchair and Ziyad looked at it as if it was the first time that he had seen it.

"This? No, I can't lay this at your door, although I did try all those years ago."

Ameesha remained silently stunned and listened in disbelief. Ziyad saw her confusion,

"I should introduce you, as you have clearly been living under the misapprehension that this man is Randolph Curran. This piece of filth is a Veddah called Randul Ranatunga, the young man who punctured my lung in a stupid fight and left me for dead."

Ameesha found her voice, "But Baba, you said that that a Veddah caused all your injuries. Randolph is no Veddah." She turned to Randolph for confirmation, but he just maintained his focussed stare on her father.

"You told the police that he was responsible for putting you in that chair. That he stole all your money."

"I told a lie. Well, a partial lie. Have you never lied, Ameesha?" He looked across at his daughter and gave a crooked smile. "Perhaps you better not answer that in front of our guest."

Ameesha took her father's advice and refrained from responding, knowing that to do so would prove his point. Ziyad kept his attention firmly fixed on the man he knew as Randul, who listened to the exchange. Ziyad addressed him, ignoring his daughter.

"I expect you are wondering why I wanted to meet you?" Randolph waited for Ziyad to provide the answer. "It is not to give approval to your dalliance with my daughter. The slut can do what she likes with whoever she likes. Even filth like you."

"Baba!" Ameesha protested, "That's not fair."

"Fair!" Ziyad twisted his neck round to direct his venom at his daughter, "You speak to me of fairness. You who attempted to steal what was not yours - from your own father. To leave him impoverished. You are a hypocrite and a disloyal child who I reject as any blood line of mine."

Ameesha subsided into silence as Randolph interrupted.

"I am not interested in your family squabbles." He turned to Ameesha, "You brought me here, Ameesha, under entirely false pretences. That was a mistake." He turned back to Ziyad, "Now, either you have business with me, or you do not. If not, then I shall leave." He made to rise from his chair only to be stopped by Ziyad's unexpectedly conciliatory tone.

"Please, do me the courtesy of staying just a moment longer. I don't want to have to detain you by force, but I will if necessary." Randolph bristled at the undisguised threat but lowered himself back into the chair to hear what Ziyad had to say. Ziyad knew that he could not physically restrain his guest but used the phrase out of force of habit.

"Thank you. Now, tell me, do you still have any of those exquisite Padparadscha sapphires that you were so kind to show me before you left me for dead?"

Randolph's face was fixed, and he sat without answering.

"You see, I suspect that there might be a more financially motivated reason for your return to Sri Lanka." Ziyad jerked his head in Ameesha's direction, "My naïve little girl here mistakenly believed that you came back for her – at her beck and call as the English say. But we both know differently, don't we?"

Randul still did not answer, preferring to let Ziyad play his hand. Ameesha sat wide eyed, trying to comprehend what was being revealed to her. She, who thought she was the Queen, had ended up a pawn in a much larger game.

"When you fled," Ziyad continued, "with my car and my possessions, you made a serious mistake. What you took was not mine, but I suspect that the contents are long gone. However, your two Padparadscha, I wonder where they are now? They were too valuable to take with you. They were too big to conceal about your person. Their rarity would be untradeable and draw too much attention to you."

Ziyad waited for Randul to comment and when none was forthcoming, he persisted, "I have had a long time to think about this. I surmise that you hid the stones somewhere and have returned to reclaim them. Do me the courtesy of confirming my hypothesis."

Randolph was unimpressed with Ziyad's theory, and automatically rejected it.

"This is all fantasy. I did come here at the suggestion of Ameesha. I had no idea she was related to you. Had I known I would never have come. I am sorry that you are disabled but you know that that was not of my doing. As for the stones, I do not know what you are talking about." Randul wanted to escape the dangerous charade in which he found himself entangled and hoped that his driver was still waiting outside.

Ziyad sneered at the Veddah's denial, "What were you up to at the Centauria Wild Hotel these last few days?" Randolph looked surprised, but not as surprised as Ameesha who waited expectantly for his answer. He sighed and stood up, ready to leave.

"You know who I am and seem to have been following me for some inexplicable reason." He spoke to Ameesha, "Yes, I came over to Sri Lanka a few days before I told you so that I could revisit some of the places that I grew up in. Yes, I am a Veddah and yes, I am Sri Lankan. But I suspect that you knew that all along." Ameesha shook her head in disbelief. "I wanted some time alone to decide if there was any future here for me."

"But why?" Ameesha asked, her whole world collapsing around her. "We could have done that together."

"Randul wanted time to collect something from his past." Ziyad was guessing but detected a rich vein of truth in his suppositions. "He didn't need you traipsing along. Did you find them?"

"Find what? What do you think I came back for?"

Ziyad looked pained that he was being taken for such a fool. Randul, the filth, believed that he could bluff it out, but Ziyad was not stupid. And now he was certain that he was not wrong.

"The Padparadscha, of course. How many were there? Four, if I recall correctly. I could hardly forget them; they were nearly the last thing I saw. You also took some valuable items that belonged to me, items that have never been recovered."

"Is that what this is all about? You want restitution for the money and gems I took, rather poor-quality gems from what I remember." Randul could not resist the insult that he knew would sting Ziyad.

"They were good stones, easily tradeable and untraceable. You stole them from me." Ziyad's voice rose in anger but immediately subsided when a voice from the entrance hall countered his claim.

"I think you will find that they were stolen from us, to be more accurate." A tall man in his fifties entered the room with a younger Arab by his side. The latter grinned at Ameesha and winked before licking his lips. The older man wandered over to Ziyad and stood just behind his chair. Neither Ziyad not Ameesha displayed any surprise at the identity of apparent strangers appearing in their house, just the timing. It was up to Randolph to ask the obvious question.

"Who the hell are you?"

"We are business associates of Mr Ziyad Al Jabri and Miss Ameesha Al Jabri, Mr Randolph Curran. Or do you answer to Randul Ranatunga when in your native guise?"

Randolph felt a quiver of fear slither down his spine. Ali continued with his explanation for their presence,

"Our two colleagues here have been assisting us in liquidating their investments to repay a long overdue debt. We've come to tie up some loose ends but could not help overhearing your interesting conversation."

Ziyad remained outwardly calm, resigned to the inevitable, while Ameesha had tears welling up in her wide eyes that stared at the two men in genuine fear. Everything was going horribly wrong, and she had lost any influence over events.

Randolph recognised Ahmed as the man in the alley, and then, suddenly, like a mental thunder-flash, he remembered. He had been the man lurking outside his shop in Mayfair, presumably tailing Ameesha who had visited that day. Randolph had become entangled in something that did not concern him and, from the look on Ameesha's face, he needed to extricate himself.

"Look, this has nothing to do with me. I think I should go." Randul started for the door once again, but Ahmed was faster and blocked the way.

"Excuse me" Randul looked hard into the Arab's eyes and knew that he might have to fight his way out. He had not had to impose himself on another for many years but knew that he was perfectly able to overcome an unarmed man when confronted with danger.

"My driver is waiting."

The younger man put his face up to Randul's and in broken English said,

"Not anymore."

The smell of khat hung on his breath and filled the air between the two men. Randolph recoiled and the Arab sneered but did not move away from the door.

"What are these Padparadscha you speak about?" Ali asked innocently.

It was Ziyad who responded, "Sapphires. Giant, valuable, glorious sapphires. They are the most sought-after gem, and also very rare. Our friend Randul has several huge stones. I am not talking about big; I am talking about world record sizes. I was just about to find out where they were hidden, when you arrived."

The older Arab turned his attention to Randolph, "Is this true? You have such gems?"

Randolph was about to issue his second denial when, with lightning speed, Ahmed produced a long blade which he put to the side of Randolph's neck. Ameesha screamed and the Arab's mouth curled into a silent snarl. He held the blade tight against his flesh, the keen edge cutting the top layers of skin, a narrow band of blood slipping along its length.

"My friend is very adept with a blade; would you not agree, Mr Ziyad?" He looked across the room at Ziyad who just nodded his head. "I do not want the same fate to befall you, so would you like to tell us whether you have the stones? Are they with you, or can get them?"

Randolph felt the keen blade slice against his flesh and demanded to be released. Ali nodded for the younger man to back off. Lightly touched the side of his neck, Randolph observed the slick of blood on his fingers.

"You might regret that one day," Randul said.

Ahmed looked disdainful and sauntered over to stand beside Ameesha who had moved from the window to slump into a shabby wing-backed chair. She watched him approach and seemed to shrink into the depths of the soft upholstery, trying to make herself as small and insignificant as possible. He stood to one side of her admiring the thin blade as he wiped the traces of Randul's blood from the shining surface.

Satisfied that it was pristine once again, he moved closer, sitting on the arm of the chair and sliding his hand to the back of Ameesha's neck and pushing her head down slightly. The blade hung loosely in his other hand and he gently stroked the flesh of her arm with its edge. Randolph could see goosebumps rise on her skin and she looked terrified. Her pleading face looked up at him and he knew what he had to do. There was no alternative.

"I did have some stones and they were pretty spectacular."

Ziyad looked smug on hearing the admission and nodding towards him, Randolph continued.

"He's right, I have come back to collect them."

A triumphant expression spread across Ziyad's face.

"Where are they?" Ali asked.

"In the Sinharaja. You'll never find them."

Ameesha whimpered as the blade slid down the front of her blouse and sliced off the top button.

"You will never find them without me. Without us," Randolph hastily added. "I can lead you there tomorrow when it gets light."

Ali thought for a moment.

"Ok. We will all stay here tonight and then tomorrow you will lead us to this place." To his accomplice he said, "Take her next door and tie her up. You," he nodded towards Randolph, "your girlfriend has been admired by my friend for some time. If you do anything stupid, I will let him have her as a plaything. You understand?"

Ameesha squealed as the young man grabbed her wrist and she looked across at her father and Randolph for help. Ziyad averted his face from her desperate stare. Randolph protested that the girl should be allowed to stay with him. Ali considered the suggestion and then spoke to Ahmed in guttural Arabic. Randolph could not understand what was said, but the younger man seemed to be arguing the point. After a sharp exchange, Ameesha was reluctantly released and pushed roughly towards the wing backed chair.

There followed a calmer exchange between the two Arabs and Ahmed seemed to cheer up, while Ziyad blanched and started to protest, his voice quavering and pleading. Ahmed advanced to the rear of the wheelchair and fiddled around with the wires attached to the battery. Ziyad attempted to move the machine, but it had already been deactivated. He looked around wildly trying to see what the man behind him was doing.

"I wanted to spare a daughter the pain of what is about to befall her father." Ali turned to face Randolph, "But you have insisted that she remains here with us."

Ali looked almost apologetic as he addressed Ameesha.

"Your father has repaid his debt to our cause and so is of little further use to us. He has betrayed his country and is a traitor to his people. In his absence he has been found guilty of treason and must suffer the consequences."

He then turned to Ziyad and spoke to him in Arabic. As he continued Ziyad became panic stricken and his face took on an ashen hue. Having pronounced sentence, Ali appeared to ask if Ziyad had anything to say. Ameesha sat weeping, her head in her hands.

Ziyad blathered, alternating between English and Arabic, the pitch of his voice rising as the young Arab placed a hand softly on his shoulder as if to comfort him. During a brief period of English, Ziyad gave a stark warning that Randul was not to be trusted in the forest. He spoke of his son's mysterious death but then reverted into Arabic, his speech becoming laboured as exhaustion set in. His breathing rasped in his throat and a dryness crept across his tongue making it difficult to get all that he had to say swiftly out into the room.

Ali listened politely, nodding now and again. Ahmed, on the other hand, disregarded the entreaties and took up a position directly behind Ziyad, the switch blade closed but held at the ready. The older man finally held up his hand to silence Ziyad, who continued to pathetically mumble unintelligible words, saliva dripping from his lips, tears leaking from his one good eye.

"Ssshhh. Shush, shush." The older Arab comforted Ziyad as if calming a distraught child. Ziyad's voice faded to a simper and eventual stillness. His one good eye swivelled back and forth from face to face, a condemned man awaiting his fate. Ali stood with his hands folded in front of him, his face sombre. He spoke in English, no doubt for the benefit of Ameesha and Randul.

"Your concerns for our wellbeing are appreciated, but we are here to tie up loose ends. We did not want sweet Ameesha to witness what is to happen next, but" he shrugged, glancing across at Randolph to re-emphasise the point, "you insisted."

Reverting his attention to Ziyad, he said, "You made a fatal mistake when you stole what was not yours. As a result, you have enjoyed a life of extreme luxury. This luxury was obtained at a cost to your comrades with whom you once fought. Many died because of your greed, and now it is time for you to contemplate their hardships as you too suffer."

He nodded to his accomplice and there was a click of the switchblade being released. With consummate ease the young Arab held the knife and swiftly nicked either side of Ziyad's neck and a fountain of blood rhythmically spurted out of each incision. Ziyad thrashed his head from side to side unable to staunch the flow, his mouth attempted to scream, but no sound emerged.

Randolph automatically leapt forward but the older Arab restrained him with a vice like grip. Ahmed tensed to stop any further intervention, his blade pointing upwards ready to strike. Randolph stood and observed Ziyad in his death throe, a mixture of revulsion and pity engulfing him as he saw a fellow human being witnessing his own lingering death, aware throughout that he was dying but unable to do anything about it.

Ameesha sat in the chair she had been shoved into, her eyes wide open, her hands held over her open mouth, gawping with mesmerising terror as her father's life ebbed away.

The fight in him weakened as the blood flowed out from Ziyad's arteries until his heart had nothing to push against and collapsed. His body slumped as if being deflated until it hung listlessly against the harness that held him in place on his chair. An expanding pool of thick, congealing blood spread on the cold marble floor forming an expanding red carpet around the silent cadaver on its immobile chariot. Randolph noticed the meniscus forming around the wheels in the silence that had engulfed everyone in the room. A harsh, metallic smell of fresh blood filled the air, mixed with a hint of urine and faeces as the sphincters relaxed within the body.

There was a strange tranquillity in the study. Each person was consumed with their own inner thoughts.

Randolph realised that he and Ameesha were also 'loose ends' that would ultimately need to be tied off once they ceased to have any useful purpose. In order to survive, he had to maintain their usefulness for as long as possible.

The fact that the two giant sapphires lay at the bottom of his bag in the hallway of the house, not twenty yards from where they all stood, was an irony that Randolph was unable to appreciate. He had no intention of relinquishing them into the Arabs hands while there was a chance of escape. If he handed them over here and now it would seal their immediate death. Each gem was a lifeline for himself, and Ameesha.

Ali remained standing in front of Ziyad as he died. He maintained eye contact throughout as he contemplated the justice of the execution. He mourned the loss of so many of his comrades who were unable to witness the retribution enacted against the traitor, Ziyad.

Ahmed did not give a second thought to his role as executioner. His mind was on what had been promised to him. He could not avert his eyes from Ameesha and the cleavage that he had exposed as a result of slicing just a single button from her blouse. What greater delights would he enjoy when she was released by Ali into his hands? How long he had waited to take the woman who had taunted him since first they had met? Lust and death were such toxic bedfellows.

Ameesha did not utter a sound throughout the unedifying scene. She was numb. She watched as if she was witnessing a piece of theatre, captivated by the waning of the life force that had once been her irascible father.

As her father drifted from life into death, Ameesha felt an unexpected wave of relief that she was free from any obligation to take up the role as his long-term carer. Despite the current perilous position she found herself in, she could not but appreciate that, as she was not the direct cause of her father's demise, half his wealth was now rightfully hers.

By the same measure, she quickly realised that she needed to maintain an alliance with Randolph, but for only two reasons.

The first was obvious, to facilitate an escape from her current predicament.

And the second reason?

Two spectacular Padparadscha sapphires that Randolph still apparently owned, and she wanted.

Now they were a prize worth fighting for.

Chapter 37

Ameesha and Randolph spent an uncomfortable night locked in a cellar room beneath the house. It had racks of fine wines and rare whisky but no water. The ground was hard stone and the temperature cool. Ameesha clung to Randolph for warmth and comfort, and he held her out of a feeling of compassion for having witnessed the death of her father.

Neither exposed their true feelings to the other, both realising that mutual support was the priority in adversity. The two Arabs had left Ziyad's body where it had died. There had been yet another short, strident altercation between the two men which Randolph had gleaned to be over Ameesha. Ahmed seemed to want to take her to one of the more comfortable bedrooms with him for the night. The older man had convinced him that that was not to their advantage and thankfully his authority held sway.

Before their incarceration in the cellar, Randolph had been led at knife point to the entrance of the house and, when the door was opened, he was told to bring the driver into the house. As he reached the driver's door it appeared that the man was asleep against the side window. He gently started to pull the door open so as not to surprise him, but the weight of the slack body pushed it from his grip and the driver fell half out onto the driveway, his throat cut. The blood had set around the wound which opened with a sucking sound as the head lolled onto the stone surface. Randolph jumped back and gagged at the unexpected sight. The young Arab chuckled and pushed him forward to pick up or drag the body into the house.

As he pulled the dead man, he looked around the grounds to the front of the house and saw the shadow of the gatekeeper slumped against the bowl of a tree, also seemingly asleep, but subjected to the same fate as the unfortunate driver.

Sleep had been impossible for Randolph as he constantly played and replayed various scenarios in his mind of what might happen in the morning. Ameesha had continued to lean against his shoulder and slept fitfully until there was a noise from outside the cellar and the heavy wooden door was unlocked and opened. Artificial light dazzled them both and they stood stiffly, Ameesha seeking to use Randolph as a shield from Ahmed, who stood back to let them pass.

Ameesha led the way up the stairs and across the hall towards the open front door. Randolph saw his bag, apparently undisturbed from where he had left it. He bent down as he passed and went to swing it onto his shoulder but Ahmed grabbed it from him. He roughly pulled it open and rummaged through the contents.

Randolph held his breath, praying that the search would not be thorough.

Ahmed was single minded in his task, believing that Randolph might have a weapon secreted in the bag. Satisfied that there were no threats within the bag, he threw it over to Randolph who let out an imperceptible sigh of relief.

As they emerged from the house into the daylight, they could see that it was heavily overcast and large raindrops had started to fall, casting dark spots on their dry clothes. Along the drive, Randolph could clearly identify the gatekeeper's body in the daylight, the front of his shirt dark with dried blood.

A people carrier was parked outside the house, and they were bundled in, Ameesha to the back with the young Arab, and Randolph in the front with Ali, who drove. The vehicle stopped at the gates and the young Arab jumped out to open them before returning to his seat next to Ameesha.

"Please do not do anything foolish, my associate is eager to get to know the lovely Ameesha better. It is only so long that I will be able to hold him back." He waited for Randul to acknowledge that he had heard and understood the threat.

The vehicle swept out of the drive onto the highway to start its long journey towards the Sinharaja Forest, Randolph giving succinct instructions along the way. He would take a route that would avoid the main tourist trails and car parks. What he had to do did not need any complications from meddling innocents.

After four hours of driving and a brief stop at a tea house, the road started to become rutted, necessitating Ali to concentrate on keeping the car out of the deep pools of water that had collected overnight. At one point they slid from one side of the road to the other and the wheels sank into the soft verge before regaining their grip, the vehicle snaking a path back onto firmer ground. The Arab fought with the wheel and cursed in his mother tongue.

While Randolph contemplated trying to take advantage of the situation, he knew that he had no way to protect Ameesha from the leering Arab sitting uncomfortably close to her. With each violent lurch of the vehicle he bumped and rubbed against Ameesha while placing a seemingly protective arm around her shoulders. She shivered in disgust and pushed him aside. He glared at her for yet another rejection, knowing that in the fullness of time he would have here begging for his mercy.

After another forty minutes of wrestling with the increasingly slippery conditions caused by the progressively hardening monsoon rain, Randolph told Ali to pull off the greasy track. The engine roared as the wheels spun across the verge and came to a halt to one side of a small clearing. The rain suddenly thundered down onto the forest. Any thought of being heard was dispelled by the noise of the water drumming against the thin metal roof over their heads. Raindrops exploded on the bonnet engulfing them in a mist of spray that obliterated their view out of the vehicle. They all sat quietly waiting for the storm to subside.

Randolph sat almost in a self-induced trance, absorbing the spirit of the forest, reawakening the life-forces that were the roots of his Veddah past. Here he was in his natural realm, the land flowed through his veins, was embedded in his very soul. Here he was transformed from the hunted to the hunter and a reinvigorated confidence swept through Randul.

Randul the tribesman. Randul the hunter. Randul the Veddah.

As suddenly as it had arrived, the rain relented and Ali ordered everyone out of the vehicle.

Randul grabbed his day bag and led the small party into the forest. In single file, they moved through the dark vegetation of the forest, twisting and turning along narrow tracks that meandered this way and that, up precipitous inclines and down into deep valleys. All the while, the thick cloud cover made the forest unusually dark, as if dusk had come early.

Randul welcomed the disorientating gloom and experienced a freedom as he ascended slick slopes and traversing rocky outcrops that dripped with water from the storm. His sure footedness, even after all these years, was not matched by the rest of his group. Everyone had to concentrate on the uneven ground underfoot for fear of falling or losing their balance. On more than one occasion the Veddah had to retrace his tracks to assist one or other of the party who had fallen or slipped. The two Arabs cursed as their clothes became encrusted in the soft mud and the detritus that covered the forest floor. None of them were dressed for hiking, least of all Ameesha who shivered in the damp environment, her thin blouse clinging to her body, her brightly coloured dress spattered with soil and torn at the hem where it had snagged on sharp protruding branches.

The terrain gradually became even more extreme as Randul lead them higher into the hills. Rocky outcrops sought to twist ankles or strain sinews, but the Arabs were hardened men and the strenuous conditions did not seem to be having an impact on their progress, much to the disappointment of Randul. Ameesha, on the other hand, was not doing well, her levels of fitness and stamina being well below those of the men. This was anticipated by Randul and helped to slow the group down, allowing the day to perniciously wane.

Ali maintained a close watch on everything Randul was doing, evidently mindful of the dire warning that Ziyad had imparted before he died. The forest was Randul's world, and Ziyad had made it abundantly clear that he had a track record of leading people into its hinterland and returning alone.

On the few occasions when it had been possible to walk side by side Randul sought to engage Ali in conversation. Anything to distract him from the gap that was regularly opening up between them and Ameesha and Ahmed. The exchanges were stilted and interrupted every time they had to take another rest to let Ameesha recover her breath.

During these breaks, Ali assumed an aloof demeanour for the benefit of Ahmed who complained constantly but, when silenced, was clearly respectful of Ali's seniority. Randul saw that the respect was not reciprocated and noted it for later. One thing was certain, Ameesha and he were far safer under the protection of Ali than his licentious, impetuous and murderously bloodthirsty younger partner. To build any form of relationship with Ali was crucial to their survival, but Randul was under no illusions that Ali was also a trained killer. That they were both expendable – 'loose ends', like Ziyad – was undeniable, and the only things keeping them alive were two exotic and exceptionally valuable stones. Ali had no intention of declaring these jewels to his masters. He viewed them as his commission for years of dedicated service to the cause and, what's more, Ahmed did not feature in his plans for the future.

The path that they travelled was up a sharp rocky incline rising above the treeline and Randul could hear Ameesha breathing hard as she fought to keep up. He increased the pace marginally, Ali matching him step for step until there was around a hundred yards between them and Ahmed, who was still guarding a miserable Ameesha. As Randul crested a ridge he pushed on a little harder. Ali looked to his right at the man setting the harsh pace and then spun around to see that the two stragglers were out of sight.

"Stop!"

Randul obeyed instantly and swung his daypack from his shoulders as if pleased for the break. He sat to his haunches to rest. Ali stood waiting and watching for the other two to catch up. His patience was limited and after a minute or two he walked slowly back towards the ridge, casting an eye back now and again to check that Randul had not moved.

Randul dabbled his fingers in the water that fell from the trees and trickled as shallow rivulets through the mica encrusted gravel under his feet. The rain made the stones glisten and their surface sparkle, even in the overcast light of the monsoon.

The strength of the rain increased again and Ali shouted down the slope beyond the crest for the others to hurry up. Randul stood, apparently impatient to move on. He slipped a couple of wet stones into his pocket and looked up to the darkening sky. There was barely an hour of daylight before night closed in.

He was surprised that he had managed to lead the Arabs this far without any apparent suspicion of prevarication. Randul had taken care not to cross paths where there might have been any distinctive features that Ali might recognise. His precautions had enabled him to pass the same area on at least three occasions.

The stilted conversations were important as a way of distracting Ali from appreciating his surroundings, while the young man was too beguiled with Ameesha as his potential prize to be aware of where they were. The wet, blouse and skirt that clung to Ameesha was all to Randul's advantage. It was the reason why he had not been the perfect gentleman and offered her a layer of his clothing to keep her warm.

Slowly the two stragglers plodded over the ridge and made their way to where Randul was casually standing. Ali also looked skywards and then to Randul, his expression one of concern and suspicion.

"We are losing the light and have been walking for hours. Where is the place that you are leading us? How long?" His English was broken and with his wariness came an edginess.

"We are really close, but I don't think we'll get back tonight. Perhaps we should seek shelter for the night." Randul looked around as if searching for a suitable site to make camp.

"No! I'm not stupid. How close?"

Randul shrugged, "Depends on Ameesha, she's tired. Ten, fifteen minutes."

"We go on and then you can lead us back to the car in the dark. Ziyad said you were not to be trusted in the forest and I want to be out of here as quickly as possible."

Randul gave Ali a querulous look as if he was asking the impossible.

"Do you have any idea how dangerous it is to move around here at night?"

Ali was unperturbed and looked to his associate to give him support, unclear as to exactly what the dangers might be. Randul played on his ignorance.

"Moving at night puts you at serious risk of attack by an elephant, leopard or a marsh crocodile. No one wanders around the forest at night."

For the first time Ali felt uncertain but maintained a brave face. He had to admit that this was not an environment in which he felt entirely comfortable. He just wanted to find these gemstones and finish what he had been sent to do. If it were not for the Padparadscha sapphires he would not be standing in the middle of an unfamiliar terrain with a dependence on a savage for his route back to the car.

Ali was becoming increasingly irritated by the young Arab constantly drooling over the woman. In his state of pent-up frustration, he was useless to him. He was just waiting for a word from Ali to defile her in ways that Ali chose to push from his mind. There were more pressing issues for him to deal with at that moment.

He would tidy up after he had the stones.

"We keep going." He waved a wet hand forward to usher Randul on. Ahmed started to complain yet again but Ali ignored him and pushed Ameesha ahead of them both.

Randul strode ahead taking Ameesha by the arm and propelling her forward. She stumbled as she attempted to keep up. Ali dropped back slightly and, out of earshot of their captives, harangued his accomplice. Randul whispered to Ameesha that she must push herself for the next few minutes as he increased the pace still further. Fear drove the woman on, taking each step with confidence in the belief that Randul had a plan that he was starting to unfold.

"You have a plan?" Ameesha said expectantly.

If truth be known, Randul had only the vaguest idea of what might ensure their freedom, but what he was abundantly clear about was that both he and Ameesha would be killed once these two assassins were in possession of the two sapphires. The only advantage he had at the moment was that he knew that they were a mere twenty minutes hard walk away from the car, and two minutes from Monkey Head Rock where Randul intended to try to split the men.

"Just do as I say."

Randul had every intention of keeping his putative plan to himself. Ameesha was as much a risk to him as the two men behind him.

The gap between them and the two Arabs and Randul widened again as Ali was preoccupied arguing with an increasingly agitated Ahmed. Randul could guess what they were debating, as could Ameesha who involuntarily shuddered, not with cold from the steady rainfall but at the prospect of Ahmed being given free reign with her. She suppressed the tears that were threatening to well up, strengthened her resolve, and concentrate on her breathing that came in short gasps as a result of the furious pace that Randul had set. All she could do was keep in step and pray that Randul had a reliable plan to divert the fate that she knew awaited her. Every time she started to lag behind he tugged roughly at her arm so that she had to trot to catch up.

This was a different man from the one she met and shared a bed with. He was unfeeling, single minded and uncommunicative. She was tired, cold and terrified.

Randul saw Monkey Head Rock ahead and checked his pace until Ameesha was close alongside. As they pulled level with the rock he whispered sharply,

"Fall down and scream."

Ameesha hesitated unsure if she had heard him correctly.

"Now" Randul hissed and gave her a rough shove. She stumbled and the Arabs saw her fall heavily, calling out as she hit the ground. Randul immediately bent down to tend to her.

Randul settled Ameesha in a seated position with her back to the rock, obscuring the lower part of the eroded face of the monkey. He attentively tried to make her comfortable and, placing his bag on the far side of the rock, glanced over the edge at the approaching Arabs. He took out a jumper to act as a cushion for her against the hard rock. Bending down behind the rock, he spent as long as he dared positioning the cushion at the base of her back.

The two Arabs arrived at the rock and Randul reverted to inspecting her ankle with a concerned look on his face. The Arabs stood looking down as he carefully manipulated her foot and pronounced that he did not think it was broken, but that it was badly twisted.

He pulled his bag over and removed a small first aid pack, ensuring that the remaining contents was stowed safely. Efficiently unwrapping a bandage he strapped up her ankle to give it as much support as he could.

"She can't go on. We'll have to stay here for the night," Randul announced.

"But we haven't got any shelter and the rain's still falling," Ahmed moaned, his machismo slipping, his nervousness at being out in the jungle at night evident.

Ali remained standing, looking down at Ameesha's ankle, unmoved.

"Stand up," he ordered. Randul turned to look up at the Arab whose impassive expression showed a cynical disbelief as to the true extent of her injuries. Randul helped Ameesha up and she stood favouring her right foot.

"Walk."

Ali nodded his head forward to show that he wanted her to parade in front of him so that he could assess the true extent of the injury for himself. Ameesha took a hobble or two, wincing with the effort, and made a good job of feigning the serious nature of her damaged ankle. Ali observed, trying to work out whether the delay was necessary. He was keen to get out of the forest and his mistrust of the softly spoken Veddah had not wavered.

"We'll rest for ten minutes. No longer." Ali paced around as his colleague took out a pouch and extracted a few leaves of khat. He rolled them in the palm of his hand and placed the green ball into his mouth and lethargically chewed.

Ali watched as Randul assisted Ameesha to settle back down against the rock. She felt a gentle squeezed on her arm to acknowledge her acting prowess. She gave him a wan smile but she was becoming increasingly doubtful that they were going to escape from their captors. There was a grim silence amongst the small party.

Eventually Ahmed sidled up to Ali and whispered to him with his back to Ameesha and Randul, who looked at each other with foreboding. Initially Ali seemed to be rejecting whatever his accomplice was suggesting but then something was said that made him pause for a moment. He walked across and addressed Randul.

"How long would it take for you and me to get to the place where the stones are hidden?" Randul did not like the implication for Ameesha but recognised an opportunity arising from the question.

"We're very close, but I don't think she can make it and get back to the car tonight. She needs to rest." Ameesha immediately realising what was to befall her should Ali and Randul leave her alone and she wrapped her soaked skirt tightly around her legs and folded her arms protectively across her chest.

"She does not need to go any further." Ali knew that his statement was literal, but then that was true for all three of his companions.

"What do you mean?" Randul asked guardedly.

"She and Ahmed will wait for us here." Ali looked at each member of the group in turn. Ameesha let out an involuntary yelp of fear and Randul shook his head,

"No. I can't do that."

"If you do not, she will be dead before morning. If you do, she might survive." Ali had moved to stand toe to toe with Randul, blocking any chance of Randul seeing the dread that spread across Ameesha's face. Ali raised his head and look down his nose at Randul, his mouth twisted down to infer that there was to be no further debate. Randul allowed the tension in his shoulders to relax slightly and Ali took it as submission.

"She is not to be touched." Randul moved aside to look directly at Ahmed who just insolently smiled back, shrugged his shoulders and spat a green globule of phlegm noisily onto the ground at Randul's shoe.

"That depends on you," he said. Randul went to take a step towards him, but Ali stepped between them.

"We're wasting time."

Randul kept his gaze on Ahmed with stony eyes.

"We're only here for the stones. Give us those and then we will go," Ali said softly into his ear.

Ameesha stared at Randul silently, imploring him not to leave her but, to her dismay, Randul picked up his day-bag and prepared to move off with Ali. Ameesha was shaking with terror, and he placed a comforting hand on her shoulder.

"We won't be long," he said.

Her eyes opened in disbelief at his callous desertion of her and she sat open mouthed as Ahmed fidgeted restlessly to one side, eager to be left alone with Ameesha. Randul raised dark threatening eyes towards Ahmed who stopped jiggling as he saw the raw hatred in Randul's face. Automatically, he adopted an aggressive pose and the knife flashed into his hand from nowhere, inviting Randul to take him on. Randul nodded his head at the blade.

"That won't help you if I come back and find that you have harmed her."

The menace in his voice weakened Ahmed's intimidatory pose and he glanced at Ali. As he listened to the exchange, Ali realised that Randul was more of a danger than he had initially thought. The Veddah are known as fearsome hunters but Ali had never come across these people. He wondered if the warnings imparted by Ziyad as he drowned in his own blood should have been treated more seriously. Whilst the girl was being held as a hostage he felt that the unarmed tribesman would be compliant at least until they returned, and then Ali would deal with all of them.

"Come." Ali ordered Randul to take the lead.

"Please…don't…," was the only words Ameesha could whisper from her quivering lips as the two men melded into the gloomy forest.

Ahmed needed no other cue and, as soon as their footsteps had drifted away, he was upon Ameesha. He moved so quickly that she had no opportunity to scream or cry out before a wet hand clamped itself over her mouth. She tried to squirm free, but he was stronger than her and he kneeled roughly pinning her against the stone. His right hand brought the glinting blade up to her eyes and held it there for her to fully appreciate the threat it held. She whimpered and sat motionless and terrified, in a state of paralysis. His breath was rank with khat, and she could smell the body odour from such close proximity to him.

He shifted his position, maintaining his hand over her mouth, pushing her head hard back against the rock face. The knife slowly moved to the front of her blouse, and he deftly sliced off each of the remaining buttons, one by one, like a cat playing with a mouse. He became more aroused as the smooth skin of her cleavage and torso was revealed. Using the blade, he very softly traced lines across her naked stomach, and it made her skin shrivel into goosebumps of fear. He forced her to slide down the rock face until she was on her back with her head cricked at an uncomfortable angle between the vertical rock face and the soft leaf litter of the forest floor.

Ameesha was petrified with terror, unable to move or call out. The Arab pushed his knees between her thighs and made her open her legs. Using his knife point like a pencil, he drew random shapes and curls on her taut skin, circling her navel, running up to her sternum and the bra that was stretched tightly across her chest. The thin blade slid up under the flimsy piece of lace that held the cups together and the keen edge released her breasts. He swept the cups aside with the knife to reveal her nipples and was lowering his head looking into her terrified eyes all the while.

Suddenly there was a single rapport from a gun. It unmistakably came from where Randul and Ali had disappeared. Ahmed froze and then suddenly jumped up, losing any interest in the half naked girl at his feet. Ameesha pulled her clothes around her and kicked out hard at his legs, catching him just under the knee. He yelled in pain and slashed through the air with his knife, passing just above Ameesha head. She quickly rolled herself into a defensive ball awaiting the welter of blows or the sharp stab of a blade in her abdomen that was sure to follow. He looked murderously down at her and the grip on his knife tightened.

Another shot rang out. He looked to left and right, confused and uncertain what to do, desperately scanning the trees all about him wondering whether the second round had been for him.

All thoughts for Ameesha were banished and he rolled to one side for cover. There was not a sound and he used the rock for cover. He continued to carefully scrutinise his surrounding for any movement, but there was nothing to be seen.

Slowly and stealthily, he left the safety of the rock and tracked parallel to the route taken by Ali and Randul. The path was easy to follow and after a few minutes he arrived at a clearing and stopped, dropping into an indentation in the ground to observe the lie of the land.

He had been unable to determine who had fired the shots. He had searched the Veddah's bag for a weapon but the sound was not that of the handgun that he knew Ali was carrying.

Everything was still.

The rain had ceased but the canopy maintained a constant stream of drips from the overhanging leaves. He waited a minute. And a minute more.

There was no sound other than the natural nocturnal noises of the forest. No breaking branches under a careless foot, the crunch of leaves, the scuff of material against an outstretched branch, the squeal of disturbed wildlife as someone scurried through the undergrowth. His eyes detected a mound to one side of the clearing, and he watched it for any signs of movement. His breathing became shallow. All of his senses were heightened by the khat.

Gradually raising himself into a low crouch he cautiously edged his way round the clearing until he was in the cover closest to the mound. He paused and listened. Upon satisfying himself that he was alone, he crept forward towards the heap that he knew from experience to be a lifeless body. The clothes were indistinguishable, but he suspected that it was Ali. Suddenly he broke cover, running fast across the narrow strip of open ground before sliding down at his partner's side.

That Ali was dead was beyond doubt. A bullet had passed through the front of his face and created a large exit hole in the back of his head. The body lay crumpled and the Arab was thankful that Ali was face down in the dirt. Even in the short time since he had first heard the shots, flies had detected a meal of epic proportions. The Arab cursed under his breath and lay close, using the body as cover while he considered what to do next.

He realised, too late, that his automatic reaction to follow in the direction of the gun shots was a mistake. There was nothing he could do here, and the girl would almost certainly have run away from the glade where he had left her. The Veddah would have returned to collect her and fled. In fact, they had all left him, alone in the forest. The dangers that Randul had warned of began to play heavily on his mind.

To his right there was a crack of a twig, and the Arab checked himself. His eyes darted from tree to tree trying to see into the dense undergrowth. It seemed to come from the path leading out of the clearing. He waited and then there was a second sound, and he was sure that he saw a millisecond flash of movement. Very cautiously, he wriggled round the remains of Ali's head and, keeping close to the ground, he squirmed his way to the edge of the thicker vegetation.

*

The gun from the mouth of Monkey Head Rock was in Randul's hand, having been removed while he settled Ameesha against the rock. He had been surprised by the speed with which Ali had moved when he pulled the weapon from his day-bag. Ali had produced a small snub-nosed pistol from a holster at the small of his back with such rapidity that Randul had hardly raised his own heavy antiquated weapon. He thought for a moment that he had made his move prematurely.

Without trying to aim, Randul pulled the trigger and the first bullet slammed into the groin of the Arab who sank to his knees in shock and pain.

Randul did not hesitate and pulled the trigger a second time.

There was a click and silence. Ali started to recover and raise his own weapon.

In desperation Randul pulled it a third time.

A flash of light flared from the end of the barrel, to be immediately followed by the roar of sound, but the next bullet had already burst through the Arab's brain before exploding out of the back of his head in a mist of blood and gore. Ali's arms flew upwards, the snub-nosed pistol arcing away from his lifeless hand as his body spun sideways and collapsed into a heap. It lay face down like a broken toy, bent at the waist at an impossible angle.

Randul had intended to double back to where he had left Ahmed with Ameesha but as he retraced his steps, he almost bumped into him moving swiftly towards the sound of the gunfire. That a huge mistake on his part, but a stroke of luck for Randul, who flattened himself against the leaflitter and held his breath as the man, only a couple of feet from him, stealthily crept past. Randul allowed him to pass as he was unsure as to where Ameesha was and so might need Ahmed. He tracked back to where Ali's body lay and saw that the younger Arab was already by the corpse.

Randul watched as Ahmed slid across the clearing floor with practiced ease. His body was low and difficult to detect at times. He had reached the trees and Randul moved on fifteen or twenty metres down the path. He had chosen this route because the way was relatively obvious, and he could maintain a watch on the progress of his pursuer. He looked down at the ground and found a suitable stick. Placing his foot across the centre, he slowly placed his weight on it until it cracked loudly.

The improvised pursuit continued for five or six minutes until the ground started to climb. Even though the Arab was good at tracking, he was unaware that he was being deftly led by Randul. By the time the sky had cleared, and the moon cast an eerie blue light across the landscape Randul had brought the Arab to the edge of the cliff from which Thinuka had fallen. At its base a river tumbled and rolled over the smooth boulders that filled the narrow gorge, its distant roar a constant background to the nocturnal noises of the forest.

Randul sank into a crevice between some rocks but Ahmed had moved away from the path and Randul momentarily had lost sight of his quarry. He waited, keeping his breathing as shallow as possible to minimise any noise. There was a very light sound of movement from somewhere but still there was nothing that he could see.

Randul shifted his position to improve his line of sight. A stone was loosened by his knee and before he could catch it, it had rolled across the hard rock and clattered and bounced down the steep slope before falling over the edge of the cliff. Randul watched as it disappeared and moments later there was a dull crack, like a rifle shot, echoing around the canyon one hundred feet below. Randul desperately tried to locate the man who he knew had been following him. The one thing that he did not want to happen had happened – he had lost sight of the Arab.

Randul had to move; the sound of the stone being displaced would almost certainly have given away his location. There was another line of rocks approximately fifteen paces away to his right and, checking that there was no sign of the Arab ascending the bluff from behind, Randul stood up and ran towards the outcrop. He had taken only three short paces before he slid to a halt as the younger man rose from behind the craggy rocks and stepped down from the uppermost edge.

He said nothing, watching Randul with caution, alert to any move he might make, noting the old revolver in his hand. The unexpected appearance of the Arab had thrown Randul off his guard and the other man covered the ground between them with incredible speed.

By the second pace Randul realised that he was the subject of a frontal attack.

By the fourth pace Randul had started to lift the gun.

By the sixth pace Randul pulled the trigger, the barrel pointing at the Arab's midriff.

By the eight pace Randul realised that the aged gun had not discharged.

By the tenth pace Randul pulled the trigger again, also with no effect.

With the twelfth pace, the Arab lunged the knife forward. Randul sidestepped and thought he had successfully dodged the blade, but the momentum enabled the Arab to shoulder barge Randul off his feet and he hit the ground hard, forcing the air out of his lungs and the pistol from his grip. The Arab said nothing, retained his footing and merely glared down at Randul with murderous black eyes. He was poised ready to launch a second attack, but he held back, willing Randul to get up.

Winded, Randul had edged into a kneeling position. His left arm felt numb from the impact until he felt the warm sensation of blood seeping down his skin beneath his shirt. He tried to lift his arm to inspect the damage, but it was unresponsive. The pain was yet to arrive, the blade being so sharp and efficient that the shocked nerve cells had yet to detect the damage.

The two men cagily circled each other, one armed with the rapier sharp knife, the other wounded and cornered. The Arab had the triumphant look of a matador knowing that he was about to dispatch the weary and weakened bull. It was an unequal match and Randul knew that this was the end. It was just a matter of time before the Arab advanced to perform the suerte de matar.

*

Ameesha sobbed openly as she sat curled into a small defensive ball at the foot of Monkey Face Rock. She tried to pull her damaged clothing together, and finally tied as best she could the shreds into a knot to cover herself. The sudden ill-advised departure of the Arab was an immense relief, but she knew that to remain at the rock would be an equally stupid mistake. She stood unsteadily, forgetting for a moment that her injured ankle was a myth.

Surely it would be futile for her to wander off in a random direction in the vain hope that she would find her way out of the forest. She did not know where she was or if Randolph, Randul, or whatever he was called, was still alive. There was no means for her to defend herself and there was only the faintest hope that Randolph would have been able to overcome both of their captors. There seemed to be no alternative but for her to follow in the path of the men. If she discovered that Randul had failed in his attempts, well, that did not bear thinking about.

Ameesha was in a quandary but she could not delay. The thought of the two Arabs discovering her meant almost certain death, but with the surety that Ahmed would have his revenge and would rape her first. He had almost succeeded once and would not fail if given a second chance. This filled her with an overwhelming sense of dread and gave her the impetus and determination to find a way out of the forest. Time was not on her side, and she could not prevaricate much longer.

She briefly, very briefly, considered just running into the forest in the hope of finding a path or road that would lead to safety. This would have been her preferred choice if it were not for the warning Randul had given about the dangers of moving through the forest at night. She knew that there were both elephants and leopards in the forest. The former aggressive when suddenly disturbed, the latter larger and more dangerous than their African relatives. She had no idea if there were marsh alligators but had no wish to find out.

She knelt in front of the Monkey Face Rock and threw aside the jumper that Randul had so carefully placed against the rock for her comfort. She assumed from his fumbling behind her that there was something under it but all that was revealed was an oil cloth that she immediately recognised from her father's safe. She quickly slipped her hand into the jagged opening that formed the monkey's mouth and felt around in the bottom, but the void was empty.

Should she assume from the shots that Randul had taken her father's weapon from the hole? If so, why was it there and how did he know? The answer suddenly dawned on her. She could not think why she had not worked it out earlier, but it was obvious to her now. This was his secret hiding place and it was not only the gun that was secreted in the void.

The Padparadscha sapphires.

This was their hiding place and he had collected them from under the noses of the Arabs. She could not suppress a sly admiration at his audacity.

So, who had them now?

She re-evaluated the odds of Randul having survived at the expense of Ali. If this was the case, then he was now hunting, or being hunted by the evil bastard who was about to rape her. Anger rose from within her, and her mind was made up. Whatever happened, she could not allow Randul to be killed. He was the one link to where her Padparadscha sapphires were.

She would not let them fall into the hands of that foul little bastard.

*

Randul felt a dizziness from loss of blood and his adversary was in no hurry to finish the job. Randul stumbling occasionally and the Arab watched as he weakened. There was no point in risking an injury. He had all the time in the world and would merely harry his victim.

He lunged at Randul and withdrew. He juggled the knife from one hand to the other to demonstrate to Randul that he could use either one to kill Randul.

Ahmed saw that the Veddah was not going to last much longer.

Equally, Randul knew that he could not wait and, breathing heavily, he sank onto one knee, his head bowed but his eyes focussed on the glinting knife blade.

The Arab approached too confidently and was taken off guard when Randul suddenly surged forward. The Arab had allowed his grip on the hilt of the knife to slacken and Randul grabbed his wrist, ducked under his held arm, while twisting his body in a rotational movement. The younger man was thrown off balance and his knife arm forced back against his shoulder joint. The blade dropped to the ground as Ahmed shrieked in pain.

He quickly recovered and, with his free hand, delivered a deep kidney punch. Randul groaned and tried to counterattack but the Arab was too fast. He brought up his knee and smashed it hard into the side of Randul's outer thigh. The blow instantly immobilised Randul's leg and this time he genuinely fell to one knee.

Randul had done his best and failed. He was set for an instant death. His breath rasped in his throat; the stab wound in his arm sending pulses of searing pain through his body. He looked up at the Arab as he walked around rotating his injured arm, as if trying to reset it from a dislocation. He maintained a careful watch on Randul but knew that this time he was incapacitated and unable to mount another attack.

Still, he had no wish to underestimate the tribesman again.

Satisfied that nothing was broken, Ahmed continued to rub his shoulder. His eyes blazed with hatred as they bore into Randul with an intensity that his adversary knew marked his end. The Arab advanced cautiously and picked up the knife from where it had fallen. He carefully cleaned the blade on his trousers, still wary of the injured man.

"I'm going to make this very painful. You're going to beg me to put you out of your misery. I know every way there is to inflict agony on a person with a blade and you are going to experience as many as I can manage. Your very soul will scream for entry into hell rather than endure what I am about to inflict on you."

Randul watched helplessly as the Arab swung his foot and caught Randul square on the chin. He fell back and Ahmed bent down and placed the cold blade beneath Randul's left eye. The salty taste of blood filled Randul's mouth and he spat out what he could.

"You will only need one of these to see what I am going to do to you."

Ahmed gently brought pressure to bear on the blade and Randul felt it puncture the skin. The sound of his heart beating and the swish of blood pumping through his arteries was deafening and Randul squeezed his eyes tight shut, but the blade kept slicing into his flesh.

Suddenly, without warning the sensation of the knife penetrating his eye socket ceased and Randul opened his eyes. The Arab had frozen as he bent over his victim, his gaze looked out beyond the ridge into the middle distance. There was an expression of stupefaction on his face, and started to turn to look behind him as he released his grip on the knife that fell to the ground in front of Randul.

The vision of Ameesha with her blouse tied across her breasts greeted the Arab, as did the muzzle of the snub-nosed pistol that had flown from Ali's hand when Randul shot him. Randul gingerly felt his upper cheek which was wet with blood and painful to the touch. He scrambled to his knees, collected up the knife and hobbled over to stand next to Ameesha.

Her voice was icy cold and without emotion, "Kneel, you pig."

The Arab lowered himself to his knees. If he felt any fear, he did not show it. But he should have. Ameesha was standing above him, her hands tightly gripping the stock of the pistol and the end of the barrel was rock steady, not moving a millimetre. In the certain knowledge that Ameesha was not going to show him any clemency, the Arab experienced a strange sense of calm, the moment before an execution. Resistance was pointless, escape impossible. His fate was sealed.

Randul recognised that Ameesha was not in conscious control of her actions. It was as if she was in a trance, the performance of one task foremost in her mind. He tried to gently restrain her, but she violently rejected any of his attempts to placate her or take the weapon from her. He locked eyes with the kneeling man who had a look of serenity on his face.

He smiled up at Randul and then at Ameesha, as if absolving them of any guilt.

That was all it took.

The bullet smashed into the side of his head and the back-spray covered Ameesha and Randul in a red mist. Inexplicably, the body did not fall but remained kneeling as if in prayer, its back rounded, head drooping, the arms slack by the side of the torso.

Ameesha kept hold of the smoking weapon and fired three more times into the crouching figure. Lowering the gun she said to Randul, "I assume you know the way out of here?"

Her voice was unemotional, flat, monotonal. She held the gun loosely at her side and turned away from Randul as if waiting for him to take the lead. He closed the blade of the Arab's knife and picked up his day-bag.

"The car is about fifteen minutes straight down that track. Follow me." Randul walked past Ameesha who did not look at him or make any move to follow.

"Straight down there?" Ameesha said pointing the pistol in the direction that Randul had indicated.

"Yes."

"Give me the Padparadscha" Ameesha nodded at Randul's day-bag.

"No." Randul had turned back to face Ameesha.

"You won't leave here with them."

"Well, that's up to you, Ameesha."

He held her gaze and then continued to walk away before freezing on hearing Ameesha shout, "Give me the bag or I will shoot you."

Randul looked over his shoulder and Ameesha stood with the gun held straight out in front of her. Randul stood and assessed the situation, not wishing to act peremptorily. She remained in the pose of a police marksman, the gun unwavering and her face determinedly set.

Using his uninjured arm, Randul slowly lowered his backpack and felt inside until he located the chamois bag. Carefully he pulled it free and opened the draw strings to allow the two gems to fall into the palm of his hand. He held them up for Ameesha to see and then put them into his pocket, his wounded arm hanging loosely at his side. Removing his good hand from his pocket he held it out, "Ameesha, give me the gun."

He walked very slowly towards Ameesha and she mirrored his pose, her hand open, the other still tightly gripping the pistol.

"Give me the sapphires."

Without altering his pace, he passed her by and continued to the side of the cliff.

"Give them to me," she repeated more urgently, not quite as confident as she was.

"You won't shoot me, Ameesha."

He retrieved one of the stones from his pocket and tossed it in the air. Ameesha caught a glimpse of a sparkle before Randul turned his back on her and threw it as far as he could into the gorge. Ameesha gasped in horror as it arced high in the air and fell. She took a step forward to try to see where it landed, but realised it was futile.

"These things have been a curse ever since I found them," Randul snarled, taking the second stone from his pocket. "It's time they were banished from all our lives."

"What the hell are you doing?" she screamed in a strident voice, panic flooding her face. She stared wide eyed at Randul.

"Don't!"

He looked at the stone in his hand and tossed it up once looking in the direction he had thrown the first. Ameesha was besides herself and made a lunge at Randul but she was too late; it had already left his hand.

"Now you can shoot me, if you want."

Randul limped painfully back past her and collected his bag. Ameesha looked from the gorge to Randul and back again in incredulous disbelief. She lifted the gun and pointed it at the back of the man walking away from her, tears forming in her eyes.

"You bastard!" She screamed, "You stupid bastard."

Her finger tightened on the trigger, her hand shaking uncontrollably.

Chapter 38

When Randolph walked into the police station, he was clear as to what he was going to say. For credibility, it was important that he kept his story as close to the truth as was possible. He had telephoned the police from his hotel immediately upon his return from the forest via a visit to the local hospital for a few stitches in his arm and under his eye. The policemen who had answered the telephone arranged for him to attend at the station first thing the next morning.

Accordingly, the Chief of Police met him and politely accompanied him into an interview room along a bland, green painted hallway. There was an air of inactivity throughout the building and Randolph could only presume that the Chief of Police had taken charge of this interview out of boredom. The room was sparsely furnished with a table and three chairs. Randolph took the far side of the table and sat facing the door. The policeman sat across the table and leant back at a slight angle to rest one arm on the edge. He had arrived at his office only shortly before Randolph. As a result, he had not had a chance to have his customary mug of tea which made him irritable before even he had started his day.

Last night he had taken the telephone call from the night duty officer that an Englishman wished to report a death. He had assumed that some relative had passed away while on holiday. Because it was the death of a foreigner, it was his responsibility to deal with the matter. He anticipated the usual Consular interference and time-consuming reports and eventual repatriation of the deceased, which was a tedious process involving a heavy administrative load. He had instructed one of his junior officers to pull out all the required forms in preparation.

Randolph sat patiently while the policeman made himself comfortable.

"You gave your name as Randolph Curran, but it seems that you are not originally from England?"

"No," Randolph had anticipated this arising and had prepared his reply while walking back through the forest. "My parents left Sri Lanka many years ago and made a life for themselves in England when I was very young."

The policeman turned down the corners of his mouth as if in disapproval, or incomprehension, as to why anyone would want to leave his homeland, particularly such an idyllic place as Sri Lanka. He made no effort to pursue this line of enquiry, much to Randolph's relief.

"I understand that you wish to report a death?" The policeman put the various necessary forms into a tidy pile and took an expensive looking fountain pen from his lapel pocket. Slowly he unscrewed the gold cap as he waited for the Englishman's response.

"In truth, there are five deaths I wish to report. Five that I know of, that is."

The reply had an electric effect on the policeman who sat bolt upright and dropped his pen onto the pristine forms, a spray of ink droplets soiling the page. He absent-mindedly brushed his hand across the page as if to clear scattered seeds from the surface. The droplets spread in fading arcs, and he muttered as he picked up his pen and furiously wrote down a short sentence.

The policeman nodded for Randolph to continue and simultaneously shouted through the door for another officer to join him. Randolph saw little point in having to repeat his story and so waited until a sallow man of around forty slid into the room and sat down next to his senior officer. The Chief pushed the ink soiled forms across to him and jabbed his finger to indicate that he was to take detailed notes of an impending confession, if a confession was about to be made. The sallow detective read the short, scribbled sentence on the ink-streaked sheet and shot a look in Randolph's direction before he took out his own cheap, plastic biro. His hand hovered over the paper waiting for Randolph to continue.

*

The solicitor's office in Columbo was hardly one that would inspire confidence in the legal services that might be available from the short, overweight man who sat behind a desk covered in files. Loose papers overflowed onto the floor and festooned the shelving that climbed the full height of the walls. The room was hot and smelt musty. It was impossible to open the windows that were jammed in their swollen wooden frames from the monsoon rain. Last night's cooking from the restaurant below combined with a bitter aroma of sweat from the perspiring solicitor. His eyes were furtive, and anxiety surrounded him as soon as Ameesha had entered the room.

Mr Andula had represented her father for as long as she could remember and, every time she met him, she felt a rising sense of revulsion. His hands were thick fingered. The gold rings on each one enveloped in soft flesh, making it impossible to remove them without the aid of a saw. An ostentatious, gold Rolex was tightly strapped to his left wrist. It glinted in the pallid sunlight that managed to pierce the veil of dirt that had adhered to the surface of the grimy windows. One pane was broken and had been covered in an old polyethene bread bag, stuck to the frame with yellowing Sellotape. The solicitor's once white shirt had a dark grey edge to the collar and the top three buttons were undone to reveal a thick mat of curling chest hairs, sparkling with minute beads of perspiration. Damp stains were visible under his arms and across his stomach where the material was stretched to breaking point and restrained by timeworn buttons.

However, despite his outwards appearance, Mr Andula was known to be a canny and artful lawyer, and these were the attributes that Ziyad had admired, particularly when he was acting on his behalf.

Shortly before his untimely death, Ziyad had made some alterations to his will and appointed Andula as sole executor to his estate. Shuffling through a thick manila file, the solicitor eventually pulled out a document that was bound by green ribbon down one long side. The paper was thick, but the document itself comprised of only a couple of pages.

The lawyer cleared a slightly larger space on his desk and laid the manuscript before him, smoothing it unnecessarily as if to delay the unavoidable consideration of its contents. He took a deep breath and fiddled with a pair of horn-rimmed glasses that hung on a cord around his neck, making no effort to place them on his nose.

"Ameesha, my dear, are you aware that your father had placed some new conditions upon the inheritance?"

"He made some reference to some conditions. Yes."

Ameesha sat upright, tense, apprehensive, with a strong desire to make this meeting as short as possible.

She had followed Randul out of the forest, the gun remaining on his back throughout, but her inability to pull the trigger, even when she knew that she was safe and could see the car, was mystifying to her. There was something that stayed her trigger finger, a stay that she could not overcome, despite her fury at his wanton act of stupidity in throwing the Padparadscha stones back into the river from whence they had been plucked.

She was apoplectic at the thought of their loss and what they would have been worth. As soon as she had become aware of their existence, she had vowed that she would own them. Any feelings that she might have had for Randolph, or Randul, or whatever he called himself, had become secondary to an overwhelming desire, an insatiable lust, to caress and embrace those magnificent stones.

And now they were gone, as were any emotional ties that might have existed between Randolph and herself. He had walked away from her, without glancing back, self-assured that she would be unable to pull that trigger. It was his supreme confidence in anticipating her failure that had eroded her own ability to take control of the situation.

She was powerless, and she had been humiliated - yet again.

Her father, Ziyad, had seen through her greed and Randul had perceived her weakness. Her only comfort was that she had had no part in the murder of her father and as such, his inheritance must fall to her. An inheritance that she had enhanced, and her father had stolen from her. She was dependent upon it to provide her with the freedom to leave the island and start a new life without any reliance on a man, any man.

"Ameesha?" the lawyer repeated, trying to gain her attention. "You do know about the conditions?" He leant forward as far as his stomach would permit. He was looking at her through long, feminine eyelashes that shaded bright, beady eyes. Ameesha returned her attention to the matter at hand.

"Yes, but those conditions do not apply. My father was killed by the two Arabs who were working for those who wanted my father dead. I had nothing to do with that and the man who killed them will be able to attest to that." Her voice rose in both pitch and volume. She was intent on showing that she was having no nonsense from this ghastly little man. Her future was not going to be compromised by him, or anyone else.

"So you say. I have not been able to speak to…," the lawyer referred to another sheet of paper on his desk, "Mr Curran as yet. But I will get a report from the police in due course."

"The police?" Ameesha was unable to hide the alarm in her voice. "What's my father's will got to do with the police?"

The lawyer viewed her with surprise, "People have died, my dear. Not least, your own dear father. Do you have no shame, my girl. No remorse?"

Ameesha hated his patronising attitude but bit her tongue, unwilling to aggravate the man who held the key to her fortune. For his part, Mr Andula was genuinely shocked at the dismissive manner with which she had treated the events of the last day or so. The details around what had transpired had only been very briefly relayed to him and he felt a great sorrow for the loss of his old client to whom he had such a great deal to be grateful. He knew a fair amount about Ziyad's business interests and, as they sat together in his study, he had listened to his reminiscences over many a glass of fine malt whisky.

It was he who had introduced Ziyad to the woman who was to become his first mistress, without any intended ulterior motive on the lawyer's part, but the liaison had been useful, albeit that the birth of the child unexpected. Ziyad had been harsh to disown the woman, but he had seen to it that the boy's upbringing was reasonable without being lavish. Obviously, it would not have been acceptable or appropriate for the boy to have had any greater opportunities than Thinuka, Ziyad's lawful son, or Ameesha.

Thinuka had developed into a wayward youth who had squandered the advantages that his father had heaped upon him. It was understandable that the deserted boy felt remote from a father figure, Ziyad repeatedly having refused to accept this role, not wishing to place himself in the public eye as a philanderer.

The boy had been monitored by the lawyer who had discreetly acted as the go-between. In a way, this role had cemented the bond between Ziyad and the lawyer. Both men were inextricably linked by the existence of the boy who had grown into a man, a man who developed the guile of his father with a wisdom, assisted by the lawyer, that protected him from the barbs and hurt of being disowned.

The strange triumvirate served the lawyer well and now he had reached the finale after years of preparation, nurturing and waiting.

Ameesha, the daughter, the woman who sat before him in avaricious anticipation, had played into the lawyer's hands without any need of subterfuge. Her greed for the wealth that her father had amassed was too great for her to wait for his death by natural causes. Ziyad had discovered that she had taken matters into her own hands after Ziyad became paralysed. She assumed control of his affairs, overseeing the liquidation of millions of dollars of assets, a role that Mr Andula had anticipated fulfilling. But that was not to be. However, by adopting her chosen course of action, Ameesha had removed any conflict of interest between the lawyer's role as Ziyad's trusted advisor and her role of his investment manager. He could observe, advise and monitor, while maintaining the trust and confidence of Ziyad, his client.

Everything had worked out rather well. Just the final details to tidy up.

*

When Randolph had completed his statement, the sallow detective had filled five pages of close script. The Chief of Police had sat spellbound by the precise and detailed account of the events in the forest and had asked very few questions throughout. The omissions from the report were few, but primarily any reference to the Padparadscha stones, which Randolph deemed as irrelevant.

The only interruption was when the Chief of Police had briefly left the room to dispatch three of his men, one to Ziyad's home and the other two to go into the forest and locate the bodies of the two assassins. He returned with two mugs of tea, one for himself and one for Randolph. The sallow detective was not felt to be in need refreshment.

"You do realise that we need to verify this information?" The Chief of Police rose stiffly from his seat and sipped his tea as he paced around the small room. He had been seated for too long and the stiffness in his back reminded him of the fact that age was catching up with him.

"When are you due to fly back to the UK?" The answer was immaterial, as the Chief of Police wished to see Randolph to leave as soon as all the paperwork had been completed and his story confirmed.

The Chief looked down at the suave man seated at the table. He was relaxed and the Chief had no reason to doubt that he was telling the truth. An innocent tourist who had become mixed up with events that were not of his making. A visit to a house that had been made at an unfortunate time.

Ziyad, on the other hand, was well known to the Chief of Police. During the course of his whisky infused visits, a payment or two had exchanged hands. On his part, he had ensured that young Thinuka's indiscretions were discreetly handled and Ziyad's premises regularly patrolled to discourage any unwelcome attention. The two assassins seemed to have slipped the net, which was an embarrassment. They were obviously professionals who would have easily eluded simple young officers who were unaware of the reason why their patrol route always covered the Al-Quadi properties.

The fact that Al-Quadi was the target for some attention remained a mystery to him, but he was not overly surprised. Ziyad's paranoia with privacy and security told the Chief all he needed to know. Whether it was fraud, drugs or extortion, the Chief could not be sure but while the regular additions to his salary continued, it was not in his interests to pursue any further enquiries. Al-Quadi made no trouble, save for allowing his son to run free, and so there was no reason to rock what had been a very profitable boat. In fact, an exhaustive enquiry into the matter might reveal matters that were best left undisturbed.

The Chief completed another silent circumnavigation of the room and then appeared to have reached a conclusion.

"The facts seem to be clear to me. The murder of Mr Al-Quadi was motivated by an attempted theft of jewels by illegal immigrants into Sri Lanka and the abduction of you and his daughter was to extract further valuable assets belonging to Mr Al-Quadi. You foiled the attempt and saved the life of a Sri Lankan citizen, for which you are to be commended."

The Chief looked hard at Randolph who wondered if this was a suggested interpretation of the facts that he was challenging Randolph to question or dispute. Either way, the summary was fastidiously recorded by the subordinate and would no doubt dictate the conclusion of the final report, regardless of any analysis of the verified facts. He put his hand on the shoulder of the sallow detective and gently patted him as one might an obedient dog, before dismissing him from any further duties. The detective gratefully collected up the sheets of paper covered in the scribbled statement, tapped them on the table to create a tidy pile and quickly excused himself from the room.

After he had gone, the Chief closed the door quietly and spoke conspiratorially to Randul.

"Such serious crimes are not often, if ever, seen in Sri Lanka. It would be appreciated if the details of this matter were to remain, shall we say, veiled? My officer will type up your statement for signature later today. Perhaps you would return this afternoon when we can tie up all the loose ends?"

Randolph had heard that phrase before and looked up at the Chief in some alarm. From the silent exchange that passed between the two of them, they understood each other.

As he emerged from the police station, Randolph took a deep breath of fresh air and exhaled in unconcealed relief. The interview had gone much better than he had expected, which was more than could be said for the one occurring in the lawyer's squalid office in Colombo.

*

Ameesha clenched her teeth together and listened with incredulity to her father's lawyer as he explained the ramifications of the most recent changes to her father's will.

"You see, my dear Ameesha," she winced as he sought to ingratiate himself, licking his saliva moistened lips in anticipation, "the conditions your father placed upon the inheritance of his considerable private fortune were in your best interests. Of course, he had hoped to witness your marriage, but sadly that is not to be possible due to the unfortunate events of the past few days."

Ameesha was confused and wondered if she should have retained Randolph a while longer. The convoluted delivery of the Machiavellian machinations of her father's mind had made the intentions obscure to her. She was impatient for a definitive answer.

"Can you just come to the point? I am currently living in my family home, but I do not have access to sufficient cash to live as my father would have wished. So, tell me, what is the hold-up in my inheriting my father's estate?"

The lawyer waggled his head from side to side as if to emphasise the tricky nature of the arrangements.

"You will inherit a percentage of his wealth subject to you accepting the choice of husband that your father has made for you." The lawyer lowered his eyes to avoid the disbelieving gaze of Ameesha, before continuing. "However, should you choose to follow your own path then you are disinherited and your portion of the estate passes to another."

Ameesha slanted her eyes as she watched the lawyer carefully, his hands shaking slightly as they brushed across the open will. The text was short and precise, but she could not understand why it had taken the lawyer so long to explain her position.

"I do not intend to marry. I thought that I might, but not now, and certainly not a marriage arranged by my father." She cast her mind back to Randolph but realised that her aspirations in that direction had been dashed as soon as she had pointed the gun at him in the forest. Her mercenary desire for the Padparadscha sapphires had exposed her true character to him and he had dismissed her out of hand.

The lawyer looked crestfallen, and his shoulders sank as he appeared to visibly deflate, swallowed into the depths of the scuffed leather upholstery of his chair. Ameesha on seeing this reaction suddenly began to realise the final denouement to her father's vengeance.

"You?" she scoffed. "He was not serious?"

The lawyer looked crushed and tried to restore a modicum of his pride. He extracted himself from the bowels of the chair into which he had previously sunk.

"It would not be so bad. I have a successful business and would provide for you." On seeing Ameesha's horrified face, he added, "Who else is going to have you? You are damaged goods."

"Well, not you, Mr Andula. I would rather die than marry you," she snapped and got up to leave.

"Then you will die a pauper," he replied, a harshness to his voice that confirmed his disappointment at her flat rejection. The lawyer also rose from his seat and tried to pull himself to his full height but remained dwarfed by the statuesque woman who had scorned him. A delightful fantasy that had preoccupied his mind since he had negotiated the arrangement with Ziyad now lost.

He had one last card to play,

"If I am to be rejected then there is nothing more for you here. However, are you not intrigued as to whom the estate passes?" Andula waddled past her and placed his hand on the door handle, pausing for her response.

"Who?"

Andula smiled at this small pyrrhic victory. Opening the door, he took a step over the threshold and found who he was looking for seated quietly outside.

"Please do join us?" Andula stepped back to allow the person who had been waiting so patiently to enter the room.

Aloka, smartly dressed in an expensive suit, swept into the office and smiled at Ameesha. He maintained a safe distance between himself and the furious looking woman who stared open mouthed at his arrival.

Words failed her and she just watched as her father's shop boy sat in the seat that she had just vacated and confidently crossed his legs, brushing a mote of dust from his pristinely pressed trousers with a delicate hand. He craned his neck round to disdainfully observe Ameesha with a victorious expression that drew the air from her lungs. She felt an acute sense of despair, of drowning in her own self-pity, her chest heaving as she fought for breath, short muscular spasms, as if she was attempting to swim in freezing water. Her eyes were dry, her gaze penetrating, a spear of hate flew across the divide between them.

Aloka turned back to face the lawyer, dismissing her presence, ignoring her ire. Andula returned to his chair behind the desk and consulted the will that had remained open on his desk. He had no need to read the relevant codicil, he knew it word for word having carefully drafted it for Ziyad only a few days before his death.

"Aloka, Ameesha has rejected the terms of Mr Al-Quadi's will and so, as you are his only son…"

Ameesha let out a squeal of surprise. Andula coughed at the not unexpected interruption and persisted.

"I shall continue. As Mr Ziyad Al-Quadi's only son, he has bequeathed to you his entire estate after all expenses have been settled, including my fees."

Andula was addressing Aloka while watching Ameesha for her reaction to his revelation. She did not disappoint, and let out another short, shrill cry before putting her hands over her mouth to stifle any further sound. She stood motionless as comprehension seeped into her confused mind.

Not only had she lost her inheritance but she also had to absorb the fact that Aloka was her half-brother, not a lowly employee. In any other circumstances she might have embraced him, and they could have shared their grief together, supported each other, worked together, expanded their business together, become rich together.

Aloka swung himself out of the chair and arrogantly sauntered over to where Ameesha stood. She watched, transfixed to the spot as he advanced before stopping and putting his hand out, palm up. Surely, she thought, he does not want to shake hands like a victorious tennis player consoling the vanquished. She looked from hand to face and when he realised that she did not comprehend what he was wanting, he simply said,

"Keys, please."

"What?"

"Keys."

"Keys to what? You already have the shop keys."

Aloka smiled,

"No, not the shop. The house."

Ameesha looked across to the lawyer who shrugged his shoulders as if to indicate that Aloka was within his rights. In a daze, she rummaged through the contents of her clutch-bag and extracted the keys. The man before her, the man she had treated as a loyal employee, slowly raised his hand and, with delicate fingers, prised the keys from her grip. Ameesha was unable to resist.

With a glare that was a mixture of bafflement and fury, hot tears burning the corners of her eyes, she turned and pulled open the door to the office before storming out, unwilling to give either man the satisfaction of seeing her crumple before them. Halfway down the stairs she grabbed the handrail for support and sank onto the bare timber tread, allowing her head to sink, stretching the tendons at the back of her neck, and she shook with self-pity and rage.

The tears had to be banished; the self-pity dismissed, both were to be replaced with a black all-encompassing vengeance, blinding her vision, overpowering her senses and seeding itself deep in her heart. 'Beware, Aloka!' she said to herself, 'Ameesha Al-Jabri is a vicious, mercilessly, vengeful woman.'

Chapter 39

Randolph sat at the bar of his hotel and ordered a drink before dinner. There was a small noisy crowd of tourists that had been to see the elephants at Uda Walawe. They had gathered around a table cluttered with half empty glasses and discarded mobile phones, photographs having been shared and experiences excitedly recounted. Randolph tried to block out the intrusive chatter and reflected on his interview at the police station. The Chief of Police appeared to have accepted his account of events without too many questions or any requirement for additional clarification.

The officer he had sent to Ziyad's home had found his body still slumped in his motorised wheelchair, desiccated of blood, a haze of flies buzzing in a cloud around him, gorging themselves on the sticky, blackening liquid that had pooled on the floor. As described by Randolph, they also located the gatekeeper and the taxi driver. The second group of policemen, sent into the forest with precise directions provided by Randolph, had taken longer to locate the bodies of the two assassins, but had eventually done so and arranged for them to be returned to the mortuary for an unnecessary autopsy.

As Randolph quietly sipped his drink, five bodies lay on marble slabs in the city mortuary. At the insistence of the Chief of Police, one specific pathologist was ordered to cancel his dinner engagement in order to work overtime and deliver a report, with the required conclusion, onto the Chief's desk by first thing the next morning. Not that there was much doubt as to the cause of death and the Chief was relieved that all the evidence to date accorded entirely with the Englishman's account of events. This reduced his paperwork, and he was all in favour of keeping the administrative workload to a bare minimum.

The Police Chief arrived early at his office the next day and was pleased to see that the pathologist had been true to his word and that the report lay at the centre of his clear desk. He placed the mug of steaming tea next to it and took off his jacket, placing it on the back of his chair, before sitting down to absorb the contents.

All accorded with Randolph Curran's statement and the case became much simpler when one of his officers placed a sheet of paper onto his desk before retiring in silence. He knew that when his boss was concentrating it was unwise to say anything that might break his train of thought. The Police Chief took up the single sheet and read it slowly. His eyebrows rose as he noted the identity of the two dead Arabs. The names meant nothing to him, nor was he concerned as to their country of origin, it was their profession that was the item that caught his eye. Trained assassins. Not entirely a surprise, save for the fact that an innocent tourist seemed to have got the better of them. He picked up his mug of tea and sipped pensively.

If there was anything about the whole affair that did not entirely tally with Mr Randolph Curran's detailed and precise account, it was his ability to lure the Arabs into the forest. What had drawn them there? Why had they bothered to go so deep into the forest with the woman and the Englishman?

He re-read the information on the sheet and contemplatively drank the remaining dregs of his cooling tea. Both men were wanted in several sovereign territories and now their careers had ended in his area of responsibility. The Americans, the South Africans, the Spanish and the Germans all had warrants out for their arrest and would seek instant deportation if they were apprehended. It was also clear that there was some sensitivity to a good many of the killings that had been attributed to them.

There would be considerable kudos attributed to those who were responsible for bringing these two international criminals to justice, but the Chief was not sure he wanted that sort of attention or acclaim. Apprehending habitual criminals was fine, but international hitmen with powerful masters who had little regard for national boundaries or a public official's privacy was not an area into which he had any desire to place himself. He did not want to start his imminent retirement in fear of appearing in the cross threads of a successor to the two dead Arabs.

No. It was clear in his mind that this affair was to be kept as far from the media as was possible. He did not think that the politicians to whom he reported would want Sri Lanka to become known as a destination for terrorists and killers. It had taken a huge effort to restore confidence within the tourist industry after the Easter Sunday explosions in 2019. That episode had killed two hundred and seventy innocent people, and no one wanted to rake up that period of their history.

He replenished his tea before drafting a sanitised report for his political masters. He would inform the overseas authorities that their two fugitives were no more, and that their demise was a matter of national security. He was sure that such a course of action would find favour with all concerned.

Lastly, there was the matter of the Englishman that needed his attention. He would make the necessary arrangements for his discreet return back to England with a warning that he was not welcome in Sri Lanka should he ever have a notion to return. In fact, he would order that all records or evidence of his presence in Sri Lanka should be removed. Similarly, he would suggest to the British authorities that when Mr Randolph Curran arrives at Heathrow, he should be quietly spirited away to wherever he came from.

*

Unfortunately, as his arrangements were being put in hand, the Chief of Police was unaware of the impact a disinherited woman who was obsessed with the restitution of what she considered to be her birth right was about to have on his time before his retirement.

Aloka, on the other hand, had no illusions as to the threat under which he was living. A dishevelled Ameesha had been seen on a couple of occasions loitering around the shop by a few of his staff. From the private safe in his office, he removed a mobile telephone that he rarely used nowadays. He picked out the numbers that he had memorised many years ago and listened to the brief message that came by way of reply. He rang off, placed the instrument on the desk in front of him and waited. It was not long before the call-back came, and he snatched up the phone and spoke briefly.

"We still have a loose end. Will you send someone?"

*

Randolph was preparing for his arrival at Heathrow when the first officer appeared from the flight deck and made his way directly to Randolph's seat in first class.

"Excuse me, sir." He bent down to ensure that his conversation was not overheard by any other inquisitive passenger. The embarkation of Randolph onto the aeroplane before any of the other passengers, accompanied by a plain clothes police officer, had sparked conjecture amongst the crew. However, they were instructed that Mr Curran was a VIP and was to be treated as such.

"We've begun our descent into Heathrow and have received a message from air traffic control in London." The First Officer glanced around to make sure that he was not being observed by anyone, rather relishing his clandestine role. "They have asked if you would wait behind and allow the other passengers to leave first. Someone will then come to collect you and escort you through passport control and customs. Your luggage will be delivered directly to a car that will be waiting for you."

Randolph smiled and thanked him. To be escorted through immigration and customs was just perfect.

Once the plane had come to a standstill, the other passengers rose as one to retrieve their hand luggage and diverse parcels from the overhead lockers. Randolph sat quietly watching the mayhem with an amused look on his face. No one took any notice of the relaxed, well-dressed gentleman who remained seated as they all trooped towards the door. They had other matters to worry about such as whether their luggage would arrive first on the carousel, and what delay they would experience as they passed through customs with the odd piece of jewellery or electrical equipment that should be declared but would be overlooked.

Randolph had no such concerns, having been escorted through all the security checks at Bandaranaike Airport with no more than a perfunctory examination of his documentation and luggage. He anticipated that the same would occur at Heathrow as a man in a dark suit and club tie peered into first-class from the main door. He spoke briefly to a young steward who pointed in Randolph's direction. There were no other passengers left and the crew watched as Randolph collected his own hand luggage.

"This way please, sir."

Randolph obediently followed and, as at Bandaranaike, the normally strict and time-consuming checks and inspections were minimal. Within the space of fifteen minutes, he was seated in the back of a black Range Rover speeding out of the airport complex towards his home.

"Good trip, sir?" his chauffeur enquired.

Randolph shifted in his seat and removed the small chamois leather pouch from his inside jacket pocket. He undid the string ties and rolled the two irregularly shaped Padparadscha sapphires onto the palm of his hand.

"Very satisfactory, thank you."

Acknowledgements

I failed dismally in the first print run of A Still Life to adequately recognise those who have been so supportive of my efforts to entertain through the written word. I hope that with the publication of this, my second book, to rectify that omission.

Writing a book, any book, is a solitary business and requires concentration and effort over many weeks just to produce the first version of the final product. It is then that the daunting prospect of releasing these early efforts to a wider readership becomes a reality. All the doubts and fears arise as you circulate the file, and then wait for the reactions and feedback.

I have been incredibly fortunate to have found an amazing group of beta readers who are critical, constructive and incredibly generous with their time. Some have strengths in analysing my storyline and finding those errors or omissions that I was sure that I had covered, while others have levels of grammatical precision that shame me in my ignorance. I have to admit that for narrative effect, I have sometimes ignored the corrections of those who have a far better grasp of grammatical English that I have ever had. These errors, and any other inaccuracies, are mine, and mine alone, and if you discover yet more anomalies while reading this book, or wish to comment on any aspect of it, then I am delighted to hear from you using the email address below or, better still, leave a review on Amazon.

But back to my happy band of helpers, my gratitude to you all is more than I can hope to express in this short acknowledgement. You are a source of inspiration and the strength that makes me continue with this strange pastime. I hope that during the course of providing your guidance to me, you get some enjoyment from what I present to you for consideration. I do not intend to embarrass you by providing full names but to Jo-Jo, Sam, James McD, James W, David, Fi-Fi, Alex and Alison, you are all heroes and this mention does not do you all justice.

Finally, Vanessa. Oh, Nessa, your forbearance, patience, calming words and, after at least seven full readings of The Sauceror's Apprentice, you are still talking to me. What you have done goes way beyond the vows that you made to me on our wedding day all those years ago. Editor, proof-reader, cover designer, coffee maker, brow soother and IT guru! Without your continued encouragement and love I would never have had the courage to complete and publish one book, let alone two.

Shall we try a third?

Vanessa, you are my Padparadscha – beautiful, unique and mystical. Truly, a jewel beyond compare.

BG Knight

March 2023

Email: bgknight2020@gmail.com

Biography

The Sauceror's Apprentice is the second novel by BG Knight, the first having been A Still Life. Encouraged by the response to A Still Life, he embarked on this latest book inspired by a trip he made to Sri Lanka in 2020.

The beauty of the island is only matched by the kindness and generosity of the people who have experienced a turbulent time over the last few years. If anyone is thinking of visiting, then they should do so.

Although BG Knight is a pen name, it is fair to give him some definition. Following a career in investment management, BG returned to writing later in life having always enjoyed storytelling in his more formative years. He works from home in Berkshire and is ably assisted by his wife and two dogs.

Visit BG's website at www.bgknightauthor.com

Printed in Great Britain
by Amazon